"Cathartic and transcendent."

—New York Times

"Exceptionally engaging. . . . Surprising plot turns and richly developed characters make for a vivid, riveting read."

—*The Washington Post*

"Gripping, thoughtful science fiction in the vein of Tiptree or Crispin. Unique, timely, and enthralling . . . absolutely beautiful. What a glorious, heartbreaking maze of a book."

—Seanan McGuire, *New York Times* bestselling author of *Once Broken Faith*

"Newman has crafted a thrilling tale of murder, mystery, and madness on a world where humanity is still its own worst enemy. Horrifying and heartbreaking in equal measure, the catastrophe driving this narrative will keep you riveted until the very last page."

—Kameron Hurley, author of *The Stars Are Legion*

"A fascinating and propulsive tale."

—*Locus*

"Incredibly well-realized world building . . . thrilling." —io9

"Builds and builds to this remarkable crescendo. . . . The ending had me breathless . . . an awesome book."

—Roxane Gay, author of *Hunger: A Memoir of (My) Body*

continued . . .

ALSO BY EMMA NEWMAN

PLANETFALL

AFTER ATLAS

A Planetfall Novel

EMMA NEWMAN

ROC
NEW YORK

ROC
Published by Berkley
An imprint of Penguin Random House LLC
375 Hudson Street, New York, New York 10014

Copyright © 2016 by Emma Newman
Penguin Random House supports copyright. Copyright fuels creativity,
encourages diverse voices, promotes free speech, and creates a vibrant culture.
Thank you for buying an authorized edition of this book and for complying with
copyright laws by not reproducing, scanning, or distributing any part of it in any
form without permission. You are supporting writers and allowing Penguin
Random House to continue to publish books for every reader.

ROC with its colophon is a registered trademark
of Penguin Random House LLC.

Library of Congress Cataloging-in-Publication Data

Names: Newman, Emma, 1976– author.
Title: After atlas: a Planetfall novel / Emma Newman.
Description: New York: Roc, [2016]
Identifiers: LCCN 2016022507 (print) | LCCN 2016028732 (ebook) | ISBN
9780425282403 (paperback) | ISBN 9780698404335 (ebook)
Subjects: LCSH: Murder—Investigation—Fiction. | BISAC: FICTION / Science
Fiction / General. | FICTION / Science Fiction / High Tech. | FICTION /
Mystery & Detective / Police Procedural. | GSAFD:
Mystery fiction. | Science fiction.
Classification: LCC PR6114.E949 A69 2016 (print) | LCC PR6114.E949 (ebook) |
DDC 823/.92—dc23
LC record available at https://lccn.loc.gov/2016022507

First Edition: November 2016

Printed in the United States of America
1   3   5   7   9   10   8   6   4   2

Cover art by Anxo Amarelle CGI
Cover design by Adam Auerbach
Book design by Kelly Lipovich

For my Mum:

*the only woman in the world who could
go through what she has and come out the other side
looking even more fabulous than before*

ACKNOWLEDGMENTS

Before I talk about this book, I want to thank the team at Roc for giving *Planetfall* such a fantastic launch into the world. It was the first time a book I have written was reviewed in the *New York Times* and the *Washington Post* and it was thrilling! I would also like to thank everyone who reviewed it, tweeted about it, grabbed their friends and made them read it (I have been told this has happened several times!). Visibility for sci-fi books written by authors who happen to be female is hard-won, and you lovely people have been hugely helpful.

I want to thank Jennifer Udden for all the usual stuff I say in the acknowledgments (still true) but most especially for the e-mail you sent me after reading the 1.5 draft of this book. It made me laugh and it made me believe I had made something I could be proud of after that hellish year.

Thanks to Pete and the Bean, as always, for keeping me fed and cuddled.

I want to offer the biggest, plumpest, cheeriest thanks to Rebecca Brewer, my editor. Thank you for asking for more. Thank you for pushing me to go deeper when I was scared to. You have made this a better book as a result, and editors don't get told that enough, in my humble opinion.

AFTER ATLAS

1

IT'S TIMES LIKE these, when I'm hunkered in a doorway, waiting for a food market of dubious legality to be set up, that I find myself wishing I could eat like everyone else. I watch them scurry past, hurrying back to their warm little boxes with their bright lights and distractions, a hot meal just the press of a button away. They'll stand there in front of their printers, watching that artificial shit being spurted out of dozens of tiny nozzles with clinical precision to form lasagna or something, and their stomachs will rumble and their mouths will water and, oh God, just the thought of it is making me nauseous. As much as it disgusts me, I envy them.

It's cold and damp, the November sun is setting in the middle of the afternoon and I am beyond tired. The satisfaction of finishing my latest case didn't last long in the face of my hunger, and I just want the truck to arrive, to buy what I need, to get home and to shut the door on it all. I'll make a casserole, I promise myself, like a parent promising a grumbling toddler he'll get a toy if he behaves. There's some beef left in the freezer. And if there's flour (I try not to get my hopes up), I'll make dumplings, stodgy and crisped on the top like the Brits make them. I haven't eaten since an early and inadequate breakfast, and just imagining what that casserole could smell like makes me close my eyes and smile to myself, just for a moment. I turn my collar up and tuck my hands back into my pockets. I'm hoping that here in this little nook no one will see me and feel they're entitled to come and talk to me just because they've seen me on the news and docu-feeds.

A woman walks in front of the doorway and looks straight at me, pausing midstride as if she's listening for something I'm about to say. I pull back into the shadows when she laughs, worried that she's recognized me, before realizing she's talking to an avatar projected by her chip. She's experiencing walking with a friend, chatting and laughing away. When I shift to the other side of the doorway she blinks with a yelp, seeing me for the first time, and mutters an apology in Norwegian.

I rest my head against the door behind me, waiting for my pulse to settle again.

"Would you like to play a game while you're waiting?" Tia asks.

"No." Now I'm the one looking like I'm talking to myself. Not that it matters. Most of the people I can see in this dingy London backstreet are talking to either projected avatars or, like me, just the voices of their Artificial Personal Assistants, delivered directly into their brains via neural implant.

"We're next to a node for a new urban-enhancement game with a free trial to—"

"No."

"Would you like me to stop making urban-environment interactivity suggestions when you are off duty?"

"Yes. Why are you making them, anyway?"

"A recent change in the licensing agreement between—"

"Save it, Tia. I don't need to know." It's the first rule of any change to a licensing agreement: it's not for the benefit of the end user, no matter what they say.

Where the fuck is the van?

I check the time and it's only five p.m. It feels like two in the morning. There's a steady pounding throb at the back of my head, and my hunger has moved from gnawing, through occasional bouts of light-headedness, to making me want to kill someone. Then I hear the low whine of the van's engine and step out as it parks, pulling my small wheeled case behind me, ready to muscle my way to the front when it opens its back doors.

Everyone in the loitering crowd has their public profile set to private, as do I. I recognize some of them from other markets. There's the man with the tiny dog that bites anyone who goes near, the little shit. There's the woman with the umbrella that's almost taken my eye out several times, and she knows she's doing it but has no fucks to give for a rival consumer. There's the old dear who looks like she could be the sweetest grandma straight out of a department store Christmas mersive advert, but I know she's just as willing to grind her bootheels into someone else's toes if they push too much from the back.

The driver gets out, moves to the side of the van and slides the side door across just enough to pull out the folding table, while his passenger jumps out and scans the street. They've just made a delivery to a supermarket down the road, one that's—like all of them—too expensive for most people to shop in. It has aisles filled with perfect vegetables and a counter with the freshest meat—actual real meat cut from real animals—all sparkling and brightly lit. I only know about it because of the mersive adverts that weasel their way in every few months or so before Tia closes the loophole they've exploited to get to me. Cooking with real, fresh food is the province of the rich. Rich enough to buy it, or rich enough to have the space for dirt to grow it, or rich enough to hire space and equipment to have other people grow it just for them.

This impromptu market is a testament to mankind's ability to exploit every possible consumer niche. The driver has come from a wholesaler who has realized that there are people willing to pay good money for the stock that the supermarkets won't take. So all the rejects get put into boxes and loaded onto the last delivery of the day, to be sold in a backstreet that smells of piss and misery. Now it's filled with people who are doing well enough to spend money on food items considered luxuries, but not quite well enough to afford to do it in a nice building with beautiful staff and real champagne given at the door.

I'm not doing well enough to have the money to do this. I've made greater sacrifices to get this food. I doubt any of the others have given up years of freedom to be able to buy a few misshapen vegetables every week. I frown to myself, trying to stop thinking that way. I try to reframe it, the way Dee would. "It was a shitty choice," she'd say. "But at least it was one you got to make for yourself."

It doesn't have the same effect when she's not here with me. No matter how much I try to spin it into something else, it doesn't alter the sheer injustice of it all. But as much as I want it to, my sacrifice doesn't give me a place at the front of the jostling throng that is slowly, reluctantly morphing into a queue. In moments I find myself behind the old woman and take care where I'm putting my feet. The man with the dog is farther back, his irritation expressed perfectly by the tiny, vicious snarling of the overgrown rat in his arms. There's a sharp, painful tap on the top of my head and I twist to see the woman with the umbrella.

"So sorry," she says with a fake smile.

"It's not raining," I say through gritted teeth.

"Oh, has it stopped?" She pretends not to have noticed and still doesn't fold the damn thing away. There's a slight narrowing of her eyes as she stares at me and I face front again, worrying that she's thinking she's seen me somewhere before.

I turn my collar up as if against the wind, but it's more to cover as much of my face as possible. Crates of produce have been hauled out of the van and the driver has cranked one open already. He scoops out a few carrots, all huge, malformed things, looking like fetishes from some ancient magical ritual. He holds one up for the crowd, who laugh when they see how much it looks like a man running, with its split root and arm-like offshoots. Turnips are dumped next to them, then onions. It's as if the universe knew I wanted to cook a casserole.

"No need to push," the driver calls. "Plenty for sale tonight. Cooking apples too, when this doughnut"—he jerks a thumb at his assistant—"digs 'em out for ya."

Tia informs me that the seller's APA has made contact and the handshake has been successful. All I need to do is pick what I want and our APAs will handle the rest. I swipe away a notification warning me that the ingredients I plan to buy will amount to an extra three hours on my contract to pay off the credit required.

The queue shuffles forward as the first purchases are swiftly made. Only four people away from the table, I'm already earmarking the ones I hope will still be there when it's my turn. The seller glances down the line, sees me and winks. A recorded audio message comes in from him moments later and I give Tia permission to play it to me.

"I got some flour in the van for you and some sugar. You need to sieve 'em 'cos they was spillages, but it's all good 'cos it's a clean processing plant. No charge. My boy'll give 'em to ya round the front of the van after you got your veggies."

Has it been sent to me in error? The message continues.

"I know you was the copper who got that bloke who was killin' the babies up north. Saw it on the feed. I know 'im, I thought, he's the one who buys me veggies. So there's extra for you whenever you come. Just don't tell no one. Next time I'll bring some beef if I can sneak it out. I got a baby grandson, see? Same age as that young lad, the last one that bastard got."

The message ends, and for the first time in years I choose to seek out eye contact with another real human being because I genuinely want to. He meets my gaze and nods and I smile. I actually smile at someone I don't know. He looks away to serve the next customer and I'm left reeling from the body blow of the first act of kindness I can remember in years.

The queue moves forward again, and even though the umbrella hits my head once more I don't have any anger left in me now. I ignore it and wait with newfound patience. There will be something left for me by the time I get there; I know it now.

Minutes pass and then the hairs on the back of my neck prickle. I have the distinct impression someone is watching me. It's not the woman behind me—I can hear her arguing with the man behind her, who's also been hit by the umbrella. It's someone else. I tuck my chin into my coat and whisper to Tia.

"Who's in this crowd?"

"Everyone within a ten-meter radius, with the exception of

the driver and sales assistant, have their public profiles set to private."

"Read them anyway."

"You are not currently assigned to a case. Please state your justification."

I can't give the real reason, so I need to lie. If I push it too far, my breach of their personal privacy will be flagged in the system. "Possible criminal activity in progress." I pause, hoping that's enough.

The gamble pays off; I'm in good standing at the Ministry of Justice and there's nothing in the system to suggest I ever abuse my privileges, so it gives me the benefit of the doubt. Tia pulls in the information that all the people around me would display about themselves if they had their profiles set to public, overlaying it across my vision as if the text is floating above the tarmac next to me. Before I even have the chance to scan the list, Tia highlights one and pulls it to the front, in line with a command I programmed years ago. That profile is now larger than the rest with a single keyword flashing.

Journalist.

Oh JeeMuh. Oh fuck, no. Not now.

The omnipresent paranoia ratchets up a gear and my palms start to sweat. He must have followed me from the train station, old-school style. I read his profile and select the link to his portfolio. He's written several pieces about the Pathfinder. Of course he has; half of the journalists alive now have written some bullshit about that crazy woman who built a spaceship called Atlas and took the faithful off into space to find God. His most recent piece is an article on the capsule they left behind to be opened forty years later that will soon be opened, the one I've instructed Tia to remove all mentions of from my feeds. The grand opening is less than two weeks away and the speculation about its contents has gone from occasional and irritating to constant and unbearable.

I force myself to appear calm, telling myself that I overreact to these people, and if I don't get a lid on this soon, it could be reported to my psych supervisor.

"Show him in the crowd, Tia."

A small blue arrow appears at the right-hand edge of my vision and I twist until the arrow disappears and a bald black man in a heavy gray overcoat is outlined in blue. He's staring right at me and just a second of eye contact is sufficient to send my heart rate high enough to flash a notification from MyPhys. I look away as fast as I can, silently hoping he'll stay where he is.

It's a ridiculous hope.

There's only one person in front of me now, and the vegetables I've got my eye on are still there. I want to run but I need the food. I add a "Do not disturb" to my personal profile but I know it won't make any difference to that parasite. If anything, it'll probably make him even more keen to bother me. Journos are twisted sods.

He's walking over and I ball my fists in my pockets. I fix my attention on the table ahead, tucking my nose beneath the top rim of the turned-up collar, even though it won't do a thing. I have to satisfy this primal urge to duck and hide somehow.

"Mr. Moreno," he says, even though his APA will be reminding him of the DND notice on my profile.

"I don't have anything to say."

"I don't want to talk to you about the case."

I channel my contempt into a long sideways glance. "I know."

"It's just a—"

"Leave me alone," I say as the person in front of me finishes her transaction.

"That's not very polite."

"Neither is harassment," I reply, and point out the vegetables I want, furious at this asshole ruining my chance to give the vendor a personal thank-you for his kindness. I pass over the small canvas bag I've brought with me and watch the carrots, onions and turnip being put inside. Even though it's gone out of fashion, I extend my hand to the seller and he shakes it firmly. "Thank you," I say to him as our APAs handle the transaction.

He winks at me again. "You need to queue properly if you want to buy," he says to the journo. "These good people have been waitin' awhile."

"You pushed in right in front of me!" umbrella lady says, sparking protests from the others behind her. As the journo extricates himself, I nip round the side of the van and collect two small sacks that I put straight into my case with more thanks to the seller's son.

I manage to get a few meters away before the journo catches up. "Mr. Moreno, I'm not like the others. I want to work with you. Surely you want some control over what people say about you? About your mother?"

"I deny permission to use any footage of this interaction or any recording of this conversation. If it's published online I'll use every fucking contact I have in the Ministry of Justice to—"

He smiles, holds up his hands as he puts himself in my way, forcing me to stop. "There's no need to threaten me. I'm not stupid. I'm not going to fuck with an SDCI, am I?"

"You already are." I move to go around him, mindful of the fact he's taller than me.

"I just want to explore the impact of—"

"Piss off." I push past him, but he follows. "I'm recording this," I say, even though he knows I will be. I still have to cover my ass.

"There are a lot of people who want to know who you are, Mr. Moreno. They want to know how you're doing. The network had more than three million messages after that first documentary was shown about you and your father. Three million people who cared so much they got in touch. Thousands sent cards and gifts. Did you know that? Just because of that documentary. Imagine what a second one could do."

That documentary. I stop, struggling to control the rage as a string of warnings from MyPhys scroll down the left-hand side of my vision. It details elevated blood pressure, increased cortisol and high adrenaline levels, forming a cold report of my need to punch this fuck into next week.

"Those people want to love you, Carlos. They want—"

I round on him, the bag slipping from my fingers, the case handle dropping into a puddle. "They want whatever the fuck you tell them to want," I spit through my teeth. "Let's tell the fucking truth for once. You want me to make you money. You're not interested in me or my story."

"On the contrary," he says, teeth bright white against his dark brown skin, "I'm very interested in why you spent all that money on a few shitty vegetables. On your pay grade? Bit indulgent, isn't it?"

I can hear Dee telling me to back off, just like she did on the first day I met her, when I almost hit the hot-houser who'd tried to make out that kidnapping us was an act of mercy. Even when Dee's hundreds of miles away, I carry her with me. I push down the rage, telling myself over and over again that he's not worth it. This journo isn't the first to harass me and he won't be the last. I can't risk a black mark on my file. "I'm going to walk away now, and if you follow me, I'll call in a team that'll make the counterterrorism forces look like the Boy Scouts."

I pick up the bag and the handle of my case and I force myself to walk away from him. I listen for his footsteps and breathe again when I realize my bluff has worked and he is walking in the opposite direction.

"MyPhys is reporting elevated stress levels," Tia says as I start to shake. "Would you like to play a game to calm you down while we walk to the station?"

"No, Tia. Call Dee for me. I . . . I need to talk to Dee."

2

I WOULDN'T CALL myself a violent man, but there are few things more satisfying than pulling off a perfect head shot from more than a hundred meters away and watching the can's metal head split open. That's when the tentacles come out and I switch to a laser cannon with a broader beam, because those things fly around so fast it's impossible to hit one at a time. When I've got a couple of good shots in, the whole creature comes out of the can to scuttle off across the red dust, but I shoot a grenade into its gelatinous rear end before it can get behind cover. Another stain on the surface of Mars and another cheer from Dee. I grin at her and holster the cannon, feeling like the fucking Don of New London, and turn to watch the scientists I've saved crawl out from the transporter.

One of them, a woman, comes over to me. I can't see much of her figure through the thick environmental suit, but she's pretty. I can't help but smile at the admiration in her eyes, blue and huge with wonder at my evident skill.

"That was an amazing shot," she says in a British accent far crisper than mine. "If you have a minute, I'd love to tell you about the new-season selection on offer at Abeline and Colson."

"Oh for fuck's sake," I say, and a dialog box pops up on the right-hand side of my vision.

Would you like to remove in-character ads?

They're not even in character. How do those gimps in marketing even think this shit works? I'm pumped up from ending a fight that's lasted at least twenty minutes, and the last fucking thing I want the character—who's obviously going to give the next bit of plot—to ask me is about whether I want to look at hand-knitted jumpers. I select the "yes" option with a flick of my eyes and confirm the micropayment.

We've noticed heightened levels of irritation from in-game ads. Would you like to remove all ads from this server connection?

Oh, I would love to, but I look at the cost and even though it isn't that much, I know I can't keep pissing away a few pounds here and there like I have been tonight. That's the trouble with these violent mersives: once the limbic system gets involved my higher cognitive functions are screwed.

"We carrying on, Carl?" Dee asks.

"Yeah," I say, dismissing the offer and its accompanying dialog box. "Sorry."

"There's another transport that was due to reach the outpost, but they haven't checked in," the scientist says, back to the game dialog, as if nothing has happened.

"We'll look into it," Dee says, and she gives me that smile, the one she always gives in between fights, the one that promises violent fun.

"Take our 'porter," the scientist says. "We can make it to the bunker from here. And then maybe afterward . . ." She looks me up and down and then fires a lustful smile at Dee. "Maybe you could both come back here for a debriefing."

"Yup, we'll do that," Dee says, and heads for the transporter's driving seat as the last of the scientists jump out the back and head off to safety.

"Did you change the settings?" I ask as I strap myself into the passenger's seat. "I thought the whole sex-starved martian-scientist stuff pissed you off."

She shrugs. "I just fancied a change. I think the shitty dialog is funny. It's like those ancient horror classics—you seen those? They were just pr0n, really. And I figured you might need to blow off some steam. No pun intended."

"Bollocks," I say, and we both laugh.

She's right though: I did need this. When I finally got through to her I was almost home, munching on a bag of roasted chestnuts from the only street-food vendor in London that I trust. By then I couldn't talk about what had happened; I'd already pushed it down too far. She could tell I was upset. "Wanna shoot some shit on Mars?" she'd asked, knowing I needed some way to vent. There's nothing better than an ultra-violent with a thin-ass plot and great rendering to help me unwind after a case. "Do you think the scientists on Mars know about this game?"

"Are you joking? Half of them probably made a stack of cash recording environmentals for the game company."

"I wonder if they play it."

She doesn't answer, focusing instead on getting the transporter over some difficult terrain. She always drives, because she's better at it than I am. I don't mind, but usually there's a turret I can man to keep me busy. These are nothing more than armored jeeps and there's nothing for me to do but wait until we reach the next set piece.

I look out of the window at the orange sky, the browns and dusky reds of the martian landscape. Even though I know I'm not really here, it's not enough to stop it seeming real. I know that what I see is simply a clever combination of images displayed into my lenses and data streamed to my chip, all conspiring to make me see and hear things that are, literally, a world away and not real anyway. The real base on Mars has been in operation for more than ten years and the planet has been studied for the past sixty-odd, and not once has there been any evidence of aliens or indigenous robots or aliens inside robots, as this game has decided upon. The only thing realistic about this is the way it looks and my brain just laps it up, happy to be tricked as my body lies on my sofa, home at last.

If I could, would I jack it all in, sell all my stuff and apply for a secondment to the Mars station? What kind of person would do that?

Someone like my mother. But she didn't go to Mars. I shudder, forcing my thoughts away from her, a flash of irritation at the journo for stirring that shit up again. I have no desire to leave Earth, no matter how many people and news feeds say I must be desperate to. I'm not the abandoned, tragic figure they want to make me, staring up at the night sky, wishing I had been taken too. Fuck that shit. I'm not what they want me to be.

"You're quiet," Dee says.

The orange glow from outside shines through the plasglass visor of her helmet, highlighting stray blond strands around her eyes with bronze and making her pale skin look like it's being warmed by the light of an ancient forge. I almost tell her about the journo, but I don't want to say the words he said. If I do that, they'll feel too real. And anyway, she's heard me moan about this shit for years; she doesn't need to hear it again.

"Must be tough at the moment," she says. "All that talk of the capsule is bad enough but that documentary on top? That's tough shit for anyone to deal with . . ."

I turn away from the fake martian scenery to look at her, feeling the stress and dread that I'd been trying so hard to escape seeping into this world too. "What documentary?" Had the journo chosen to leave out the fact it had already been made? Or is this another one?

"Shit. You didn't know?" She bites her lip.

"What documentary?" There have been several over the years, each one a punctuation mark at the end of some tenuous anniversary. The first was when I was ten. *After Atlas* it was called, and the researchers who made it harangued my father into a nervous breakdown. And that fucking journo had the gall to try to make out that it was a positive thing.

"Well, it's forty years since they left, and with the capsule being opened and . . ." She doesn't need to finish the sentence. "I saw it come up on the schedule at work. I didn't know whether to tell you or not. I thought they might have been in touch."

I draw in a deep breath. "Someone hassled me on the way home tonight." I don't mention the food market. Dee wouldn't understand. "He said something about a documentary, but it didn't sound like it had been made yet."

"Oh, it's definitely been made already," Dee says. "They didn't even e-mail you?"

"They probably tried." My job is tough and I didn't choose it, but one perk is better than most at my pay grade: I can buy top-level personal security for only a fraction of its market value. It's enough to keep the bottom-feeders from finding where I live and hacking my stuff in the cloud and making my life even more hellish. They always find a way to my public in-box though, the one I have to have by law. And at every shitty anniversary or reminder of the day Atlas carried its crew off to follow that lunatic to find God, the in-box is bombarded by interview requests. My APA filters it as best as its algorithms can, but there's always someone who manages to get through to me. If it weren't for Dee and her kindness, I wouldn't even have this break. I can't afford a private gaming server, and Christ knows how she can on her pay grade. No, I'm not going to cast my professional eye over that puzzle. I'm just glad it's only the in-game ads bugging me and not some twat trying to get a sound bite in the middle of a firefight.

"But don't you want to make sure they tell the truth?"

"They're not interested in that, Dee. They're interested in a narrative."

"But don't you want that narrative to be true?"

I frown at her, but she's keeping her eyes on the dust and rocks ahead, steering the transporter toward a bright dot on the horizon. "I don't give a shit about what anyone thinks."

"Yeah, but the last one said you had ongoing problems as a result of—"

"Show me a person who doesn't have ongoing problems and I'll show you an AI. What's it to you, anyway?"

She glances at me, smiles a little, but something about this is making me uncomfortable. "I just worry about you. Look at you. You're skinny as hell. You eating properly?"

I let my raised eyebrow express how unimpressed I am. "Dee, I always eat properly."

"You're too thin. It must be the stress. I'm not having a go, Carl—I can only imagine how awful it must be. Shit, the things they say about your mother—I mean, that would upset anyone."

The things they say about my mother. They did upset me when I was a child. I believed them. Before I had the means to filter the news feeds like I do now, I saw what the world thought of a mother who left her baby behind to travel on Atlas. There were chat shows dedicated to decrying her decision, and features on the worst mothers in history in which she was always in the top ten. It didn't matter that others on that ship had left children too. Five toddlers, ten teenagers, many more adult children. As a baby, I was singled out. And all the other children had been left behind by their fathers. It was as if the media had so much more outrage to pour upon an absent woman than all those absent men.

Everybody judged her as the worst of humanity. I wasn't old enough to realize that those fucking leeches didn't have a clue what my mother was thinking when she left on that ship. And just as much as they hated her, they pitied me. I was incapable of understanding that, to them, I wasn't a person but rather a character in a melodrama of their making. Nothing more.

"Carl?" Dee's voice is as gentle as it always is, but she wants me to say something and there's nothing I want to share. "Don't you want people to know what their bullshit can do to someone?"

I don't even want to think about this anymore. I scan the surroundings for anything hostile, hoping for something to pop up that I can shoot. I don't understand why the level designers have allowed such a huge gap between action. The next station still looks miles away, a tiny cluster of lights in the distance. Surely something is about to land and open fire or roll out from behind a rock and take out the engine? It's like it wants me to sit here and be bored while Dee . . .

While Dee interviews me.

I don't say anything for a moment, getting a handle on the anger. I can't believe Dee would have anything to do with those parasites. It's us against them, surely, like it's always been. Right from the moment I met her.

A flash of the inside of the shipping container all those years ago, dark save for a single bright coin of blue sky in the roof at the corner. The smell of vomit and urine. The sound of someone weeping in the corner; others muttering to each other in a language I didn't understand. Hands were wrapped around my fist, holding it still.

"I could have had him!" I yelled into the darkness, the face in front of me nothing more than a glint of light from watery eyes.

"He would have killed you." Despite the circumstances, I was elated to hear someone else speak English. "Calm down. We haven't been shipped out yet."

"So we need to get out before that happens!" I was a teenager, still bruised and bloodied from trying to escape and being rounded up and thrown into the container with the other nonpersons. We'd been tricked into going somewhere with a rumor of paid work off-grid, then rounded up like stray dogs and treated just the same. The woman in the darkness had stopped me from hitting the man who'd thrown us in there. I had almost punched her out instead.

"No, it's a good thing. I heard what they're planning to do. We're going to be hot-housed. If you mark yourself out as violent, it'll be worse for you."

"Hot-housed? What does that even fucking mean?"

The hands tightened around my fist and her voice lowered. "It means we have to be smart. You've played games, right? Mersives?"

"Yeah," I lied.

"This is no different. You keep quiet, learn the rules, do the right things at the right times. We get it right, we'll win the game. Understand?"

"No."

"Willing to learn?"

"I guess."

The hands shifted until only one held mine. I uncurled my fist and she shook my hand, mingling our sweat. "My name is Dee."

"Carlos."

She pulled me closer until I could feel her breath on my ear. "I'll watch your back if you'll watch mine."

And she did. Dee taught me how to navigate that appalling gov-corp-sanctioned "solution" to the problem of nonpersons on the streets: the hell of hot-housing. On the first day there they told us that we were lucky. That we had a way to become part of society again, and with a place in society we would have rights once more. The hot-housers neglected to mention that those rights would be owned by whoever bought us at the end of our time there, when we'd been sorted and had a value assigned to us and the debt we'd accrued during our imprisonment had been fully calculated.

Hot-housing was nothing more than a prison that had been monetized more creatively. Every aspect of our life controlled. What we did. What we ate. What we learned. Later, what we thought and felt. Life was the inside of a cell or the inside of the machine (even now the hairs on the back of my neck prickle at just the thought of it) or the inside of a virtual training space.

None of the outer doors were locked. They didn't need to be. Every morning when our individual cells were opened, they'd make us walk past windows to get to the mess hall, just so we could see what was outside.

Miles of barren wasteland. Toxic earth, ravaged by defunct industry from the previous century and too expensive to clean up. In the sky above it, dozens of drones set to patrol in the hope someone would try to escape, funded by the sorts of people who looked for cheap acquisitions for their brothels or labs or other sordid uses.

We were the lucky ones, as they told us every day, because we were bright enough to be trained and strong enough to take the drugs that enabled us to cram ten years' worth of education and training into less than two. Yeah. So damn lucky.

Dee had been right; being hot-housed was like a game and it had clear rules. Not that there was any enjoyment in understanding that the only way to win was to make ourselves too useful and valuable to sell into menial labor or other terrible places we only heard rumors about. It meant we left that hell with bigger debt; after proving our value we had to pay for the training that enabled us to reach our potential, but, as Dee said, at least after we served out our contract we'd be in a better place to enjoy our freedom.

I used to hate how seeing her again brought it all back so sharply. Now I appreciate how it helps me to remember we survived.

Looking at her now, in the driving seat, I doubt my suspicions. Surely it's the same as it always was. Surely I'm just being paranoid, the harassment earlier setting me on edge. But this doesn't feel right. I check my thinking, looking for the assumptions and gaps in the data. It leads back to the same conclusion: she's trying to interview me for someone else.

"Stop the 'porter."

"Why? I can't see any—"

"Stop the fucking 'porter, Dee!"

The tires skid and she kills the engine. "What?"

"What's going on? You've never talked to me about this stuff before, in all the years we've known each other. Five years ago you didn't even mention the thirty-fifth anniversary fuckery they were churning out on the feeds—you just met me online and we shot the shit out of stuff."

"Look—"

"Then you invite me here, just as all the capsule bullshit gets fired up again, offering a sanctuary from the public servers. There's no way you can afford this, Dee, not unless you've got into some seriously dodgy shit, and you're not going to risk a black mark."

"Carl, you're—"

"And now you're asking me the kinds of questions a hack would, while the game gives you an oh-so-convenient pause in the action. Did you really think I'd fall for it? It's clever, I'll give you that. No breach of privacy per se; no need to do anything to my accounts that could be traced. No, they just used you to get to me the old-fashioned way. Nothing illegal whatsoever."

Dee's shoulders slump and she holds up a hand to me as she looks away, whispering, presumably to whomever is backing this sorry exercise. It's probably some journo or one of the researchers for that damn documentary she brought up. Yeah, they always try to snare me with the whole "Don't you want to tell your truth?" line.

"They say they just want one exclusive interview, Carl. Not about the capsule. About Alejandro and the Circle. Just one interview and then this server space will be yours for the rest of your life—full privacy, no ads, any game you want."

I laugh because if I don't, it'll come out some other way. I've never even mentioned the Circle or Alejandro to Dee; no way I'll talk to strangers about them. "Tell them to go fuck themselves."

Dee's eyes move as if she's doing something with a dialog box and she takes off her helmet. "Carl," she says, reaching over to touch my arm. "They'll draw up a contract promising to show you the edited footage before it's released. It's the best way for you to have a voice in this madness. You can't just keep running away from it all the time. It just makes them more interested in you—don't you get it?"

"Not you too." My voice cracks and I look away from her, the old, familiar bitterness of betrayal flooding back in.

"These people are different. You'll have complete control over what they put out on the feeds."

"I already have control. I choose who to talk to and who to keep out. It's none of their goddamn business." I move away from her. "I won't forget this. End game and exit."

3

WHEN I COME back into my body I ignore the MyPhys recommendation to remain lying flat for at least sixty seconds, and sit up. There's a moment of dizziness and a residual sense of disconnection that makes me shake my hands and feet as if I've been out in the cold.

I'll watch your back if you'll watch mine.

It feels like something has been pulled out of my chest and left an aching hollowness. All these years later and I thought Dee was still watching my back, the only person in the world, literally, that I could call a real friend. The self-pitying misery twists into anger, settling into a more familiar shape inside me. What else did I expect to happen? This is the way the world works! I was stupid to think she would be different.

"Come on," I say to myself. "Get up. Fuck her! Fuck all of them!" I squeeze my eyes shut, digging down into myself and that well of self-reliance, a strange comfort in this realization that Dee has fit the same pattern as my father, as Alejandro, as all of them. "I don't need any of them," I whisper to myself.

I take a moment to look around myself, making sure I'm fully oriented back in my apartment and that my brain is in sync with reality again, before heading over to the kitchen area. I need a practical task that can absorb some of this useless emotional energy. I know I'm pushing the emotional shit down and I know my psych supervisor would berate me for it, but what the fuck else am I going to do? Smashing stuff up or crying or talking it out isn't going to change what my best friend just did to me.

I fish out some cubed beef and stock from the freezer and dump them in the microwave. "Defrost," I say, and leave it to do its thing as I prep the vegetables.

My ex would start complaining at this point. "Why don't we go to La Casa?" she'd say. "We could have anything we like for a tenth of what this costs."

"But it's printed," I'd say, and the old argument would start again.

"There's nothing wrong with printed food. Stop being such a caveman, Carl."

"No. If you want to eat with me, we eat real food."

It never would have worked. She was great company if we were doing something together, like dancing or sim-diving or whatever new thing she'd found to get her adrenal gland working again. But it was the quiet times when the gulf between us was far too evident. She'd make jokes I didn't get because I just didn't have the same kind of life as her on too fundamental a level. When she had been a teenager, finding boyfriends and trying to study during blackouts caused by mass riots, I was in the Circle, digging fields on the other side of the world and pretending to pray. She'd grown up during the transition from pseudodemocracy into neoliberty, experiencing the varying crises caused by the shift from state governance to gov-corp management firsthand, while I'd been held in a cocoon of cult worship. How the hell could we understand each other?

"Who are you, Carl? Really?" she said when we broke up. She'd started asking about an article on me that was making the rounds online. "'Cos you keep telling me that you're not who they say you are, but every time I try to figure out whether there's anything more to you—"

That was when I shut the door in her face, having pushed her out of my flat. I handled that badly. But I can't deny the relief when her noise was gone. And I can't say I've really missed her since. I'm just glad she signed the NDA so nothing about what we did together or how crap I was to her at the end made it online. Those fucking documentary makers would have had a field day with it.

I'm gripping the knife too tightly. I draw in a deep breath and release it slowly. Why am I even thinking about her? Between our incompatibility and the change made to my contract a couple of years after we split up, that relationship was doomed. Back then, the corporates followed advice based on a social algorithm that apparently recommended allowing assets to have friendships and even date. It prevented long-term psychological issues or something. Then the corporates decided it was cheaper and less risky to allow assets access to gaming platforms where they could have virtual relationships instead. The same parts of the brain get stimulated without any risk of an asset falling in love and becoming difficult; problem solved. Only someone who has never been owned by another could balance that equation.

My contract has always prevented full-time cohabitation,

as they call it. A tidy corporate phrase encompassing love, security, friendship and the chance to discover something special enough to make an asset rage against his contract. That's what it comes down to in the end. And that's only the first of more than fifty clauses detailing all the other things I'm denied. The right to have children. Discussion of my contract with anyone other than my owner or their representative. The right to own property . . . The list goes on.

I don't look at that list anymore. I've grown out of seeking emotional self-destruction. But even now the doubts are slithering in, making me question whether ignoring the hellish foundation my life is built on genuinely equates to coping. What if I just keep looking the other way until one day it comes crashing back in? I'll be sent back to the testing center to be "recalibrated." No. I can't let that happen. Deep breaths. Hold the knife more gently. Chop the fucking vegetables.

"Tia, find me something to listen to. Something with a bit of oomph to it."

My APA selects a favorite of mine: an old album by an obscure Russian nova-punk band that self-destructed in an all-too-predictable fashion. I chop the carrots, and without a case to occupy me, my thoughts drift back to Dee, and another burst of anger flares through my chest. I'm not going to be able to let this go. She means too much to me.

It obviously wasn't mutual. We went through the stress, the fear, the abuse—all that hot-housing did to us—together, and then she throws me to those fucking dogs hungry for the next story. And for what? Did they offer her the same private-server deal they tried to buy me with? How long has Dee been reporting to them?

I put the knife down and press my fists into the worktop. I have to accept Dee told them everything about me that she could. As a fellow asset, she can't have told them about my status or about the hot-housing, so realistically, the most they could know is how I approach a few games. I didn't spill my guts to Dee as we played. Far from it. I just have to let it go and be thankful that I figured out the trap in time.

It doesn't make the betrayal any easier to deal with though.

"You haven't checked the stream for seven days," Tia says. "Would you like to review your settings?"

"No."

"I could suggest new people to connect with," Tia presses. "Or perhaps we could discuss a way to make your experience more convenient or enjoyable."

"No, Tia, it's fine. Everyone's talking about that bloody capsule, and when you filter that out, there's not much left."

"There are several trending tags that might interest you: #shut-upaboutthecapsule, #boringcapsuleisboring, #anythingbut—"

"Nothing social tonight, Tia, thanks." I'm not sure what the masses enjoy more: being swept into a fervor about the latest big story or the backlash against it. It all ends the same way: by the time whatever is being hyped actually happens, most people have used up all the fucks they could possibly give about it.

"Would you like me to review the filters in place on your public in-box? You have received new messages since you last checked your mail."

"All asking for interviews or some statement about the capsule?"

"All except one has been filtered into the 'Journalist shit-bags' folder. Would you like to—"

"I'm not interested."

"Would you like me to summarize the latest papers published in *Applied Psychology*, *The Criminal Mind* and—"

"No!" JeeMuh, I'm annoyed at an APA. I need an early night.

"Would you like me to make fewer suggestions?"

I start peeling the potatoes, wondering how to reply. I should keep up-to-date with things better than I have been of late. It's good to keep up with the latest research and think pieces by the greats in the field. But on these rare evenings of downtime between murder investigations, it's the last thing I want to do. I should keep an eye on current affairs too, but with the news feeds full of crap about the capsule and all the markets, tech and financial, wanking themselves senseless about what could be inside it, there's nothing left of merit. Tia is one of the highest-level APAs for both work and personal use, but it can be overzealous in trying to connect me more. It's only following protocols established from a combo of my psych supervisor's recommendations and my own profile settings, but sometimes it feels like it's nagging me.

"I don't mind suggestions," I reply. "I'm just not interested in anything except making this casserole right now."

I know I'm an outlier. My ex used to have ten conversations on the go while taking a shower—even while taking a dump. It's not like I can really jump into the stream anyway, not with my job. I'm always holding something back, even though I have permission to use a legal pseudonym for recreational use online. It's not the same when you know anything you say or do is being recorded and could be reviewed at any time by your owner. I can see why the hard core go to such lengths to create illegal online identities. The freedom that true anonymity would give must be intoxicating.

I'm quieter online than most. I guess some of Alejandro's teachings sank in deeper than I'd like to admit. It's then I realize he taught me how to cook this casserole and I shake my head. I'm not the product of tragedy the media hacks want me to be. Another selfish bastard did far more to make me what I am now than my own parents.

"Tia, has Alejandro Casales said anything about the capsule?"

"Yes. He made a public statement on arrival in London."

"He's in Norope?" My heart judders in my chest. Has he finally come to find me? No. He probably doesn't even remember me now. Only a narcissistic twat would think someone as high-profile as him would give any fucks about me. I know I'm just another piece of human wreckage he's left in his wake.

"Yes. He arrived in London eight days ago and made the statement at the airport. Would you like me to play a recording of the footage?"

I don't want to hear his voice again. I don't want to see his face. Why did I even ask? But I have to know now. "Just . . . read it out to me with your voice."

"Upon arrival at Heathrow Airport, Alejandro Casales said: 'I don't have anything new to say about Atlas and the one they called the Pathfinder. All I have is hope that whatever she left us in that capsule nourishes humanity. I know there are so many who hope it will contain answers, but to those who seek them I say this: look inside yourself. The answers to these questions are probably already within you, waiting to be heard. Turn off the distractions long enough to listen.'"

Even with Tia's voice it makes me clench my teeth. It sounds like the kind of preachy bullshit he'd say. "Why is he in Norope?"

"He hasn't made any statement to that effect, nor answered any questions about his visit," Tia replies. "Eighty-two-point-five percent of all mentions regarding his visit make the assumption he is here for the opening of the capsule."

That's bollocks, I think. For one thing, the capsule will be opened in Paris, Europe, so why fly into the capital of Norope? Relations between the two great gov-corps are better than they've been for a while, but back before England became part of the union between the former UK and the Scandinavian countries, there was always a vast political gulf between the island and mainland Europe. Landing in London when you're as famous as Alejandro Casales is like flicking all the balls in Europe without even trying. He used to be one of them, after all. And for another thing, there's over a week to go. Half of the news feeds have got that number ticking down in the corner of their broadcasts. Millions of people, every day, are counting off the days to what many are calling the event of the century. Others are calling it the end of the world, but then there's always someone counting down to that. Whether they believe it's going to reveal secrets that will change the world or just a picture of Cillian Mackenzie with his middle finger thrust in front of him, everyone is talking about it online. Except me.

The irony is, if I had true anonymity out there, I'd probably want to talk about that fucking capsule too. As much as I try to keep any and all reminders about it away from me, I can't stop my thoughts from drifting back to the bloody thing. I was only six months old when it was buried by the Pathfinder and her project/PR manager. What did Lee Suh-Mi and Cillian Mackenzie decide to gift to the poor bastards they left behind? The fabled coordinates to God and enough technical knowledge to build another huge ark and follow them? That's what most people seem to be hoping for: a new age of interstellar travel and space exploration. That's because they're idiots. There's no way we have the resources to devote to such a huge project, not after the damage from the '30s. There's no way to mobilize a build like that without taking critical materials and man power from something else, and there just isn't the slack anymore. The last thing that even came close was the Mars expedition and that hasn't made enough money to recoup costs. No profit means no more gov-corp interest, and that means it won't happen.

And what would be the point of trying to pursue Lee's crazy followers anyway? There's no guarantee Atlas made it, even if God was waiting for them at those coordinates. The Pathfinder and those stupid enough to follow her are probably all dead, frozen and floating in a huge man-made failure. I can imagine my mother's face, gray skinned and white lipped, eyes staring—

A loud buzz makes me jump and the knife slips. A red bloom sinks into the potato on the chopping board as I inspect the cut. Another buzz.

"What is that?" I ask Tia.

"The doorbell."

"You're shitting me."

A new icon labeled "DOORCAM" flashes in my right-hand field and I select it. My boss is standing on the doorstep, pressing the button for a third time. Fuck! Did she find out I was at that food market? As the buzz fades she looks straight into the cam and raises an eyebrow. I've been living here for more than five years and no one has ever rung the bell. I didn't even know there was one.

"Open the door for her," I say, hurriedly rinsing the cut. Knowing her, she'll take the stairs even though I'm five floors up. Enough time for me to put on some trousers and a clean T-shirt, if this bastard cut stops dripping.

"MyPhys, does this need stitches?" I stare at the long slice down the edge of my left forefinger.

Tia's voice reports back. "MyPhys recommends thorough

cleaning of the wound and application of a medi-strip. The injury has been logged in your medical record and you will be notified should there be early indications of infection." When I don't immediately move, Tia adds, "There's a box of them in the bathroom cupboard."

I leave drops of blood on the flooring as I dash in there and rinse it. Another drop splatters the white porcelain as I pluck a strip from the box and tear off the protective film with my teeth. There's immediate relief once I've pressed the gelled side against the cut as the local anesthetic does its work.

There's just enough time to dress properly and wipe up the blood from the floor before the knock. I run a hand through my hair, realize I haven't shaved and then open the door.

Roberta Milsom looks exactly as she always does: her hair is cut shorter than mine, in an Afro style, dark brown skin, no makeup. What you see is what you get with her and I like that. She gives her usual nod and steps inside without bothering to wait for the invitation to do so. We both know it would be superfluous, and if she's anything, she's efficient.

"Caught you out, did I?" she says, taking in the medi-strip and the fold creases in my T-shirt that haven't had a chance to drop out yet.

"Yes, ma'am," I say, standing straighter out of habit. "I was cooking."

"I'd heard you do that," she says, walking in, her boots making a gentle clumping sound.

She doesn't ask if she's disturbing my plans. That's irrelevant. I'm always available, as per the terms in my contract. Milsom knows there's no one else here because she would have checked beforehand. She doesn't apologize for the intrusion because she has every right to summon me any time of day or night, regardless of what I might feel about it. What I don't understand is why she's come in person to do something she usually handles with a message.

That fact makes me tenser around her than usual. I follow her down the hallway, watching her sweep her trained eye over everything. She's thinking it's too big a place for me, that it's an indulgence on my part that she would never permit herself. But she won't say that. There are professional boundaries, after all. Just like everything she's looking at, it doesn't really belong to me; it's being paid for out of a negotiated extension to my contract. I'll be paying for the rent on this place as part of my contractual debt for many, many years. At the end of it all, I'll walk away with the clothes on my back—nothing more. I'm not going to extend my contract for paintings and ornaments and clothes I don't need.

"I'll get to the point," Milsom says, even before taking off her coat. "There's a case but it's complicated. I'm going to shut down your APA while I brief you."

Another first. The tension knots my shoulder muscles. I don't keep a cluttered border in my UI field, not like some, only a tiny icon in the bottom right for me to select if I want to do anything in silence instead of the voice interface. When it disappears I realize how deeply I'd become accustomed to it.

"Are you worried about a security breach?"

She doesn't answer, just tosses her coat onto one of the chairs. "Aren't you going to offer me a drink?"

I want to quip that she said she was going to get straight to the point but I daren't piss her off. She's honest-to-God nervous and I know that something big is coming. "Should I get one for myself too?"

She nods. "Make them large."

I open a bottle of wine, having finished the whisky last week, and pour two large glasses as she settles herself in another chair, all the while taking in the Spartan decor and sleek storage. This could be anyone's apartment, I think, imagining seeing it through her eyes for the first time. No photos, no ornaments, not even any art.

I take the wine over to her and sit opposite. She takes a sip and then downs a good slug of the stuff. It irritates me that she isn't savoring it; the bottle, being the real deal, costs just shy of a week's worth of debt. I hide the fact I'm trying to breathe in the aroma—she'll only think I'm some pretentious tosser—and then take a sip myself, letting the flavors spread across my tongue before swallowing.

I'm ready for something shitty—some celeb knocked off in a corporate's house, that sort of thing. I wait as she considers the best way to start.

"Alejandro Casales has been murdered. We want you to lead the investigation."

4

"WHAT?" I SAY dumbly, like all the people I've had to inform of the deaths of loved ones.

"The head of the Circle cult has been murdered, Carlos. We need you to head up the case."

The second time she says it I can get ahold of it, understanding the words but not believing them. She said "head of the Circle cult" as if I'd needed a clarification, as if I were somehow magically capable of forgetting that man.

As clearly as I see her now, I see Alejandro the day I met him more than thirty years ago. I opened the door to him, ashamed because I knew he would notice my clothes were dirty and that the hallway carpet was covered with filth. The sun was behind him and he towered over me, like he'd been sent by the Greek gods I'd been learning about.

"Ah, good morning, young man."

"We don't want to buy anything and we don't believe in

God," I said, having learned it from my dad before he'd stopped talking.

"Just as well. I'm not selling anything and I'll never tell you what to believe," he replied. "My name is Alejandro. You must be Carlos." His voice was deep and gentle, the kind I wished my father had.

"Do you know my dad?"

"I need to speak to him. It's very important. Is he at home?"

"He doesn't talk to anyone. Are you police?"

A laugh. "No."

"Bailiff?"

"You seem very young to know a word like that."

I'd learned it from the television. I had it on twenty-four hours a day and not on the children's channels. I needed to hear other adults and it comforted me. But there had been one vintage show about people who didn't pay bills and had their stuff taken away, and the idea had taken root in my brain. My dad didn't get out of bed, so surely he wasn't paying our bills. I was convinced that one day large men with clipboards and corporate baseball caps would turn up and take everything away. I was too young to realize that no one used clipboards anymore.

"He doesn't talk to anyone," I repeated, and started to close the door.

"I need to talk to him about your mummy," he said, and the door swung back again, letting the sunlight spill over the grime around my feet. "He'll listen to me. Only five minutes, and then I'll be gone and I promise I won't take away any of your stuff."

"Pinky promise?"

He held out his hand, baby finger extended, and let me interlock my own with his. Satisfied, I stepped aside and let him in.

Inside the house, with the sunlight shining onto his face, it all made sense. Same dark brown eyes, same dark brown hair, same olive skin. He was a long-lost uncle, one I had been wishing for so much, come to sweep us away to his gigantic estate and make everything better.

Oh God, how could I have been so right and so wrong?

There's a moment when something threatens to surface and I lock it down, shifting into professional mode. No room for that shit right now, not with her watching me.

"Carlos, I know you were close to him, and I know this is hard and that's why I'm running this by you off the record first. I don't want this to be the first black mark against you, if you can't handle it. That wouldn't be fair."

I frown at her. Is this some sort of . . . caring? "What are the details?" I ask, wanting to put this back into a framework I can understand.

"He was found in a hotel on the edge of Dartmoor."

"Dartmoor? What was he doing there?"

"We don't know." Another pause. There's more and it's bad and I just want her to tell me straight. I can't make any demands though. It's the first time she has ever considered my feelings and the only time I don't want her to. "Carlos, he was hanged, drawn and quartered."

Automatically I go to activate the icon that's missing. I've heard that phrase before but I can't place it.

"What have you got from the scene?"

She looks down; at first I think she's accessing something but she's retrieving the wineglass, stalling again. "We haven't had any SOCO access to the scene yet."

"Why?"

Her lips, thin already, almost disappear as she presses them tight together. After a beat she says, "Lawyers. A fucking army of them. Look, like I said, it's complicated."

"Lawyers? How can anyone interfere with a crime scene? That doesn't make any sense. When was he found?"

"Two days ago."

"What the actual fuck?"

She holds up a hand. "Spare me. I'm just as pissed off as you are. This is a clusterfuck—there's no other way to describe it. I'll fill you in on the details on the way to Devon if you take the case. I just need to know if you can handle this."

Can I? I don't want all this shit dredged back up, not now when it feels like everyone else in the world wants to do the same. But the thought of someone else handling this is worse than the stress of doing it myself. I'd only end up obsessing over it even if I turned it down. And I don't want that black mark either.

"Yes," I say, with certainty. "It's mine. I can handle it."

I have never seen her look so relieved. "Thank fuck for that," she whispers, and drains the glass.

"Collins could have taken it if I'd said no," I say, standing a moment after she does. "She's excellent."

"She couldn't." She scoops her coat from the chair. "You're the only one the lawyers would agree on. Now get your stuff. We're leaving."

It takes only a couple of minutes to pack; I hadn't fully unpacked from the last case, which had taken me up to Scotland. I travel light anyway. I take the bags of flour and sugar out in my bedroom, not wanting to explain them to Milsom, and hide them under my bed. As I stuff clean underwear into the side pocket of the mini case, my APA comes back online.

I call up the v-keyboard and type in a query for Tia, taking a moment to select privacy mode so Tia won't give the results through any of the apartment's speakers for Milsom to hear. "Define: Hanged, drawn and quartered." It feels like I'm researching something distant and unimportant. I just can't believe anything about what I'm doing could be related in any way to Alejandro. Surely there's been some sort of mistake.

No. The Ministry doesn't make mistakes like this.

"A method of execution used from the thirteenth to eighteenth centuries in which the condemned was drawn to the location of the execution on a rudimentary litter pulled by a horse, then hanged without a drop to prevent the neck from being broken. Before death, the condemned was cut down and his genitalia cut off before he was disemboweled. His intestines and heart were burned, major organs removed; then he was beheaded and the body cut into four quarters."

I sit heavily on the edge of my bed, swallowing down the burning sensation rising from my stomach. Was this really what had been done to him? After steadying myself I call up the keyboard again.

"Was this how they executed murderers?"

"This manner of execution was reserved predominantly for crimes of high treason or spiritual treason."

"Spiritual treason?"

"Refusing to accept the church sanctioned by the monarch and state. During the 1500s approximately one hundred Catholics were hanged, drawn and quartered in Tyburn, London, after refusing to renounce their faith."

"You said 'his'—what happened to the women?"

"They were burned at the stake."

"Why?"

"To preserve modesty."

"JeeMuh," I whisper. They had some fucked-up ideas about modesty back then. Perfectly fine to butcher someone in public, but any hint of seeing a nude woman was obviously improper.

I swipe away the virtual keyboard, not wanting to keep the boss waiting. Before I leave my bedroom I take a moment to compose myself. The start of a case always fires me up, gets my brain fizzing with questions and potential avenues of inquiry. But this time it's all churned up in a mess of emotion. I need more distance from this but I'm not going to get it. I hold my palm flat in front of my chest, shut my eyes and push my hand down slowly as I breathe out, imagining my core being calmed by the movement. I will learn the details, I will work the case, I will identify the murderer. I've never found a puzzle I couldn't solve. This is no different.

MILSOM is waiting in the hallway by the front door, gazing at the wall without seeing it, tiny movements of her eyeballs suggesting she's reading something. I approach, her eyes flick up to the far top right and then she blinks, seeing me. She looks at my bag, the one given to me when I left the testing center almost twenty years ago, but says nothing. It's scuffed but still does the job.

"Ready?" she asks, and I nod. We leave as Tia shuts down the heating and the lights and locks the door behind us.

We descend the staircase in silence, the elevator not even given a glance, and emerge into the courtyard outside the apartment block. The wind cuts through my coat and I turn up the collar. A few stubborn leaves are still clinging to the plane trees that edge the perimeter, their fellows now slippery mush collected in the gutters around the car park. I hate November.

"I parked round the corner," Milsom says. "Your space was taken."

"I let my neighbor's daughter park there. It's safer for her. I don't need it."

Milsom stares at me for a moment and then heads toward the gates. Tia opens them ahead of us and I turn to look back at the ground-floor window behind us. Sure enough, the building manager is watching us, probably wondering why a police protocol opened the gates a few minutes ago. I give him a wave but it isn't returned. Sour old bastard. The sooner he's replaced by something with a good-manners subroutine, the better.

"Nice place," Milsom says as we leave the courtyard and the din of London's sprawl comes crashing in, no longer held at bay by the noise suppressors built into the perimeter.

I just nod. I'm too tense to cobble together some small talk. I need to get to work.

A car from the Ministry is parked down a side street, sleek, compact and ubiquitous. It's one of the hybrid models with both automated and manual driving capabilities. I don't hold a license for the latter, not that it would make much difference; Milsom would never let me drive anyway.

Her APA unlocks the car as we approach and I put my bag in the boot as she gets in. I savor the last few moments of silence as I walk round to the passenger's side. I feel like I'm standing on the edge of a pool, taking a deep breath before diving in. I open the door, plunging in.

"Automatic, social," Milsom says to the car's AI, and the engine starts. There's a pause as she does something with her APA and a map is projected onto the windshield. I see a red line snaking across the south of England from East London to Devon. Milsom approves the route, the map is replaced by a translucent pale blue line projected to appear as if it overlays the tarmac ahead of us, and we snap our seat belts into place so the car will pull away.

Once we're moving, my seat slides back from the dashboard,

swinging round to face Milsom's seat, which is doing the same. The rear bucket seats are folding away to make more space now that the car knows there are only two passengers. The windscreen is on my left now, her chair slightly closer to it so we both have room to stretch out our legs.

"I'll keep this as a verbal briefing on the way to Devon," Milsom says. "I know you get travel sickness if you do too much AR."

"I might have to face forward when we get to those rural roads," I add.

The car has taken us to a main road and the traffic is thick, all the bumpers mere centimeters from each other as the Met Traffic System manages the individual car AIs set to a compulsory automatic status. It's nearly midnight, and it'll be a couple of hours before this is all cleared through and the Met TS will let people drive manually again.

Milsom is calling up data, seeing things that I cannot. I look past her shoulder to the car next to ours. Four men—maybe two couples, from the way they are acting—are all facing each other, playing some sort of game that's apparently hysterically funny. Tia thinks I'm interested in them and pings their AIs. All four are set to public and social, and I hastily set my own to private as I skim their details. I'm not the least bit interested but am grateful for the brief distraction.

"The victim was found in a room at the Moor Hotel, in the living-room area of the largest suite there." Milsom's voice snaps my attention away from them and back into the car. "The victim." That's what he is now. It stings, but I wrestle it into place. Easier to use that than Alejandro or even Casales. The first tiny bit of distance I can get. "It's a five-star place, very exclusive, and prides itself on being old-fashioned."

"In what way?"

"Human staff, even the cleaners. Some other quirks you'll see when we arrive."

"Who found him?"

"A woman sharing the suite with him, someone from the Circle that traveled with him from the States. Selina Klein. The lawyers have prevented us from getting her background."

I shake my head in disbelief. "On what grounds?"

"Potential of religious persecution."

"And why the fuck has the Ministry not blown that bullshit out of the water?"

Milsom frowns. "I know our people are working on it. All indications are that the lawyers are being deliberately obstructive. Everyone knows we have the right to investigate a murder committed in our country in the manner we see fit. But the Europeans are throwing their weight around, as well as the Yanks. I know he's high profile, but they're taking the piss."

"The Europeans too? On what grounds? There's no way there can be any jurisdiction bollocks going on here. He's not even a citizen anymore."

"That's what I thought," Milson says. "They claim he's still legally a citizen of Europe and they've sent a bunch of lawyers willing to prove it and slow everything down as much as they can. It's because of the Circle though, let's face it: it all comes down to money. They have so much property all over the world, particularly Europe, it's no surprise the legals are sniffing about. The only good thing about it is that they've got all the guests, employees and their ISPs bound by a gag order, so we won't be harassed by the press as soon as we arrive."

I nod. "Good to hear. Hopefully they'll all be too distracted by the capsule to go sniffing around police contacts."

Milsom nods in agreement, but we both know the media vultures will be circling long before we want them to be.

"We've managed to secure assurances that Klein will not leave the hotel, nor will any of the other guests that need to stay, until we give the go-ahead."

I can see why they would have to secure that for Klein: as a member of the Circle she won't be chipped. "Why not just pull the data from the other guests' APAs?"

"Several are unchipped. There's a Brit who had to have hers removed on medical grounds a few months ago. Like I said, this place is old-fashioned and caters very well to those without personal APAs. The rich ones anyway."

"You said the lawyers have kept the SOCOs out too. Is . . . his body—"

"The parts have been removed," she says quickly. "No international laws can stop that or stop the recorders going in. Which they have. The virtual scene is ready for you once we're out of the car."

"But no actual people have been in there."

"No police. The scene's already been contaminated. The hotel manager, for one, and a cleaner have been in there— thankfully they had the sense to not clean the mess up, but they trampled through the room to get to the bedroom."

"Why?"

"The woman, Klein, was hysterical. Let me take you through what we know from the start. The victim and two traveling companions—Selina Klein and Theodore Buckingham— checked into the hotel eight days ago. Casales secured a standard room and the Diamond Suite for a two-week stay with the option to extend. He shared the suite with Klein and the room was for Buckingham. Apparently he didn't know how long he was staying, because no date was set for the return flights. For five of those eight days the victim was in London, and the other two at the hotel. We don't know what Casales was doing in

London yet, for obvious reasons. He returned to the hotel on Sunday afternoon, they all dined together in the restaurant and Casales and Klein retired to their room at ten p.m.

"At approximately nine thirty a.m. on Monday morning, one of the cleaners was working in a room down the corridor and heard screaming coming from the suite. He rang down to reception and called for the manager, who came at once. They let themselves into the room after knocking a couple of times and entered the crime scene. The cleaner rushed straight out of the room and vomited in the hallway after seeing the state of the body. The manager crossed the room to the bedroom, as Klein was standing in the doorway, screaming. She managed to push Klein back into the bedroom and shut the door before Klein collapsed."

It didn't sound like the kind of crime a woman would commit. Something was missing—that much was clear. How could a man be murdered and hacked into pieces while a woman slept next door? Had she left at some point later that evening, to come back and discover the body in the morning?

"The local police were called, as was an ambulance," Milsom continues. "Klein was treated for shock, and the local bobbies secured the scene as best they could. They piped it through to the Ministry at ten-oh-one a.m. By ten twenty-three a.m. a memo came through from Number Ten to the Ministry, instructing that other than securing the scene, having it recorded and removing the body parts to a nearby morgue, no further investigation was permitted to take place without express permission. Not even a postmortem."

"Has that ever happened before?"

"Once, but not for a murder. Back in the late thirties there was a break-in and suspected burglary in London. In the first twenty-four hours there were more lawyers on the scene than coppers, apparently."

"For a burglary? Where? One of the Ministries?"

"No. Cillian Mackenzie's pied-à-terre in Mayfair. The Euros were convinced sensitive documents were there, ones owned by Lee Suh-Mi. She was a European citizen so they felt they could wade in. That's the trouble with all these bloody lawyers. They build in the loopholes when they're on the right gov-corp committees so they can exploit them later."

Just the sound of Lee and Mackenzie's names makes the muscles in my lower back knot up. "Has anyone said why there's all this crap for this case?"

"The Yanks are arguing that as the Circle is based in the States and the victim had a religious visa, they are obligated to ensure the investigation proceeds with proper attention to their wishes. The fact he's worth billions of dollars probably has something to do with it too. The Euros are saying that as the victim was actually a citizen of Europe, they have to represent his family and ensure the investigation proceeds with proper attention to *their* wishes."

I can hear the frustration in her voice, and I share it. "Still doesn't make any sense," I say. "How can it be against their wishes to catch the one who did it? Their delays are only going to make that harder." I pause, remembering what she'd been like when I said I'd take on the case. The relief. "Wait. The delay was because they were arguing about who would head this, and they settled on me?"

She nods.

"The Yanks know I don't believe in any of that cult shit, don't they?"

Milsom swipes away something from her personal display

and looks at me properly for the first time since the briefing began. "You know what they're like. How can they trust us godless Brits to treat this with the sensitivity it needs? You were in the Circle, you left but it wasn't acrimonious. They think you'll be sympathetic and that you'll know how to treat the grieving. The Circle aren't the most cooperative people in the world."

"Don't I know it." I try not to imagine what they'll all be like when they get the news. I try not to think of my father, weeping. I fail.

"Now, we know you're too professional to let any history with them interfere with the job, so no complaints from our end on that front."

I don't say what I'm thinking. It would be unwise to respond to what lies beneath those words, but I know it. They know I won't risk doing anything less than the cleanest, deepest investigation I'm humanly capable of. I can't risk anything less than that, as their property. I'm prepared to extend my contract in order to eat proper food and live in anything bigger than a broom cupboard, but not for sloppy work.

Sometimes I try to imagine the day my contract ends. It's getting harder. I've added more than fifteen years to it already, between paying for my flat and buying fresh food over the years, and there's likely to be more added if the food prices keep going up. The last time I asked Tia to check, I'll be in my mid-eighties when I'm free again. I'll never have children—I've made peace with that now—but maybe one day I'll be able to live somewhere with a garden. I'll be old but skilled enough to still have some consultancy work to pay for the space to grow real food. Hands in the dirt again. Doing something real. No people around. Yeah, that's the dream. Strange how the things we rail against and hate in our youth can be the things we crave as we get older.

"The Euros," Milsom continues, "feel you are uniquely placed with regard to your history with the Circle, but they also like the fact you used to be a European."

Until the Ministry officially bought my citizenship—and my rights—from them. I keep that bitter thought to myself.

"It helps that you and the victim were born in the same region of Spain too."

"Neither of us have lived there for more than thirty years though."

Milsom's shoulder twitches into a dismissive shrug. "As long as it matters to them, I'm not going to raise that. I'm just glad they actually managed to reach an accord. Otherwise we would have ended up with some god-ugly compromise, probably a multinational team and multiple agencies. At least this is tidy."

I nod, making sure that my expression remains neutral, just like Dee taught me all those years ago: *"Never let the fuckers see how you feel."* What I'd mistaken for tact and a mote of caring about my emotional state was simply a way to soften me up and keep it off the record so they could spin any line they liked if I had turned it down. I can't figure out if I'm more pissed off with Milsom for the manipulation or myself for thinking that she cared. There was no need to handle it this way; they could have forced me. But the Ministry prefers to keep our relationship as polite as possible, no matter how sordid its foundation. Nobody does emotional distancing from reprehensible behavior better than the British, after all. Besides, they need me to be one hundred percent engaged with this case. No doubt there will be more scrutiny than normal, and normal is bad enough.

"It's going to be a tough one," Milsom says.

"I can handle it," I say, and I'm not bluffing. In all honesty there's a part of me actually looking forward to this. A brief moment of concern that I'm some sort of sick bastard passes when I realize it's the puzzle part of my brain that's getting excited, which was identified as one of my most profitable qualities and was honed by the hot-housers. It'll come down to attention to detail and logic, the things I feel most comfortable with. "What resources do I have?"

"Grade-A expense allowance, most of which will go on that hotel on the days you stay there," Milsom reads from a note in her visual field. "Priority-one access to the Met AI, the Norope AI and an open channel to the US FBI AI, along with a human contact there and in Europe. The details are with your APA now. The visa for your trip to the States is already being processed, as is the one to Europe." At my frown, she says, "He wasn't chipped. Depending on what you find, you may need to work up a deep background with a bit of legwork, particularly in the States. It's not like we can just ping an AI for the Circle."

I'll have to go back there, the one place on Earth that I swore I would never step foot in again. I suck in a breath between my teeth as a sinking dread settles in my stomach. I'll have to see my father again.

"Get some rest," Milsom says. "You're not going to get much once we arrive, and I have a stack of pendings I need to deal with."

I agree and ask the car AI to shift my seat into a resting position. Tia sends my personal preferences to it, and it swivels around to face front again as Milsom's turns in the opposite direction until she is facing the rear window, giving her more space to move her arms about in communication with her APA in silent mode.

The traffic is easing the farther we get away from the center, and I see the car with the four-man party in it pulling away as its lane increases speed. One of them, a black guy with a shaved head and a neck thick with muscle, smiles at me as our eyes meet accidentally. I wonder where he is going and Tia tells me instantly, reading the destination from his social profile. I close my eyes, thinking of my old life in which little social mysteries were nurtured like fragile seedlings, safe from the trampling of overzealous APAs.

5

WHEN MILSOM SHAKES my shoulder, I think it's my dad waking me and, for the briefest moment, that we're driving across the Southwestern American wilderness. I haven't thought about that journey for years. I sat on a box in the front seat, too short for the seat belt without it. Dad was stimmed and tense, terrified the long, straight roads would make him fall asleep at the wheel. I still had Bear then; I'd held him tight for days of travel, the only constant while everything changed around me.

When I take in the sight of wrought-iron gates looming out of the darkness beyond the car's headlights I'm fully oriented again and grateful that I didn't dream about Alejandro. I dismiss Tia's dialog box asking if I need more prolonged stimulation, as if the mild adrenaline burst of waking in a car with my boss on the brink of the highest-profile murder case of my career to date isn't enough. I'm alert enough for now. Tia informs me that it's just before two in the morning.

The gates open ahead of the car and the seating starts

shifting itself back into its default orientation. I realize Milsom hasn't driven us down here, which is unusual for her. I guess she had a lot of admin to attend to on the way. That and the fact her APA would have overridden any request to drive manually after that glass of wine.

The car takes us along a long, winding drive, the kind reserved for the sort of place owned by people who want you to spend the last minutes of your journey appreciating just how rich they are. Either side of the drive is hemmed in by trees made naked by winter, catching just enough light from the car to look like they're straight out of some cheap horror mersive. The tarmac is covered with twigs, and I see a few broken branches pushed to the side of the road. A storm must have come through.

"There will be some legal documents to sign when we arrive," Milsom says.

I frown at her. "Send them to me and—"

"They need to be witnessed hard copies," she cuts in. "The lawyers are waiting up for us."

"That's why you came down here with me?"

She nods. "When I'm certain everything is compliant, I'll leave you to it." My shoulders drop an inch with relief. I was starting to think she'd be watching over my shoulder the whole time. "But I'll be checking in," she adds, as if sensing it. "More often than you'll like."

"Like being a rookie again."

"No, Carlos. Not at all."

I want to explain what I meant, but I don't bother. I shouldn't have been flippant. I'm more tired than I think.

Milsom sends over the digital versions of the contract I'm soon to sign, and when Tia offers to review it, translate the legalese and then summarize it to me, I accept. In seconds a list of bullet points stream down the left-hand side of my vision.

"This contract is . . . insane." I look at Milsom.

"I know. I reviewed it on the way down."

"Will it get in the way of how I usually work a case?"

"Not as far as the Ministry lawyers or I can tell," she replies. "It's mostly about privacy and ownership of information that emerges from the case, but with three different parties all claiming rights and needs that must be respected, it's bloated as hell. Just send me anything in the first instance, as you would with any other case of this level. If it looks dicey, I'll let the lawyers worry about the contractual obligations. As far as I'm concerned, we go in there, we pay these parasites some lip service and then we can get on with our fucking job."

"Um . . . you know that this is being recorded." Even if I had a normal contract with the Ministry, we'd still be on the record now, seeing as we're here on Ministry business.

She grins in a way I've seen only once before, and just like back then, I'm glad I'm not the one who has pissed her off. "Yep. I know."

As weird as all of this is, I'm reassured by what she's said. I'm used to walking into difficult situations, being in the specialty that I am, namely murder cases that are highly sensitive and complex. These days, "sensitive" means "something that could cause the Noropean gov-corp a serious loss in profits, for whatever reason." And "complex" usually means "a case that can't be solved by reviewing cam and local-node data for all of five minutes." With all the data available to law enforcement these days, it's more economical to train a very small number of specialized detectives with high-level skills and move them to wherever they're needed.

Simple cases are handled by local police, as they should be. I never arrive at a place where things are simple or going well.

Sometimes it causes friction; the local DI never likes some outsider sticking his nose in, let alone one who answers to a line of command plugged straight into the top levels of the Ministry of Justice. Sometimes they think I'm there to just swan in and make them feel like they can't handle a case. With this one I don't anticipate it being a problem. The local police here will have figured someone like me would be sent as soon as the call came through from the hotel. It was probably a relief.

I call up my v-keyboard and instruct Tia to operate in full predictive mode, as is my preference when working a case. It's tiring, having to filter out a greater amount of information pulled from the Web, but Tia is getting pretty good at working out just how much I want to know. Besides, it means I can look a lot of things up with just a thought, rather than having to v-type or speak. More than once it's saved my ass in difficult conversations when I've had to bluff knowing more than I should have.

Before the hotel even comes into sight, Tia informs me that the handshake with the hotel's local node has been successful and case protocols successfully implemented. Now every chipped person I interact with will have a notice displayed when they look at me and when they speak to me, warning that any footage recorded either purposefully or passively will be reviewed by the Ministry's AI and could be used in a court of law. It does nothing to help more subtle lines of inquiry, but it does mean that if anyone tries to film me and send it to those documentary makers, the Ministry will shut them down faster than I could say "piss off." That's one of the things I love about this job: when I'm on a case, no one can fuck with the Ministry's highest-level privacy protocols.

The Moor Hotel is a leftover from a bygone age, a time when people built houses without worrying about ecoregulations and sustainable materials. It's three stories high and there are more than a dozen windows on both of the upper floors. The roof is tiled with slate and doesn't even have any solar panels fixed to it. That alone speaks of exclusivity; a portion of the exorbitant costs must go toward the exemption certificates required to maintain period buildings in a manner sympathetic to the time of their construction.

Tia deduces my interest in the building from the amount of time I spend looking at it and provides me with an Augmented Reality overlay as the car slows to a stop. Late-Georgian construction, original stonework, built by a family who made their money from a combination of tin mining in Cornwall and slavery run through Bristol. How many people suffered, how many probably died, so that family could live in luxury? I wonder whether any of the current hotel guests are paying for their rooms with modern equivalents. Less than a second later I have to dismiss Tia's offer to pull the hotel-guest records for my perusal. I'll look at them when I'm more fresh.

Milsom gets out and I pull my bag from the boot. The bitter cold and gusty wind make me feel even more awake. Even though we're standing right outside the hotel there hasn't been any kind of welcome ping, nor have any details about my room been sent to Tia. Maybe this is what Milsom meant when she said it was old-fashioned.

The car's door locks make a gentle clunk as we head up the steps to the main entrance. The warm glow spilling onto the steps must be a welcome sight for the usual weary arrivals. For me, it signals the beginning of the hard work ahead.

"Good evening."

I start at the sound of a real voice as we enter and realize that the door has been opened by a human being, standing there dressed like a character from an RPG set in the early twentieth century. I stare at him a little too long and his smile becomes strained. Tia misinterprets my focus on him and a bio flashes up to the right of his head, which I file for future reference.

"Welcome to the Moor Hotel, sir," he says. "I hope you enjoy your stay."

I've never stepped inside a hotel with even reception staff, let alone someone paid to just open the damn door. Isn't that what local nodes and motors are for? All the places I usually stay at on the job are the sort of functional midlevel corporate places where you can go through an entire stay without meeting a flesh-and-blood employee, if you're happy to eat printed food.

"Ah, Deputy Commissioner Milsom and SDCI Moreno, welcome."

The female voice pulls my attention away from the doorman, to his relief. I catch up with Milsom, who's several steps ahead of me, being greeted by the hotel manager.

Even though she looks like she's in her late forties, the bio Tia displays next to her reveals she's just turned sixty. Her skin is a dark brown, makeup subtle but effective, her straight black hair pulled back into a no-nonsense ponytail. Her suit is simple, bespoke tailored and made of cream fabric. Her high-necked blouse is open at the collar and the same dark blue as her high-heeled shoes. She cuts a smart figure. I'd expect nothing less at this sort of place.

"Ms. Patel," Milsom says, "thank you for staying up so late."

"Please, call me Nadia." She steps forward and shakes my hand after Milsom's. "It was the least I could do. I understand you're going to be in charge of the case."

I nod.

Her smile is warm and hotel-genuine. "If there's anything you need, please don't hesitate to ask."

"I would like to speak to you first thing in the morning," I say, aware that Milsom is giving me her "end this conversation" frown.

"I'll be in my office from eight a.m. It's just over there." After pointing out a door on the other side of the lobby, she turns to Milsom. "The legal team is in the meeting room, waiting for you. I'll show you the way."

There are potted plants, black-and-white marble floor tiles and framed oil paintings, giving the lobby the feel of a stately home that just happens to have a reception desk in its hallway. It smells of money and cleanliness.

I try to picture Alejandro here, sipping coffee in the bar I can glimpse through glass in a large set of double doors we pass on the way to the meeting room. The mental image seems a mockery of all I knew him to be. Had he changed so much in recent years? There was a time when he deplored these kinds of places and the people who chose to frequent them. It's easier to imagine his rambling tirade against it, delivered with a softly spoken intensity that made his damning words all the more powerful. He was a man you leaned toward to hear better, a man who would welcome the movement like you were being brought conspiratorially into a huddle to hear a secret that could change your life, when it was just as likely he'd recommend a way to cut a vegetable more efficiently.

It hits me that Nadia saw his body, and I have a sudden urge to find that room and see the crime scene for myself. Why am I being led down a corridor in the small hours of the morning to see a troupe of feckless legal monkeys when I could be getting started? How can days have gone by since his death and even more time be wasted now?

"Is this really necessary?" I ask Milsom quietly. "Wouldn't it be better to see—"

"Do you really think I'd be doing this if it wasn't?"

The tone of her voice tells me all I need to know about how frustrating the past forty-eight hours have been for her. The fact she's had to leave London to deliver me to the lawyers is bad enough. I regret my question.

I use the rest of the time en route to ground my thoughts. I've felt on the back foot since the moment she arrived at the apartment, and now, on the brink of starting the investigation, I feel horribly underprepared. Usually I've reviewed extensive data before even arriving at a scene, even had conversations with the local officers and got a feel for what to expect. This feels wrong on some deep level. I feel like I've been thrown into a mersive without knowing what it's supposed to be about.

Nadia knocks once on a door at the end of the corridor leading from the lobby and opens the door for us. She stands aside, giving me another one of those "don't hesitate to ask for help" smiles, and closes the door behind us once we're inside.

Three men and two women are seated at a conference table and all stand when we arrive. I see that papers have already been laid out along with honest-to-goodness fountain pens. I can't remember the last time I made a nondigital signature. For a moment I wonder if I can even remember what mine looks like, and Tia "helpfully" displays a copy before I blink it away.

Introductions are made, more for the recording of the meeting rather than need, as our APAs handle digital handshakes and name exchanges by default. I let Tia remember the names and faces for me, disinterested by the suits creating this final obstacle. Two of them are from the Ministry and look the most relieved to see us. One represents the Circle, one the flimsy connection to Europe, and the third Norope. All of them look tired.

"Everything as I was briefed?" Milsom asks the man from the Ministry.

"With one last-minute addition," he says, firing a glance at the woman representing Europe. Then he looks at me. "You'll be required to make a regular report on your progress and be available to answer any questions."

"I was expecting that," I say, looking at Milsom.

"Not to your superior. To the gov-corps our colleagues represent. In person."

"But that's"—I bite back the first five expletives that come to mind—"highly irregular," I finally say.

Milsom looks like she could kill someone. Neither of the gov-corp lawyers meet her glare. The American representing the Circle looks tense and a little embarrassed when I look at her.

"It's what's on the table," says the European lawyer with a distinctly Spanish accent.

A message arrives from the Ministry lawyer, who has been silent so far, sent to both Milsom and me. Sign it, for fuck's sake, otherwise we'll be here another two days.

Milsom's nostrils flare. "If any of you interfere with SDCI Moreno's work, it will only delay the answers we all want."

"It's just a matter of keeping involved parties informed of progress," the European says. "And it will all be kept in the strictest confidence. The NDAs we've drafted up for the parties involved are robust."

Milsom picks up the pen like it's a dagger she's about to plunge into the woman's chest and slaps it into my palm. I try to pull off the cap before realizing that it's one of those heavy, expensive ones that have caps that need to be unscrewed. I feel like an idiot and silently curse whoever still makes these stupid pens just so lawyers can feel special, because it takes a fucking age just to get the cap off. They probably bill people for the time it takes them to do it.

I scrawl my name a dozen times, under the direction of the Ministry lawyer, give an entirely superfluous digital signature via

Tia, then press both of my thumbs onto the portable Ministry of Justice identity-verification box to provide a thumbprint with the one on the right and DNA sample from a drop of my blood extracted from the one on the left. I also manage to avoid making snide remarks about their ancient identity protocols. When it's all done, the cap of the pen screwed back on and the pieces of paper shuffled back into order, there's a palpable shift in the atmosphere.

"Thank you, ladies and gentlemen," says the man from the Ministry, and the European lawyer gives a curt nod before practically bolting from the room. The Noropean leaves after shaking hands and the American lawyer does the same. They leave together, continuing some previous conversation about reindeer steak, of all things.

The woman from the Ministry stretches. "What a bloody nightmare that was. And before you start, Deputy Commissioner, we did the best we could to get those assholes out of the way as fast as possible so your man can start work." She looks at me with tired eyes. "I hope you're as good as she says you are. I don't want to have to go through this bullshit again."

"He is," Milsom says.

The best that money could buy. I finish the sentence in the privacy of my skull. For anyone else at my pay grade, a compliment from the deputy commissioner would be a welcome rarity. For me, it's meaningless; there's no mythical promotion to be craved, no commendation mark that could count toward a performance bonus. Just the pressure to do my job perfectly in order to avoid an extension on the contract. And, beneath it all, my own pathetic need to see the puzzle solved. When it comes to the Ministry of Justice, I am exactly what they want me to be and I can't do a fucking thing about it.

6

FROM THE WARMTH of the lobby I watch Milsom and the two Ministry lawyers drive off, and my guts relax again, feeling like they drop lower in my abdomen by centimeters. Finally I can get started.

"Only the one bag?" Nadia asks, looking at the small case that is probably less than hand luggage for most people, and I nod. "I'll show you to your room," she says, unhooking a key—*that's actually made from metal*—from its place on the wall behind reception. She smiles at my disbelief. "A lot of people are surprised by this."

"What if I lose my key?"

"The door can still be opened by your chip. 'So what's the point of the key?' you might ask." She rounds the desk and comes to my side, gesturing toward a lift in the corner of the lobby. "Romance."

"I don't understand."

She presses the button to call the lift. "The romance of a

bygone age." She dangles the key from its weighty brass fob, catching the light. "I think we lost something in the rush toward ease and speed and convenience. Something up here." She taps the side of her head. "And here." She places the same hand over her heart. "The sense of physical security provided by a key one can hold in one's hand when staying somewhere unfamiliar is very powerful."

For the first time, something of this place makes sense in its intersection with Alejandro. He was always talking about that kind of bullshit. He never admitted that having a neural chip made thousands of everyday things easier. How many times did he say that the modern world was forcing people to lose the art of connection? *The art of connection?* Bollocks. Only a privileged twat could say something like that. JeeMuh, if we still had to investigate every murder with unchipped police—and unchipped perps—it would take months. Only people in little bubbles of wealth and comfort have the luxury of thinking that way. Alejandro lost touch with what the world is like for most people a long time ago.

I follow the manager into the lift and she presses the button for the third—and topmost—floor. The interior is all brass and mirrors, gleaming just as much as the lobby did, not a speck of dirt in sight.

"Breakfast is served between seven and ten a.m. on week-days, eight until eleven at weekends. All of the food is locally sourced, ethically and sustainably produced and prepared by hand by our chefs."

I have to remind myself that I shouldn't enjoy this place too much.

"There's room service too," she adds. "Available twenty-four hours a day."

Of course, Tia could pull this information from the local

node, but this is all about Nadia filling the silence with something safe. A world-famous man has been murdered in her hotel and she doesn't want to talk about it with a detective in a lift. She's so poised and her portrayal of serenity in the provision of comfort for others is so convincing that I wonder how hard she works to maintain it. I suspect I would learn more from a conversation with her outside of the hotel and her princely domain, when she has to work with unfamiliar scenery and unreliable stagehands. I'd at least learn more about what she's really like.

That's how I'd play it if she were a suspect, but right now she isn't. There are some proprietors who would relish the opportunity to create something that would draw clients with a taste for the macabre to their establishment. She isn't one of them. This place is too polished, too perfect and too comfortable in the illusions it already sketches for its guests to need anything else. The questions I have for her can wait until morning.

With a bright ping the lift stops and the doors open. A wooden plaque on the wall opposite provides directions for rooms "1–6," "7–12" and the "Diamond Suite." I look in its direction as we step out into the corridor and see police tape across the door. A bored-looking constable straightens as he sees me and gives a curt nod, which I return. Every couple of years there's a debate about whether a human police officer really needs to be posted outside a crime scene. It's only at the most serious that they're posted and it's just a matter of time before it's phased out altogether. I'm glad to see him, even though the poor bastard's feet must be killing him and he must be bored senseless with his chip in duty mode.

"I hope you don't mind being on the same floor," Nadia says, following my gaze. "I moved all of our guests onto the floor below, you see. We had room, with it being out of season. Thankfully."

"It's fine," I say, glad that no one else will be snooping around as they go to and from their rooms.

"I've put you at the far end." She gestures for me to walk with her in the direction opposite the crime scene. "The local police left a bag for you. I've taken the liberty of bringing it up to your room."

"Thanks." That'll be the paper suit and shoe covers left by the SOCO in the hope that all the legal nonsense resolved itself before they came back in the morning.

The walls are horizontally divided by a thin strip of painted wood that Tia unhelpfully tells me is a dado rail, with blue flocked wallpaper covering the lower half and cream paper the top half. The light fixtures are small chandeliers benefiting from the high ceiling, and the carpet is a thick, deep blue with a spring to it. It looks newly refurbished, no worn patches on the carpet down the central strip, no scuffs on the walls and no chips in the paintwork. There's no sound save the padding of our shoes against the pile and then, when we get to the end of the corridor, the wind gusting outside the window.

"There was an awful storm last night," she says as she unlocks the door of room 12. "It still hasn't blown itself out."

The room is larger than the footprint of my entire apartment. I see a bathroom through a partially open door on the left-hand side and, in addition to the sofa and two armchairs, everything else I'd expect to see in a hotel except for the usual black screen that makes up part or all of one of the walls.

There's a four-poster bed I feel embarrassed at the thought of sleeping in, and a huge window with a padded seat below it covered in cushions. Somber oil paintings of Dartmoor are counterbalanced by thick gilded frames, and the wardrobe is more ornately carved than anything functional has any need to be.

"If you want a screen," she says, "there's one retracted into the ceiling. Just press the remote control by your bed or your APA can ping the local node with hashtag 'screen twelve.'"

Remote control? I put my bag next to a chest of drawers that looks like it could be worth more than the car I arrived in and pick up the slender rectangle of black plasglass. I haven't held one of these since I was a child. At my touch a series of buttons ghost into view, waiting for a fingertip to make contact with one of them. There's one to call down to reception, the remote control doubling as an external mobile phone for guests who aren't chipped.

"If there's anything you need, please don't hesitate to contact reception at any time, day or night."

I put the remote control down. "Actually, there is something. Has the key to the Diamond Suite been given to the policeman outside it?" Even though I know it can be opened by my chip, I don't like the thought of a physical key being anywhere else.

She nods. "Yes, and the spare one too."

"Thanks," I say, and she smiles again. Her face must ache by the end of the day.

"I hope you can enjoy your stay, despite the circumstances," she says, and leaves after placing the key to my own room on top of the chest of drawers.

The door shuts with a muffled clunk and I'm alone again for the first time in hours. I was tired before Milsom arrived at the flat. Dozing in the car has done nothing except knot some muscles in my neck. My eyes are starting to feel gritty, and I look at the bed, resisting the urge to test how soft it is. If I sit down I might not get up again.

"Tia, download the case file from the MoJ. And grab all the data from the hotel node for the entirety of the victim's stay and the time since his body was found up to now, and stick it in a subfolder called 'Hotel local data' in the case file."

I clench my fists at the thought of the time wasted so far. The murderer is probably long gone. I hold on to the fact that it's hard to stay hidden for long without extensive preparation, and from what I know of the murder, it doesn't seem like a professional hit. My money is on stalker or crime of passion, but as I know next to nothing so far, that could easily change.

I need to understand why this happened to the man I once loved more than my own father.

I'm torn between getting deep into the data and seeing the crime scene for myself. It's a purely psychological need; there's nothing there that I won't be able to review virtually, thanks to the recorders. On some base level, I need to believe this has actually happened. And I want to see it before the SOCO arrives and deploys a forensic team. I look up who the local one is and see that he's already been pinged. He and the team will be here within the hour, and my mind is made up.

"Okay," I say to both Tia and myself. "Let's give you some stuff to do while I check out the room. Pull information on all the guests who checked in either just before or during Alejandro's stay. I want a separate list of those who checked out between ten p.m. on the night of his murder and when the hotel was locked down by the local police the next morning."

"You should sleep," Tia says after confirmation of my orders scrolls past on the left-hand side of my vision. "Your cognitive processing will be reduced and reaction times slowed should you stay up without—"

"Shush," I say. "I'll get some sleep—don't worry. I just want you to be doing something useful while I'm asleep."

"I have already completed the tasks you assigned."

"Good. Has the MoJ assigned me a dedicated case space on the server?"

"Yes. Confirmation came through zero-point-zero-three seconds after you signed the contract. Would you like me to port over your preferred settings and load the case information into it?"

"Yeah. Render a full VR mock-up of the crime scene from the recorder data. I'll look at that in the morning. Show me the list of checkouts in the window between murder and lockdown."

There are seven names and one leaps out instantly: Theodore Buckingham, one of Alejandro's traveling companions. He checked out at 5:03 a.m., only seven hours after the last time Alejandro was seen alive by anyone other than Klein. Tia has also flagged pending requests from the local police to intercept the seven people, which were blocked by the MoJ, stating that no action could be taken without the contract being in place.

"It's in place now, you bureaucratic fucks," I mutter, and resend the local police requests with my own appended and an additional note to get a manhunt team onto Buckingham as priority. Odds are that one of those seven people is the murderer—probably Buckingham, seeing as the vast majority of murder victims are killed by people they know—and he is now outside of my reach. "Tia, how often are requests from local police blocked by the MoJ?"

"If you're more specific I can—"

"In murder cases with the request being the location and potential interception of individuals placed in the vicinity of the crime."

"This has only happened on three occasions."

"Which cases?"

"You don't have the grade clearance for me to be able to dig down. Would you like me to send a request to Milsom?"

A cold, heavy stone is forming in my stomach, no matter how much I try to keep myself from leaping ahead and forming conclusions before I have all the data. All of this stinks of obstruction at a high level. Everyone knows how critical it is to move fast, and everyone in that room downstairs knew that every minute they argued, the perpetrator was getting farther away.

"Would you like me to send a request to Milsom?" Tia repeats.

"No," I say.

I need to work the case like any other, and not just because the MoJ has my balls in a vice. I need to work out what happened to Alejandro and why, and keep my casework clean as a whistle. But there's another investigation starting here and I need to keep that locked away in my own thoughts, away from Tia and anything else that could form a data trail.

I suck in a deep breath through my nostrils, aware of the tension building in my body. I can't let this suspicion interfere with my job here. I hold my palm level with my chest and slowly move it downward, imagining the churning in my stomach being smoothed away by the motion as I breathe out.

I will learn the details. I will work the case. I will identify the murderer.

Then I remember Dee taught me that when I nearly broke in hot-housing. I shove all thoughts of her aside. I can't be distracted now.

"Tia, pull the data from the corridor cams on this floor between nine thirty p.m. and nine thirty a.m. on the night of the murder. Isolate any footage that contains people and show me those sections with a time stamp."

All public locations have to be recorded by law, including the corridors of hotels. There are discussions about whether individual rooms in hotels should also be declared as public spaces, but there's still far too much resistance from higher-ups in the gov-corp who depend on hotels for their love affairs. It's the reason why there's been a resurgence in rooms with interconnecting doors: easier to sneak someone in from the room next door without risking being caught on camera in the corridor.

Moments later Tia has the footage ready. There's a few seconds of Alejandro going to the Diamond Suite with Klein, followed by Theo Buckingham, who goes into the room next door. The footage jumps to 5:03 a.m. the following morning, when Theo Buckingham leaves his room with a small wheeled case. The next person seen in the corridor is one of the kitchen staff leaving a breakfast tray outside of room 9 at 7:00 a.m. "Tia, I want you to send the data from the hotel node to the MoJ AI to check for signs of tampering, especially of the corridor cam footage."

"Done."

It's almost three in the morning, but I know I can't go to sleep until I've seen the room myself. I open the bag left for me by the local police and pull out a pair of gloves from a box inside. I see a few paper suits in cellophane and the proof-of-tampering seals are reassuringly green. I dig out a pair of shoe covers and then hesitate over one of the suits. No, I'll just look from the doorway. It's too bloody late to do more than that and I want to be fresh tomorrow.

I physically lock the door of my room behind me, thinking about what Nadia said about the feeling of holding a real key. I turn it over a few times in my palm, feeling the weight of the brass fob as I drop it into my pocket.

When I pass the lift a warning flashes across my vision. If I wasn't expecting it I might have missed a step. Restricted zone ahead. Your movements are being recorded by the Ministry of Justice.

For anyone else in the hotel—apart from the copper—the message would continue to scroll across the bottom half of their vision until they walk away again. For me, thankfully, it stops, having satisfied Tia that it is active and all is as it should be.

"Good evening, sir," the constable says.

Tia flashes up his bio next to his head with a brief career summary. Five years on the force, clean record, probably promotion within two years. Wife and two children. Impressively high gamer score on the Mars game I was playing earlier. Bastard. I'm glad my profile will be locked to him and he won't see how pathetically low mine is in comparison.

"Good evening, PC Radley. All quiet up here, I assume?"

"Yes, sir. They cleaned up some vomit in the hallway out here—the one who found the body threw up, you see. I said it was okay to do that, as it was outside of the scene." He pauses, nervous that I'll disagree, then continues when he sees I don't mind. "The hotel owner and a cleaner went to room twelve earlier, to get it ready for you. Other than that no one's been up here since the guests were cleared off this floor. Do you want to go inside?" He's looking for a paper suit, worried he'll have to say something awkward.

"I just want to look from the doorway. The SOCO should be here in the next half hour with his team."

Radley steps aside and pulls the tape off as I put on my gloves and shoe covers. I instruct Tia to switch on the lights in the Diamond Suite and also unlock and open the door so I don't have to touch anything. There's a solid clunk from the door as the lock is opened from within and the door opens just a crack.

"Would you like me to present an enhanced view of the room in line with the coroner's record of the body?" Tia asks.

"Give me a minute to look at it normally first," I say, and press on the door, near the hinge in a place where most people don't touch, to push it open.

The smell hits me before anything else, the residual stink left behind by bowels voided upon death. Radley walks away a couple of steps, making out as if he's stretching his legs a little, giving me privacy perhaps, but probably just getting away from the stale air seeping out of the doorway. I give myself a moment to get used to it and then push the door farther open.

At first all I see is the bloodstain, the shock of it making everything else fade into the background. *Alejandro's* blood. Most of a large Persian rug in the center has had its vibrant colors obliterated by a dark brown stain, as has a good portion of the cream carpet around it. I see dried droplets of blood on one of the walls and a few on the sofa cushions.

After a few moments I blink and start to see the whole room. It's effectively a living room–cum-study, with a door to the bedroom on the left, which is open. I can see a four-poster bed in there with rumpled sheets and some clothing on the floor. There's a bathroom off to the right of the living room and probably an en-suite off the bedroom too.

It's huge and sumptuous and a world away from what I'd expect Alejandro to choose for himself. The Circle was against technology—against being chipped in particular—so I can understand his choice of hotel to a certain extent. But the luxury is jarring. Why come to *this* hotel and sink himself into a lifestyle he ridiculed and railed against?

In the Circle I knew, the one I endured, it wasn't just a rejection of invasive technology; it was all about simple living.

Simple living to the point of discomfort. We lived in dormitories with hard beds and drafty windows that rattled in the winter storms. We wore clothes made with wool and cotton we grew, spun and wove ourselves, a simple sweater taking hours and hours of effort when one could be bought for a negligible amount of money. Even the sheets I slept on had been spun and then woven by someone in the Circle. Alejandro always talked about how knowing who made the things we used and wore was somehow better than convenience. He was under the impression that spending hours toiling away like it was the fucking dark ages was a way to stay connected to the difference between need and want and to teach ourselves about the true value of something.

This room is filled with all the unnecessary luxuries and conveniences of modern life that would have made the Alejandro I knew launch into an epic rant. What changed? Is the Circle just as different now? Or maybe this is proof of what I've always suspected: everything he said in the Circle was bullshit and every chance he got, he came and stayed in places like this.

A chair is on its side next to the rug. There are no other signs of a struggle. Tia, determining that my minute is up, overlays the images of the various body parts as recorded and then recovered by the coroner. I take in a leg, an arm and then my eyes settle upon the back of Alejandro's head, severed at the neck and resting on one side near the desk, over a meter away from his torso.

Sweat breaks out on my forehead and my pulse races as I swallow down a sudden rush of saliva. I've seen horrific things in reality, in AR and in mersives, but never done to someone I knew. Never to someone I once loved. I hold my breath, forcing myself not to vomit, not in front of that copper.

I can feel myself pulling back, almost like I am physically stepping away. The rush of emotions is being pushed down before I even have time to name them all. My professional defenses and years of training are kicking in, forcing me to look for details instead of the whole while the rest of me, the man who knew the victim, recedes along with the urge to throw up.

"Tell the SOCO I'm in room twelve if he needs to see me urgently. Otherwise I'll be with him at seven a.m. and I'll buy him breakfast."

"Right you are, sir," Radley says, replacing the tape after the door swings shut on its weighted hinges.

I get back to my room and before I have a chance to take off the gloves I think of the space between the head and the torso, the way the neck just . . . ended in nothing, and then I'm heaving into the toilet.

Fuck.

I pull off the gloves, clean my teeth, take off my shoes and get into bed fully clothed, in case the SOCO is a belligerent bastard and thinks I should lose just as much sleep as he. I wonder how Dee is before remembering that I'm angry with her. I try to think about killing aliens on Mars, about what I'll have for breakfast, about how soft the bed is. The constant stream of crap acts as a buffer long enough for my body to calm down and fall into a restless sleep.

7

I WAKE BEFORE my alarm, surprised to have got any sleep at all. I don't feel rested though and stagger to the shower as Tia combs the news feeds for any keywords related to the case.

The shower area is about the same size as my entire kitchen. Tia has already updated the settings for the room to comply with my preferences and the shower starts running as soon as I enter the bathroom.

"How long before premium rate kicks in?" I'm tempted to treat myself to an extra minute.

"There's no limit on water usage," Tia replies. "It's included in the room price."

I stand under the showerhead and let the hot water pummel my scalp. Nothing about the murder has reached the press. Yet. I check the case folder as I wash my hair.

Somewhere between reminding myself of the details and sorting tasks by priority, I realize I haven't heard the sound of Alejandro's voice since I left the Circle. He'll never say anything again. The thought hits me so hard I have to slap my hand against a tile to steady myself. An awful, churning grief builds and I lock it down as swift as I can, as I learned to do so well when we were being hot-housed. These emotions won't serve me now. I can't let a moment of nostalgia cloud this investigation and add years to my contract. I ask Tia for a summary of overnight case developments and listen as I rinse the shampoo away.

By the time I'm rinsing the shower gel from my body, I know how the next few hours are shaping up. The SOCO is going to meet me in the restaurant downstairs with a preliminary report in half an hour. All of the guests—except one—who checked out in the murder time window have been tracked down and the unchipped ones are being interviewed as I shower. The prime suspect, Theo Buckingham, remains at large.

If he were chipped we'd have him by now, but he'll still be picked up by the end of the day. There are just too many cameras, either embedded in buildings or in people's retinas, for him to remain at large for any longer than two days. Even if he manages to disguise himself, his first transaction will be picked up and flagged as priority information to the manhunt team.

He's a US resident—and not widely traveled, according to the file the US gov-corp sent overnight—so it's unlikely he'll have any criminal connections sophisticated enough to give him a means to pay for food and travel off-grid or under an alias. He can't buy anything without using his thumbprint, thanks to being here under a visa and unchipped. There's a flag on the system, so the MoJ AI will be alerted as soon as his thumbprint-authorized purchase pings the visa-tracking system. Eventually he'll either try to buy something in a moment of stupidity (which is surprisingly common) or he'll try to steal something. Either way, as soon as he goes near anywhere that sells or serves food, he'll be picked up on camera anyway. He's probably already been recorded dozens of times. Like all criminal investigations, it's simply a matter of knowing where to look in the mountain of data. If those legal assholes hadn't put themselves in the way, there would be a lot less to comb through now.

Once I've checked in with the SOCO I'll interview Klein and see what she noticed during the time Alejandro was sharing the suite with her. I'm hoping she'll be able to fill in the blanks in terms of motive, having traveled with Buckingham too. Milsom said she was treated for shock when the cleaner and the manager discovered the body the next morning. I need to understand why she didn't raise any alarm during the incident itself. My first guess is a sleeping tablet, but still, someone being violently murdered next door should have woken her up; most legal drugs for insomnia trick the brain into going to sleep, not staying so deeply under that you can sleep through a man being hacked to pieces next door. Could Buckingham have drugged her? If that's the case, there's more planning involved in this than a crime of passion would suggest.

I check the case file and see that the doctor called to treat her took a blood sample that has been withheld from processing by the legal crap. I put in a request for it to be screened for drugs and add a priority tag, and dress for breakfast.

"Would you like to review the mail in your public in-box?" Tia asks.

"Later," I say. "Delete any that are in the 'Journalist shitbags' folder."

"Those messages have only been filtered. Would you like to review the contents first?"

"No," I say, and pick up the key to my room. "There's nothing they can say that would interest me."

"Deleted," Tia says, and I smile at the thought of their little electronic hooks being blasted away. I'm not a fish to be caught with promises of truth or money. I think of Dee, manage the flash of anger, and lock my door behind me.

THERE are more people than I expect there to be in the restaurant at seven a.m., and every single one of them stops eating or talking to stare at me when I walk in. If I'm still here this time tomorrow, I'll order room service.

A waiter greets me as everyone realizes they're all staring at me and return to their conversations, some with another person actually sitting across from them at the table, others with a person eating somewhere else. A couple of them are staring at the space above the empty seat opposite them, their chips projecting an image of their conversational partner sitting at the table with them. I've never been able to bring myself to do that, even though these days everyone is used to people looking like they are children having a tea party with imaginary friends. I hate conversation over food and regret setting up a breakfast check-in with the SOCO. This is work though, and I just have to deal with it.

I give the waiter a polite brush-off, slightly freaked out by the enforced in-person interaction. It's so much noisier here, what with several unchipped guests actually talking to each other and asking the staff questions usually handled by APAs.

Tia picks out the SOCO for me, a man already giving one of those awkward waves made redundant by the bio Tia flashes up for me. The dark circles under his eyes make me appreciate the poor five hours of sleep I managed to get. I head over, studiously ignoring conversations about the capsule and someone saying they recognize me from somewhere before being rapidly shushed into silence by their companion, probably thanks to the MoJ warning flashing up.

The SOCO is called Alex Jacobs and he's a small man, one who looks like he might have overcompensated in the gym for his lack of height and then let himself go in his fifties. I see from his profile that he's very experienced, has multiple positions on various procedure advisory boards and is a member of a chess club. No gamer score; both of our bios are set to professional information only, and as we're effectively of equal rank Tia isn't pulling more. I wonder what kind of stuff he plays when he's not in the mood for chess. I get the feeling he's not a shooting-alien-robots kind of guy.

"Good morning," he says, and stands to shake my hand. "I ordered coffee. I hope you don't mind."

"Not at all," I say, and sit down. "Want to sort out the food before we get to business?"

We both choose a full English breakfast from the menu that has been printed out on an actual card instead of appearing as an option to select via my APA. My stomach rumbles as the waiter writes our order down on a small notepad with a pencil. It looks like a theater prop. I've only ever seen a waiter do that in mersives. In fact, I can't remember the last time a waiter took my order. Usually they just turn up with the food a while after Tia has put my order in.

Alex is staring at the notepad too, shifting in his seat as if he's worrying that he has some important line to deliver or plot to introduce in a play he didn't sign up to act in. When the waiter goes he looks relieved and drains his coffee cup.

"You get to stay here, then?" he asks.

"Yeah. Weird place."

"There are worse kinds of weird," he says, and looks away, then upward, and I know he's accessing notes. "Okay. You know what I'm going to say first."

"Something about why the hell weren't you allowed in there earlier? I know, I know. Believe me, I'm just as pissed off."

"I'm not going to give you a hard time about it," Alex replies. "I heard about the lawyers. Okay. So we're on the back foot. The blood soaked in and dried but the patterns are still there. Some interesting stuff on that front. I've added it as a layer to the recording files, fully tagged. I've been told you prefer to examine the details of a scene in VR."

"I'll look around the room itself too."

Alex nods. "I've prepped an AR layer for in situ use too."

"What about DNA?"

"Nothing unexpected. Matches with the girlfriend, the victim and the bloke who was in the room next door . . ." His eyes flick up and right again. "Theo Buckingham. There was a hair from the hotel manager near the door, as expected because she contaminated the scene, and some cells from the cleaning staff in the corners. We had to hunt for that though. They keep the place very clean. There might be more DNA on the body, of course, under the fingernails and so forth."

"The pathologist should be sending in preliminaries this morning," I say as our breakfast arrives.

"I think an ax was used to chop the body up," Alex says, starting on the pile of scrambled eggs with an enthusiastic stab of his fork. "There are marks in the carpet and the rug. I tagged those too, of course. If it weren't for the soundproofing, it would have been heard in the room below. There was a renovation in the hotel a decade or so ago and they put it all in then. That soaked up the blood and bowel contents too, otherwise the manager might have had some distressed calls. They still might have heard a few thuds though. Takes a good wallop to get through bone and—"

I lay my fork back down again and he notices the way I am pressing my lips together, trying not to let the nausea overwhelm me.

"Sorry. Thought you'd be pretty used to this stuff."

"I knew the victim."

To his credit, Alex looks appalled. "Crikey. Sorry. I had no idea. And the MoJ still assigned you? That's . . . a bit cold."

I don't offer any comment, electing to sip some water rather than explain why I had no real choice in the matter. The food looks delicious and the smell was divine before my stomach turned. The bacon has been cooked to perfection, the eggs look light and fluffy and the mushrooms gloriously dark and succulent. I will never forgive myself if I push this to one side.

"Anyway, it's all tagged on the new layer," Alex says quietly. "And you can always ping me if you have any questions. Anytime."

He changes the subject then and I allow myself a few deep breaths. The visceral reaction to this case disturbs me. I thought it had been trained out of me. I suppose there isn't enough training in the world for when this shit is personal. I've got to get a handle on it though; I can't act like a fucking rookie every time some detail comes up about his body. *The* body. I resolve to return to my room as soon as breakfast is over and just look at all the details until the shock is out of my system. I need to desensitize myself before the pathologist calls in.

The SOCO is a boring man, all too happy to chatter away as long as I nod and make the right kind of grunt in the right places. His total lack of need for any kind of articulate response is glorious. My stomach settles and the food is even better than I'd hoped for. It's all I can do to not moan in pleasure at each mouthful. How the people around me manage to chat at the same time as experiencing this astounds me. Philistines.

No. Privileged. This is the quality of food they're accustomed to.

Alex gets a message as he's starting the last sausage and makes his apologies. My hope that he'll leave it behind is dashed when he plucks it off the plate with a wink and walks out. I can't help but respect the complete absence of fucks he has for the appalled faces around him as he leaves, taking a bite of it like a kid at a carnival.

The empty chair he leaves behind is a welcome sight. That was one of the daily irritations of life in the Circle: communal eating for every meal.

"You'll get used to it," Dad had said as we stood in the doorway to the hall filled with long tables and benches. "You probably shouldn't have been eating by yourself all the time before anyway. This is better for you."

"Why?" I was eight years old, thousands of miles from home and the most important possession I owned had just been taken from me. His knowing what was better for me seemed ludicrous.

"It's good to be social," he said. Like he'd forgotten the fact he hadn't left the house for more than two years before Alejandro turned up, and had barely spoken to me the whole of that time.

"I don't want to talk to anyone." The people sitting at the tables looked weird. Their hair was strange, their clothes, the sound of their voices. A lot of them were speaking English and I still wasn't comfortable talking in anything except Spanish. Other than a few babies, the other children looked at least ten years older than me. That was a relief though; I would have been forced to sit with another child my age, as if a shared age would make it an easy or pleasant interaction. "I just want to talk to Bear."

"We talked about that. He isn't good for you. Don't you remember what Alejandro explained to us about the chip inside it? That bear was made to record everything about you so bad people could use it to sell you things and tell you what to think after putting a chip in your head." He tapped the top of it so hard it hurt. "You need to forget about that bear and talk to real people now."

That's when I started to cry.

"Excuse me."

I blink away the memory, disturbed by how vivid it was after so many years of distancing myself from that time. There's a man standing next to my table.

"You're the policeman investigating the murder, aren't you?"

He's in his twenties, far too tanned and handsome for me to take seriously as anything other than a model or actor, and dressed in the latest fashion of a high collar, slim-fitted shirt and fat, luxurious tie-cum-cravat. His trousers are narrow enough in the leg to show off his sculpted calf muscles, and the toes of his boots are so pointed they look ridiculous. His voice has had any sort of regional accent trained out of it.

Tia flashes up a notification that this guest's face is being matched to the identity profiles of the unchipped guests. A second later a name floats next to his perfectly coiffed auburn hair: Travis Gabor, twenty-nine years old, resident of London.

"Yes," I say, once his name has come up. "But you should know that—"

"Good," he speaks over me, eyes flicking back to the entrance of the restaurant. "So you'll need to interview the guests who aren't chipped, right? Like in *Marple 2070*?"

"Yes, but—"

"I need you to interview me last," he says in a whisper, after leaning down to fill my nose with expensive aftershave. "It's absolutely—"

"There you are!" A man's voice rumbles from the door to the restaurant. It isn't that he shouts; it's just one of those voices deep and naturally loud enough to cut through anything.

Gabor stands straight too quickly and runs a hand through his hair, whatever product he used making it fall back into exactly the same place as before.

"You need to understand that anything you say to me is being recorded and can and will be used as evidence in this investigation, should it become necessary," I'm finally able to say as Gabor gives a reluctant wave to the man on his way over, making the wedding ring he's wearing glitter and catch my eye.

Tia informs me of the other man as he marches toward us, glowering. Stefan Gabor, a billionaire with a financial empire so vast and complex people make both fictional and investigative mersives about it. Nothing else is visible in his profile, and Tia informs me that her attempt to drill down to anything more than just his name has resulted in an automatic notification from his legal department that a formal request will have to be made.

I hate dealing with these people.

No, I hate dealing with people, but the rich ones are the worst.

I look for a family resemblance but can't find it in the jowly man in his forties; the only thing they have in common is the tan. It seems that Stefan is happy to wear his wealth around his waistline as well as in his expensive suit. He's dressed far more conservatively than Travis is, the only flash of ostentatiousness in the form of a diamond tie pin with a rock as big as a sugar cube, and a glittering wedding ring. I make the connection about half a second before Stefan's hand cups Travis's right buttock and squeezes hard enough to make a tiny squeak slip from Travis's throat.

"Ask him, did you?" Stefan's voice is so low I can feel it in my stomach, like a bass beat in the car. Before Travis has a chance to answer, Stefan looks at me. "I take it you told him how ridiculous he's being?"

I pause, fully expecting Stefan to answer both questions without any need for my input. Men like him sail through life having a dialog with only themselves, punctuated by minor interruptions from others.

Stefan continues. "I told him it isn't anything like that ridiculous *Marple* game and that he doesn't have to stay here to be interviewed." His hand squeezes tighter and Travis stands on tiptoes, jaw clenched. "I think he wants the attention. I'm sorry he wasted your time, Officer."

"Inspector," I correct, just for the hell of it. I look at Travis, past the tan and the absurd hair, and see the desperation in his eyes as he stares down at me. "Actually, I would appreciate getting a statement from Mr. Gabor."

"That isn't necessary," Stefan says, releasing his grip on his husband's arse so he can fully concentrate on the onslaught he's about to give me.

"As the SDCI in charge of this investigation, and in accordance with the Noropean law and with the endorsement of the Ministry of Justice, *I* am the only person in this room who decides what is necessary and what is not."

"It's not convenient for us to stay another day," Stefan says, reddening.

"I can stay and you go back to London, darling." Travis's voice is higher, more strained than when he spoke before. "I wouldn't want to be any bother. And I could do with a couple more days here, to rest."

Stefan's upper lip curls downward. "You're better now." He pauses, frowning. "I can leave Frostrup here to—"

"Don't be silly. You need Frostrup more than I do." Travis reaches over and fiddles with the tie pin. "You worry too much, darling. I've got the 'pad and the headset. I can ping you every hour if you're worried."

Stefan looks back at me. "Can't you take a statement in the next hour?"

"I'm afraid not," I reply truthfully. "It would be this afternoon at the earliest."

"I'll speak to the commissioner about this, over dinner," he says, and I smile.

"You do that, and please pass on my regards to her."

Stefan walks away and the waiter who has been lurking nearby, nervously waiting for an opportunity to seat the Gabors, shows him, with some relief, to a table on the far side of the room.

Thank you, Travis mouths before Stefan clicks his fingers toward him in irritation.

I watch the man-poodle return to his master before I return to the last mouthfuls of my breakfast. Everybody is on a leash. Some are more obvious than others.

8

I'M GLAD TO be back in my room after breakfast. I felt Travis's eyes on me as I left, the tug of his neediness. I don't think for a moment that he has anything to do with the murder, nor do I think there's any need to hold him here for interview, but there's something going on with him and I can't walk past a puzzle without trying to fit in a piece or two. Besides, I never pass up a chance to irritate people like Stefan, who think they can intimidate me with their wealth. It's petty and I'm not proud of myself, but I still enjoy it.

"There are fifteen new messages in your public in-box," Tia tells me as I lock the door. "Would you like to review them?"

"All from journos and Web monkeys? Tia, for the last time, just put them in the shitbags folder and don't bother me with their crap again."

"Thirteen have been filtered and are requesting a quote or interview for the capsule event. One is from Dee Whittaker. Subject: 'Sorry.' Would you like me to open it?"

"No," I say, pulling off my shoes and taking off my suit jacket. "Delete it."

"Would you like me to notify her APA that you have deleted the message unread?"

"No, for the sake of fuck, Tia. Just butt out, okay?"

There's a pause, and that stupid bit of my brain that anthropomorphizes Tia makes me think I've offended her. *It.*

"Why did you ask me that anyway?"

"I'm adhering to the parameters outlined in the latest update from the Ministry of Education for individuals who have been through the accelerated-learning and assimilation program. There's a concern you shut people out too readily. Would you like me to outline the changes made in the last update?"

"No."

"Would you like me to summarize the concerns that led to the change in your social interaction parameters?"

I pull the belt from my trousers and throw it across the room more forcefully than I intended to. "I don't think this is the time, do you, Tia? I mean, there's more important stuff to review than the latest interference from my psych supervisor, isn't there? Like, I dunno, the dinner menu or—I know!—the massive fucking murder investigation."

"You are shouting at me," Tia says. There's no hurt in its voice—it's just as steady as normal; I disabled the fake-emotion option—but I still feel bad. "You are under increased levels of stress. Would you like me to schedule an appointment with your psych supervisor?"

Just the memory of that man's voice makes me want to break something. "No. Thank you." I draw in a deep breath, hoping it will calm me down. The last thing I need is for MyPhys to start flagging up stress symptoms outside of the expected range. I don't want anything like that on my record during this case.

"What about the other e-mail? You only mentioned fourteen of them."

"The remaining e-mail is from a journalist but does not mention an interview request nor the capsule. As it mentions the location of your current investigation, I have flagged it for review."

I frown. Has the murder been sniffed out already? "Okay, show me."

> I need to talk to you urgently about the reason you're in Devon, off the record. Don't include this in your investigation file, otherwise we will both be at risk.

I sit on the bed. "Tia, tell me about the person who sent this."

"Naal Delaney. Thirty-five years old, citizen of Norope. Winner of the Webben Prize for outstanding investigative journalism. Independent, writes for four Noropean news agencies, predominantly on organized crime and corporate espionage. Level-one personal data–protection license. Banned from entering Europe and any business premises owned by European gov-corp subsidiaries."

Great. Now I have to speak to a journo for work, just when I thought I'd be safe from them for a few days at least. I have to follow this up. Delaney could simply be trying to get my attention by being deliberately obscure, but mentioning my current location—which would be hidden from any public-profile data—suggests something genuine may be behind this. Whether Delaney wanted this incorporated into a formal investigation or not, that's what's going to happen now.

"Did any of the other e-mails from journalists that I've deleted come from Delaney?"

"Yes. You have deleted three requests for an interview sent by Naal Delaney."

"Are they still on the cloud?"

"Only the time stamp and sender address, not the contents. Would you like me to adjust your settings?"

"No, that's fine." I can't afford the amount of storage space it would require to store all my junk mail at the level of privacy and protection against hacking I'd require. "How many days ago did the first one sent by Delaney arrive?"

"Six. Sent at fourteen twenty-one on Thursday, November twelfth."

That was after Alejandro entered the country and a good couple of weeks after the rest of the journos started harassing me again. "And is . . . Hang on. Is Delaney male or female?"

"Delaney is registered as gender neutral."

"Is ze on any MoJ watch lists?"

"No."

"And no word of the murder has got to any of the news agencies ze works for?"

"Nothing has been reported."

I stare at the carpet long enough for Tia to start pulling up information about the fibers and manufacturing technique. I swipe the information away. Just because some hack thinks something is urgent doesn't mean it actually is. Delaney could have had someone tip hir off that I was here in an official capacity without knowing anything about the reason why. I'm already two days behind in this investigation. I don't have time for journo games right now. "Tia, set a reminder for me to reply in a day, okay? Now, is the VR crime scene up-to-date with the latest files from the SOCO?"

"Yes. Would you like to enter it now?"

"Yes."

"Please sit or recline in a comfortable space and confirm that you are not operating machinery."

"JeeMuh, Tia, can't we just skip this bollocks? I know the drill and you know I'm not operating anything or driving a vehicle."

"I'm sorry, I'm not authorized to override safety checks tagged 'critical.'"

I sigh. "I confirm I'm not operating machinery. I am not driving a vehicle. I do understand the risks of entering a fully immersive virtual environment and that prolonged use can increase the chances of heart attacks, depression, PTSD and a whole other list of side effects of which I am totally aware."

Tia displays the list of risks and waits for me to consciously select the "I have read and understood this" box before it goes away. I lie down on the bed, wishing I was getting ready to play instead of going to see Alejandro's dismembered corpse.

I close my eyes and for the briefest moment I wonder what Dee said in that e-mail, and then the darkness becomes bright and I am standing outside a door with a Ministry of Justice logo on it.

I'm standing in a gray corridor that looks very much like the real corridors in the depths of the MoJ headquarters. It's only here to ease the transition into the crime scene; I could just float in darkness before entering the room but I don't like that disconnection from reality. I know some inspectors prefer to have the building in which the crime scene is located rendered around it, but I don't do that unless I have to. I don't like walking through places in the real world that I've just been walking through in my virtual server space. I did it once, when I was a rookie, and then spent the rest of the case finding myself questioning whether I was really in the actual building every time I went back to the real crime scene. There's no faster way to a special kind of madness when you find yourself asking your APA to confirm that you're not in VR every five minutes.

I rest my hand on the door handle and ready myself. I will see Alejandro's dead body in there and it will be in pieces and his head will be detached from his body. I will see the blood and the echoes of the violence done to him. It will be distressing. It will not break me.

I open the door.

Inside is a perfect replica of the Diamond Suite, recorded by the MoJ recorders less than an hour after the crime had been reported to the police. The recorders are nothing more than drones that take thousands of ultra-high-res pictures of a crime scene, enabling the MoJ AI to replicate it in detail in a virtual space like this one. The drones are perfect for the task; they fly in, don't touch anything and don't contaminate. Unlike the police photographers of the past, there's no risk of them missing any details; every square inch is considered equally critical and recorded perfectly. I can zoom in, remove objects, highlight details—anything I like here. And all without the duty plod staring and offering tips like they so often do.

It's so accurate, it's easy to believe that I'm in the real room, aside from the fact there are no smells. They're piloting a scent recorder and replication process at the moment, but it's still not reliable enough to use in an MoJ investigation. I don't think it matters in this case. I take a step farther in and shut the door behind me, glancing at the doors to the other rooms, the desk, the seating area . . . all the places my eyes can rest before I have to look at the body.

The blood on the rug is darker, slick in places where it has soaked the carpet so much that it's coagulated on the surface. In places it mixes with the contents of his bowels, voided upon his death. I'm grateful for the lack of smell. The chair, on its side, rests to the left of Alejandro's torso, the shirt he was wearing now missing sleeves. I stare stupidly at the top buttons of his shirt, left open at a neck that stops far too abruptly in a hacked stump.

My gaze tracks across a leg, still sheathed in a trouser leg left tattered at the top. It looks unreal, like some sort of bizarre mannequin accident. The foot is covered by a sock and I look for his shoes. They are paired and placed neatly together by the side of the desk.

There's a constriction in my throat, the sense of something building in my chest, and it's hard to breathe. A physical pulse of grief passes through me like a cold wave crashing through my body from the depths of my stomach, up toward my chest, threatening to burst out of me with a brutal, animal force. Then, just as quickly, it's gone and I sag, nothing more than a strangled groan making it out of my mouth.

I force myself to look at the back of his head.

His hair is slightly shorter than when I last saw him, and peppered with gray strands that force an appreciation of how long it's been since then. I don't know if his eyes are open or whether there is an expression on his face. I'm not ready to look yet.

Something is missing. I walk up to the edge of the rug, inches from one of his hands. When I see the signet ring I realize that it is his left. His right arm lies past his torso, as if tossed there, at least a meter away. I see the marks in the rug that Alex mentioned and wonder where the ax is now—and where it came from in the first place.

"Open case notes, new file: 'Interview reminders.' Heading: 'Manager.' Do they have an ax in use within the hotel? Perhaps the grounds. Check groundskeeper or gardener equipment."

"Noted," Tia says.

It's not the thing that was used to kill him though. He was hanged first. I look up at the light fixture, the cracks in the ceiling rose from where his weight must have pulled the cable and damaged the plaster. A short length of cord remains, hanging from the knot that secures it and ending in a frayed stump that has clearly been cut. I look around the room and check the SOCO's notes on evidence retrieved. No noose or remainder of that cord has been found. Alex reported that one of the curtain cords was used and has made a note of the length based on the other of the pair left hanging beside one of the closed curtains.

I pull at the tie at my throat, loosening the knot, and undo the top button. In this virtual space I could be naked if I wanted to be, but I stay in the suit, in the clothes I wear when I work.

I call up the layer the chief SOCO talked about and select the voice option for the tags, and a few places in the room glow faintly. I point at the stains in the carpet, now edged in a pale blue light, and hear his voice.

"You can see the blood soaked into the carpet—I'd say at least two or three pints in this stain alone. From the distribution I believe the body was dismembered here and then the limbs thrown to the positions you see here, rather than pushed or pulled. The head was removed last, I'd wager, judging by the spatters on the face and neck, but that will need to be confirmed with the pathologist's report."

The remainder of the cord hanging from the light fixture is tagged. "Only the victim's DNA has been found on the knot securing the cord to the light fixture. Of course, that could have been left when the victim closed his curtains, but from the amount of skin cells caught in the fibers, I believe the victim tied the knot and tested its strength."

Alejandro was made to hang himself? At gunpoint, presumably? I make a note and then point to the tagged chair. "Due to the height of the ceiling and the deduced length of the cord, the victim—if my earlier assumption is correct—would have stood on this chair to tie the noose to the light fixture and also would have had to stand on the chair in order for the noose to be placed around his neck. In addition, the murderer would have had to stand on it to cut the victim down. No dirt from outside is on the chair cushion, which suggests the murderer's shoes were very clean, were house slippers or were not worn at the time. Due to the cushioning foam beneath the upholstery, no measurable impression has been left."

Something is niggling me but I don't focus on it yet. I want to get all the data first. I point to tagged spots of blood and listen to the chief SOCO describing how the distribution of the blood spatter supports his idea about where the body was cut up. "In addition," the recording of his voice continues, "it's clear the chopping took place in a localized area, presumably after the victim's death, as there are no blood spots elsewhere, caused by attacking a moving victim, for example."

Last is the brown stain on the rug. "Piecing together the residue detected at the scene and the images from the recorders," Alex's voice says after I point at it, "reveals that the body was cut down after death, as the torso partially covers the contents of the bowels that were released when the victim died, as is common in hanging. Feces have run down the leg and dripped—"

I cut off the audio, having taken all I need from that tag already.

Something about this case feels . . . off. Usually when I look at a scene I can mentally reconstruct the murder in minutes, often sooner. Here, I feel like I have the pieces before me but I'm not confident about how they fit together.

"Tia, come and talk this through with me."

Tia's avatar walks round, as if she has been standing behind me the whole time. She's dressed in a three-piece pinstripe trouser suit and flats, her skin the same olive as mine and her black hair pulled back in a bun. Her face is attractive but generic, one of the thousands of pre-generated avatars available that's nice enough to look at, but not so gorgeous that it would be distracting. She's too perfect to be truly realistic, but here, fully immersed in a virtual environment, she's convincing enough for me to feel like I have an old-school police partner to bounce ideas off of. Exactly as the MoJ programmers intended it. It's so much cheaper to have a virtual partner than an actual human being.

"Lay it out for me," she says, pulling a line from one of the cheesy mersives I've played lately. "What have we got?"

"We've got a murder that just doesn't feel right," I say.

"Is this something to do with your gut intuition?" She seems just as unimpressed with me as I am with myself. I hate this nebulous shit, but nine times out of ten, that niggle in the gut is worth listening to.

"Yeah," I say, struggling to drill down into some detail. "He was hanged first, right? Chief SOCO thinks Alejandro tied the knot up there because of the DNA residue. Now, let's say I'm Theo and I come in here to kill him. Why the fuck would I get a curtain cord and make a noose out of it, here, in this room?"

"Why not bring one from your room?" Tia asks.

"Right. If he didn't bring one from his room, it suggests it was unplanned. Does that mean they were talking and then Theo decided to kill him out of the blue? If that's the case, why a noose? I mean, he must have had a gun or something to make Alejandro tie it up there and, presumably, put his head through, because the victim wouldn't have done that willingly. But how the hell would Theo have a gun anyway? The Circle hate them, he couldn't have brought one through security into the UK and I doubt he'd have any criminal connections good enough to obtain one or a print pattern either. Without a gun, Theo wouldn't be able to knock him out and then, I dunno, lift him up there to kill him. That's just craziness."

"Tying a noose and forcing the victim to hang himself at gunpoint doesn't match with your hypothesis about this being a crime of passion," Tia says.

"Agreed," I say, scratching my chin. "And the rest of it . . . Why has the body been cut up? It doesn't even fit with being drawn and quartered. For one thing, Alejandro was dead when he was cut up, judging by the spatters and lack of evidence of a struggle. For another, there's nothing here that suggests his genitals were removed—though I guess the pathologist will have to verify that. But by the look of his trousers, they were just ripped at the top of the thighs when the legs were severed. And there are too many . . . pieces to follow 'quartering' too."

"The bowels appear to still be inside the torso," Tia says, looking down at it. I don't know if she's programmed to look at the thing she is referencing, having pulled that fact from the initial report to the MoJ made by the police officers on the day, or if she has actually deduced that from what is being shown here. APAs are so good these days it's impossible to know unless you program them. "If the murderer was trying to follow the historic technique of hang, draw and quartering, they would have removed the bowels while the victim was alive."

"Okay, so what it looks like we have here is a forced hanging that obviously required premeditation, followed by some batshit chopping up that seems very passionate." I shake my head. "No, it just doesn't fit together."

I look at the cord hanging from the ceiling and another explanation presents itself. Before it's even settled into place I'm shaking my head for a different reason.

"What's wrong?" Tia asks.

"Nothing," I say, dismissing the idea of suicide. Alejandro would never end his own life. "I don't have enough data. I need the blood-test results from the girl he was sharing the room with, for a start, and more information on Theo. He has to have been pretty fucking disturbed to do this to someone he practically worshipped. Something must have pushed him over the edge."

"Perhaps they argued," Tia says.

"Perhaps." I stuff my hands in my pockets, trying to understand the last hour of Alejandro's life. What state of mind would a man have to be in to come into his cult leader's room, force him to hang himself and then feel compelled to mutilate the body like this with the girlfriend asleep in the room next door? If Theo drugged her, that would suggest premeditation again and I can't make that sit comfortably against this chaotic brutality. The limbs haven't been arranged, just tossed aside. There's no other meaning here, no pattern left in the positioning or the blood. It speaks of someone filled with uncontrollable rage.

"Maybe it's not Theo," I say. "Maybe the girl did it. It would explain how she could sleep through it—in that she didn't—and why no one went in or out of the room in the murder window. Maybe Theo heard it and ran, thinking he was next."

"Theo has made no efforts to contact the police," Tia says.

"Maybe he can't handle it." I shrug. "He could still be in shock."

"But if this theory is correct, you are assuming Theo saw what happened to the victim," Tia says. "As the door to this room wasn't opened between the time the victim and Klein entered the suite and the time the cleaner discovered the body, how did Theo see what had happened?"

"Were any calls made from the room that night?"

"None," Tia replies.

"He might have heard the latter stages through the wall," I say, looking at the wall next to the bedroom door. "Am I right in thinking that's the back of the en-suite bathroom in his room?"

"Yes. According to the renovation notes placed in the case file by Alex Jacobs, primary SOCO, soundproofing was placed in the walls between rooms."

"Enough to block out loud thuds?"

"I don't know. Would you like me to run a simulation and calculate the number of decibels any sound from this room would reach in Theo's room?"

"Yeah, do that."

"Assuming the sound of the body being cut is of comparable volume to a log being split by an ax, within an error range of plus or minus twenty decibels, the number of decibels reaching Theo's room would sound like this in the minimum range." She claps her hands and there is the softest thump, not even as loud as a normal clap would be. Not nearly enough to alert him of anything untoward. "And like this at the topmost range of permitted error." The second clap is louder, but still not enough to wake someone. And even if he did hear it, why not come to the room and check?

"Of course, all of this is assuming the security video is clean," I say. "Klein may have tampered with it."

"Members of the Circle are renowned for lack of technical skills," Tia says.

"Yeah, but some are latecomers. Klein might have been in tech before she joined them. Has the US gov-corp released her details yet?"

"A formal request hasn't been made since the legal obstructions were removed."

"Fuck. Then make it. I want her background as fast as possible. Theo Buckingham's too."

"Done."

I need more information and none of it can be found in this room. I look at the back of Alejandro's head, trying to force myself into going and looking at his face, like I have with every single victim I've ever seen. But my feet just don't move.

"Tia. The victim's face . . . Is it . . . Are his eyes open?"

She walks around the fallen chair and crouches down in front of it, just like I should. "Yes," she says. "Would you like me to describe the effects of the hanging on his skin and blood vessels?"

I shut my eyes, wishing I could have done the same for him, wishing there was no need to. "No," I say. "Exit crime-scene simulation."

9

I DON'T REMEMBER anyone openly sleeping with Alejandro back when I was in the Circle. That's not to say it didn't happen; most of my time there I was either too young or too angry to notice social signals with any subtlety. He was a handsome, charismatic guy. No doubt men and women all but threw themselves at him all the time. I'm curious to see what it was about Klein that made him pick her out from the faithful to travel all this way with him.

Her background file arrives as I'm putting my belt back on, trying to shrug off the sense of physical disorientation following the immersion. I ask Tia to read me the pertinent details as I splash my face with cold water. Her full name is Selina Jane Klein, a thirty-year-old divorcée originally from upstate New York. According to the file she used to be chipped and had a high-profile job in one of the thousands of data-management firms on the East Coast of America. I scan her resume and former job profile. Nothing there suggests she has any specialties that would make it easy for her to doctor the security footage, but I'm going to keep an open mind. She might have been working with someone else or she might have learned it outside of work. Either way, being unchipped, she would have to have some sort of portable unit to even access the local node, and nothing in Alex's report lists anything like that found in her room. For the first time I wonder whether she and Theo actually worked together and if he took such a unit with him.

I review the medical file citing removal of her chip for "reasons of psychological well-being" a month after her divorce was finalized. Two months after that, her official residence became that of the Circle. That was three years ago.

I shrug on my jacket and drop my room key into the pocket. Before I saw the crime scene in detail, I was all but convinced Theo was the one who did it. Now she is equally in the frame, at least until the blood analysis comes in.

"What's the ETA on those blood test results?"

"The sample is currently en route to the pathologist's lab, where it should be tested immediately," Tia replies. "I estimate two to three hours."

Of course, out in the sticks like I am here, there are no administrators with twenty-four-hour schedules who'd be able to physically find and package up the sample the moment a request comes in. The request must have been picked up this morning, hence the delay. Toxicology tests used to take weeks, apparently. At least I don't have to wait that long. I leave my room.

Klein has been put in a room on the second floor at the other end of the hotel to the Diamond Suite, almost directly below my room. There's a local copper on the door, making sure she doesn't leave and that no one interferes with her while the investigation is under way. The copper, a freckled redhead who looks like he's barely old enough to wear a uniform, reports that no one has been in or out and that he personally has checked all daytime room service before it goes in and when it comes out.

"Hardly touches a thing," he says. "I wondered whether I should tell the doctor that came to see her on the morning it all kicked off, but then I heard you were here so I thought I'd tell you, sir." I have the feeling he's enjoying being on the periphery of such a high-profile case.

I don't want to do anything to tarnish that. "Thanks for letting me know, Constable."

He opens the door for me after a brisk knock and I go inside. The curtains are drawn against the milky November sunlight and the air is stale. In the gloom I can make out nothing more than a shape on the bed. A tray of untouched morning pastries and fruit is on the floor beside it, illuminated by a rogue shaft of light poking through a gap at the top of the curtains.

"Ms. Klein?" I say, closing the door behind me. "Are you awake?"

"Yeah." Her voice is flat.

"My name is SDCI Carl Moreno. I'm running the investigation. Do you mind if I open the curtains?"

"I guess not."

I draw them back and hear her moving in the bed behind me. When I turn, I see that she has shifted out of the brightest patch, keeping her face in as much shade as possible. I pull back the other curtain and then there's no shadow left for her to hide in.

The bedside table is covered by a small mountain of used tissues and the bin nearby has a scattering of more, balled up, tossed and fallen short of their target. A glass of water is perched on the bedside table, holding some of the tissues back from falling off the edge, and has specks of dust and a hair floating on the surface.

She pulls herself up into a sitting position and I see she's wearing a hotel dressing gown over a silky nightdress. Only the counterpane covers her, the room too hot and stuffy to merit the use of all the sheets and blankets on the bed. I'm struck by how incredibly pale she looks, her cheeks drawn, brown eyes bloodshot and puffy. Her hair is a tangled mess of brown curls that tumble chaotically to her shoulders. She pushes some of them back away from her face as she squints at me and I note how well manicured her nails are. Not something I remember any of the women in the Circle having when I was there.

"Do you mind if I stay in bed?"

I shake my head.

She looks at the tissues and frowns. "Sorry about the . . . mess." Her voice is hoarse.

"Do you want some water?" I ask, and she nods.

I take the glass with me, letting some of the tissues tumble silently to the floor, rinse it out in the bathroom sink and refill it. There's a packet of complimentary toiletries, unopened, next to the tap. All of her belongings are still in the Diamond Suite and will be until I sign off their removal.

The room is smaller than mine, the bed just a standard one without posts. It's still opulent and just as pristine in the areas untouched by her grief. I hand her the glass and she manages a weak smile of thanks. She drains it and I refill it without asking.

"I guess you want to talk to me about . . . him," she says as I pull a chair over from its place beneath the desk and sit next to her by the bed.

"In accordance with Noropean law, you need to understand that anything you say to me is being recorded and can and will be used as evidence in this investigation, should it become necessary."

"Okay. What do you wanna know?"

"Let's talk about you first."

"I was sleeping with him. Let's just get that out in the open, straight off the bat. I know you Brits get all antsy about that kind of stuff."

I don't bother to tell her I'm not the typical British citizen, whatever that's supposed to be. "Is that why you came with him to Norope?"

She nods. "Yeah. Well, partly. I really wanted to come with him. I've never been outside of the States. He said I could travel on his visa as an assistant." She looks past my shoulder, out of the window. "I can't believe this is happening. I keep expecting him to come through the door, to tell me it's all some fucked-up mersive or something. Not that it would even be possible."

"You had your chip removed," I say. "Was that to join the Circle?"

"I was going to do it anyway." She brushes back a few curls that have fallen forward again. Her fingers are trembling. "He just gave me another reason to do it."

"He recruited you personally, then."

She nods, her eyes sparkling with tears. "In New York. He was on a tour, doing talks, you know. I went to one. It was . . . a tough time for me and he was the only person on the god-damn planet making any sense."

I nodded, wanting to give her the impression I understood. And I did. Alejandro had a knack for finding the most vulnerable at the lowest point in their lives and making them think he had all the answers.

"My divorce was being finalized at the time. I had some difficult choices to make. I didn't want to be chipped anymore, but if I trashed it I'd be trashing my career at the same time. He showed me that choosing to live unchipped wasn't about what I would lose, but about what I would gain."

"What career was that?"

"I was an information architect and UX specialist. I created intuitive hierarchies and data-filing systems and designed user interfaces for corps managing massive data sets. It was a good job. Well paid. I was climbing the ladder with the rest of them."

No wonder Alejandro plucked her from the crowd. She's attractive, even now; back then she probably stood out more. Well educated, successful, technical background. Those were his favorites. People who had seized all they could from modern life and were still left empty. He liked them even better if they had been broken by it too, like my father had been.

"The US gov-corp file says you were married. Did your husband object to your joining the Circle?" I know that's unlikely, timing wise; I just want to hear what she has to say.

"Oh, all that happened before I even met Alejandro. My ex-husband was the reason why I didn't want to be chipped anymore."

"I thought the US antistalking laws were pretty robust, especially in divorce cases."

She fishes out the end of the dressing gown's belt from under the cover and twists it around her fingers. "No. It wasn't that." After a long pause she shrugs to herself. "You'll dig it all up anyway. He fell in love with his APA and I found out." She mistakes my silence for disbelief. "I know, right? I mean, what kind of fucking world is this where a guy can choose a woman who doesn't even exist over someone real who loves him?"

Now I see where the modern world broke her just enough for Alejandro. "Was it a difficult divorce?"

"Aren't they all? At first he denied it, but I knew. I overheard him talking to her when he thought I was in a mersive upstairs. He'd started internally projecting her avatar, you know, to make it seem she was like a person, there all the time. I mean, JeeMuh, it was like having some goddamn ghost in the house. I freaked out when I realized, and he promised he'd only do it when he was alone. But it was already too far down the road by then. I heard him talking to her like she was real. I mean, we all do that, right? But talking like she was a real person he *loved*. She was just a projection from his own chip. He was such a fucking narcissist."

"And when you challenged him . . ."

"Oh, he carried on denying it, but I knew. A friend of mine is a lawyer specializing in virtual-adultery cases so I went to her. She knew a sympathetic case officer and I presented my suspicions and the evidence I had. It was enough to file a demand to have a third party examine the data held in his cloud and rule whether there was an unusual amount of activity . . . types of activity . . . Stuff. You know."

"And they reported back to the case officer that he was spending too much time with his APA?" I'd heard about cases like this springing up more and more. It wasn't a criminal act, but even if it was, I wouldn't want anything to do with it.

Her forehead crumples as she frowns at the toweling twisted around her fingers. "More than that. He was spending time with her at the same time as me. At the same time as us making love. He was having sex with me while he was superimposing me with her avatar. JeeMuh." She rubs her free hand over her face, shaking more now. "It was a goddamn nightmare. And the lawyer he got was so good. Argued it was all totally understandable because of some Jungian anima crap that I still don't understand. I moved to New York, my life totally falling apart, and I met Alejandro. And we talked. I mean, really talked. He listened to me. And when I'm with him, he's really with me, you know? He's totally present every—" She stops and her face crumples. "Oh God. He's gone. I can't believe he's gone."

She breaks down in front of me. I watch her fumble under her pillow for a tissue and blow her nose. I've seen some pretty damn convincing acts in my time, but my gut tells me she's genuinely upset. I can't eliminate her based on that though, and there's still a lot more I need to know.

"Sorry," she mutters, wiping her top lip. "I just . . . I just can't stop crying. What will we do now? How can we go on without him?"

"The Circle?"

"Yes. There's so much . . . so much to be done and I don't know how we'll . . . ." Her voice cracks and I fight the tug of memories trying to pull me back to that place where people thought he was the center of the universe. I feel a flash of hatred toward her for being so broken by the loss of him, for needing him so much when he was just a man who scooped up the human detritus from the edges of society and fooled them into thinking they were part of something special. I pause as the feeling subsides, giving her a chance to compose herself too.

"I need to ask you some more questions," I say. "Why don't you try to eat something? You'll feel better for it."

She leans over the side of the bed and looks down at the tray as if lumps of clay are sitting on it. She finally reaches down and plucks a small bunch of grapes off the plate. "What do you wanna know?"

"Why were the three of you here in England?"

"Alejandro used to travel quite a lot. There were donors all over the world, people who believed in his message but weren't ready to come to the States. There was someone in London he had to see, someone very rich, I think. That's the impression I had, anyway. He didn't talk about the details."

"But why stay in a hotel hours away from London?"

"He said it was a good place for people who aren't chipped. And it's private too. It would have been a circus if we stayed in London this close to the capsule being opened and all. He said the press here wouldn't see him as himself, but as one of Cillian Mackenzie's rejects, so he wanted to keep a low profile. This place has lots of famous people staying here. The staff are used to getting rid of the press."

I think of the doorman. It seems plausible enough, but there are many high-security hotels in London. Perhaps there was another reason he picked this one, one he chose not to share with her.

"Did he meet with this person in London?"

She nods. "He went last week."

"By himself?"

"Yeah. He went up on Wednesday morning and came back"—she looks up at the ceiling—"on Sunday afternoon."

"Didn't you want to go with him?"

She nods again, twisting the cord. "I had the feeling he didn't want me there though. He organized a tour for Theo and me, up to Bath and Stonehenge—you know, tourist stuff. Like he wanted us to not feel left out when he was obviously leaving us out of his London stuff."

I stay quiet, feeling there is more she could say about this. Sure enough, the pressure of silence makes her draw in a breath.

"I wondered if he was going to see a lover. He said he couldn't tell me about it because the person he was seeing wanted it all to be secret. He . . . I dunno. It seemed to me like it was a big deal."

"Did he seem nervous about the meeting?"

She shrugs. "I guess. Tense, maybe."

"And when he got back from London, how was he? Did he mention if the trip went well?"

She looks back down at the dressing-gown cord and then disentangles her fingers to pluck a grape from its stalk. "I don't think so. He didn't seem himself. He went for a really long walk the day he got back. Said he had a headache and wanted to get some fresh air, and when I asked if I could go with him he said he wanted to be alone. That wasn't like him. I wondered if he was getting sick or something. He didn't want to be with me much at all. Nor Theo. And Theo being Theo, he thought I'd said something to upset Alejandro."

I see the first signs of animosity when she speaks about the other person from the Circle. I want to keep her focused on Alejandro for now. "And what about the rest of that Sunday? How did Alejandro behave?"

She frowns at me. "I haven't heard anyone outside of the Circle call him that. It's kinda weird."

I silently admonish myself. "It's what you call him," I say, covering myself. "How did he seem that last afternoon and evening?"

She rolls the grape between her fingers, as if the idea of eating it hasn't even occurred to her. "Distant. Distracted, I guess. It wasn't a good day. I guess . . . I guess it stirred up some stuff for me, being with someone who didn't feel fully present."

"What do you mean by that?"

"Like he was off in deep thought, meditative almost, but at random points in the day. I thought he was bored of me, if you really want to know the truth. I thought he met a lover in London and when he came back to me, I didn't measure up anymore." She drops the grape onto the bedcover. "I tried to talk to him about it but he denied it. But I knew. I know what it feels like to be replaced."

She starts to cry again, scattering the grapes as she searches for a clean tissue. I recall a box in the bathroom and get it for her, which she accepts gratefully.

"You know, I've started to wonder if he wanted to bring me at all," she says after blowing her nose again. "I think back and I can't remember him being all that keen, you know? Theo definitely thought I shouldn't have been here. Have you seen Theo? How is he holding up? God, I haven't even thought about him. He must be—"

"He's missing," I say, and she looks genuinely shocked.

"For how long?"

"Since the night of the murder. Do you have any idea where he might have gone?" She shakes her head. "Any distant relatives, any friends he made while you were touring?"

"No, none," she says, and then pales further, until she looks like she could faint. "You don't think Theo . . ."

"He is a suspect."

"No, that's crazy. He loves Alejandro just as much as I do. Did. Shit."

"In the same way?"

"He wasn't gay, if that's what you mean. At least, I don't think he was."

"You seem uncertain."

She wipes her nose, the skin around her nostrils reddened. "Theo is . . . What's the best way to put this? Pretty repressed. He might be gay, but if he is, he's the last person on Earth who'd admit it. He's got issues, you know?"

"No. Tell me about him."

"He joined the Circle years before I did. He always traveled with Alejandro. He was there when I met him in New York, but I didn't notice him. I mean, no one else is in the room when Alejandro turns on the charm, you know?"

Oh, I did. But I didn't show her that I knew. "Go on."

"Theo saw himself as Alejandro's personal assistant, I suppose, when he traveled. Not so much back home. He was so pissed when I told him I was coming with them to England."

"You two didn't get along?"

"Oh, most of the time everything was fine. I guess he didn't like the thought of having to share him, especially not with the whore of Babylon."

"He called you that?"

She smirks. "Not explicitly. Theo came from a hard-core religious sect in the Deep South. For him, the Circle was, like, the most progressive place ever. He never missed the personal tech because he didn't grow up with it. Apparently Alejandro spent a long time helping him transition out of their brainwashing, but some of those ideas never go away. I don't think he liked the fact we slept together." She shakes her head. "He was pretty childish a few times here, before Alejandro went to London. Sulking at the sight of us together, like a kid. Jealous, I guess." She looks back up at me. "Oh, but he isn't a horrible person—don't get me wrong. We had a nice time touring, when it was just the two of us. I guess he could relax when Alejandro wasn't there. I really don't think he did . . . that. I mean, no one who actually knew Alejandro could do that to him, surely?"

"Theo checked out just after five a.m. on the morning the murder was discovered," I say, and she visibly shudders. "Did he mention leaving early? Was he scheduled to go on any trips without you?"

"No. We were only supposed to be here another day or two. Alejandro said he hadn't made up his mind, but it wasn't going to be much longer. Theo wouldn't have risked going away by himself that close to our departure. He wouldn't have wanted to inconvenience Alejandro."

"I'd like you to talk me through the last night you had with Alejandro," I say, keeping my voice soft. She's more open than most—being American certainly helps—but she could close up any moment if she feels threatened.

Her eyes well up again and she looks up at the ceiling. "He was pretty low at dinner. Distant, like I said. Theo was struggling with it too and being an asshole to me. I guess he thought we'd had a fight or something and obviously it would have been my fault. Alejandro said good night to Theo after dinner and said we should have an early night. Theo stomped off back to his room, probably because he thought Alejandro meant more than he did. We went back to our room about nine p.m. No, maybe it was closer to ten. I don't know exactly."

"And how was Alejandro when you were alone?"

She wipes her nose and sniffs. "He said sorry. I asked him what for and he said he hadn't been himself and it wasn't fair to me and that he was sorry for that. I was relieved. I asked him if he wanted us to be over and he . . ." She stops, frowning into the space behind my shoulder. "He seemed sad. He said it wasn't the time to talk about it and that I looked tired. I was. I took a bath. I don't know what he did while I was in there. I got dressed for bed and went into the main room to see if . . . if I could take him to bed. He kissed me, but not like he wanted more. He had a drink, whisky I think, but he'd made me a chamomile tea. He said I should go to bed and took the drink through for me. I . . . I got into bed and he sat on it next to me, stroking my hand. He told me to drink up and that he'd tuck me in. Like I was a kid, almost. I got sleepy. I guess the bath and him being there kind of relaxed me. I drank the tea, he kissed me good night and tucked the sheets around me. And the next thing I knew, there was this man yelling in the room next door. I felt groggy, like I was still jet-lagged. I thought I dreamed it or something. I think I went back to sleep—that sounds crazy but I did—then I heard the door again and I got out of bed, and the hotel manager was telling someone to get out of the way, from the door into the suite. I got out of bed and went to the door and I saw his . . . I saw his foot."

She breaks down again, this time sobbing uncontrollably, sometimes almost screaming into the tattered tissue in her hands. For a moment I wonder whether to move over to the bed and hold her, but decide not to. She's too vulnerable and I'm not the right person for her to cling to. Instead I go to the door and the constable stands rigid to attention when I open it.

"Ms. Klein needs psych support right away. She's been by herself too much already."

"Sorry, sir. I was told that no one—"

"Not your fault, Constable, but see to it, would you?"

"Right away, sir!"

I leave him outside and return to stand by my chair. She's on her side now, fetally curled around a pillow, her distress muffled. The dressing gown has slid from one shoulder, reveal-ing a dark bruise the size of a thumbprint on the front of it, a couple of inches above her armpit. I lean over and look at the back and see four smaller bruises, just as black.

"Ms. Klein," I say gently, but she doesn't hear me. Now isn't the time to ask about them. I stand there, a reluctant wit-ness to her world imploding, until a psych-support officer arrives with a small leather case and a professional smile. I leave him to do his work after saying a superfluous good-bye and thank-you to the second victim of the crime.

10

I GO BACK to my room to decompress and review the interview. Tia has automatically transcribed every word and added text, audio and full video copies to the case file.

I play back the audio a couple of times, paying extra attention to the pauses, the words that are strained and where the silences are the longest. Her account doesn't match up with the briefing Milsom gave me in the car. I need to interview the cleaner later anyway.

I get Tia to call Alex for me and he accepts a voice connection immediately.

"Good morning again," he says.

"Is now a good time to come over to the Diamond Suite?" I don't have to ask permission, but I have the feeling things will go more smoothly if Alex feels he's the rooster there.

"Of course. They did leave that bag in your room, didn't they?"

A gentle way to remind me to suit up. "Yeah," I say. "I'll be there in a minute."

I double-check that the tamperproof seals are still reading green when I pull them from the pack left for me the night before. "Tia, call Nadia for me."

Nadia accepts voice connection in 1.5 seconds, as if she has been waiting for my call. "Good morning, SDCI Moreno. How can I help you?" I can hear that smile as she speaks.

"Do you have a gardener here?"

"A groundskeeper, yes. He has an assistant too."

"Do they use an ax?"

"Yes. They— Oh." She's realized why I'm asking. "Would you like me to check if they still have it?"

"That would be great, thanks. If it's where they expect it to be, don't touch it or let them touch it. In fact, take one of the constables with you. I'll send one down to your office now."

At least she's levelheaded. I assign the copper who was guarding Selina's room after reminding him about evidence protocols, and he's barely able to keep his voice from squeaking.

There's always a point early in an investigation when it feels like the information that needs to be checked and folded into the case is expanding exponentially. Just that one conversation with Selina has opened up a new facet that creates many more questions than I woke up with this morning: Alejandro's London trip.

It might be unrelated. It could have everything to do with the murder. I have to turn over every stone at this point, with everything still wide-open and Theo still out there somewhere. Selina said Alejandro behaved differently after the trip and that alone is enough to justify following up on it.

"Tia, put in a request with the MoJ for all of Alejandro's visa details, including the temporary credit assigned to him at the border. I need all the transactions he made during his trip to London pulled and put in the case file in a new folder called 'London trip,' okay?"

Alejandro being unchipped has made this part easier; all unchipped visitors to England are assigned temporary credit for use during their stay to make transactions seamless when they spend any money in the country. Without having a chip to handle it all, they provide a thumbprint instead and the visa system processes it. Of course, it will only provide part of the picture—the person or people he saw there may have paid instead—but it should at least give me a few places and times to narrow down the data combing. Just one transaction will enable me to get a visual on him, and identification software is so good now the MoJ AI will be able to track him across London for me, assuming he didn't go into any black spots.

There's the outside chance he had access to illegal credit. There's an entire criminal subculture that specializes in hiding transaction activity in a cashless society, after all, but I'll worry about that if something unusual becomes apparent.

I take a moment to mentally run through the morning so far, certain I've forgotten something. Travis Gabor comes to mind. "Tia, pull any data on Travis Gabor, will you? I'd like to see his chip activity before it was removed, and the reason why it was taken out."

"Stefan Gabor has placed a formal legal-request clause on his husband's data. Would you like me to initiate the request process?"

Gabor doesn't have any legal right to stop me from reviewing the data; he's just putting an extra layer of fuckery into the mix so that if I turn anything up that could incriminate him, he has a heads-up. What it does force me to do is justify the search, right from the start, more explicitly than I have to usually. I'm tempted to drop it; I don't think Travis is involved, but something about the way that rich bastard is trying to make my job harder pisses me off just enough to not let it go.

Besides, it's not like this case doesn't already have an army of lawyers swarming over it already. I'd like to see Gabor trying to block three gov-corps at once.

"Yeah, do that. Ping one of the MoJ lawyers who was here last night."

"The MoJ lawyers will want a justification for—"

"Tell them the justification is that some billionaire twat thinks he can fuck with the MoJ. And if that's not justification enough for coming up with some legalese bullshit—like they are paid to come up with every day—then they can call me."

"There are several expletives in your response. Would you like me to present your request verbatim?"

"No. Of course not. Make it all nice and polite, Tia."

"Done."

Of course, my conversation with Tia is now sitting in an MoJ data bank, and if things turn nasty with Gabor it could be raked up to paint me as a belligerent bastard with an ax to grind. But it won't. I'll just scan the data, let Travis have an extra night in the swanky hotel without any abuse from his husband and then it will all be over.

OUTSIDE the Diamond Suite I show the green seal on the paper-suit packet to the duty officer outside and then put it on in front of him. After doing the same with the packet of full bootie-like shoe covers, I pull on a pair of latex gloves last and go inside.

There's a team of six people at work in the room, all dressed like me, in paper suits, and not one of them is Alex. In a corner farthest away from the place the body was found is a portable bank of testing equipment at hand to extract DNA from any samples and then check them against the National Genome Database.

A woman looks up from the desk and shouts through to the bedroom, "The SDCI is here, boss." The others in the forensic team take a brief interest in me then, a couple giving me a polite nod and a smile; the rest offer nothing more than a blank stare before returning to whatever still holds their attention.

"Ah." Alex appears at the doorway to the bedroom. "Come through. I'll show you what we're working up in here."

There are two more from his team in there, both men, both too engrossed to look at me. They're dedicated, that much is clear, but then so much is riding on this case being wrapped up neatly that their reputation is on the line. They probably won't see another case that's this high-profile for years, if ever.

"Only Klein's hair is in the bed," Alex says. "The victim didn't sleep in it, since the sheets were changed the morning before the murder."

I nod. "I just interviewed her."

"So you'll be interested in the cup we found in the bathroom."

I follow him into the en-suite, telltale signs of forensic examination and dusting all over the mirror, the sink and the marble slab it's set into.

He points at a porcelain cup that I recognize, the same type as in my room, provided with the tea and coffee facilities. "She drank from it, but his prints are on the cup too. I put it back where we found it so you could see it in situ. From the positioning, I think he made the drink and gave it to her; both of their prints are on the handle and his are more smudged there. Then he carried it into the bathroom and put it here, when it was empty and not too hot to hold on the sides rather than the handle."

"Chamomile tea?"

He nods. "The tea bag is in the bedroom bin, so he left it in there to steep, as the kettle is in the main room."

"Any residue?"

Alex grins. "Oh yes. It's in the machine at the moment, but my money is on a heavy sedative." He glances away for a second before looking back at me. "The analysis should be done in a few minutes, but I'll bet you a hundred quid that it's Zopadril, a sleeping drug widely used in the US."

"I'd accept, if betting on evidence outcomes didn't contravene MoJ conduct guidelines." The grin drops from his face and I smile. "It's okay—I know you're only joking. I'm not that uptight." It's only partly true; he doesn't have to watch his own conduct as closely as I have to. "What makes you so confident?"

"We found a bottle in the drawer over there." He points to the bedside cabinet on the far side of the bed. "Prescribed to him, according to the label."

I scratch the back of my head. That doesn't sit right. Alejandro was so anti-drugs—anti-anything that interfered with the natural workings of the brain, be it a physical chip or substances that altered neurochemistry. "Who prescribed it?"

"A doctor at the Chicago airport walk-in clinic. Apparently it's prescribed to help with jet lag. Thing is, it looks like he didn't take any for jet lag at all. Only three of them are missing from the bottle and we know he didn't take them; the capsules were emptied into the tea. We found them in the bin with the tea bag, partials of his prints all over them."

"He gave her three times the recommended dose? Shit, was he trying to kill her?"

Alex shrugs. "Maybe. She wouldn't have been able to taste or smell it, so it's a good choice from that perspective. Anyone with very low blood pressure could have been killed by that dose, but she's young, fit and healthy. He obviously wanted her out for the count though. Puts her out of the frame, I reckon."

I nod in agreement. It could also explain the discrepancies in her account. "I'm just waiting for confirmation from a routine blood test taken when she was treated for shock but, by the sound of it, there won't be any trouble detecting that sort of dose."

"The question is, I suppose, why he drugged her," Alex says. "If she'd been sleeping normally, he might still be alive now. But that's for you to worry about." The grin returns. "There was something else I wanted to flag. May be nothing, but still, I like to be thorough."

He leads me back into the main room. "Clare," he calls over to a black woman in conference with one of her colleagues. "Come and tell the SDCI what you found earlier."

She comes over quickly, looking surprised to have been picked out. She's in her forties, I think. It can be hard to tell with hair covered up by these suits. Tia confirms, uninvited, that she's forty-two. "Morning," she says to me. "I was going over the desk. There's hotel stationery in the top drawer for the use of the guests. I had the idea that, in a place like this, they may have a set number of paper sheets and envelopes provided every day, replenished with the cleaning routine."

I nod, impressed. "Go on."

"I checked with one of the cleaners and he told me that they always make sure there are five sheets and five envelopes, and a spare ink cartridge for the fountain pen. Well, the cartridge is still in the drawer, but the pen is missing, along with one sheet and one envelope. According to the cleaner, he didn't have to replenish the supplies in the desk at any point during the victim's stay here. There were five of each, and the pen, in the desk on the morning before he was killed."

"Good work," I say.

Alex smiles warmly at her and I find myself altering my impression of him. He's still dull, but at least he gives credit where it's due and is proud of his team. "Thanks, Clare," he says, and she returns to her colleagues.

"So I take it there's no sign of the letter or the pen?"

Alex shakes his head. "We tried the blotter to see if there are any impressions left, but with it being a fountain pen, the applied pressure was too weak to leave anything we could detect."

"Okay. Anything else you want to flag?"

"Not right now. I'll add everything to the VR file and the AR layer, tagged. We should be wrapped up by about five o'clock this evening."

As I'm saying my good-bye I get a ping from Constable Riley, the one I sent to assist the hotel manager. I send back a "Will be with you shortly" and leave the suite, peeling off the protective clothing in the corridor outside. The duty officer takes it for me and I thank him, impressed by how attentive these coppers are.

I reply to the ping once I'm back in my room. "What is it, Constable?"

"The groundskeeper's ax is missing, sir. It's usually locked away in a shed, but the day of the murder he left it in a log by accident. He said the storm blew up faster than he thought it would and took a gate off one of its hinges, which he had to see to right away, as it was blocking access to the back of the property. He didn't realize the ax was missing until we checked the shed."

"Right—"

"I . . . Sorry, sir, I have more information."

I smile to myself. "Go ahead, Constable."

"The ax was only bought a month ago, so I took the liberty of calling up the purchase record with the hotel manager. I've put a picture and description of the exact, ummm . . . model of ax into the case file."

"Excellent work," I say, meaning it.

"Thank you, sir." He sounds quite breathless. "Anything else you need me to do, sir?"

"I'll get back to you." I end the call and ask Tia to put a commendation mark in Constable Riley's file. "Call Alex, Tia."

Alex accepts voice contact immediately. "Something come up?"

"Potentially. There are details in the case file of an ax, which is currently missing from the gardener's shed."

"Fantastic. I'll see if it matches these marks in the rug. I'll get back to you ASAP."

I sit on the edge of my bed and rest my head in my hands as I think things through. Why drug your own girlfriend? Why handwrite a letter?

The idea of suicide returns and initially I resist it. Then the training kicks in and I pull myself up. The resistance to the idea is too automatic to be objective.

Selina said Alejandro was acting strangely. That when they spoke before she went to bed he seemed sad. He drugged her and didn't even bother to rinse the cup. No, maybe it wasn't carelessness; maybe that was deliberate. To show she was incapable of waking while he hanged himself.

"You're considering case elements," Tia says, having identified keywords from my thoughts, just patterns of electrical and chemical activity it reads all the time. Normally it's only filtering for commands and the need for the v-keyboard and the like. Now I'm on a case, the brain activity created by keywords relating to the case are also attended to. "Would you like to enter a summary in the case file?"

Alejandro would never kill himself. No. I can't think of a reason why he would go against such a fundamental belief. Either way, I don't even want that word associated with him. "No."

Of course Milsom pings me at that moment. I stand before I realize it, even though her location reads as "London, MoJ." I accept the request for voice contact.

"How's it going?"

"Good."

"Suspect?"

"One of the people from the Circle, traveling with him." No doubt she's already scanned the case file. She wants to hear which details I choose to place emphasis on. "Theodore Buckingham. He checked out in the murder window. The manhunt team is on it. We've all but eliminated the girlfriend and I think we've identified the weapon used to chop him up; I'm just waiting on a confirmation from the head SOCO."

"Good. You getting the help you need?"

"Yeah. The local team is very strong, very sharp. I'm impressed, actually."

"Anything you need from me?"

Some fucking time?

"No, thanks, boss."

"Tread carefully around the Gabors. One of them is friends with the commissioner."

"I need to be thorough, ma'am."

"There's thorough and then there's avoidable legal action. Understand?"

"Perfectly, ma'am."

"I need you to give me an interim summary by lunchtime."

"That's less than twelve hours since I had sign-off to investigate!"

"I need to feed the dogs, Carlos. Otherwise they start

barking. Just clean up the case log and expand on the critical details—I can see it's all in there."

"Understood."

She ends the call and I sit back down again. Should I have told her what I fear? No. Not yet.

A message pops up from Alex. Just three words. It's a match!

I get Tia to notify the local force coordinator that I need a murder-weapon hunt. Even though that ax wasn't used to kill him, it was used to mutilate his body and could be covered in some solid evidence.

It's almost lunchtime. I find the room-service menu and start salivating at the options.

"I have an update on Travis Gabor's data," Tia says, and I put aside any thoughts of steak and dauphinoise potatoes. "The legal team secured access. The chip was removed four days ago on medical grounds. Suspected infection of the synaptic interface."

"I've never heard of that."

"It's very rare. Only one case per five hundred thousand, usually within a week of first insertion."

"How long had Travis been chipped?"

"Since age sixteen, as per Noropean law."

"What about the data? Anything come up that's pertinent to the case?"

"Yes. In the past three months prior to removal of the chip, eighty-six percent of Travis Gabor's Internet information searches were about the murder victim; a further ten-point-five percent were searches for information related to the Circle. His APA was instructed to notify him of any reports that Alejandro Casales was traveling outside of the United States. In addition, Travis Gabor has made repeated contact with an individual who works in visa control. He was informed when the victim's visa was approved and also sent details of his travel itinerary. This is illegal activity. Would you like me to inform the data-control department at—"

"No, not now," I say, amazed at the results. "Did the Gabors book into this hotel after Alejandro made his reservation?"

"Yes."

Was Travis stalking Alejandro?

11

I FILL THE kettle from the bathroom sink and switch it on, trying to work out where Travis fits into it all. Why come and beg to be interviewed if he was involved? Does he want me to think he's guilty?

Either way, the data can't be ignored. He's still lower priority than Theo and seems to have no desire to leave the hotel. In fact, he seemed much more interested in being forced to stay.

I ping Constable Riley and ask him to make sure Travis Gabor doesn't leave the hotel and to keep a record of his movements. Tia is already tracking all activity going through the local node as standard and will continue to do so until I lift the status of "crime scene under investigation." I make a note in the case file that Travis will be interviewed and a recommendation that the information about his search behavior be kept from his husband. Any hint of a potential scandal and Gabor will try to shut this thread of the investigation down faster than I could say "billionaire bastard."

I dunk the tea bag in a cup of hot water, watching the brown cloud spill from it. I think about Alejandro making that chamomile tea and try to imagine any other reason he'd want to drug Selina. I don't think for a moment it was attempted murder; he had enough capsules to do that and with the drug being masked by the tea, she wouldn't have been able to taste a higher dose.

I picture Alejandro in the main room of the suite, her in the bath, him breaking the capsules open and tipping them into the cup. If I were him, why would I want to keep her asleep so deeply she couldn't hear anything?

The image of the severed rope hanging from the light fixture flashes and I push it away. No. Something else could have happened before that point. Perhaps he planned to leave and didn't want her to wake and find he hadn't come to bed yet. Or perhaps someone else was coming to see him there in the suite, away from the public spaces and their cameras.

Travis, maybe?

I squeeze out the bag, drop it in the bin and find fresh milk in the tiny fridge hidden away in a cupboard. There are bottles of booze in there too and various snacks. Just as I'm replacing the milk there's a notification that new data has arrived.

"What is it, Tia?"

"Blood-test results for Selina Klein are in. Zopadril, a heavy sedative drug licensed for use in the United States, was detected at levels above the recommended dose. The doctor has appended a note, stating that it's his belief that nothing could have woken her properly for at least ten hours since the time of ingestion, and that it accounts for the grogginess observed the following morning. He also recommends that any testimony given regarding events within the first two hours of being woken be treated as unreliable."

That's that wrapped up, then. "Remove Selina Klein from the potential suspects list."

"Done. I have also communicated with the MoJ AI. There is evidence of tampering with the camera footage seized from the local node."

"This is my unsurprised face," I say. "Anything else said about it?"

"The footage has been referred to the specialist team for human review."

"Something unusual must have been flagged up, then. Any idea when they'll feed back?"

"No estimates have been provided. Average response times during periods with comparable caseloads range from twenty-four to forty-eight hours. As the priority tag has been retained, a reasonable estimate would be between twelve and twenty-four hours."

Someone deliberately removed the images of whoever went into that room after Selina and Alejandro retired for the night. Whether it's the same person who went in there and murdered him or just an accomplice remains to be seen.

"Tia, does Travis Gabor have any technical training that could enable him to tamper with that footage?"

"Travis Gabor was an employee of a digital-security firm for a period of nine months, three days following his graduation from Cambridge University."

He's the first person in the case file with the potential to have the relevant skills. "Oh fuck," I say, regretting that stupid outburst before. "Ping Milsom for me. Tell her I need to meet with her in my MoJ server space."

It's more secure than having a conversation here and I need to see her face when I tell her. She agrees and within minutes

I'm back in the virtual Diamond Suite. She's already there, standing at the edge of the room, hands in her pockets.

"So what's rattled you?"

"Let's talk in there," I say, pointing to the bedroom, and she follows without a word. I shut the bedroom door behind us, blocking off the view of the carnage. "I want to talk to you . . . as close to off the record as I can."

"That bad?"

I nod. "I don't mind this being on the MoJ server—I just don't want it to end up as evidence outside."

"Okay. I'll see to it, if I think it's necessary."

"It's Gabor's trophy husband. He was digitally stalking Alejandro Casales for months before he had his chip removed—removed for a reason that sounds flaky as hell. He's the only person in the frame who could have the skills to tamper with the video cameras in the lift and corridor outside the crime scene."

"Oh shit," Milsom groans. "This is the last thing we need."

"It's early days, and Travis Gabor isn't trying to evade investigation. I only prodded because things seemed weird when I met him at breakfast. He asked to be interviewed last. I'll add that conversation to the case file, now it could be relevant. I just wanted to flag it up with you, since it looks like it's going to turn into something."

"It's turning into another splinter in my arse—that's what it's turning into," Milsom mutters. Then she looks at me. "You were right to do that. I'll go and speak to legal, see if they can isolate the investigation data so none of Gabor's lawyers can start weaseling their way in before any charges are made. I'll go and brief the commissioner too. She needs to know what's ahead."

"Should I keep it out of the interim report?"

She considers it for a few seconds. "No, you have to put it in. He's on the suspect list now. We're legally obligated to report everything to the parties at that meeting last night. If it came out later that we held something back from the first report, we'd be fucked. It's not ideal, but they are legally bound to keep it all confidential, so we just have to hope the investigation wraps before any of them are tempted to tip off the Gabors that Travis is in the frame."

"Stefan Gabor must have multiple business interests with all three gov-corps," I say. "There could be some conflicts of interest ahead."

"There always are when you deal with people like that," Milsom replies, a grim set to her jaw. "No getting away from it. The best way to handle this is to do a flawless job as quickly as possible, okay?"

I nod.

"So, what does your gut tell you, seeing as we're speaking candidly here?"

That damn word comes back to me again and I know I have to tell her, for the same reason I can't keep Gabor out of the interim report: it could come back to bite me later if I hide it any longer. "I think there's a real chance we're looking at a suicide and subsequent mutilation of the body."

I've never seen Milsom look genuinely shocked before. It's disconcerting. "How much of a chance?"

I pause, not wanting to paint myself into a corner. I don't want to put a number on it; it's just where my gut is pulling me. No. There's no way he'd do that. No way. I'm probably just missing a piece of the puzzle and I bet Theodore Buckingham has it. "I . . . I'm just saying that this isn't shaping up to be a straightforward murder case," I finally say.

She nods slowly, and I think through what I just said, hoping I've covered my bases well enough. "Any other bombs you need to drop?"

"No, ma'am," I say. "But there is one thing . . ." I check to see how hostile she looks and judge that this is as good a time as any to ask. "I put in a request to legal earlier, to get Gabor's data."

Milsom folds her arms. "Go on."

"Well, the way I put it to my APA wasn't as polite as the wording that arrived with the lawyers. If this thing with Gabor pans out and . . ."

"You're worried you could look bad?"

"Yeah. I took a dislike to Stefan Gabor and it . . . may come across, should that exchange with my APA come out in judicial review."

Milsom smirks. "Not like you to make a mistake, Carlos." She lets me fret for a few seconds before saying, "I'll pull it—don't worry. I don't want it to cause any strife either. Now get back to work and contain this shit storm as quick as you can."

She disappears, not bothering to maintain the internal reality of the simulation. When I come back to my body my guts start cramping as my mental state is fully reconnected to my body again. The stress of confessing my mistake to Milsom makes me shake. She didn't mention any mark against me in my file. That doesn't mean she won't put one there. A black mark puts another year on my contract. Three black marks and they'll send me in for "calibration." I shudder at the thought of it. Like all expensive property, I'm kept in good working order.

I sit up and perch on the edge of the bed. I hold my palm in front of me and move it downward slowly, breathing out, pushing it all down. The case is the most important thing to worry about right now.

"A message arrived while you were immersed," Tia tells me. "From Dr. Palmeston, the pathologist assigned to the case.

She says that her preliminary report is ready and you are welcome to visit her at the lab."

"Tell her I'll be there as soon as I can."

CONSTABLE Riley gives me a lift over to the outskirts of Newton Abbot, where the pathologist's lab is. Riley chatters about the case, brimming with an enthusiasm I just can't muster. The lab is just like every other I've ever been in: spotlessly clean, clinically intimidating and brightly lit. The only thing this one has that I haven't seen anywhere else is a fish tank. It jars me as I enter the pathologist's lair, the tiny flashes of blue and bright purple catching my eye as the fish dart from one side of the tank to the other. There's a plastic treasure chest belching bubbles every few seconds and a model diver tangled in the underwater plants.

A misshapen body is covered by a sheet on one of three slabs and the two others are empty. Standing next to it, absorbed in a virtual task I can't see, is a white woman in her late fifties, just below six feet tall, her gray hair cut into short spikes and the tips dyed red to match her lipstick. She's wearing a white lab coat, buttoned up, leaving only a pair of burgundy trousers in sight and glittering red boots wrapped in the same plastic covers I wore over my own shoes earlier. Her profile has its privacy settings dialed high, so all I get is her name, Dr. Linda Palmeston, and confirmation of her position as head pathologist for the region.

"I would have gotten to it earlier," she says, still with her gaze in that strange middle distance where her APA interface sits. "Only some bloody conker slashed my tires and I had to change them. Little shits who live at the farm down the road. I got them on camera this time though. Just finishing up here, then I'll be with you."

"What car do you drive?"

"Car?" She wrinkles her nose, making the tip of it look sharper and more pronounced. "Bike. Vintage Ducati." She grins. "Gives me more pleasure than my husband ever did."

I wasn't expecting a bike. Vintage motorcycles are rare and require special licenses obtained after high-level driving and safety exams, seeing as they don't have an AI to take over should there be any need. Only the most dedicated bother with them these days.

"I knew someone who rode a Harley," I say.

The nose wrinkles again. "Old man's bike. Can't see the sense in sitting back like that with your arms in the air like some pillock. I mean, if you're going to drive an armchair, at least be comfortable." She blinks a few times and looks at me properly. "Well, hello at last. Sorry about that. Just wanted to get some tests set up for the stuff I'll be doing this afternoon."

"Dr. Palmeston—"

"Call me Linda, for Christ's sake." She looks at my face and then up and down my body. "An SDCI, eh? All the way from London. Well, aren't I honored?"

I smile at the sparkle in her eyes. "Not in the least. Call me Carl. You said you had a preliminary report ready?"

"That I did. I like a man who gets straight to the point. Alex called me earlier, said you knew the victim."

I nod.

She moves over to the top of the slab and takes hold of the sheet. "This isn't going to be easy, no matter how toughened you are. If it's too much, just say. I'll keep it as quick as I can."

I appreciate her sensitivity, but it still embarrasses me. "I've seen the body in a VR sim, as it was found."

"Never the same as seeing it here," she says. "I closed his eyes, if that helps."

"Let's just get this done."

She pulls back the sheet and I see Alejandro's face for the first time. I'm glad she closed his eyes. The waxy skin, the butchered neck and gap between it and the top of his torso are bad enough. I can't stop my eyes from moving down his body, seeing the other gaps caused by the mutilation. His genitals are shrunken and don't even look real, more like something crudely shaped and stuck on the outside of his body with macabre absurdity. His legs are tilted onto their sides without any attachment to the body to hold them in place, pulled over by the feet.

"The victim was hanged and died from asphyxiation caused by the cord around his throat. You can see the petechiae on his face here around the mouth and eyes. The blood has drained somewhat but there was also the telltale discoloration and congestion picked up by the recorders that fits with that too. Now, here"—she tilts his head to the side and points to a place on his neck—"is where you can see a textbook inverted-V bruise on the neck, caused by the cord. This tells me it's not strangulation."

I nod. "Otherwise it would be a straight line."

"Bonus points to the SDCI. Now, there's no way for me to tell if he was unconscious, strung up and then died or if it was suicide, but I know there was a chair at the scene he could have used. No note found, I take it?"

"No. But evidence one might have been written and removed from the scene."

She nods. "I wouldn't bet either way yet, if I were you. But, if you're a betting man, like Alex is, I would say suicide. There's no head trauma, so he wasn't knocked out first, and no signs of any struggle. Now, I still need to look at the organs and do a full workup, so he might have been drugged, but he's a big guy. Six foot four, weighs a hundred eighty-three pounds. That's a lot of weight to get into that position without some sort of pulley."

"There's no evidence of one," I say.

"Of course, someone could have had a gun on him," she says, "to force him to hang himself, but if they did, they didn't tie his feet or his hands once he was in the noose."

"Okay. Anything else turn up?"

"Nothing beneath the fingernails or on the hands except for trace amounts of Zopadril powder."

"I've spoken to Alex about that. He drugged the woman he was sharing the room with."

"Ah, so I shouldn't be surprised if it's not in his system—that's good to know. That was an outside chance I had in mind—his being drugged, then somehow hoisted up." She shrugs. "If nothing else crops up in the rest of the autopsy, I would say it was a straightforward suicide followed by the obvious mutilation of the body." Linda pauses, glances up at me and then back down at the body. "I did check for any sexual activity or signs of rape. There aren't any."

I press my lips together for a moment, then ask, "Is the murder window still accurate?"

"Yes. Some point between eleven p.m. on Sunday night and two the following morning. If those bloody lawyers hadn't kept us out, I could have been more accurate, but that's the best I can do with the information I have."

I nod, and seeing that I haven't got anything to add about the lawyers, she carries on.

"Alex sent over the details about that missing ax and it matches with the cuts left in the body around the joints that were severed. If you look here"—she points to a cut in the left hip—"you can see where the ax bearer missed the mark and swung wide. From the mess he or she made, I'd suggest they weren't used to using one. I think they started with the right leg—there are more cuts and failed attempts on that side. Then the other leg, right arm, left arm then head last. I'm only going by the number of failed cuts, you understand, and blood spatters. With the victim already dead at the time of the cutting up—thank goodness—there aren't any other physiological markers I can go by."

"Anything else you can tell me about the ax wielder?"

"Maybe later. I'm going to map all of the cuts into the VR autopsy suite and run some simulations. I should be able to give you an approximation of their strength and a decent crack at which hand he or she favors."

"So you think a woman could have done that?"

She smirks at me. "I'd be able to. It was a sharp ax. There was obviously some passion behind it. Keep an open mind."

She draws the sheet back over the body and I feel a palpable physical relief.

"Tea before you go?"

I shake my head. "I'd love to but I've got to get an interim report to my boss as soon as I can."

"You can use the room through there to do that." She points to a door beside the fish tank. "It's got a good sofa. I'm making myself a cuppa anyway." She comes round to my side of the slab and gently guides me toward it. "I've got some gingerbread too. I make it myself. I'll get you some."

My lips and fingertips are tingling. It's chilly in here, and as I let her steer me I appreciate just how cold it is for the first time. I start to shiver. "Well, if there's gingerbread," I say as my teeth start to chatter. "I'll stay for one cup."

12

I GET BACK to the hotel with a stack of homemade gingerbread in a plastic tub, the interim report filed and acknowledged by Milsom and a smile on my face. MyPhys has logged mild shock but nothing so prolonged that it would merit any fuss, thanks to Linda's intervention. She even invited me out on the bike later, saying it would be good for me, but I had to decline. I said the case was too high profile and needed a fast turn-around. I didn't tell her that the terms of my contract prevent me from pursuing any extreme sports or traveling in or on vehicles with a safety rating below five out of five. The MoJ wouldn't appreciate its property being broken.

I have steak in my room, listening to some old Chinese electropunk Tia has suggested I might like. I turn it off after the first mouthful of the steak, wanting to devote my full atten-tion to the experience, reveling in my solitude as the flavors play across my tongue. If I tried to buy a steak like this in London it would cost two months' worth of my "salary" and

I'd have to cook it at home, as none of the restaurants that serve this stuff would let the likes of me through the door. When I finish the last of the potatoes and deliciously crisp mange-tout I stare at the plate for a few moments before licking it clean. And that is why eating alone is always best.

I've indulged myself enough. As my body digests, I take my mind back to the MoJ server space and open my personal incident room. I spend half an hour or so mocking up a virtual board like the old-style mersives always have, just so I can stand back from it and look at what I have so far.

In terms of a murder case, I have fuck all. In terms of a suicide there's a lot more evidence, but that niggling sense of missing something critical still haunts me.

"Tia, come talk this through with me."

She walks up to my side from behind me in the same three-piece pinstripe as usual, her flats clicking on the parquet flooring. "So, what do we have?" she asks.

"The victim drugs his girlfriend, either hangs himself or is forced to do so; then his body is cut up. Now, there are gaps in this big enough to drive a truck through. For one thing, the camera footage of the lift and corridor outside have been altered to hide whoever went into his room after he and Selina retired."

"It would also disguise the victim leaving the room and returning before his death, or being returned already dead," Tia notes, programmed to extrapolate logical possibilities from the information available.

"Right. Now, I would guess that whoever chopped him up also tampered with the footage. That same person might also have forced him into that noose, but there's no evidence at all to support that."

"The only DNA within the room is that of the victim, Selina Klein and Theodore Buckingham," Tia reminds me. "As Klein has been eliminated, the only other person the evidence can potentially place at the scene in the murder window is Buckingham."

"But Buckingham has no tech skills at all, so if he is behind all of this, he would have had to get someone to doctor the video, and who the hell would do that? Even if Klein could have helped afterward, she was too doped up to be able to hack the local node while Theo was still in the hotel."

"Travis Gabor could have the technical knowledge to hack the node," Tia says.

"Yeah. Where does he fit in?" I scratch my chin, feeling the stubble just starting to surface. "He was stalking the victim. What if he went to speak to him that night? It's a potential motivation for the victim drugging Selina, if he didn't want her to know or overhear. If Travis entered the room early enough in the window, he's a better suspect than Buckingham. But if Travis forced him to hang himself and then mutilated him, why did Buckingham check out at five in the morning?"

"Travis Gabor is very wealthy," Tia says. "Perhaps he paid Buckingham to remain silent, or to leave."

"Or terrified him into it." I try to reconcile the tanned fashion victim with the idea of a brutal killer. Appearances can be deceiving, especially when it comes to high-functioning obsessives. "Crimes of passion often follow periods of stalking," I say. "But forcing Alejandro to hang himself seems so much colder than the rest of the crime."

"There is insufficient data to form a case against either Theodore Buckingham or Travis Gabor," Tia says.

"Yeah. I need to learn more about Travis's movements that night. Tia, pull the camera footage from the entire hotel from six p.m. the evening of the murder through nine thirty a.m. the following morning. I want you to map out the movements of the victim, Theo Buckingham and Travis and Stefan Gabor, as far as you can. While you're doing that, I'm going to see if I can find out anything more about Theo."

AFTER a brief conversation with Nadia about her staff, I go down to the small conference room she offered for my use and wait for the first person to arrive.

There's a knock on the door, rather timid, less than five minutes later. A tall man enters, dressed in a black suit, with brown skin and very short black Afro hair that is graying at the temples.

"Ms. Patel said you needed to talk to me," he says in a deep baritone voice. "I'm Marcus Magill. I was on the desk overnight when . . . the thing happened."

I gesture toward one of the chairs on the opposite side of the table. "Sit down, Mr. Magill. Could you confirm you've given consent to have this interview recorded for use by the Ministry of Justice?"

"I did, just now, on the way here," he says, jerking forward when he realizes he should sit down. There's a sheen of sweat on his high forehead and he looks like a man about to be condemned.

"There's nothing to worry about," I say. "I just wanted to speak to you about the shift you did from ten p.m. to eight a.m. three nights ago."

"I was on the desk," he says. "Mostly. A few times I went into the back office, but the desk would have pinged me if someone came into the lobby, so I know I didn't miss anyone."

"Have a glass of water," I say, pouring one for him. He takes it with a shaking hand.

"Am I in trouble? Only, I love working here. I've been here for years. Was there something I should have done differently?"

I smile, trying to reassure him, but it isn't enough to penetrate his anxiety. "You're not in any trouble, Mr. Magill. I just wanted to ask about the guest who checked out at about five o'clock that morning."

"It was three minutes past," he says, twisting the glass of water on the table in front of him. "I looked it up on the way. I'm not allowed to record when I'm on duty, but there are cameras in the lobby. I can get the files over to you if—"

"That's all in hand. Why aren't you allowed to record personally?"

"It would be a breach of privacy. It's about keeping the trust of our guests. Ms. Patel is very strict about it. She says the people who come to stay here want to get away from all that. The local node checks uploads, just in case anyone is tempted. There was a girl who started working here last summer—I don't remember her name. Anyway, this actor came to stay and she tried to record him secretly. She said it was only for her own use, but she was still sacked. Ms. Patel really laid into her. Could hear the yelling from the lobby, I could."

He's starting to relax. Good. "Why do you like working here?"

"I won't lie: the pay is good. And Ms. Patel is one for detail and things being done well and I like that. She notices the things I do and she says so, and there's not many who do that these days. Sick pay is generous; holiday too. And we all know each other. We get a meal per shift here too. Good food. Proper stuff, you know. Like my mum used to make."

That surprises me. I wouldn't have thought there'd be enough surplus to sustain that. "Is there much turnover of staff?"

"No. A lot less than most other work at this pay grade, you know. We all know how good we got it here."

"It was Theodore Buckingham who checked out that morning," I say, and he tenses, knowing I'm back onto the important stuff. "What can you remember about him that morning?"

"He was out of breath," Magill says, looking up as he recalled. "I remember thinking that he looked like he'd been running around or something. Bit sweaty too. I remember him wiping his lip"—he swipes the back of his hand across his top lip to demonstrate—"like that a couple of times. He said he wanted to check out. He only had a small bag with him, carry-on size. I asked if he wanted his suitcase brought downstairs from his room and he looked surprised, like he'd forgotten it. He said yes and that he wanted a taxi into town. Ms. Patel told the other police, the ones looking for him, about the taxi company."

I nod. "Yes, the manhunt team has all the details. Did he say anything else?"

Magill thinks hard, staring at the table as he does so. "No. I asked him if he'd had a pleasant stay—I always do—and he just looked at me. It was a bit strange, like he was distracted. I saw on the system that he arrived in a party of three and asked if the other two people he arrived with were planning to leave early too. He just shook his head and said he'd wait outside for the taxi. The room was already paid up to the end of the week, so he didn't have to settle anything. I just asked for the key and told him the remainder of the room fee would be repaid, minus the deposit for each day, but he didn't seem to care. Then he went outside and walked up and down. Bob was on the door that night and we both looked at each other—I remember that, because it was about minus one and freezing out there. It was still really windy too. That storm hadn't gone through. It was still gusting out there."

"How long was he waiting for the taxi?"

"About twenty minutes. He came back in twice, asking if it was coming, and I said, 'Yes, sir,' and gave him ETAs, and then he went back outside. He must have been frozen by the time it came. When it did, he just got in with his hand luggage and the driver nearly left without the suitcase—Bob had it with him in the lobby. It was like he forgot about it again. Truth be told," he says, leaning forward, "I thought he must have had a fight with his boss, or that lady who was with him. He didn't look happy most of the time they were here."

"Anything else you remember about him? That night he checked out, or any other time during his stay?"

He frowns at the glass of water, deep in thought. His eyebrows suddenly jerk up and he looks back up at me. "Yes, actually. He smelled of shower gel, the stuff from the guest bathrooms, and I remember thinking he was mad going outside with his hair still damp in that weather." He frowns again. "I suppose that isn't very interesting. Lots of people shower when they've got a long journey ahead. Sorry."

"You've been very helpful, Mr. Magill. Thank you."

He stands uncertainly. "Is that all you need, then?"

"Yes, thanks."

He is the epitome of relief as he leaves the room.

It certainly sounds as if Theo Buckingham was distressed. Could he have showered to wash off the blood?

"Tia, put me through to Alex."

"Afternoon," he says after accepting voice contact.

"Alex, Theodore Buckingham's room, the one next to the Diamond Suite. Have you checked it out yet?"

"No. I wanted to get this suite done first. Has something come up?"

"You didn't mention any footprints, even though there was all that blood."

"We think there was one that the ax wielder must have

noticed and scrubbed at with a cloth or piece of clothing. Then he or she probably took off their shoes."

I get up out of the chair. "The desk clerk noticed Buckingham's hair was wet when he checked out. I thought maybe he showered off the blood after—"

"I'll get a team in there right away."

There's a knock on the door as I end the call and the cleaner enters, a short, rather pale man with a slight build in his late forties. He has a shock of black hair and dramatic eyebrows that haven't seen any grooming in those forty-odd years. I scan his profile, see nothing unusual and gesture for him to sit down as I do so. "Thank you for coming to see me, Mr. Tregowne."

"Ms. Patel said I had to," he says with a broad west-country accent. "I'm supposed to be at home."

"I won't keep you for very long. Could you confirm you've given consent to have this interview recorded for use by the Ministry of Justice?"

"I have, with pleasure. I wanna do my bit."

"I wanted to ask you about the man who was staying in room two, next to the Diamond Suite."

"Not about the murder?" His bushy eyebrows dip as he frowns at me.

"I've read the statement you gave to the local police on the day. I may need to ask you more questions about that, but now I want to focus on the man in room two."

"I cleaned that one before I went into the Diamond Suite," he says, and inwardly I groan. Judging from the rest of the hotel, Alex's team will be lucky to turn anything up. "That bugger stole the towels. All of 'em. I had to put it in the log. And to think, these people have everything but still steal. Terrible, ennet?"

"Did he leave anything in the room?"

Tregowne tugs at an earlobe as he considers this. "His bed was a mess—didn't even straighten that, but they don't often. There weren't nothing in the bin."

He looks at me as if that's significant. "Is that unusual?" I ask.

"Well it is, matter of fact," Tregowne says, straightening himself in the chair as if he's about to deliver a proclamation of great import. "See, I empty the bins by takin' the plastic liner out, then I sprays it and run round with a cloth, then I put a new liner in. Weren't no liner that day. Put it in the log, I did. I put everythin' in that. Ms. Patel likes the details, she does. I reckon he pulled it all out, though why he'd want to travel with a bag of old tea bags and cotton wool, I dunno."

"Those were missing from his room too?"

"Oh yessir. All the tissues. All the cotton wool. I assume he used some of it. Bloody cheek. Only thing he left were the shampoo and shower gel, but there was hardly any left anyway, so I had to replace them. Put that in the log too, I did."

Everything is pointing toward Theo again. "Did you ever meet him?"

"Room two, you say?" Tregowne leans back, tugging his earlobe again. "I did, now you say it. Was the first mornin' they was here. He wanted to know where the room's uniport charger was, you know, for portable units for thems that aren't chipped—that sort o' thing. It's tucked away in one of the desk drawers. I showed him and he said thanks. He seemed nice enough."

"This was over a week ago," I say. "What made it stick in your mind?"

"Oh, it didn't. I just looked over my log before I come in 'ere. I put it in the log, I did. All the guest questions and comments go in there. Ms. Patel says it shows where the hotel needs to be better-like. She's a sharp 'un."

"Did you ever see anything being charged?"

He shakes his head.

"Anything else in the log for room two while Theo Buckingham was there?"

"He liked his tea and coffee. I thought the Yanks only drank coffee but he took a liking to the tea too. Didn't touch the drinks in the fridge. Liked the cheese snacks more than the rest. That's about all I can tells you 'bout him. Was he the murderer, then? Only I was wondering that myself. Don't like the thought of no one running about at large who does that sort o' thing to people. B'ain't no natural thing."

"We're on the case, Mr. Tregowne. Thank you for your help."

He stands. "Was a terrible shock, seein' that. I won't be cleaning on that floor again. Ms. Patel said I don't have to. I reckon it'll be haunted now."

I fail to think of a response, and realizing that I'm not going to comment, Tregowne goes to the door, gives a polite nod and leaves. I look out the window, seeing the sun break through the cloud for the first time in days. "Let's go for a walk," I say to Tia. "I want to look at where the groundskeeper left the ax before it went missing," I add. I wouldn't want anyone to think I was taking some time out for myself, after all.

13

THE GROUNDS OF the hotel are divided between neatly manicured formal gardens close to the building and a few acres of
meadows and woodland. I stand at the back door as I button
up my coat, acclimatizing to the crisp air and taking in the
various paths I can choose to walk. Tia lays out a route to the
gardener's shed with a pale blue line overlaid across my vision,
and a second in purple directing me to the log the ax had been
left in before it was stolen. I follow the purple one first and it
takes me through a geometrically patterned formal garden
made of clipped box hedges that come up to my knees, gravel
paths and flower beds lying fallow for the winter. In just over
two minutes at a very leisurely pace I reach the fallen tree on
the other side of a bigger path that leads residents round the
edge of the woods toward the nearest meadow. Most of the
branches have been lopped off. Tia highlights the indentation
left by the ax, taken from the constable's report.

I turn and look back toward the hotel. Theo's room overlooks this side and he could have seen the groundskeeper working on the tree from his window. It's also in full view of any of the second- and third-floor rooms on this side though, and the restaurant. Any of the guests could have seen that ax left here.

"Looks like the sun is going to come out after all." An unfamiliar male American drawl comes from behind me.

I turn and see a tall, broad-shouldered man with sandy blond hair and the kind of large, square jaw I'd expect from across the pond. Tia takes a beat longer than usual to pull up a profile that is irritatingly sparse. Mark Collindale, USA. His privacy settings must be dialed up very high to evade an MoJ check. A line is added, pulled from the local node, detailing that he checked into the hotel at six a.m. today. Either way, his chip will have given him the standard MoJ conversation-recording warning.

"Maybe. Can I help you?"

"I'm the liaison from the US gov-corp. I'm here to help in whatever way I can."

I don't believe that for an instant. He's nothing more than a sanctioned spy, here to check up on the investigation in the absence of the lawyers. "Some confirmation of that would be useful." I wait while he looks away and a confirmation-of-identity ping comes through to Tia, who verifies it with the MoJ. "I submitted my interim report earlier," I reply. "I take it you've read it?" When he nods, I add, "So you know I have all the support I need from the local authorities."

"Walk with me?" He gestures down the path, toward the meadow. The last thing I want to do is talk to this guy, but I daren't risk a complaint to Milsom that I've been uncooperative.

"I don't have long," I say, trying to manage expectations as politely as possible. "You understand that there's a lot to follow up on."

He starts off away from the house. I feel short walking next to him, and I'm just under six feet tall. He isn't dressed like a thug, even though he has the body of one. His coat is black cashmere, very expensive, the scarf a muted tartan and his trousers a dark charcoal gray. His black brogues aren't suitable for anything other than gravel and concrete paths, so I doubt we'll walk anywhere other than the formal garden.

"Your interim report just presented the facts," he says, looking ahead.

"It's too early for speculation," I reply.

"But I'd value your opinion. You're very experienced and knew the victim. You have more insights than you put in the report, I'm certain."

This is not a conversation I want to have, let alone be recorded and later pulled apart by lawyers if something goes wrong. I'm used to answering questions without giving too much away—I learned that pretty damn fast once I left the Circle—but he wouldn't be here unless he wanted something specific. I don't have time for these games anyway. "Is there something you're worried about?"

"'Worried' is a strong word."

I sigh and leave the silence to tease something out for me, as Dee taught me so long ago.

"Any lesser investigation would be drawing conclusions already," Collindale says, clasping his hands behind his back as he strolls. "I'm glad you haven't been speculating about suicide. I imagine that's because you knew the victim and his beliefs."

"Why are you glad about that?" I keep my eyes ahead too, as much as I want to watch for his reaction. My instinct is to be careful about eye contact here, but I can't quite decide why.

"Because it makes it far less likely that you'll look for

evidence that supports that theory and thereby overlook the rest."

"I run a thorough investigation with every case," I say, trying to keep pride from tightening my voice. "Regardless of the victims and their beliefs."

I see him nod from the corner of my eye. "Then you won't shy away from looking into Gabor further."

"No."

"Have you interviewed him yet?"

I bite back a comment about my schedule and priorities being none of his business. "Not yet, no."

"Then you won't know that a friend of his husband came to meet the victim in the first week of his stay, and then a second time the day before his death. Someone from a Spanish subsidiary of the European gov-corp."

I stop and look at him, feeling the sucking pull of muddy inter-gov-corp politics. "I'm sure the victim met with lots of people. That's why he came over to England. It certainly wasn't for the weather."

Collindale smiles, his teeth predictably white and perfect. "I just thought you should know about it, and the fact that Theo Buckingham was spotted meeting with that individual in private too."

He's trying to sway me into focusing my investigation down this route. Irritated by this bullshit, I think back to how the conversation started and decide to risk being direct. "Why are you really worried about the possibility of suicide?"

He frowns and turns up his collar. "Looks like the sun isn't coming out after all," he says, glancing up at the clouds thickening once more. "I look forward to your next report, SDCI Moreno."

I stay where I am and watch him go back toward the hotel.

It's no surprise that the gov-corps are starting to look for ways to smear each other, and the US must have hated Europe getting involved right from the start. I'm angered by the fact they're willing to stoop so low so quickly. Once he's inside I turn my back on the building so no one can read my lips.

"Tia, note in the case file that the US is worried about the suicide angle."

"Done. Would you like me to add a transcription of the conversation with Mark Collindale?"

"Yeah, but tag it as something to be excluded from the next interim report."

"Done."

I pause before going back into the hotel, thinking about the likely suicide. It would be very much against Alejandro's beliefs and would go against everything he's said about it in the past, very publicly. But people change. There are so many things that have cropped up, so many tiny details that have jarred with the memories and internal construct I have of the man, it's possible this aspect of him had changed too. If it was suicide, what could possibly have happened to outweigh the principles he so firmly held? And why would it bother the US gov-corp enough to have their liaison bring it up with me?

"Tia, don't request this information from the US gov-corp contact, but how much money does the Circle bring into the States every year?"

"Would you like me to pull the data from an Internet search?"

"Yeah, that's fine." As long as Collindale doesn't know I'm looking into this straight after our conversation, it is.

"Drawing upon thirty-five sources with a credibility score between ninety-nine-point-five and ninety-nine-point-eight, it is speculated that the Circle brings approximately five hundred million dollars into the country per year."

"JeeMuh!" I thought it would be in the thousands. "Where the fuck does all that come from?"

"Thirty-five percent is estimated to be donations from supporters around the world. The remainder is a combination of assets transferred from private estates relinquished to the Circle upon full membership and earnings from patents shared with the US parent gov-corp."

I think of my dad and the pathetic sum of money he brought with us, having failed to hold down a job for years after his breakdown. Even that tiny amount was something I so desperately needed and yet was denied to me when I left. I don't realize I've balled my fists until the knuckles start to throb. I take a minute to get a handle on the anger before moving on. The case comes first.

"Does the Circle pay taxes?"

"Yes, at the reduced rate for religious organizations: five percent on total yearly income."

"You mentioned patents. What kind?"

"Would you like me to compile a list of those detailed in the public domain?"

"Yeah." I walk a little farther down the path and find another log, this one with a shallow depression carved out and smoothed to form a rudimentary seat positioned to take in a view through the gate to the meadow. I perch on it as the data comes in, ordered hierarchically in broad divisions, with the option to drill down. The top-level categories are predominantly engineering disciplines along with energy harvesting and storage.

"And these are patents filed by members of the Circle?"

"Yes. Some transferred along with financial assets upon acceptance into the Circle; some filed during membership."

"That doesn't make any sense. They join the Circle to get away from tech, not carry on their research."

"Would you like me to verify the data with the US gov-corp patent office?"

"No," I say instinctively. My gut is telling me to go carefully here; it's clear money has something to do with the US gov-corp's concerns. Are they worried that if Alejandro committed suicide the Circle would disband and they'd lose that income? No . . . Five hundred million is a lot of money but only a tiny fraction of the numbers they deal in every day. Something to do with these patents, then?

"Urgent call incoming from DS Talbot, head of the manhunt team," Tia says, and I accept voice contact.

"SDCI Moreno. What is it?"

"Sir, we've found Theodore Buckingham. He's dead."

14

BY THE TIME Constable Riley has driven me through Ashburton, I've been fully briefed by DS Talbot. She tells me how they traced Theo's movements from the taxi driver's dropping him off in the town center early in the morning two days ago, having picked him up on the public cams fairly quickly. After stashing the larger of his two cases—now in the possession of the manhunt team—behind a set of bins in an alleyway, he wandered up and down the high street as if looking for something. At seven a.m. an old-fashioned corner shop opened, once the province of paper newsprint and magazines. Now it's a hub for package deliveries ordered via the Internet and a local-information board for those incapable of accessing the Internet. When I comment that I thought everyone was online now, whether chipped or using portable devices, Talbot tells me that it was written into the town bylaws to provide public copies of critical announcements in the shop after the local rag shut down and the unchipped protested, some violently.

In a snippet of film retrieved from the shop's cam, Theo, with his hand luggage trundling behind him, looks at all the small ads clustered around the local gov-corp branch's announcements displayed on a screen that takes up most of the wall. The ads are nothing but text boxes in a variety of mostly ill-chosen fonts. Something clearly catches his eye as he stops in front of one. His lips move, as if he is repeating what he is reading to commit it to memory. Then he leaves a disappointed shop owner, who probably hoped Theo would be tempted by one of the many snacks and drinks available at the bank of food-printing machines that fill the rest of the shop. I'm briefly distracted by the fact there is even a shopkeeper there. So many of the shops in London haven't had human staff for years.

The manhunt team tracked him leaving the town after consulting a local map pulled from his hand luggage that he forgot or simply abandoned in the alley. After an analysis of the ads displayed in the area he was looking at in the shop, it was simply a matter of following up.

My car pulls up outside the cottage in which Theo's body has been found, one of several advertised on that board as short-term lets for people who still want to visit the area in the off-season.

"Shall I wait here for you, sir?" Riley asks. I'm tempted to bring him in with me, show him how things are done, but I need all of my attention on the case.

"Yes, please," I say, and leave him and his disappointment inside the car.

The wind whistles and tugs at the door when I get out. Aside from the road there's nothing but the moor in all directions, bleak and miserable. I have a sudden desire to be back in London, walking through dense streets held snug by skyscrapers and filled with people. Not even Tia can find something interesting to tag as I scan the gorse bushes and stubby grass.

DS Talbot is waiting outside the cottage, wearing a thick, padded jacket over her suit. The profile flashing up next to her as I approach her tells me she's thirty-two, has risen through the ranks with a number of commendations and is a member of a local amateur dramatics society. I don't select the option to find out more about her previous stage appearances.

She has a narrow face with rather sharp features and dark brown eyes. Her hair is mostly tied back, apart from a few mousy brown strands teased loose by the bitterly cold breeze. She weighs me up with tired eyes and folded arms. "Any questions before we go in, sir?"

"You seemed to cover everything about him getting here on the way over. Anything else I should know?"

"Not about the manhunt, sir—it was straightforward once we got the shop's footage. It involved some legwork, as there are a few places on his route that aren't covered by cams, but we got there without having to ask for satellite data, thank God." When I frown at the comment, she adds, "Can't stand the paperwork when we have to pull data from another agency. MoJ backing or not, someone has to make sure it's all done properly."

I have a sudden appreciation for how advanced Tia is. "So, he walked a few miles to get here, found that the cottage was still empty and broke in?"

"Yes, sir. Round the back. No other buildings overlook it, and it's remote enough that few people travel the road onto the moor here. He picked the perfect spot, really. He must have been serious."

"Serious about what?"

"Committing suicide."

"He went to a lot of trouble doing something he could have done at the hotel," I say as she leads me round the back to show me the evidence of the break-in. "Taking a taxi, finding some-where on a notice board, walking—what?—five and a half miles in freezing weather?"

She shrugs. "Perhaps he didn't intend to do it when he left the hotel but then had a change of heart. It's a lonely place up here. Left alone with his demons . . . I suppose they won."

The back door is open, the wood splintered around the lock. An officer posted outside of it with a nose reddened by the cold hands us both paper-suit packets and shoe covers. We both shrug off our coats reluctantly and prepare ourselves for entry.

As I put on my suit, Tia pings for a house AI but there isn't one, just a basic local node to access the Internet and manage the household devices. As standard procedure, Tia starts down-loading all the data from the node over the past three days.

"Any house cams?"

"One, by the front door. Nothing useful on it. It's probably why he went round the back."

"Have you found the local node's hard drive?"

She nods.

"Take it in as evidence."

"Sir?"

"It could have been tampered with. The cams in the hotel were."

She reddens. "I've been focused on the manhunt—sorry. I should have—"

I wave a hand and mutter that it's perfectly understandable, disliking the way my status makes people so afraid of slipping up. "Have the recorders been in?"

"Yes, sir. The SOCO team is in there now."

We step inside, avoiding the protective plastic that has been laid over footprints already tagged by the chief SOCO. She leads me through a small kitchen replete with an old-fashioned butler sink and state-of-the-art food printer. One of the forensic team dusting it for prints glances at me and then goes back to his task.

I pause to focus on the printer, making the duster shift uncomfortably, thinking I'm taking too much interest in what he's doing. Instead I'm signaling to Tia that I want the printer data, and in seconds I see a confirmation that the file is available for me to read at will.

"Sir?"

Talbot is waiting by a door at the other end of the kitchen. I move over toward her and she takes me into a dark hallway with a dingy carpet covered by the same plastic, though there are no footprints or anything else tagged here yet. The wallpaper is a tired beige with thin cream stripes. A staircase climbs at my left, so narrow that a rope hung from loops forms the handrail instead of wood. It's cold and smells damp.

"This is a holiday cottage?"

"At the low end of the market, sir. Not really a surprise it's empty at this time of year; I doubt many people come back twice. There's rustic charm and then there's . . . this."

"Where is the body?"

"Through here, sir."

She goes to a door at the far end of the hallway that is ajar and pushes it farther open. I can hear a bustle of activity within, including Dr. Palmeston's voice as she asks someone to find her a cup of tea before she has to kill someone for it.

She's the first to look up when I follow Talbot in and she grins. "Sharpen up, you lot. The big cheese from London is here now." She winks at me. "And he'll need a cuppa too—it's bloody freezing in here."

Two SOCOs look at each other until one of them, a young man, tuts and leaves the room.

"Come over and see for yourself," Linda says. "Afternoon, Talbot. How are the rehearsals going?"

"Good, good," Talbot says, staying back.

There's not a lot of room in the small lounge. It's cluttered with a large sofa and two armchairs, as well as a modified log burner and two display cabinets filled with china and miscellaneous crap. As I move round the sofa to join Linda, Theo's body comes into view, curled on his side, wrapped in a duvet with a cushion under his head. He looks asleep. A whisky bottle is lying on its side on the floor next to the sofa. A dark brown stain on a grubby beige rug begins at its neck.

"About two days," Linda says, predicting my first question. "Sometime in the first night he was here; certainly no more than three meals were printed. I reckon he got the whisky from duty free, as I haven't seen that single malt for sale around here."

"The people in the Circle are teetotal," I say, crouching to look at him more closely.

"Oh. Maybe it was a present for someone. I won't be able to confirm it until I get him to the lab, but it looks like he used it to swallow a whole packet of paracetamol and another of ibuprofen." She holds up an evidence bag with empty blister packs inside. "These were next to the bottle. And this."

She hands over a second bag to me, containing a note.

I killed him and I can't live with myself. I'm sorry.

The scrawl is written in pale blue ink on a page ripped from a notebook. "Where's the pen?"

"Haven't found it yet. Looks like a fountain pen to me. We

haven't gone through the bag yet; we've only been here half an hour."

She moves aside to point at the armchair behind her and Theo's hand luggage resting on it, still zipped up. On the other side of the room DS Talbot kneels down. "There's something under the sofa, sir. It could be a pen."

"Can you fish it out?" I ask the remaining SOCO, who is already opening an evidence bag, ready for the task. In less than a minute I'm looking at a fountain pen through the plastic, and Tia confirms it is the same make as the one missing from the Diamond Suite. I frown at it. Why take a pen from the hotel room of your victim? Did Theo plan his own suicide so far ahead? "Can you open the case next, please?" I say to the same officer, and he nods.

"Of course I'll go over him properly once he's at my lab, and once I've finished the autopsy on the victim we discussed earlier, but it looks pretty straightforward to me. Nothing to suggest anything other than suicide, anyway. Are you happy for me to move the duvet and do a quick check-over?"

I nod and move out of her way, giving the evidence bag and the pen it contains to Talbot. The SOCO unzips the case slowly and carefully, as if expecting a snake to burst out of it, and then lifts the top flap.

"Shit," Talbot whispers at the sight of the bloodied towels crammed into the case, the same fluffy cotton as the ones from my hotel bathroom.

"Bag them now," I say to the SOCO once he moves again, having remained still enough for his retinal cam to record the contents. "I want to see what else is in there."

He pulls the top towel out and drops it into one of the larger evidence bags. The second towel is pulled out and dropped in too, revealing a hand ax still covered in spots of blood and a section of severed curtain cord with a knot still tied in it.

Linda has been watching too, distracted from Theo after hearing Talbot's surprise. "There's your weapon," she says confidently. "That blade is the right length anyway. And the cord he was hanged with too. Jackpot. I'd like to take both back to the lab with me, please."

"The ax matches the one missing from the hotel," I say after Tia's confirmation. "Talbot, what did your team find in the suitcase he left behind the bins?"

"Clothes, a few souvenirs from Bath and a couple of paper books about the city—the kind they sell in the tourist shops there, sir."

"You're certain?"

"I opened it myself, sir," she says, still staring at the ax.

"Bag both of them," I tell the SOCO, and he lifts the ax out from the very end of the handle in the hope of not smudging any prints. Once the cord is bagged too I say, "Look inside the wash bag."

The SOCO does so. "Toothbrush and paste, shaving gear and a bottle of something." He pulls it out. "Tylenol."

"That's a painkiller in the US," Linda says, but I already know. "The ibuprofen and paracetamol are Noropean brands," she says, holding up the blister packs in the evidence bag.

"It doesn't make sense," I say. "Why buy paracetamol when he already had Tylenol in his bag? They're the same thing. He might not have known that, I suppose."

"He didn't buy them after he left the hotel," Talbot says. "Perhaps he bought them in Bath, when he got the books. I'll look that up."

I nod and turn back to the SOCO. "Anything else in there?"

"A small plastic bag," he says, lifting it out carefully. "Contains a used disposable razor blade, used tissues, several pieces of cotton wool with blood on them, couple of cotton balls—"

"That's from the hotel bathroom bin," I say. "Bag it. Anything else?"

He drops it into another evidence bag. "A few pieces of unused cotton wool and some tissues. Nothing else, sir." I watch him run his hand around the loose pocket in the inside of the lid and shake his head.

"Were you expecting a gun?" Linda asks.

"I wouldn't have been surprised, but no, I was hoping for something else."

"He didn't buy the painkillers," Talbot says, bringing her attention back into the room. "He visited Bath with Selina Klein, but she didn't buy any there either."

"Could they have been found in the cottage?" the SOCO asks, and Talbot shakes her head.

"It's illegal to store any drugs, legal or not, on premises rented out to the public. Not even a tube of antihistamine cream or antiseptic."

"He must have taken the ax from the hotel room. Perhaps he stole the pills from the victim," Linda offers without convincing me, and, by the look of her face, even herself. "We'll lift whatever prints we can from them. The boxes haven't turned up yet. There may be something of use there."

Talbot nods. "We might be able to trace the transaction through the bar code, but it'll take some time. Thousands of boxes of those pills must be sold every day."

I agree with her; there are lots of people who still don't trust their printers when it comes to drugs, so the mass-manufactured tablets are still widely available. "Anything on his person?" I ask, looking over at Theo's body, the blanket now moved to the end of the sofa, revealing a plain green jumper and jeans with mud spatters around the hem.

Linda checks him over and shakes her head. "Only an old-fashioned wristwatch. Nothing in his pockets."

"Coat?" I ask the SOCO, and he goes off to find it as his colleague returns with two steaming mugs of tea.

"You are a brilliant officer with a fine career ahead of you," Linda says to him as he hands a cup to her. He smirks as he hands the other to me.

"If only it were as easy to impress Alex Jacobs," he says, and Linda frowns at him.

"Do not take your superior officer's name in vain," she says, all mock sternness, and then slurps loudly from the mug.

"I found his coat," says the other officer from the door. "His passport was in one of the pockets, nothing else. I've bagged it and the coat."

I sip the tea, discover it's a chemical copy from the printer rather than the real thing and set the cup down. I look at Theo, the ax in its evidence bag and the whisky bottle on its side. Everything lying in front of me says "suicide." Too loudly, perhaps.

"Are you happy for me to take the body from the scene?" Linda asks. "Would be good to get the poor bugger somewhere useful."

"Yeah," I say, and she leaves the room, slurping the tea as she goes.

"You're not happy with it, are you, sir?" DS Talbot says. "The painkillers are bugging you."

I nod, but they're not the only thing that isn't ringing true here. "I need to know where they came from. I have other leads to chase. Can I leave it with you?"

She straightens, as if deriving some pride from the fact I need her. Perhaps she thought that finding Theo Buckingham meant the end of her involvement in the case. "Of course, sir. Would you like direct updates or should I just put them in the case file?"

"The file is fine, unless it's something critical. Make sure forensics goes over the local node's hard drive too, as well as sending the data to the MoJ. Oh, have the cottage owners been notified?"

"Yes, sir. They live down in Cornwall. Not best pleased, but they know there's nothing they can do. There's an estate agent in the town who manages the property and I got full sign-off from them regarding removal of any property relevant to the case."

"Excellent," I say. "I'll leave you in charge of the scene. I'm going to have a look around the rest of the cottage before I go."

"The SOCO did a quick check, sir, and he doesn't think Buckingham went up there. No dirt from his shoes are on the stairs, anyway."

I glance back at Theo, noting his shoes are still on his feet. It looks odd, with him curled up as if taking a nap. I try to imagine him hacking Alejandro's body to pieces with that ax and simply can't. I left the Circle before he joined so I have no idea what he was like, even how he spoke, but what could move a man to that violence after being so close to someone for so long?

I know the answer to that. Jealousy. Desperation. Hatred. So close to love, so easily reached from a place of devotion. What could have tipped him over the edge into those dark waters?

Linda comes back in with a body bag and an assistant. I leave them to it and climb the stairs.

The air is stale and smells of mold. There are only two bedrooms and a bathroom, all of which haven't been redecorated in the past twenty years. There's certainly no sign he came up here but I look through the drawers and wardrobes anyway, under the beds and in the bins. Nothing.

I go back down the stairs and wait as the body bag is carried out. Linda says good-bye, and I return to the living room to find DS Talbot standing where she was before, this time absorbed in an invisible task with her APA.

"There's something I want you to check before I go," I say, and she blinks at me. "Did he dispose of anything in the town as he left?"

She shakes her head slowly. "No, sir, I'd remember that. And once we found him here I got one of my constables to retrace the route he would have taken, just to look out for anything unusual. Of course, that was a couple of days ago. Do I need to sweep for something in particular?"

I shake my head. "No. I don't know what it is yet. Thanks for your help. Keep up the good work."

She smiles, softening the sharpness of her features.

I leave the cottage, feeling more dissatisfied than I should, having found the prime suspect and the primary weapon. I have to report it to Milsom, but I know what she'll say and I don't want this case to close yet. Something was missing back there and I can't shake the feeling it's critical. Why would a man ask where a uniport charger is unless he had something to charge? And that being the case, what would a man who comes from a place where technology is shunned want to charge in the first place?

15

MY BODY IS back at the hotel, my mind in the MoJ server space, this time in Milsom's virtual office. I don't want to be in either place. Milsom's arms are folded and she's giving me that look, the one that makes sweat gather on the small of my back. The look that says, "Give me one good reason not to put a black mark in your file." One good reason stands between me and another year added to my contract.

I need to change tack. "I'm not saying anything except that Theo's suicide doesn't ring true for me. Whether the case stays open or not . . ." I hate the words falling from my mouth. Every goddamn particle of me wants the case to stay open. It is far from resolved. ". . . is entirely up to you, boss. All I'm doing here is voicing my concerns. I'm not going to be another splinter in your arse about this."

She leans back in her chair, an old-fashioned leather one with brass studs running round the edges where the leather meets the wood. A perfect reproduction of the real chair in her real office in London. One she shares with ten other people at her pay grade, reserved solely for the rare occasions when they want to chew someone's ear off in person.

The rest of the room isn't an exact replica though. Here, in her own virtual space, she can have things on the walls, personal effects on the large wooden desk. Not that she does, of course. That would be unprofessional. I don't even know if she has a partner, where she lives, what she does in her spare time. She has ruled my life for almost twenty years and I know as much about her personal life as I did the day I met her.

There is only one picture on the wall behind her chair. A block of red three meters high and two across, with a band of dark brown at the bottom and a tiny black square on the far left-hand side, sitting on top of the brown. Its lack of detail infuriates me. Fuck modern art. Fuck this office. I want to bang my fist on the desk like in some cheesy mersive, yell that the case needs to stay open if she's interested in knowing the truth. I want to shout that I need to be left to do my job, dammit, and that all the pen pushers and bean counters—and whatever else those lone DCIs say in these situations—need to butt out and let me get the job done. But I stand here, feet exactly half a meter apart, hands clasped behind my back, standing straight, waiting for her decision in silence.

"Finding the prime suspect dead is a critical milestone," she says, her voice less confrontational. I don't allow myself to relax. "There's no way we can stop the meeting and we can't keep the details out of the file, obviously." She steeples her fingers. "Off the record, I acknowledge your concerns. But it doesn't change the fact that we're under immense pressure to close this case as soon as possible. It's just a matter of time before the press blow it open, and while we can gag the Noropean press, we can't do the same for Europe and the States."

"But couldn't their lawyers—"

"No. They've made it clear they're not prepared to do that. It costs too much money, for one thing."

This stinks. The press is just a collection of subsidiary companies owned by other subsidiary companies, all answering to their respective CEOs at the top of the respective gov-corp branches. If all three groups can collaborate enough to cause all the hell they have already, a mutual agreement to gag the press should be a piece of piss. Yes, it costs money, but money that's just being moved around from one part of the beast to the other. At the end of the day, gov-corps always balance their books.

"They'll want a verbal summary from you, being the lead investigator," she continues. "Stick to the facts but downplay the parts that concern you."

I press my lips together, look down at the edge of the desk and the oak-leaf detail carved into the edging. The original is old enough to be real wood that was actually carved by a human hand. Someone who would have taken pride in his work.

"I'll handle any difficult questions," she says, and stands up. "I know you're not happy, Carlos, but for what it's worth, you've done a great job on this case."

Have I? I've only just started and she's talking as if it's the end. There are more questions than answers, and the thought of leaving these loose ends to be buried in a digital footnote at the end of Alejandro's life makes my stomach churn.

I realize she's looking at me expectantly. "Thanks, boss," I say, and she gives a slight smile of satisfaction. Yes, your dog is lying down and rolling over.

"It can't have been easy. I'll send a note to your psych supervisor to recommend a session or two to make sure nothing lingers from this."

A memory of Dee returning to the communal break room

after a session with her psych supervisor flashes through my mind. We were in the final stage of highly specialized hot-housing, one that few people reached. Our future owners had put down a deposit on us and detailed how our skills were to be tailored to their requirements. They weren't just buying people with the exact skill sets required; they were buying people who could never resign early, who would never qualify for a pay raise and never use their training to jump ship to another gov-corp for a higher pay grade and better conditions. With extraordinarily limited rights of our own, we could be worked harder, for longer hours, in whatever conditions they chose.

Dee—who read up on these things in far more detail than I ever did—explained to me that my future employer was the best I could ever hope for. As an SDCI, I would be exposed to sensitive information, so my contract would be nontransferable. All I needed to do was keep the Noropean MoJ happy and I would serve out my contract for the next fifty years and then be free.

It was an intensely stressful time. I was reciting Noropean law in my sleep, going through conditioning to ensure good behavior around superiors and being trained in data-mining techniques. Dee, with her sharp eye for human behavior and social structures, had been bought by a media company that combined entertainment with "social education and behavior refinement." As she put it, "They make people laugh while programming them to be good citizens." She'd laughed at the horror on my face, that moment I realized that all the shit Alejandro had been preaching at me was true. I asked her how the psych session was.

"I just pretend I'm in a shitty RPG," she said, stabbing the buttons on one of the food printers. "If you choose the right responses, they leave you alone." She turned to me then, shot that smile that always made me feel better, like I wasn't the only real person in the world. "I'll help you if you like. Then they won't put you in the machine again, and you'll qualify sooner too."

"How do you know all this?" I asked, and she shrugged.

"Obvious, innit? We're resources now. Resources that got mined and sold and are being made into something else. Just like a game. I don't wanna grind at this level for any longer than I got to. Fuck that shit. If we gonna have to do what we're told for the next fifty years, I want more interesting orders. Know what I'm sayin'?"

I didn't, back then. I was still reeling, still fumbling my way back into the world after the hell of getting out of America, of escaping from one exploitative asshole only to find myself in the clutches of another. If it wasn't for Dee putting her faith in me and keeping me sane, I would have been stuck in hot-housing for another year, maybe more.

I don't even know if I could have survived that last phase.

It wasn't the performance- and memory-enhancing drugs; the hot-housers managed the side effects well enough. It wasn't even the occasional beating from another inmate, which happened when they flipped out and I was the nearest viable target. It was the constant cognitive dissonance of being so desperate to get out yet too scared to leave. Of being so afraid to fail yet wishing I did so it would all stop. Of being told I was lucky when I was being abused. Of hearing I was a valuable asset when I was being treated like a fucking object. I had no idea what my future was going to be like; I'd forgotten what life outside hot-housing was really like. What if I didn't meet the expectations of the Noropean MoJ? How would the money they'd spent on buying me be reclaimed?

"The thing to remember, above all else," Dee said as she

plucked some artificial shit out of the delivery hatch in a little paper tray, "is that no one gives a fuck about you. There are a million of you, of me, all ready to take our place if we bomb out. And it could be a lot worse."

"Am I supposed to feel lucky? I never wanted this," I said, and she smirked.

"Neither did I. But I want the alternative less. This is the best we got right now. If we play this game right, in fifty years we'll have real choices. And if we play this game well, those fifty years won't be so bad, neither."

"They'll still own us," I said, gripping the edge of the table I sat on.

"Dump that anger, sunshine. Someone always owns you," she said. "No matter who you are. Deal with it."

I miss her. I was too harsh. She has the same pressures as everyone else. That one slip with the journo shouldn't cancel out everything she did for me. I'm a fuck sometimes. I need to call her after I've dealt with this.

Now, looking at my boss, I take a breath to say a session with the pysch supervisor won't be necessary, but Milsom wouldn't have said that unless she'd already made the decision. She must have seen the entries in my MyPhys file detailing the vomiting incident, the mild shock and the stress at various points.

I consider the sparse branches of the decision tree ahead of me and put on my best grateful smile. "Thanks, boss. I'm sure that will be helpful."

"WELL, this is a relief to everyone involved," says an American man whose pay grade is so far above mine and privacy dialed so high that Tia has nothing to display about him. "A crime of passion—very tragic. Obviously Theodore Buckingham had issues with the relationship between Casales and Klein. We'll arrange for both of the bodies to be transported back to the Circle." He gives a nod to the lawyer representing them, her face pinched with worries that she doesn't express. "And, of course, we'll compensate Norope for the use of—"

"I'm sorry to interrupt"—the man's opposite in Europe, a petite blond-haired woman with a French accent, holds up her hand—"but you're talking as if this is over."

The sight of the American's teeth, just as even and white as those of Collindale, who sits beside him, doesn't make his smile any more convincing. "It is. Buckingham admitted to the crime. His suicide is tragic, but it's the end of the road. Sometimes these things are just as straightforward as they appear to be. Crimes of passion are often committed by someone known to the victim and—"

"Don't insult my intelligence," the French woman says. "Have you read Buckingham's background? He came from an extremist sect that has codified misogyny to the extent that an unmarried woman having a sexual relationship is practically a manifestation of Satan on Earth. Do you really think that a man who grew up in that environment would take out his jealous rage on the *male* participant in the extramarital relations? The man he all but worshipped? No, he would have killed Klein."

She focuses her pale blue eyes on me. I've barely spoken since I gave my brief, horribly edited summary of the case to date. "Don't you agree?"

I feel Milsom's glare like a sunlamp, making my cheeks burn. "In my experience, women do bear the brunt of the anger in crimes involving sexual jealousy, but we can't be sure that was Buckingham's motivation. It could have been a matter of attention without a sexual element."

"Did you hear that?" the French woman says with arched eyebrows. "He said, 'We can't be sure,' and that is my concern exactly. We do not know enough about Theo Buckingham to understand the motive here."

"Listen," the American says. "I don't need to know what he felt when he hacked that poor bastard to pieces. I'm not interested in what he was thinking when he fled the hotel and went and killed himself. The facts are all that matters here, and the facts—"

"Are woefully incomplete," the woman, whom I'm starting to see as my savior here, interrupts. "Perhaps you haven't had the opportunity to read the entire case file"—she flicks a disparaging look at the American, whose jaw clenches—"but anyone who has can see several avenues of inquiry that our investigator hasn't had the opportunity to pursue yet."

"*Our* investigator," the man from Norope says with unsubtle emphasis, "was tasked with finding the murderer of Alejandro Casales, which he has done, in less than twenty-four hours."

The French woman redirects her attention to the Circle's representative. "Are you satisfied with what you have to take back to your client? Would you be able to answer all of their questions honestly? If Buckingham's family disputes this result, do you think a judicial review would conclude that all avenues of investigation leading to the inference that he is guilty have been adequately completed?"

The Circle's lawyer clears her throat and gives a nervous glance toward Collindale. Interesting. "I would anticipate dissatisfaction from both the Buckingham family and members of the Circle."

The lawyer next to the Norope representative, one I recognize from the first night at the hotel, has been typing at her v-keyboard throughout. A message arrives from her, sent to both Milsom and me. This investigation is costing Norope approximately £10,000 per hour. Shut this down now.

"In terms of a path to prosecution there is nowhere else to go," Milsom says. "Buckingham is dead. No one else is under suspicion. I can't see what would be achieved by continuing the investigation at this point."

The French woman looks up and to the right as she holds up her hand. The lawyer who represented Europe at the first meeting is also seated beside her, staring into the middle distance, attending to something else. "I understand this is a costly process," the French woman says after a few seconds, as if the private message has been intercepted and she doesn't care that we know. "But it will be even more costly if a civil case is brought against the Ministry of Justice with claims of negligence."

"The Circle will not bring that charge against the Brits," says the US gov-corp rep far too confidently, and the Circle's lawyer's eyes flash with anger. "It wouldn't be in their best interests to do so."

"But the Buckingham family comes from a very wealthy sect," the Circle's lawyer says. "Litigation would be a concern."

I have the feeling she would suggest it to them herself, just to get at her countryman for treading on her toes.

"And Europe is willing to share the costs of extending the investigation, as per the original agreement."

Milsom and the Noropean reps look at one another. This is my chance. Alejandro deserves better than this shoddy, half-baked investigation.

"I wouldn't need much more time to follow up on a couple of things," I say, trying my best to weather Milsom's glare. "I work fast. You've all already seen that."

"I suggest we consult within our respective groups and reconvene in ten minutes," the Noropean lawyer says, and all agree.

Milsom looks at me like her favorite dog has shat on the rug in front of houseguests. "You'll be informed of the decision," she says, and with a flick of her finger I'm booted out of the simulated room and back into my aching, sweating body on a hotel bed in Devon.

16

I WASH MY face and try to disentangle what needs to be done next from my sense of dread. I may not even be allowed back on the case. After that meeting, my gut instinct is that they're going to give me enough extra time to satisfy the Europeans but not nearly enough to finish this to my satisfaction. I need to prioritize.

Theo's death has the feel of a staged tableau. All the props point to suicide but are slightly off. The whisky, plausible enough for use in suicide but too special to have been bought in Ashburton on the way to the cottage, from a distillery that doesn't have any of its products licensed for printer replication. The painkillers, again so plausible, but why take paracetamol and ibuprofen when there's a bottle of Tylenol in his wash bag? I need to get the suicide note compared with an example of his handwriting, but whether it matches or not it won't give me much more to go on. The only thing I can be certain of is that Theo knew what happened to Alejandro that night; otherwise he wouldn't have checked out in such a state. What I don't know is how much of a part Theo played in his leader's death. It will take time to work out what happened to Theo in that cottage and I'm not prepared to spend it when Alejandro's death is still unresolved. I don't even know if he committed suicide. Even though Theo's note confessed to killing him, how would he have forced Alejandro to hang himself? The only weapon associated with Theo is the ax, and that's hardly the most effective tool to threaten someone into a noose.

I don't even know whether Theo went into Alejandro's suite within the murder window. This is ridiculous.

"Tia, send a note to the MoJ specialist data team saying the hotel-cam results are needed as soon as possible, as the case has become time sensitive." I sigh, hearing my own words. All of the things they examine are time sensitive. "No, dump that. Send a note to Tim Halliday in Data Retrieval and—"

"Tim Halliday no longer works in the Data Retrieval department," Tia says. "Would you like a list of current employees at your pay grade and below?"

"Have I worked with any of them before?"

"No."

"Don't bother, then."

Fuck.

I leave the bathroom and go to the bedroom window. The wind is easing now and one of the gardeners is picking up twigs and detritus from the ornamental garden. I wonder if he enjoys his job. Can he derive satisfaction from tidying something that will just get covered with shit again the next time a storm goes through? Maybe he'd prefer to manage the kitchen garden they have on Mars, safe beneath the dome, where none of the violent storms can disrupt perfection.

Would I be happier down there, raking leaves? Maybe I was

wrong to shine as bright as I could in the first phase of hot-housing. Maybe I should have ignored Dee's advice, kept my head down and been sold into menial servitude instead of this fucked-up social twilight of having everyone think I have status and authority when I'm nothing but a slave. So few people serve out indentured contracts at my pay grade, it wouldn't even occur to them that I'm one of those unfortunates they only hear about in the most sanitized terms.

All this time I've been working so hard to make as much of a life for myself as I can, my only choices reduced to the food I put in my mouth, and all along Alejandro was raking in that money, living in luxury hotels, free to do as he wanted.

I hate him just as much as I ever did. It doesn't smother the need to solve this though. That conditioning runs too deep. Was I always like that or was it trained into me? I push my palm down in front of me, imagining the emotions pressed down below it, leaving clarity behind. The question of the uniport charger bothers me the most. I need to know why Theo wanted to use one.

Selina. I need to talk to her.

I grab my jacket and the room key, lock the door behind me and go down to her room. Riley is back on door duty and straightens up as I approach. I nod as he gives me a brisk summary about the psych-support officer visit and then I knock on the door.

"Come in," Selina calls, and I enter.

The curtains are pulled back now and she is out of bed, still in nightdress and hotel dressing gown. At least she looks like she's showered. She's sitting at the dressing table, scrunching handfuls of her damp, curly hair in a towel.

"Is it Theo?" she asks, twisting round to face me. "Have you guys picked him up?"

"We have an idea of where he is," I say. I don't want to trigger any more crying, not when I need her to be clearheaded. "I wanted to ask you about something he brought with him to the hotel."

She puts down the towel and tightens the cord on her dressing gown. "Sit down if you like," she says, waving over at one of the plump chairs. "What kind of thing?"

I sit on the edge of the cushion, leaning forward. "Something that would need a uniport charger."

She smirks. "Not Theo. Surely you know that we don't have personal consumer tech in the Circle. It causes too many distractions from the real—"

"So you didn't see him using anything at all that could need one?" I don't need to hear Alejandro's indoctrination spewed back at me right now.

She shakes her head.

I think back to the interview with the cleaner and Tia helpfully pulls up a list of bullet points extracted from the interview for the case file. They float over the carpet as I look down, checking that my memory is correct. Yes.

"The first morning you were here at the hotel, Theo asked a member of staff where the uniport charger was in his room."

Selina looks genuinely surprised. "I can't think why. He didn't even use any tech before he came to the Circle. At least, I don't think he did. Oh. No, maybe I'm getting him mixed up with Nick. Yeah, Nick's family were like the Amish; Theo's were just bigots. Either way, none of us brought anything like that with us."

"You're certain?"

"Yeah, I went through security with him. He brought clothes and books—that's all. The guy at customs said he hadn't held a paper book for years. Philistine."

I lean back and press my palms together. This missing piece feels significant. There has to be a reason. "He didn't buy anything in Bath or at the Stonehenge center?"

"Nothing that would need a charger. He bought some touristy junk in Bath and a couple of books. I bought some chocolate and tea for some people in the Circle who are Brits, and a book about Stonehenge from the shop there."

So he didn't acquire something later. I'll review his transactions to confirm, but I see no reason for her to lie. "Did he go out anywhere without you or Alejandro?"

She shakes her head. "No. When Alejandro was here Theo was always nearby, and when he went to London we were together every time we left the hotel. I guess he could have gone out without me at some point—there was time—but he wasn't the most curious guy on the planet. He was happy enough to stay here."

Then why ask for a charger when they arrived? Assuming he had tech on the morning he asked, the only logical explanation is that he obtained something between customs and arriving at the hotel.

"Did you have much time in the Chicago airport after checking your bags?"

"About an hour."

I sit forward again, feeling a flicker in my chest that I'm closing in on something. "There are shops there. Did Theo buy anything that he might have put in hand luggage?"

"Not that I remember."

"Were the three of you together for the whole of the wait?"

She looks up at the ceiling. "No. Alejandro wanted to go to the walk-in clinic there. He said he hadn't been sleeping well and that the trip was only going to make it worse, so he got some pills to help him sleep and cope with the jet lag. I went with him—I hate airports and didn't want to be left with Theo—and Theo said he was going to have a walk around before being cooped up in the plane."

"How long were you at the clinic?"

"About half an hour. There were a few people ahead of us."

I stand so quickly, she starts. "Thanks. That's very helpful."

"When will I be able to get my bag back? I'd like to get dressed."

"Soon," I say, heading for the door. I pause with the handle in my hand and look back at her, sitting on the dressing-table stool, looking utterly lost. "I'll come back and see you as soon as I can. I'm sorry about the delay. Sit tight. It won't be long now."

You've got one hour to come up with something to convince me there's a case to pursue.

Milsom's message arrives while I'm jogging down the corridor back to my room, having instructed Tia to liaise with the US gov-corp's AI and pull camera footage from the Chicago airport departure-lounge shopping area in the time frame Theo would have been walking around, along with his transaction history. I need both to prove it was actually him buying whatever it was and not a fraudulent transaction.

An hour is a ridiculous compromise. Were it not for this new lead, I'd still be waiting for the full postmortem on Alejandro, the report on the cam footage and any developments in tracking down the drugs in Theo's "suicide," unable to make any real progress at all.

But now I have something. I know it. All right, Milsom, I'll show you just how good I can be.

The data comes in as the door to my room shuts behind

me. Milsom wasn't lying when she said they'd arranged an open channel; I was expecting at least a little bit of resistance.

"Okay, Tia," I say, pulling off my shoes and lying on the bed. "Open case notes, new file: 'Theo in Chicago airport.' Put the transaction and camera footage you just got from the States into it and put the transaction data on a virtual printout for the board in my case space."

I go through the tedium of the preimmersion checks as fast as I can and then I'm in my space on the MoJ server, standing in front of the board I made in my personal incident room. A new piece of paper is pinned to the bottom and I pull it free from the virtual drawing pin.

Theo made two transactions while Alejandro and Selina were at the clinic. The first was for a bottle of Tylenol. The second was for two RV 314 Pro items bought from a consumer-electronics store. Bingo.

I use the time stamp from the transaction to narrow the search in the camera footage, and within fifteen minutes I have a detailed account of Theo's movements in the airport shopping area and irrefutable evidence that he bought two tiny cameras with built-in microphones, small enough to be hidden easily. They're marketed as being perfect for home security, as they're too small for burglars to see and therefore disable. It's ridiculous; most burglars use scramblers that disrupt the camera data sent to the local node on shoddy Wi-Fi connections, but my guess is that most people buy these things for spying on lovers rather than home security. And that's exactly what I think Theo wanted them for.

I know the cameras are no longer in the Diamond Suite; the SOCO team would have found them with the standard equipment used to detect anything that connects to a local node, from a chip in someone's head to a camera's data feed. If Theo placed them inside the suite to spy on Alejandro and Selina, he took them with him before he left.

"Tia, pull up the marketing info and technical specs for this camera model and put them on the board for me."

A new sheet of paper appears. I pin the transaction summary into a new location and pluck the technical specs from their pin. The store he bought these from sold a dozen different models. What was it about this particular camera that caught his eye?

Scanning the dry specs, I realize I'm approaching this the wrong way. Theo wouldn't have known a thing about cameras. It could have simply come down to how the box looked. The security camera in the airport shop is at the wrong angle to look at the stock as Theo made his selection; all it shows is the side of Theo's head as he dithers in front of the display, pulls a couple of packets from the shelf and then takes them over to the payment station for people who aren't chipped and don't have a personal device that can handle a transaction. He looks just like any other middle-aged man trying to hide his bald patch, having chosen a lifestyle that prevents him from learning about all the ways that baldness can be fixed now. There's the briefest thought that I'm watching a man who is now dead. I don't allow myself to dwell on it.

"Tia, pull the spy-camera stock list from the Chicago airport store and show me the packaging for each of the models on the wall over there, like they'd be displayed in a shop."

The blank wall on the other side of the room is replaced by a generic store display, populated with the different models sold by the Chicago airport shop. It's not perfect; there's no way to know which models they put at eye level and which they put at the bottom, hoping to influence sales, but it will have to do. I walk over to it, letting my eyes drift from one box to the next. Each one is a riot of color and bioplastic, shouting about the virtues of the tech that is too small to see without bright concentric circles printed on the packaging around them or luminescent arrows pointing to the transparent dots that can be stuck "ANYWHERE!" while being "100% RELIABLE!" and producing "PERFECT RESOLUTION TO ZOOMS OF 1,000%!" It makes me feel tired just looking at them.

It doesn't take long to see what the chosen model has over most of the others: two mini screens that allow footage to be watched live or recorded without the need of a personal chip. I swipe away the other cams that don't offer that feature, leaving the ones Theo chose and one other pack. Both contain the cam dots with built-in mics and screens that can be placed up to fifty meters away. The one he chose has a couple of boasts on the front that are missing from the other. "No chip? No problem!" and below that: "No need for personal cloud storage!"

I pick up the packet and turn it over, looking at the claims in more detail. There's an interface through the screen for the unchipped and free cloud storage of up to one terrabyte with an automatic backup facility.

I grin. With any luck, that free storage allocated to the cams Theo bought will still have everything he recorded on there. It's just a matter of tracking it down.

It would be much easier to go through the US FBI contact, but I hesitate before instructing Tia to connect us. In that awful meeting, the American made it clear they didn't want the investigation to go on. If they catch wind of what I could be about to dig up, they might block it before it gets to me.

"Tia, track down the details about this cam company. See if it has any Noropean connections."

"The parent company is partnered with a Noropean company that provides the cloud storage bundled with the camera."

"Perfect." It's time to throw my weight around.

It takes longer for me to find the right person to speak to than getting him to release the data to me. It's a simple-enough matter, as I already have the individual camera sales information and the location of the local node through which the data was sent to the cloud storage. Theo just skipped through the options to protect that storage at the setup stage, probably not even fully understanding what it was, and mercifully was too upset and clueless to remember to go and delete it all when he fled from the hotel. It's just been sitting there in the cloud the whole time, not even password protected.

Once I have control of the account and Tia has made a copy to my secure MoJ account and put a second copy in the case file, I make sure the data trail is in place to prove provenance, and then delete the unprotected data. I don't want that employee to get curious and have a peep during his lunch break. It's happened before; a few years ago, footage of a club where a killing spree took place was uncovered by a security-firm employee, who then released it online. When he was prosecuted for failure to release sensitive data to the MoJ, the reason he gave was wanting to make something go viral. It hadn't even occurred to him that the grieving relatives could be distressed, let alone all of the other problems it caused.

Footage of Alejandro's hotel suite in his final days would probably be the only thing that could go viral enough to stop the world from talking about that bloody capsule. I won't let that happen though.

"Tia, trash the shop-display mock-up and project the footage from Theo's cams onto that wall. And give me a comfy chair, please." I don't care that she's just going to trick a set of neurons into firing; I want to feel as relaxed as possible when I watch this.

A large brown leather armchair appears so fast I don't register the exact moment I start to believe it's there. I sit down, aware of a reluctance to open the file, just for a moment, before instructing Tia to find the cam data from ten p.m. on Sunday night.

"Play the footage from both cams side by side," I say, and clasp my hands tight together. "How long until I need to report to Milsom?"

"Ten minutes, twenty-five seconds."

The plain white wall in front of me turns into a screen with a vertical divide. I look at the left-hand side first. There was a camera in the main room of the Diamond Suite; as far as I can tell Theo stuck it to the door frame of the main bathroom, about waist height. I imagine him leaning against it with studied nonchalance, probably in conversation with Alejandro, hands behind his back as he pressed it home. Against the white paint of the door frame, such a small translucent dot would easily be missed by the resident guests as well as the cleaning staff.

The desk is in full sight, along with the sofa and chairs and part of the sideboard that hides the tea-making facilities and minifridge. The door to the bedroom is out of shot, as is the main bathroom and door out into the hotel corridor.

On the right-hand side, the cam footage is showing the bedroom that Selina and Alejandro shared. Neither of them are in sight of either cam, presumably not yet returned from dinner. Tia is displaying the time stamps for me in the bottom right-hand corners of each feed and both are ticking away the seconds. Theo managed to position the dot slightly higher on the door frame into the bedroom, and I imagine him pretending to lean, perhaps, sticking the second dot in place during a conversation or a moment when the other two were distracted.

Why do this? Did he spy on Alejandro every trip they made together? If that was the case, surely he would have just reused the equipment. Then I remember Selina mentioning them going through security together. Perhaps he had to dump the cams every time so he didn't have to find a way to hide them at the Circle and get them through customs without Alejandro spotting them.

"Tia, I want you to identify the other flights Theo made with Alejandro over the past three years and check those times and dates against his transaction history. Did he buy spy cams on any other trips?"

"There are no records of Theo making any purchases of consumer tech over the past three years at any airports."

"Any time at all over those years?"

"No transactions of consumer tech found within the dates provided."

"Is this the first trip that Alejandro made with Selina?"

There is a pause of a couple of seconds as Tia pulls data I haven't requested before. Again, I'm grateful for the open channel to the States. "Yes. Selina Klein has not traveled on any domestic or international flights since a flight from New York to Albuquerque, New Mexico, three years, two months and five days ago."

She has to be the reason for Theo's behavior. Was it a voyeuristic thing? A dark extension of an obsession with Alejandro? Or did he have something for Selina and wanted to see the way she behaved in private? Perhaps it was as simple as a sad man wanting to see an attractive woman's underwear.

Working that out at this point will be difficult, and right now I don't have the time.

"Tia, fast-forward until there's movement on the left-hand cam."

The time-stamp speeds forward until 10:08 p.m., when a figure crosses the main room in front of the camera. It's Alejandro.

I thought I was ready to see him again.

It feels like the core of my body has been turned into paper and then scrunched into a ball. A thousand unspoken conversations that I've imagined having with the man on the screen tumble through my mind like rubbish being tipped out of an industrial waste bin. And then it hits me, right in the chest: the simple, immovable, undeniable fact that I will never be able to heal the wound between us and it will go on existing, outliving him and eating at me, until the day I die too.

"The food here is so good," Selina says moments before she walks into shot, and it's enough to pull me back to this chair that doesn't really exist and the job that so definitely does. There's the sound of the door into the suite closing behind her and she stops, right in the middle of the shot on the far side of the room, looking at the back of Alejandro as he leans against the desk. He hasn't said a word yet and I find myself bracing for the sound of his voice. "Headache again?" she asks, and rests a hand on his back.

"I'm sorry," he says, and I wish he were saying it to me. That was all I wanted to hear for so long, and it's on a fucking video being spoken to someone else.

"What for?" Selina asks, and Alejandro turns to face her.

He's still handsome, perhaps more so; something about the salt-and-pepper hair that lends him more gravitas. His hand twitches forward, as if he's about to reach out and touch her but thinks better of it. "I . . . I haven't really been myself and it's not been fair on you. And I'm sorry. I'm sorry if I've made you feel . . . insecure."

Selina pulls off a chiffon scarf, something I wouldn't associate with someone from the Circle, and lets it pool on the desk
next to Alejandro. "I'm gonna ask you something and I want
you to be straight with me, okay?" He nods and she stands
straighter, as if readying herself for battle. "Do you want us
to stop being lovers? Is that what this is all about?"

He looks at her as if . . . as if he knows she's got a terminal
illness or something, as if he knows something tragically sad
about her that she is utterly unaware of. "I'm not like your
husband. There isn't anyone else."

"I thought you were with someone in London."

"Not like that."

"Like what, then?"

"Nothing like that."

"You didn't answer my question." I can hear the strain in
her voice. She is so in love with him and he seems painfully
aware of that. It isn't reciprocated. He cares for her, that much
is obvious, but it's not love in the way she would want. I don't
think he's capable of focusing his passions onto just one person.
Was not capable.

"This isn't the time to talk about it."

"So when is?" She's trying so hard to be patient when she's
so desperate for something, anything, to indicate there's something real between them that might survive the crisis. How
many people have I seen look at him like that? I know the
bitterness of that place, that desperation.

"You look tired. I'm . . . I'm tired too. It isn't the right time
for this conversation."

There is such a weight behind his words, as if he is having
to force them from his lips with the bellows of his lungs, pushing them out through strength of will. There used to be such
an energy to him, such vibrancy, it was impossible to be in a

room with him and not feel it too. Was he depressed? Ill? Something was very wrong.

"I'm gonna take a bath," Selina says, and I want to shout at her and make her turn around and press him to talk. It's a purely selfish desire. I want the mersive story options to pop up and let me choose to pursue the conversation rather than backing off. I want to make her ask the questions raging inside of me. But this is just a messy, dissatisfying slice of reality that has already happened. She walks away from him.

"Five minutes until Milsom's hour expires," Tia says, and I sit up, rubbing my hands over my face to break the spell that the magic of voyeurism has cast upon me.

"Speed it up," I say. I could report to her with just the news of this footage, but I want to go to her with something so fucking compelling there won't be any debate about the case staying open.

At double speed, Selina undresses in the bedroom as her bath fills with expensive water. I've never had a bath in my life. Even at the Circle the only option was a water-conserving shower. She's clearly making the most of her stay.

In the main room of the suite, Alejandro stays in front of the desk, arms crossed, staring at the carpet. Once Selina leaves the bedroom and goes into the en-suite, he closes the door to the bedroom and goes back to sit at the desk and rest his head in his hands. He's pale and more inwardly focused than I ever remember him being. There's a moment when his features crumple, and I adjust the playback speed and rewind back to the moment his face changed.

He is starting to weep.

My own throat tightens and I put a hand over my mouth, feeling like his distress is somehow leaching into me. Something terrible must have happened. In London? Some part of me, deep down, is frightened by this display of vulnerability in a man once god-like. If life can batter someone like Alejandro into the state he was in that night, what hope is there for the rest of us?

I still love him. Underneath the rage, the injustice, the betrayal, there is still that bright core of adoration he planted so deep inside. I want to touch his shoulder, make him look up at me like I looked up at him when he found me hiding in a storeroom, sobbing over the remains of Bear. My father had torn him open in front of me, pulled out the data chips and circuits housed inside and stamped on them as I'd screamed.

My father was a murderer. I was hysterical, clutching fake fur and stuffing and shattered silicon, mourning the death of my only friend. Bear hadn't just been something to cuddle. Its AI had kept me alive when the printer broke down back at the house in Spain. It had tried to get the authorities to come, identifying my father's neglect as harmful to my health, but the state was breaking down and everything was in chaos. "Don't worry, Carlos," his soft little synthvoice had said. "Even though the nice people can't come to help, we can fix the problem together. Tell me what happens when you try to print your food."

I'd been eating nothing but an oily slop with lumps of powder for days and it was making me ill. Bear talked to the house AI when it became apparent the printer's usual diagnostics had broken down, and made it order replacement parts. Printer renewables were one of the few things still being delivered, as critical as water supply, with provision enshrined in basic human rights. Bear sat on a stool, watching as I opened the box I'd found on our doorstep, and told me how to fix it. I tried to share the bread I printed with him once it was fixed and he'd made sounds of enjoyment, the tiny motors in his mouth mimicking chewing.

After Alejandro came and spoke to my father, somehow

bringing him back into the world, I clung to Bear when the house was emptied, in the taxi to the airport, on the plane as my father shivered and stammered in the seat next to me. I hadn't let go of him until the day we arrived at the Circle and he was taken from me.

It took me two weeks to find where my father had hidden him. It took two minutes for my father to realize where I was and destroy him.

Alejandro's hand on my shoulder made me look up into eyes that were filled with love and sadness. "Come outside, Carlos," he said. "Bring him with you. Let's find a place to lay him to rest and I will tell you a story under the stars."

"Just us?"

"Just us."

A movement on the screen pulls me away from the memory of him. Alejandro has calmed enough to wipe his cheeks and lean back in the chair. He looks up at the ceiling and then at the curtains. His lips are thin, pressed together by the decision being made, the one I can see in his eyes. The one that invites death in.

"Four minutes," Tia says, and I realize my hand is still clamped over my mouth, as if I'm unknowingly trying to keep something trapped inside. I force myself to take a deep breath and look away from the screen.

"Pause footage."

I don't want to watch anymore. I know what he's going to do and I can't bear the thought of sitting here, separated by an impenetrable barrier of time and space, to witness his suicide. But there is no choice here. I will have to make a full report. I will have to form a clear narrative and be ready to answer questions. But I know that I'll never be able to unsee what I'm about to and I need a moment to compose myself.

"Three minutes."

Fuck.

"Open a channel to Milsom."

"Are you about to amaze me, Carl?"

"I hope so, boss. I've managed to retrieve spy-cam footage recorded in the victim's suite in the murder window."

There's the briefest pause. I clutch at the sense of her being surprised and I let the tiniest feeling of triumph bloom from it.

"Well, what does it show?"

I shake my head. She had been waiting for me to expand upon it. Milsom could never really be shocked into silence. "I'm still reviewing it. It took most of the hour to get it." If I tell her now that it looks like it was suicide, loose ends or not, she'll shut it down within another hour. "I need an extension."

"Make a full report as soon as you can. I'll expedite the data analysis on the hotel and cottage local nodes, and I understand the pathologist is wrapping up now too. You should be able to put it all together by early evening."

I look at Tia's time display; in the incident room it's presented as a wall clock. "I've got another five hours, then?"

"Let me know if you need longer," she says, and I feel the pressure easing slightly. "But the sooner this is wrapped, the better."

There's no encouragement, no acknowledgment of this breakthrough. She's still angry at me but I don't think it's black-mark levels anymore. "I'll do my best," I say, and she ends the call.

Alejandro is frozen on the screen ahead of me, his face still turned toward the curtains. I make a note of the time stamp and enter a bullet point alongside it: contemplating suicide?

Perhaps making the notes I'll need for the report is the best way to pull myself back and look at this with a bit of professional distance.

Who the fuck am I kidding?

"Resume playback."

I watch him get the sleeping pills from the bedroom, return to the other room and put the kettle on. He stares at the bottle as the water comes to the boil, perhaps wondering if it's an easier route to take, perhaps still making up his mind. He prepares the tea for Selina and pours in the contents of three capsules.

He takes the cup into the bedroom, sits on the bed and waits for her to come out. He seems calmer now. He manages a smile for her when she emerges wrapped in a towel, water steaming off her skin, which is pink with heat.

"I made you some tea," he says, handing the cup to her. He watches her drink, thirsty from the heat of the bath, and takes the cup from her. As she dries her hair he puts the cup in the en-suite, out of her sight.

"Perhaps we could go for a walk together tomorrow," she says, when he comes back into the bedroom. When he doesn't reply, she goes over to him, wrapping her arms around his waist. After a beat he returns the embrace, his face turned away from the camera, hers obscured by his arms. He kisses her hair, her hands run down his back and she kisses his lips, but her attempts at kindling some passion between them are soon ended by him breaking away.

She stands there, clutching the top of her towel as he pulls back the sheets.

"You look tired," he says. "Why don't you get into bed?"

She lets the towel drop, standing in front of him naked for

a moment, but his eyes resist the pull of her body. Silently, she slips between the sheets, her eyelids already looking heavy. "I am pretty tired, actually," she says, yawning.

He sits on the edge of the bed again, tucking her in paternally. She reaches toward him and he takes her hand, kisses it tenderly. "Good night, Selina," he says as her head sinks into the pillow.

In less than a minute she is out cold. He presses his fingers against her neck, checking her pulse, before holding the palm of his right hand just above her mouth and nose to feel her breath. Satisfied, he leans over and kisses her once on the lips. "I'm sorry," he whispers, and turns off the light.

17

I PAUSE PLAYBACK to make notes, having realized I haven't made any more formal entries into the file since the one about him looking at the curtain. I'm losing my emotional distance. It feels like I'm trying to sketch a drop of water while holding back a bursting dam. I go back and identify time stamps for each bullet point, knowing all the while that I'm putting off watching the rest as much as I'm being diligent.

The shape of Selina's drugged body can just be made out in the light thrown from the doorway to the rest of the suite. She went to sleep hoping she could find something to bring Alejandro back the following day, only to wake up and see all that blood, all that violence, in a beautiful room they had shared. No wonder she was hysterical. "Tia, connect me to PC Riley."

"How can I help, sir?"

"Riley, check with SOCO that they've finished with Miss Klein's belongings, and if they have, make sure they're brought

down to her new room. Tell her she can dress and pack to
return to the States, but I need to see her before she can leave.
I'll be coming to see her in the next hour or so."

"Yes, sir."

I close the channel. I know SOCO will have finished with
her stuff—none of her clothes or belongings were in the main
room—but I didn't want Riley rushing up there in his enthusiasm and pissing Alex off by encroaching on his territory.
Hopefully Selina will start to feel a little better when she gets
her things back. I'll sign off permission for her to leave once
I've broken the news about Theo to her and gotten her to sign
a cast-iron nondisclosure agreement.

"Resume playback."

Alejandro closes the door to the bedroom, goes back to the
desk and opens the drawer. He pulls out a piece of the letter paper
the SOCO told me about along with the complimentary fountain
pen, the one we found with Theo's body at the cottage.

He writes slowly and carefully, pausing often. Sometimes
it looks like it's to find the right words; sometimes it looks like
he's trying not to weep again. The movement of the pen across
the paper is obscured by an ornamental vase filled with silk
flowers, so there's no hope of trying to render a three-
dimensional reconstruction from the footage and thereby discover what he wrote. It's not always reliable anyway, with
handwriting being such an individual thing.

He fills one side, turns over and finishes a few minutes later.
I daren't speed up the footage for fear of missing some subtle
detail or noise from elsewhere in the suite. The sound of the
scratching of the nib across the paper knots muscles in my
neck. I try to pull back, making a couple of notes and obser-
vations, but it's like fiddling with a cuff while waiting for a

public execution: something tiny and ridiculous in the face of impending horror.

Alejandro screws the lid of the pen back on and lays it beside the letter. He spins the chair until he is at a forty-five-degree angle from the desk and stares intently at the cream carpet, so still and introverted that if I didn't know better, I'd think he was reading something displayed by a chip. His hands are shaking. Mine are too.

Finally, he stands, nodding to himself. Is he still making up his mind? He picks up the other chair near the desk, the one that was on its side in the center of the room when I last saw it in the VR mock-up of the scene, and moves it to beneath the ceiling rose.

I look away, my throat constricting again, a pressure building behind my eyes. I recall my father sitting on the bed in my dorm at the Circle, hunched over with his back to the door, Alejandro sitting next to him with a hand on his shoulder. Even as young as eight I knew I was about to walk into a room where something significant was happening, so my feet stopped and I stayed still and silent, unseen.

"I wanted to die." My father's voice was clogged with phlegm and unshed tears. "I wanted to but I was too scared. That's the only reason."

"No, not the only reason." Alejandro's voice was so deep, so strong in comparison.

"I didn't stay alive for Carlos." My father's voice cracked, unable to stay steady beneath the onslaught of emotion. "I didn't even think about him most days. I'm a terrible person! A terrible father!"

He broke down, leaning into Alejandro, who put his arm around him. "The healing starts here and now, for both of you," Alejandro said. "And don't be afraid. You'll never feel that way again."

"But how do you know that?"

"Because you have left the place without hope behind you. You don't live in that place anymore. You say you were too scared to kill yourself. I don't think that was the only reason you're here now."

"I don't believe in God, Alejandro. I told you that."

Alejandro laughs, squeezes my father with that easy physical confidence he had then. "You're still here because some part of you held on. Even though you were hurting, even though you couldn't conceive of an end to that pain, you. Held. On."

"Did you come close? Before? When *Atlas* left you behind?"

"Yes," Alejandro replied, a new, darker tone beneath his voice. "I thought it was all over. I couldn't see a way forward. But I could never kill myself. I have a contract with God. And I know you don't believe, but I do."

"I wish I did," my father said, sitting back up again to blow his nose. How disgusting I found him then! "I don't believe in anything. No. That's not true. I believe in you, Alejandro."

"And now I have a contract with you," Alejandro said, pressing a hand over his own heart. "Here. I will never let you down."

And my father broke down again and Alejandro held him like a child, and I watched from the doorway, wanting to be held like that too, hating my father for making me feel that way. When Alejandro noticed me, my father still sobbing into his chest, he held out a hand to me and I stared at it, wanting so much to take it yet unable to move my feet. *Come and put your hand in mine,* the look in his eyes said. *Let me give you a place to feel safe again.*

"Carlos!" The sharpness in my father's voice made me jump and look away from the pools of Alejandro's eyes. "What are you doing spying from doorways!"

I ran as Alejandro's hand dropped onto the bed, and my father apologized for having such a broken child.

I look back at the screen and try to reconcile the memory of that man, the rock for so many people, with the one I see unhooking the curtain cord. I want to ask him about those contracts he held, written indelibly in his heart and theirs, and why he is destroying them. Is all that love not enough? Is devotion inadequate? What couldn't they give him in the end? Was his ego such that it created some sort of emotional sinkhole, all that love pouring into him, only to be sucked away by some invisible cavern beneath the surface, in his soul?

I take a breath to shout at him, to plead, and then I am looking away again, gripping the arm of the chair as the chaos inside me reaches a peak and then the training kicks in. The recalibration machine did its work, all those times before Dee taught me how to avoid it, and it feels like a rubber band inside me is stretched to its fullest extent and then snaps me back, away from the roiling mess of emotion, like a leash pulling back a slavering hound.

I swallow down the lump in my throat and look at the time stamp in the corner of the screen.

I will learn the details.

"Ten thirty-eight, victim detaches curtain cord from hook and places on chair in center of room."

I will work the case.

"Ten thirty-nine, victim pulls off shoes and places next to desk, paired, in location as recorded and confirmed by the primary SOCO."

I will identify the . . .

"Ten forty. Victim fashions noose from curtain cord and secures to light fixture. Tests the knot."

. . . the murderer.

"Ten forty-one. Victim stands on the chair."

I have never found a puzzle I couldn't solve.

"Victim pulls on noose to test strength of light fixture."

This is . . . This is no . . .

"Why are you doing this?" I am on my feet, shouting at the man who is already dead as he puts the noose around his neck.

"Please provide more detail," Tia says.

"Dios perdóname. Envía la carta," Alejandro says, and kicks the chair away.

I drop back into my seat as he drops from the noose and something inside me breaks. I double over and clutch my stomach at the sound of a momentary choked gasp from the screen. The sound of plaster cracking, of fabric rustling with the frantic, jerking movement of his body, and I can't hold it back any longer. The cry that bursts out of me is so loud, so alien to me that a part of my mind steps out from itself to listen and wonder at the sound I'm making, and then there is nothing but a torrent of rage-filled grief.

"WOULD you like me to open a channel to your psych supervisor?"

When I look up I see that the footage has been paused. I look at the clock but the second hand has stopped moving. Everything has been paused. Tia must be working out whether to boot me back into my body.

"No."

"MyPhys reports increased levels of cortisol and your neurochemical—"

"Just leave it, Tia."

"Are you in distress?"

I take a deep breath, hoping that as my body does the same on the bed in my hotel room, my efforts to calm myself here will have an effect. "I'm okay. I don't need to speak to my psych supervisor. This . . . this footage is difficult to watch, that's all."

"Is your ability to continue with this case impaired?"

That jolts me into sitting straighter, the threat of that black mark rearing once more. "No. It's not. I'm okay now."

"Would you like me to resume the footage from the last time stamp detailed in your notes?"

I push myself back farther into the chair, having nearly slid off it. "Yes, thank you, Tia," I say in the calmest voice I can muster, trying my best to ignore the desperate urge to terminate this immersion and run away. Not that I'd be able to go anywhere. I can't run from my own chipped brain.

I call up my v-keyboard, needing something to justify looking away from the images of the screen in case this immersion comes under judicial review. I need to lock this shit away deep inside myself. If I fuck up and my loss of control comes up in a case audit, I could be looking at another five, if not ten, years added to my contract. There is a moment that feels like a yawning chasm inside of me, in which I face the possibility that I'll never be free, that I'll die under contract never having felt freedom again. Dying before I've had a chance to wake up one morning and decide what *I* want to do, to pull something out of the soil that I've grown myself, to eat without having to accept that the decision to buy one meal is also the decision to remain an owned asset for even longer. Focusing on the footage is easier than facing that.

Alejandro's body swings back and forth. The room is silent except for a steady patter dripping onto the carpet from the bottom of his trouser leg. I don't look at his face. Instead I note the time of death and look at the note and pen on that room's desk as I wait for Theo to arrive.

"Envía la carta," he said. "Send the letter." But to whom? Selina is asleep and there is no one else in the room. Does he mean the letter on his desk? He doesn't have an APA to instruct and there's no evidence that he is recording himself with a portable unit. What does it mean?

Two and a half minutes after his death, there's the sound of the lock tumbling in the door to the suite. It opens and closes swiftly and so quietly I doubt it has been locked again. Expecting Theo, I am amazed to see a woman enter the room wearing a black, tight-fitting cap that covers all of her hair, a hotel bathrobe over silk pajamas and soft-soled slippers covered with a plastic bag similar to what the SOCOs provided for me. She's petite, probably not much over five and a half feet tall, with light brown skin.

She makes no attempt to cut him down and resuscitate him; she just stands there for a moment, looking annoyed. Then she heads toward the bedroom door and is out of shot until the door opening on the bedroom cam reveals her entering the room. She stands at the end of the bed for a few seconds, then lifts the cover to reveal one of Selina's feet. She blows softly on the sole, and when Selina doesn't move, risks touching one of her toes. Once she has pinched one and seen that Selina is actually unconscious, rather than asleep, the woman leaves the room again and shuts the door. When she doesn't come back into shot I assume she has paused there for some reason.

"Tia, identify the woman wearing the hat."

"Jessica Arlington."

Arlington's bio floats over the dark half of the screen. South American visiting Norope on a tourist visa. Checked into the hotel the day after Alejandro arrived and checked out twenty-six hours after his death, with permission of the local police, once she relinquished permission to track her movements via her chip, on the proviso she doesn't leave the British Isles. They should have kept everyone at the damn hotel here until I arrived, even the ones that were chipped!

"Where is she now?"

There is a pause. "Arlington's last recorded Noropean location is Heathrow Airport, yesterday afternoon, three-oh-five p.m. Her destination was—"

"Hang on. She wasn't supposed to leave the fucking country! Who authorized that?"

"I'm sorry. I am not at liberty to disclose that information to you."

That suggests someone very high up in the MoJ. She comes back into shot again, crossing the room at the very edge to stand a little way away from Alejandro, staring at his face in a way that chills my very core. Then her head moves as her gaze tracks downward and I realize she's filming him with her retinal cam. Is she some sort of spy? A sicko filming something for her own twisted pleasure, or to be sold for an obscene amount of money? The Americans don't want anyone to know Alejandro committed suicide. Did she know that and make a remarkably fast decision to blackmail them?

No. It's all too ridiculous.

A sound of a door opening down the corridor and footsteps running toward the Diamond Suite makes her pad silently and calmly into the bathroom, going out of shot once more. The door to the suite bangs open and there's a horrified cry off screen.

"Oh God, no! Alejandro! No, no, no!"

Theo runs over to him, wearing only a hotel dressing gown, grabs his legs and tries to lift Alejandro to take the weight off the noose, without success. Panting as if he's running a marathon, Theo checks for a pulse and then staggers back, shaking his head. "Selina!" he calls, and then barges into the bedroom to shake her roughly—the position of his hands corresponding with the bruises I saw—and then let her drop back onto the pillow, oblivious.

He abandons her, going back into the main room to stare at Alejandro as he literally pulls at his hair with distress. He starts scanning the room for something and notices the note on the table. As he reads, he pales and starts to cry, shaking his head and muttering denials. He flips it over to read to the end, sits heavily in the chair and bawls into his hands.

There's no sign of the woman in the bathroom making an escape. Theo wipes his face with a sleeve and stands. "I can't let . . ." he says, his voice drifting off as he looks at the body again. "You fucking bastard!" Theo shouts. He grabs Alejandro's room key from the desk where he left it and runs from the room.

I make notes, keeping the emotions at bay with the need to observe and record details that may seem like nothing now but could be everything later. But even as I type I know there is nothing in this footage that will convince Milsom that a murder case even exists anymore. The only hope I have of being able to pursue anything after my five hours are up is getting enough on the mystery woman to convince the gov-corp that there is more than just a suicide here.

"Tia, is there anything in the local node data about where

Arlington was between ten thirty p.m. and eleven p.m. on Sunday night?"

"According to the data from her chip, she was in her room from ten p.m. to eight fifteen a.m. the following morning."

She must be the one who doctored the local node data to hide the movements in and out of the Diamond Suite that night. And she's good, because anything less than that would have been uncovered by the AI analysis. Only the most capable digital criminals can trick the AIs.

She doesn't leave the bathroom for the next five minutes, apart from a brief trip to check on Selina's unconscious state. I can only assume she's waiting for instructions—I can't think of any reason she would stay there. Unless she is waiting for someone else to arrive.

Arlington is back in the bathroom before Theo returns with the ax from the log. He rights the chair and stands on it to cut Alejandro down with the blade, taking the weight of the body on his shoulder to lower it to the ground reverently. Dropping the ax as he steps down from the chair, Theo sinks to his knees and takes Alejandro into his arms, weeping into his chest as his head and arms flop back, slack with death. The sound of his pain is horrendous. It has invisible claws that reach into me, hoping to drag its twin emotion from inside me. I swallow a few times, look away from the screen to make more notes, thinking about how to present my report in a vain attempt to keep enough of me removed and my emotions in check.

When the worst has passed, Theo lays Alejandro down again. He stands, looks around and heads toward the remote control he's spotted on the sideboard. He's changed his mind before he even picks it up, looking back at Alejandro and biting his thumbnail like a child who has discovered something awful and doesn't know who to tell. He jerks, as if remembering something. Using a tissue fished from his pocket, he plucks out the room-key fob and wipes his prints from it before laying it on the desk.

He goes back to the ax and picks it up. He stares at Alejandro for what seems to be an interminable length of time, emotions flitting across his face like clouds on a windy day, always changing and threatening to burst before passing just as quickly. "I can't let . . ." he mutters. "I can't. They can't think that . . ."

He swipes the letter and pen from the desk and stuffs both into his pocket. Every few seconds he shakes his head, the horror of the situation pulling him taut between warring impulses.

Theo turns and stands over Alejandro's body. "You said you would never leave us." His face distorts into something disgusting, something bestial. "You said you would never leave me behind."

The first blow of the ax makes me physically jump. I look away, making frantic notes, speculating about Theo's mental state and his desire to hide the suicide from others complicated by his sense of betrayal. My words are distant, impersonal, a barricade I cower behind as carnage unfolds on the screen. Each blow is accompanied by a sickening thud and squelch that makes my stomach heave, forcing me to suck in deep breaths through my nose in the hope that my body in the hotel room won't vomit. Theo's crying is periodically strangled by effort, until it just stops partway through. I look up to see him as pale as a death shroud, spattered with blood, nodding to himself. "This is actually brilliant," he whispers. "You've been murdered. They'll never know, Alejandro. I won't tell them—I promise."

Something inside him has broken. He completes the grotesque task in silence. When it is done, the rug and carpet soaked with blood and him looking like the murderer in the story he's concocting, he pulls the noose from the neck in a direction that should be impossible. He staggers back, knocking the chair over again. He sees a partial footprint caused by a misplaced step and rubs the bottom of his foot with his sleeve and then the print itself to make it into an unreadable smudge.

He hobbles away, taking care to keep on the ball of his right foot so no residual blood wiped from his heel will touch the carpet.

Without looking back, he goes out of shot and the door shuts properly behind him. The room looks exactly as I recall it from the recorder data.

Arlington emerges from the bathroom and stands just inside the doorway for a few moments, taking it all in. Then she picks her way around the edge of the room, taking care not to touch anything and not to tread in any of the bloodied areas. She goes around the far side of the desk, heading toward one of the arms, I think. She crouches down, pulling a small pouch from her pocket, her back and dressing gown obscuring whatever she does with Alejandro's remains. I make a note that something was done and suggest DNA theft as the most likely act. Just as carefully, she edges around the room and leaves. I make a note of the time stamp and have Tia play the rest of the footage at four times normal speed. I sit back and stare at that room, at the back of Alejandro's head and the shining slick of blood as something dies within me too.

18

I COME BACK into my body to find my throat raw and my ears wet from tears that ran down my face while I was lying down. Full immersion stops me from running around or hitting things while my mind thinks I'm somewhere else, mimicking the brain's dreaming state, but it can't stop crying or vomiting. The chip has to leave critical bodily functions like those alone.

For once, I actually lie there for a few minutes, as guidelines suggest. My stomach feels tight and hollow with the need to eat, without any appetite to do so. I have a headache, probably from the knotted muscles in my neck, and my throat feels thick and clogged up like a pipe furred by limescale.

I try to tell myself that nothing has actually changed. I knew he was dead. I already suspected suicide. I still feel shocked though. I didn't really believe it on some level.

The minutes are ticking away and I need to make a decision. If I report in now, Milsom will close the case. The MoJ doesn't actually benefit from investigating whether a US citizen really committed suicide, so they'll wrap that up too. It won't change anything, after all.

The woman, Arlington, will probably settle the question of who doctored the local node data. She's long gone, and there's nothing I can actually do save report her actions and leave the decision to track her internationally up to whoever it was all those pay grades above me who let her leave the country. Something about that stinks, but she didn't kill him either. The thought of Alejandro's DNA being sold to the highest bidder sickens me, but there's always a risk of that when you're as high profile as he was. I don't let myself speculate about what the buyer might do with it.

I should file my report and walk away. Selina can go home and try to put herself back together again. The Circle will collapse or evolve. Either way, it makes no difference to me.

But I don't start the work. I stare at the ceiling, questioning my inertia. I have fewer than five hours and no case to pursue within them. What I really have is freedom, of a sort. No. I can't even let myself believe that. Even if I spend that time staring out of the window, at some point I'll have to justify the time spent. If Milsom thinks I just pissed about during an official investigation period, it'll be a black mark. Five hours being miserable are not worth a year added to my contract, even when those five hours are spent in luxury. I should start the final report.

I get as far as opening my notes before the minuscule motivational spark fizzles out. I don't want to write the final report because, for me, this isn't over. I need to know what was in that note. I need to know what drove him to do the one thing I would never have thought him capable of. I need to understand why he said "Send the letter."

"Tia, pull the transaction data from Alejandro's London trip and show me the list with time stamps and locations alongside what he paid for."

He was there for only five days but something critical happened. He met someone or a deal—or an affair—fell through, or something simply didn't work out the way he needed it to. Selina said that when he got back he seemed preoccupied and wanted lots of time alone. Whatever happened in London put him into some sort of crisis, and perhaps the time alone was to try to work out what to do. When no solution presented itself, he decided it was better to die.

I scan the list Tia presents and it looks like any wealthy man's trip to London. He stayed at the Savoy and ate there once per day, and the other meals were in a scattering of top-end restaurants within a couple of miles of his hotel. He dined alone, judging by cost of the meals, which I didn't expect, suggesting that whatever meetings took him up there were the sort that had no room for fine food and wine. Perhaps he wasn't there to see someone after all. There's nothing on the hotel bill to suggest he was sharing the room with anyone else, but he or she could have had their own room.

I dig deeper into the data, looking at the individual restaurants without any particular line of inquiry in mind. I look at his first lunch there, unfamiliar with the restaurant name. It specializes in Thai cuisine, which surprises me. I thought he didn't like it. I look at the dinner he ate on that same day, this time at a place I've heard of and always wanted to eat at. He ate the dish they're famed for: steak with—

Wait. He was vegetarian.

A meat dish is listed in every meal. With the three dinners he had in the city, he had two glasses of expensive wine. He didn't drink.

I sit up and swing my legs off the bed. Did he even go to London? Is all this data just bullshit?

"Tia, I need you to identify the safety cam that would have covered the entrance to the the White Lotus restaurant in Maiden Lane, Covent Garden. Pull the footage from this time window." I look up the time stamp for the lunch transaction, work out a reasonable window for him to have arrived and eaten and give the times to Tia.

I have a wash and change my shirt. I need to see Selina again anyway.

"The footage is available for review."

"Okay, Tia, I need you to run a recognition filter through it and isolate any footage of a man fitting Alejandro Casales's height entering the restaurant within that time frame."

I knot my tie, feeling the thrill of another fold of the puzzle being revealed. This is an indulgence: Milsom and the MoJ won't have any fucks to give about why he committed suicide, but I'm willing to argue that it's relevant to the case, no matter how flimsy the connection is. It's not like it's using extra officers or anything.

Even though Selina is dressed by the time I get to her, she's still pale and looks far from okay. Her case is on the bed, mostly packed, a new box of tissues sitting beside it.

"Mr. Riley said I might be able to go home soon," she says as I close the door.

"That's right," I say. "I just have a couple of things I need to talk to you about first."

She sighs, from exhaustion rather than irritation, and nods. "Take a seat."

We sit in the two armchairs, occasional weak bursts of sunshine poking from behind the clouds. I realize I haven't eaten lunch yet and the sun is already sinking toward the horizon. I hate November.

"Regarding Alejandro, did he have any special dietary requirements or eating habits?"

She frowns at the question. "How can that be relevant?"

"Please answer the question."

She shrugs. "He never ate meat, but that wasn't an allergy thing. It's part of our commitment to life at the Circle. He didn't go for very exotic food, but then he ate paella and always laughed at me when I said that was exotic." Her smile is feeble beneath the weight of her grief. "He didn't drink at all. I like a glass of wine when I can get one, but generally there isn't any alcohol at the Circle."

I nod. "I have something to tell you that will be difficult to—"

"Theo's dead, isn't he?"

I sit back, wondering if that came from a fear that had been stewing during her solitude or if somehow it had gotten back to her. "He was found dead, yes. A suspected suicide."

She nods, her brow creasing as she looks down at her hands in her lap. "I want to cry, but I don't think I have any of that left in me. Theo was a pain in the ass a lot of the time but he wasn't a bad person or anything. Did he do that to Alejandro?"

"He was involved, yes."

She looks up at me. "'Involved' is an interesting word to use."

"I can't discuss that any further at this time. I'm sorry."

She nods. "I'm just the girlfriend, I know. Listen, this is an amazing hotel but right now I want to be anywhere but here."

"I understand. The US authorities will make sure you get back home safely as soon as possible. I just need you to sign an agreement that you won't disclose any details regarding your trip here or what happened to Alejandro to anyone other than myself or a representative of the Noropean Ministry of Justice."

"What about if the cops ask me about it back home?"

"They won't. You'll be escorted by a liaison who will make sure that no one bothers you."

"And what about the Circle? They'll want to know. They'll *need* to know."

I have no idea how the lawyers will want to play that, but they'll brief Collindale or whomever else they trust to get her home again. "Your US gov-corp liaison will be able to advise you about that on the way home. No doubt as the shock subsides you'll have a lot of questions. It's best to direct them to that individual. He or she will be fully briefed." I stand. "I'm sorry this has been such a traumatic trip for you," I say, immediately regretting the words. There's nothing I can say that will sound genuine or anything less than absurdly inadequate.

Nevertheless, she seems to appreciate the clumsy gesture. She stands too and holds out her hand, which I shake. "Thank you for . . ." She trails off.

"I'll have PC Riley bring you the paperwork. It's just being printed now."

She nods, wrapping her arms about herself. "Will this . . . Will it get easier?"

I pause by the door. "It will settle into place. Be less raw. But it will take time. I can have some victim-support literature . . ." This time I don't finish the sentence. Trotting out some bullshit doesn't feel right. "It's going to be hard as hell, for you and for everyone else at the Circle. More for you though, going through what you have here. Get help if you can."

When I touch the handle she dashes forward and puts a hand on my arm. "I can't help but . . . It wasn't my fault, was it? If I'd just woken up a bit sooner, if I . . . if I'd heard something, I . . ."

The sleeve of my jacket crumples under her grip. "It wasn't your fault, Ms. Klein. I promise."

"Did Theo do that to him? Why?"

I feel like I'm staggering into quicksand. Normally I wouldn't hesitate in explaining what happened—she needs to know—but with all the lawyers and nondisclosure clauses in that damn contract I signed, I'm not sure if I can give enough detail to satisfy her. "I'm afraid I'm not able to discuss the details with you. Ask your liaison. I'm sure they'll be able to answer your questions."

The desperate hope in her eyes fades when she realizes I can't release her from that burden. I feel like a complete bastard, but it's not worth the risk. Her hand lets go of my jacket sleeve.

"Have a safe journey home," I say, and leave.

PC Riley is outside the door, accepting a sheaf of papers from the officer who was guarding the Diamond Suite earlier. "The NDA for the unchipped lady, sir," he says. "The SOCO team have finished at the suite now."

A message to that effect from Alex arrives as he says it. "Good."

The lift pings at the end of the corridor and both police officers smile at whoever comes out. I twist around to see the hotel manager looking relieved to see me.

"SDCI Moreno, could I have a word with you in private, please? Something's happened that I think you need to be aware of."

I nod and head toward the lift with her. She presses the button for the ground floor. "Is it regarding the investigation?"

When the doors close, she turns to face me. "In a manner of speaking. It's a member of my staff. She's been approached by a journalist who seems to know that Alejandro Casales was murdered here. She's been offered a not-insignificant amount of money and other perks in return for information. I thought you should know."

A flash of anger makes my face feel hot. "I take harassment from the press very seriously, Ms. Patel—Nadia. Thank you for bringing this to my attention."

"She's waiting in my office," Nadia says. "And is happy to cooperate fully. Will you be able to deal with the journalist on our behalf?"

"It would be my pleasure."

THERE are two cafés in Ashburton, and I didn't pay any attention to either of them when we drove through it earlier on the way to the cottage in which Theo died. I'm sitting in the one that serves real coffee made from ground beans rather than a bunch of chemicals mixed with caffeine and water. It's five times the price, but it's worth it. The man behind the counter smiled at me when I insisted upon a cup of the real stuff, giving me that gentle nod that people share when they meet another person who understands this need for real things.

"Those are homemade," he says proudly as he brings a small plate of biscuits over with my cup. "I baked them this morning. Free to customers who order the proper coffee."

I thank him as a woman sitting at the table next to mine sniffs. "No one can tell the difference, not really," she announces to anyone who cares to listen. The café owner rolls his eyes but doesn't challenge her. "Waste of money if you ask me."

I've learned not to reply in these situations. It's never really about the taste; it's about the perception of wealth, and anything to do with that makes people twitchy about class. Even though this country is part of Norope now, even though England exists only as a name and the borders are essentially meaningless between it and Norway, Sweden and the rest, the specter of class still haunts the British-island psyche. There may not be lords anymore, but there's still hierarchy. She probably thinks I'm on a pay grade far higher than hers, earning more than I should and showing it off. With both of our profiles set to private, there's only the purchase of this coffee for her to form her opinion of me. My suit is as generic as they come, my hairstyle functional rather than fashionable, my shoes clean and nondescript. She has no idea that I'm a smartly dressed slave and nothing more.

She's looking at me, perhaps hoping I'll argue. I turn away from her and consult the map Tia has readied for my perusal as she strikes up a conversation with the café owner about what will be found in the capsule. She speaks with the authority of the ignorant, churning out the same old shit that's been filling the feeds. To my disbelief, the owner engages with her, evidently just as excited about what will be found inside. Safe in my highly filtered bubble, immersed in the case, I'd forgotten the depth of the fervor about its opening.

I tune them out as best I can, focusing on the map instead. The other coffee shop is only fifty meters away from the café I'm in, and seated inside it is a recently promoted trainee chef called Sondra who decided her job was more valuable to her than the reward offered by the journalist we're both waiting for. Nadia Patel has the most loyal staff I've ever seen. I'm sure Sondra will be rewarded, but whether that's enough to keep her calm while she waits in the private room upstairs, alone, is anyone's guess. She wanted to insist on meeting in the café downstairs, but I pointed out to her that a journalist trying to buy information is unlikely to do that in a place where the conversation could be recorded by a dozen other patrons. "Go along with whatever ze suggests," I said to her. "Meeting in the room ze hired isn't an issue because you won't be alone. I'll be watching; I'll be thirty seconds away, okay?" The poor kid looked like she was going to be sick.

On the map, a small red dot moves down the high street toward the other café. It represents pings sent to the cloud via Naal Delaney's chip, the journalist who presumably thought it was a good idea to wheedle information out of the hotel staff when I failed to respond to any of the emails ze sent over the past six days.

Delaney knows that anything to do with the Moor Hotel and what may have happened inside it is off-limits to journalists. There's an automated message that will alert hir chip within a hundred-meter radius of the hotel, and it pops up with any related search. In attempting to bribe an employee, Delaney is at best breaching good-practice guidelines (only if their conversation is about anything other than the murder) and at worst committing a criminal offense. I often expect the worst. This is one of the rare times when I'm hoping for it.

The red dot pauses outside the other café and then goes inside.

Are you prepared to record your conversation and submit the live feed to the MoJ for consideration? I text Sondra.

Yes. I don't want to lose my job.

You won't. Sit tight, I'll be there in a couple of minutes. Find out what ze wants to know and what you would get for it.

K

I need to give Delaney time to proposition the girl explicitly before I can go in and throw my weight around. Someone else at the hotel must have revealed something to make ze so keen to find out more information—Delaney wanted to speak to me about being in Devon after all—and Nadia wants me to find out who that loose-tongued employee was. It's just one of several questions I plan to ask.

The coffee is smooth and rich, on a par with what the hotel serves. Tia deduces a pleasure rating from my reaction and gives me a notification informing me that, using one of my MoJ-approved online identities, she has rated the café on my behalf with five stars and left a comment about how good the real coffee is. I hate that instant-feedback shit—that's why I've handed it over to Tia to handle when lots of people still do it by hand—but it means a lot to little places like this. The man behind the counter starts humming a cheerful tune and I have the suspicion Tia just made his day.

Tia flashes up a notification that the live feed from my spy in the other café is available to watch. I lean back in the chair, savoring the warmth from the cup cradled in my hands and the aroma wafting up from it. I select the link.

The room in which Sondra waits is for private parties. There's a food and drink printer in the corner and chairs stacked along one wall. The wood paneling isn't good enough to give it class and the beige carpet and brown wallpaper aren't nice enough to give the place warmth. There's an old-fashioned hatch in the wall with presumably a kitchen on the other side of it, a leftover from the days when parties would have needed a catering space before people could just print whatever they like. Maybe the café owners are hoping that one day that hatch will be classed as a quaint vintage feature.

Sondra stops looking around the room, having been unable to find anything interesting to focus on, and instead looks down at the liquid in her mug trying to pass itself off as tea. She's seated at the only table in the room and another chair has already been set out for Delaney. She swiftly looks up toward the door at the sound of footsteps approaching it. The doorknob turns and then the feed goes down.

19

TIA GIVES A status update, telling me the live feed was cut off at the source and that it's trying to reestablish contact. The little red dot has disappeared from the map too.

Was permission withdrawn?

No. Data cut off at source.

Fuck.

I abandon the rest of the coffee and run out, crossing the street to sprint to the other place. I should have expected this. I've grown complacent, having Tia; I should have guessed that the journo would have some sort of privacy tech and that Sondra's APA wouldn't have been able to do anything about it. But this is more than that: from the way the feed just cut, it suggests Delaney didn't ask permission to interfere with Sondra's chip. Regardless of what ze says to her about information on the hotel and the police, I can see another case building, one involving illegal overriding of permissions and data-upload prevention.

As I push past a man walking his dog and somehow taking up most of the pavement in the process, I get Tia to contact the owner of the second café, a standard warning that I'm about to enter the premises, as I believe a crime is in progress, and that they are not to interfere in any way nor notify any of the patrons. The days of flashing an ID card are long gone.

The café is fairly busy, much more so than the one I was just in, with a woman behind the counter staring at me, pale faced and shaking.

"I'm going upstairs," I say to her. "Don't let anyone else go up there. Is there a kitchen next to the private-hire room?"

She nods. "I didn't know anything was—"

I'm already heading for the stairs at the back of the room, my profile still set to private, leaving Tia to gather the standard commitment allowing anything discovered on the premises to be recorded and potentially reviewed by the MoJ, including the exchange I just had with her. By the time I'm halfway up the stairs, the owner has granted all permissions and added a personal note stating she'll do anything to help.

I pause to take off my shoes and carry them up the rest of the stairs with me. The door to the private room is shut, as expected, and I see another door to the right, farther along the landing. The air is stale and laced with a musky perfume. There's a cord with a Staff Only sign hanging from it strung across the landing, which I step over as silently as I can. The carpet out here looks new and I wonder if the floorboards have just been renovated, as, mercifully, not one of them squeaks. I can hear a conversation taking place but not clearly enough, and I daren't go right up to the door and press my ear against it. I need to hear hir offer Sondra the bribe, just to really make sure ze is screwed.

The door to the kitchen creaks quietly as I open it, so I make a gap just big enough for me to slip inside and leave it ajar behind me. It's a small kitchen containing a sink, ancient microwave with a film of dust on it and a kettle that isn't even plugged in. Boxes of protein tubes, vegetable oil and chemicals for the food-and-drink printer are stacked high and I have to squeeze past them to get to the hatch. I manage to make it to a cramped nook with just the thin wooden hatch doors between me and what I hope is a crime in progress. The voices are easier to hear now, Sondra's high and reedy with stress, Delaney's reminiscent of a male contralto and pleasant to listen to. It sounds like Sondra is telling hir about what she does in the kitchen at the hotel. At least she's remembered my instructions to answer any questions about her job that she would feel happy talking to anyone about. I had a feeling the journo would start gently, not going straight into the deal without trying to put her at ease and taking the opportunity to gather any background too.

"There aren't many places that give you the chance to learn that kind of stuff," Sondra is saying.

"It's nice to see someone passionate about their work."

I start recording, wishing I could add a visual to it more useful than a glorified storage cupboard, but it'll have to do. A message pops up from Tia.

Unable to record. Running diagnostics. Diagnostics inconclusive. Unable to connect to cloud for further guidance.

Shit. Whatever Delaney is using has an area effect, something good enough to bugger Tia up, which is worrying.

"I'm so glad you decided to meet me," Delaney says, and I focus back on the conversation.

"You said it would be worth it."

"Do you play games, Sondra?"

Sondra hesitates. "What kind of games?"

"RPGs? MM mersives? Or do you love solo shooters?"

"Oh! Yeah, course I do. I like racing games, not shooters. What's that got to do with this?"

"Don't be so nervous! You've gone so red!"

"My boss . . ."

A chair creaks and Delaney lowers hir voice. "Don't worry about that now. She isn't here. If you tell me what's been going on at the hotel—why the police are there and if it has something to do with one of your . . . high-profile guests—I'll give you a dedicated server space that will be yours for the rest of your life. Full privacy, no ads, any game you want."

The hairs on the back of my neck prickle. I've heard that bribe before.

There's a long pause. Sondra is probably wondering why I haven't sent any messages since Delaney arrived and doesn't know how to respond. I doubt her chip even knows it's been cut off.

"Haven't you got to say anything about my offer?"

"I need to think about it. I feel a bit sick. I've never done anything like this before."

"There's no way anyone will find out it came from you," Delaney says. "I just need to know if something has happened to Alejandro Casales."

"Um . . . who?"

Her ignorance isn't convincing. I make my way back to the kitchen door.

"You know who he is. Look, as soon as the police leave it'll be all over the streams. Telling me a few hours before then doesn't make any difference to anyone else. You won't be breaking the law just by telling me if Casales is the reason the police are at the hotel. And you'll be able to play any racing games you like, ad free, years before you'd be able to afford that level of privacy."

I put on my shoes and without giving any fucks about being heard, leave the kitchen, jump over the cord and go into the private-hire room.

Sondra jumps out of her chair and hurries over to me. "Can I go now? I'm going to be sick."

I nod and she runs out of the room, leaving Delaney in the second chair. I shut the door behind me and go and take Sondra's place.

Delaney has shoulder-length brown hair, large brown eyes made striking with a hint of makeup and high cheekbones. There's a dusting of stubble on hir chin and a thin sheen of sweat erupting on hir forehead. "SDCI Moreno, I presume."

"Whatever you're running to block recording, you need to turn it off."

"They said you were good. I didn't realize how good." Ze seems preternaturally calm.

"Stop fucking with me and turn it off, or I will haul you in to the MoJ and they can crack your skull and pull your chip for me instead."

"I was hoping to have a conversation about Alejandro Casales with you. I would much rather have it in private. If you ever cared about him, you'll want it to be private too."

This is not how I expected it to go and it gives me pause. Most people caught using illegal privacy tech would be shivering with fear by this point. I fold my arms. "If you're thinking that I don't have any proof of your actions here today, you

should be aware that eyewitness testimony from an MoJ employee of my pay grade is held as fully admissible without any
corroborating recordings or—"

"I know the law. Sir. Give me five minutes, please. Then
you can do whatever you want to do with me and we'll leave
it in the lap of the lawyers."

Leaning back in my chair, I consider the options and decide
I have nothing to lose. I'm already skating on the edge of my
remit and, strictly speaking, should be reporting to Milsom.
But I don't want to be pulled back to London before I have a
chance to have a late lunch at the hotel. And I'm intrigued.
"All right. Five minutes."

"Is Alejandro Casales dead?"

Images hit me in staccato, of him writing the suicide note,
of him testing the knot, of those spasmodic jerks as life was
choked from his body. A surge of unfocused anger at being
reminded when I only came here to finally get one of these
fucking journos back for all the years of harassment makes me
want to punch hir. "I can't believe this, I—"

"Because if he is, it hasn't got anything to do with whatever
the Americans are saying. Or the Europeans, for that matter."

The anger subsides and with one deep breath it's back under
control again. "I'm listening."

"If I tell you this, I'm putting myself at huge personal risk.
I'd like some sort of guarantee this won't go further than us."

I shake my head. "You can't play the 'protect me for some
nebulous reason' card and the 'illegal privacy tech that protects
you right now' card in the same round, I'm afraid. That's not
how this game works."

Ze looks down at the table, hir lashes long and dark against
hir cheeks. "I don't think you're involved. I can't find any other

connection between him and you apart from when you were a child at the Circle. But the Ministry of Justice brought you in specifically, so there might be something I've missed."

"Oh for the sake of fuck, Delaney. I haven't got all day."

"Alejandro Casales didn't come to Norope to schmooze wealthy nutjobs into donating their money to the Circle. I'll tell you why he went to London specifically, if you agree to overlook what happened here today."

I laugh without mirth. "You are fucking joking. You know, I think it'll just be easier to deliver you to the MoJ, get them to extract the data while they're investigating that tech of yours. You'll lose your journalism license, of course, and get busted down about twenty pay grades, but maybe you'll be able to find a job shoveling sh—"

"Casales paid five hundred thousand pounds to a criminal organization I've been investigating for the last year to get illegally chipped. That's what he was doing in London."

I am reduced to staring at hir. It's such an outlandish thing to claim, such a ridiculous thing to say about Alejandro that all I can think is that it's true. Delaney certainly believes it, and there are a million better lies to tell about a man who thought personal chips were the worst invention since the atom bomb.

And then I remember what Selina said about him once he returned from London. How distant he was. That he complained of headaches. It's a common side effect in those chipped late. Too much concentration to cope with in the early days. I experienced it myself—I should have recognized it! It just never even occurred to me that he could be chipped. That was sloppy.

"That criminal organization has ties to someone very high up in the Ministry of Justice," Delaney continues. "That's why I'm nervous about telling you. But if you're as clean as your professional record suggests, I would keep this information out of your case file."

"That's why you wanted to speak to me about Casales?"

Ze nods. "I wanted to see if there was anything you could tell me about the Circle to explain why he'd do this. I don't know how he got in touch with the crim-org or how he even knew they existed."

"I haven't been a member of the Circle for more than twenty years."

"Yes, true. But you're the only person who's managed to leave it in that time too." Hir eyes look back up at me and the desire to ask more questions about me plays across hir face before ze straightens up, refocusing. "Have the Americans killed him?"

"I can't discuss the details of this case."

"But he's dead, isn't he?"

I give the slightest nod. "Why do you think the Americans would want him dead?"

"He fell out with them. With the parent gov-corp, this is. He wasn't getting on too well with Europe either. That's why he had to go to London. The crim-org he paid is one of the very few that have no ties outside of Norope."

"I want some names."

"I can't do that."

"Seriously, don't fuck with me on this."

Ze laughs. "No, really, I'm working for someone on a far higher pay grade than your commissioner, and they won't appreciate the time and paperwork involved with telling the Ministry to fuck off out of this. Casales is just one of hundreds who've bought this crim-org's services. I know that they definitely aren't the ones who killed him."

"So this was just a loose end for you?"

"Sort of. The day after they chipped him, the place that did it was torched and the one who chipped Casales was killed. Needless to say the data trail was wiped clean too."

"And you think it was the Americans who did that?"

"I know it was. They sent one of their best to tail him. She gets the job done."

I wonder if he means the woman I saw in the spy-cam footage. "Short woman, very petite?"

Ze nods. "So she did it?" Ze looks away, shaking hir head. "What a waste. Will you be going to the States to pursue this?" Before I have a chance to answer, ze holds up a hand. "No, forget I asked that. You can't talk about the case and, besides, what's the point? If it goes that high Stateside it's case closed, isn't it? Fuck."

It feels like ze is ten steps ahead in a thread of this investigation that I haven't even had a chance to start yet. And I'm never going to get to start it. But the Americans didn't kill Alejandro. He did it himself.

"Do you know why Alejandro and the US parent gov-corp fell out?"

Delaney shakes hir head. "I would dearly love to. All I know is that the Europeans were hoping to take advantage of it. They were courting him at the Moor Hotel—you must know about that."

Not as much as you do, I think. Time to blag. "We know about the Gabor connection too."

Delaney's upper lip curls. "That toad has his fat fingers in far too many pies, particularly European ones. If it wasn't for his bit of fluff, he'd live over there—I'm sure of it. No wonder the Americans killed Casales. Better than him defecting to Europe and getting into bed with Gabor."

It feels like I'm sitting on top of an iceberg, having sketched out the top and pretty damn proud of myself for managing to draw a hidden crevasse or two, when all along there's far, far more hidden beneath the waterline.

"This illegal chipping operation," I say, resting my elbows on the table. "Do they provide cloud storage too?"

Delaney nods. "Of course. They hack your transaction history to make it look like you're having a great time in London while you're having the op, and once it's done they give you cloud storage and however many online pseudonyms you're willing to pay for. It's a great service, if you don't mind funding worse crimes and being vulnerable to their hacks, that is."

"I'd be willing to overlook today if you gave me a lead to where their cloud servers are based."

"If you're looking for Alejandro's data, don't bother. The server was in the building the Yanks torched."

I frown. I know enough to never take journalists at their word. Does ze have access to it? But if that's the case, why sniff around down in Devon when the answers would be in his data anyway?

"How long ago did the arson take place?"

"It was Sunday afternoon. You can check with the local police. It was a warehouse in Wandsworth. The official line is that it was an illegal porn company making hardcore mersives involving some dodgy stuff. That way it's perfectly reasonable that there won't be gigs of online complaints about loss of service. No one would admit to losing access to *Sexy Goat Farm Three* or whatever."

If ze is telling the truth and Alejandro did get chipped, whatever he uploaded to the cloud has to be out there somewhere, even if the server running his cloud storage was destroyed. No one runs cloud storage off just one hardware network.

"I need some names, Mir Delaney."

"I'm sorry, I can't. But how about this: you forget about today, and then I'll owe you one."

I arch my eyebrow into as sardonic a statement as possible.

"Believe me," Delaney says with a wide smile that reveals even, white teeth. "When you're elbow deep in an investigation that's going to flick the balls of America's best assassin, the European oligarchs, Gabor and potentially Norope's most dangerous crim-org, you may well need to call in this favor."

If hir boss is higher than the commissioner, that may well be true. I have the sneaking suspicion the privacy tech ze is using may be something known to higher-ups who are turning a blind eye. "Tell me which member of staff told you something was going on at the hotel and you've got a deal."

Delaney laughs. "A contact overheard a conversation between two local bobbies having a cuppa downstairs a couple of days ago. Tell Nadia Patel that her little empire remains intact."

I stand. "All right. It's a deal."

Delaney flops back in the chair with relief as I head for the door. "Oh, Mr. Moreno, there is one question I'd like to ask you."

If you ask me what it feels like to be left behind by Atlas, I'll fucking bust your ass, I think as I turn to face hir.

"Is the food at the Moor Hotel as good as they say it is?"

"Better," I say, and leave. Once I've reassured the café owner and gone outside, I ping Dee. I feel bad that I never got round to messaging her before I need her. I expect her to ignore me, but she responds straightaway.

Carl! Am I forgiven?

If you tell me about the journo who set up that shit show you put me through.

A pause. You should've said yes.

Dee, seriously, I need to know right now.

Some neuter called Naal Delaney.

And when did ze get in touch with you?

The day before our last game session together. It wasn't
some epic conspiracy. Ze sent me a message, totally out of
the blue. We had a coffee together. I only agreed to meet hir
because I thought ze wanted to talk about this new show
they're launching on the network, and I realized, like, five
minutes in that I was so totally fucking wrong. When I
started to leave ze said I could have this server space if I
pulled you into a game and got you to agree to an interview.
I said you'd never agree but ze said I'd have the space for a
year just for trying.

You sold me out.

It was a really shitty thing to do, I know. I just . . . I really
wanted my own space. No one watching. You know what
that's like, Carl. Look, if I could go back to a save point and
play it through again, I'd do it totally differently.

Oh, really?

Yeah. On a second play through I'd have told you about it
straight up, and cooked something up with you so you'd
agree to the interview and just give him a gig of shit. Then
we'd both have the server space and zero guilt.

I can't help but smile at that. I should have listened to her instead of treating her like the rest of the assholes. She's not like them. Fuck knows where I'd be without her. K, Dee. Next time I have a free hour I'll ping you and we'll go back to Mars.

Fuck, yeah! Later K

I've always told myself I don't need anyone else and yet something inside me eases. That bond between us means more to me than . . . than anything else I can think of. And now I can trust her again, it's like I have a safety net once more, or perhaps a touchstone, freeing me up fully to pursue the case.

My stomach rumbles as I reach the car. For someone prepared to offer that information, Delaney didn't ask many questions. I get inside, glad for the silence and solitude but still feeling like there is far more here than I'm aware of.

Worried the gap in the constant background recording the MoJ expects from Tia will raise difficult questions, I check to see if there's any escalation from the MoJ AI, only to find that Tia didn't even report it. According to the logs, there was no interruption, as if I'd stayed in that pokey kitchen for the duration of the conversation and then left. JeeMuh. Whatever Delaney uses is better than any other illegal blocking software I know of. Ze could have killed me and nothing would have been flagged up until I didn't report in.

Was Alejandro really chipped? I put in a call to Linda, hoping she won't mind being disturbed at the lab. She accepts voice contact straightaway.

"I've finished the PM on Casales," she says. "I was just starting on Buckingham. Did you need something?"

"I was wondering if Casales was chipped."

"No sign of that," she says cheerily. "Not a sausage. Why'd you ask? I thought his cult was famously antitech?"

"Just checking," I say, and start the car. It's only when I'm two miles out of town that I remember I was supposed to take Sondra back to the hotel with me.

20

BY THE TIME I get back to the hotel I've chosen what I'll have for a lunch so late, it's barely worthy of the name. Reviewing the menu was far more enjoyable than enduring Sondra's sulking. I don't know whether she's upset that I had to go back to get her, or that she lost out on a dedicated gaming space. I don't particularly care. The job was done and I say as much to Nadia when I deliver Sondra to her office. I leave them to whatever conversation they need to have and put in the food order at reception on the way up to my room, keeping my head down and eyes fixed on where I'm going so no one else has a chance to initiate a casual conversation. I look at the dark circles beneath my eyes in the mirrored elevator interior and wonder if I'll be sleeping in London tonight.

The top floor is silent with the SOCO team gone and the police officer who was guarding the Diamond Suite now reassigned. I pause, feeling a short-lived temptation to go back to the suite. Unable to think of a decent reason why—knowing that wallowing in grief is far from decent—I carry on to my room.

I'm filled with the need to occupy myself to stop thinking about Alejandro's last act. I check my messages, deleting all of the ones in my public in-box without reading them and studiously avoiding any news feeds, to protect my blood pressure after seeing just the top trending headline. Someone in Korea is claiming that the famous Pathfinder was his half sister and that she told him the contents of the capsule before she left Earth. Fresh meat for the media vultures to feast upon, and another reason to avoid the mainstream for as long as I can.

My MoJ in-box has two messages of note: Selina Klein is on her way to Heathrow, Collindale escorting her, and the data team have finished reviewing the hotel and cottage local-node hard drives.

I shrug off my jacket, pull off my shoes and flop onto the bed. I'm less interested in the hotel-cam data now that I know what happened, but I check that it fits with what I'll be putting in the report nonetheless. The notes from the data specialist make interesting reading: original data fully destroyed both locally and on the cloud, which is rarely achieved by the average hacker, and new data expertly inserted to make the hotel corridor look inactive after Selina and Alejandro went to their room. Interestingly, the team also uncovered evidence that data being uploaded to the cloud was being monitored by clandestine software added on the same day Arlington arrived at the hotel, software with a "distinctly American signature," notes the report.

A thrill pulses through my chest. If Alejandro was chipped, he would be uploading to the illegal cloud space via the local node, and perhaps Arlington was monitoring what he sent. If he uploaded something suggesting he was about to kill himself and she saw that, it would explain why she knew he had just hanged himself. She certainly couldn't have known about Buckingham's spy-cam footage, otherwise she would have destroyed that data too.

No. Linda said there was no sign of Alejandro being chipped. Either Delaney was wrong about what Alejandro paid that crim-org for, or ze was lying. Why lie about that though? Alejandro's final words would make far more sense if he had been chipped; he could have been instructing his APA to send a letter digitally.

This hint of a greater puzzle than the one I have solved still irritates me. I feel like I stood back from the table for a moment, seeing the pieces I'd fit together with a short-lived pride, only for Delaney to come along and tell me it's only one corner of the picture. I force myself to remember that either way, it hardly matters in terms of my official investigation. It's time to write the report.

With my meal due to arrive any minute, I sort through my notes rather than getting deep into the writing. Just as I'm about to review the data from the cottage's hard drive a request for voice contact comes in from fucking Stefan Gabor, of all people. I reject the call, with no small amount of satisfaction, and go back to the data report.

Again, the cam footage has been tampered with and it's the same digital signature as that of the hotel. It takes only a few minutes to review Arlington's registered-location pings at the hotel, cross-reference them with the public nodes that run along the Ashburton high street and figure out that while she hacked the hotel node to make it look like she was in her room the whole day after Buckingham checked out, she was actually trailing him to the cottage. Maybe she didn't know about the public nodes—they don't have that system in the States—or maybe she just didn't care once she knew the lawyers were stalling everything long enough for her to do whatever she did and get out of the country.

I pull up the visa transaction data for her trip and see that she bought a bottle of that same brand of whisky found with Buckingham at Heathrow on the day she arrived. I also note the purchase of a packet of ibuprofen and paracetamol and smirk. All too easy to find the needle when you know exactly where to look in the haystack. I make a note of the connection in the case file and speculate that she went to the cottage to confront Buckingham, who may not have needed much persuasion to kill himself. Maybe she held a gun on him. Again, tying the loose end gives no real satisfaction. The only part of the puzzle left—why Alejandro killed himself—is the one I'll have to fight to put together.

My food arrives but before I remove the shining metal dome from the tray, I let Tia pass on the voice mail just left by Gabor.

"My husband tells me you still haven't interviewed him. This is unacceptable. It's almost the end of the working day and I do not want to be told that you didn't get round to him today. Make this your priority, as he is required in London."

"Overprivileged asshole," I mutter to myself. Interviewing the trophy husband had slipped my mind; once I had Buckingham's spy-cam footage it was clear the younger Gabor had nothing to do with it after all. He probably insisted on them staying at the same hotel in the hope of being able to meet the object of his obsession.

"Send a message back to Stefan Gabor," I say to Tia as I shake out the linen napkin and lay it across my lap. "The investigation is currently at a critical phase and the interview with his husband will take place as soon as it is convenient for me."

"Should I apply courtesy protocols to the message?"

"No. Just send that." Fuckers like him don't deserve courtesy.

They never give it to anyone else so why should he get it back? I smile at the thought of his jowls turning red as he reads my slap-down. I'll interview Travis Gabor after I've drafted the main body of my report. I doubt anything he says will merit inclusion in the final draft.

My smile widens when I lift the metal dome and the smell of the pork belly wafts up. I'm able to gaze at it for a couple of seconds before the cutlery is in my hands. The pork is so tender and succulent that I have to close my eyes to devote my full attention to it. Oh God, if only there could be some sort of development that would persuade Milsom to give me another night in this place.

I lick the plate clean, and then out of nowhere I am crying at the thought of Alejandro never being able to experience any sort of pleasure again. I set the plate down and rub my eyes, trying to push the grief back in its box. I'm just tired—that's all. A good night's sleep and I'll be able to handle this better.

The twilight is deepening into darkness outside and I dread the thought of having to leave the warmth of the hotel to return to London. I have three and a half hours left and I need to get back to the report, but instead I start on the strawberry pavlova I ordered for dessert. Surely if the report takes a couple of hours I'll be able to have dinner here before I leave?

A low rumble coming down the road drags my focus from the meringue and cream (real fucking cream!) and I go to the window. A single bright light pierces the gloom, traveling the wooded road up to the hotel. A vintage motorcycle. I spoon the last mouthfuls into my mouth as the rider parks, glittering red boots sparkling with the light that spills from the lobby. Linda. I lick the small plate clean as she pulls off her helmet, revealing her spiked hair, and slip my shoes back on as she heads for the door into the hotel.

She's at the reception desk when the elevator doors open onto the lobby and she waves with a broad, warm smile. She's carrying a small plastic box and holds it out to me as she approaches. "You heard the bike?"

I nod and take the box. "What brings you here?"

She shrugs. "Well, I finished the second PM and I was on my way to visit my niece and it's not too far from here, so I thought I'd drop off the spare gingerbread." When I look down at it, she adds, "For you to enjoy in a quiet moment. I can only imagine how tough today has been."

"Thanks."

"My niece is actually my grandniece, but that just makes me feel so bloody ancient. She's adorable. We write silly little stories for each other."

I blink at her. "Oh. That's . . . nice." I can only imagine how awkward my smile has become. Is this some sort of weird, clumsy pickup attempt? "You finished that second PM quickly."

A slight flush rises in her cheeks. "It was very straightforward. Suicide, from the pills and booze, as we thought. I've put the reports in the case file. Nothing of note, really." She looks at the box in my hands for a long moment and then back at my face again. "Well, it was nice to meet you, Mr. Fancy London Pants. Sure you don't want a spin on the bike before I go?"

I pat the air with my free hand. "No, no, you go on ahead without me. And thanks, Linda, for this too." I hold up the box.

She grins. "My pleasure," she says, and puts the helmet back on. "Don't let that get stale," she says through the visor, pointing a gloved finger at the gingerbread.

I wave her off from the doors and go back to the elevator. Just as I'm about to press the button to call it, a text message arrives from Milsom and I almost drop the gingerbread. My heart hammers as I open the message, as if she knows I've been dragging my heels and just ordered a meal that costs more than a week's allocation.

Interview Travis Gabor NOW and eliminate him from the investigation as soon as you can. I've just had his husband mouthing off at me and I don't want to hear that man's voice again.

I allow myself a sigh, a mixture of fatigue and relief, and head back to the reception desk. Magill, the man I interviewed earlier, smiles at me. "Is Travis Gabor in the hotel at the moment?"

"I know he went out for a walk earlier, but he may have returned while I was on my break." He consults a screen below the desk's countertop—all part of the hotel's vintage charm, I suppose—and nods. "He ordered a meal from his room fifteen minutes ago, sir."

"Which number is it?"

"Number six on the second floor, sir. Would you like me to call his room?"

"No, it's fine. He's expecting me."

A tray is resting on one of the hotel trolleys just to the right of the door to room six. Another very late lunch, probably because he was out walking. When I met him in the restaurant I wouldn't have pegged him as the sort of person to don walking boots and go trudging about the bleak countryside in November. I knock on the door and lift the largest of the two silver domes in the hopes of deducing what he ordered.

I find a full plate, the steak untouched and tragically cold. It's then that I see the cork still firmly in the neck of the champagne bottle.

This time I hammer on the door. "Mr. Gabor?" I call through the wood.

No reply.

And then I see him, clear in my mind, hanging from the light fixture, just like the man he was stalking. That was why he was so keen to be left behind by his husband, a man he was clearly afraid of—because he planned to kill himself.

"Tia, open the door to room six, second floor. Justification: suspected suicide."

The lock clunks and I push open the door. There is no body swinging from the light and I release the breath getting stale in my lungs. Stepping inside, I pull the door closed behind me.

"Mr. Gabor?"

There's no one here. No one alive, anyway. I cross the room to the en-suite and find that empty too. An assortment of hair-product bottles are scattered on the marble shelf next to the sink, a couple on the floor. Has this place been turned over?

I go back into the main room. The bed is unmade and a pair of socks and underpants lie on the floor beside it. A compact leather-covered box for carrying jewelry when traveling lies on the dressing table. I go over and open it. It's filled with cuff links studded with precious stones and a limited-edition Cartier watch. Flipping it over, I see it's been engraved. "My darling. For all time. S." I shiver and close the box.

A clothes hanger is lying on the floor next to the wardrobe and one of the doors hasn't been closed properly. Expecting a body, I open it carefully with the tip of my thumbnail, only to find a few pairs of shoes, a few shirts and a pair of trousers that's been mostly pulled off the hanger and left dangling by a belt loop. I breathe out heavily. I need to get a grip on myself.

Two heavy-duty cases are stacked on a luggage rack in the corner, and from the weight of them, they're empty. I see a slipper poking out from beneath a corner of the sheet hanging down from the bed and search for the other but it's nowhere to be found. When I move the bedding to search under the bed, I reveal a slab of black plasglass lying next to one of the pillows, presumably the device Travis was using to connect to the Internet in the absence of his chip.

Leaving it untouched, I go back to the bathroom. There's no sign of a toothbrush, paste or shaving equipment and no wash bag tucked into the corner anywhere. A gentle melody from the bedroom draws me back to the bed to see a call coming in from the husband. I stay a few paces away, repulsed by the picture of Stefan Gabor, topless and licking his lips.

When the music stops I assume Stefan has given up and cut the call, but then I see a notification flash up in a dialog box, too fast for me to read it, and then I hear Travis.

"Hello, darling."

"Has that useless man interviewed you yet, or do I need to call Barbara again?" So Stefan really is on first-name terms with the commissioner.

"He said it would be soon," Travis replies, and I call up my v-keyboard.

Tia, intercept the call coming into Travis's slab. Where is Travis speaking from?

Only one incoming call detected through the local node, from Stefan Gabor, Tia reports. I cannot identify his location without explicit permission via his lawyer. Would you like me to request permission?

No. Travis is routing his call through the slab; track where *his* call is coming in from.

"It had better be soon." Stefan's voice is more a growl. "I'm sending the car down for you, Boo. I need your arse in London. I'm hungry."

Travis Gabor's responses to the incoming call are generated by the Artificial Personal Assistant. Presumably programmed in advance by Travis to trick his husband into thinking he's still in the hotel.

"There are a thousand restaurants in London, Boo Boo," the fake Travis replies.

"I'm not hungry for food," Stefan says. "I miss you."

"I miss you too, darling. I'll see you soon. Don't worry about a thing."

"The car will be there in two hours," Stefan says. "In four and a half I want you on the bed in Mayfair, naked."

"Anything you want, master."

There's a sigh, heavy with lust, and the call ends, much to my relief.

"Tia, review the cam footage from the second floor of the hotel and the lobby for the last four hours. Isolate any footage of Travis Gabor."

I sit on the edge of the bed, smiling to myself. So Travis found a way to leave his odious husband. That was the only reason he asked to be interviewed and why he specified it should be the last one I did, to give him time to escape. He must have been planning it for months, perhaps even searching for Alejandro so much to lead his husband to think he'd run off to the Circle when he started investigating his disappearance. Clever. I underestimated him.

Tia shows me footage of Travis leaving his room more than two hours ago with a sleek backpack and stout boots on his feet instead of those ridiculous shoes he was wearing in the restaurant this morning. I watch him go into the lift and then the lobby's cam picks him up leaving the elevator. He pauses to have a brief conversation in the corner of the lobby with Collindale, of all people, and then he leaves after they shake hands. It's the last time he was in the hotel. Magill simply assumed, thanks to the preplanned meal order, that Travis had returned from his walk when he was away from the reception desk.

Why Collindale? The American liaison went out of his way to try to get me to investigate the Gabors—no, Stefan in particular—so what was that exchange about in the lobby?

"Tia, have flights been arranged for Selina Klein to return to the States today?"

"Yes."

I double-check her status via the MoJ case file and see that she was officially transferred into the care of Collindale on behalf of the North American gov-corp, to be escorted back to the Circle.

"Did Collindale sign off on the flight booking?"

"Yes."

"And how many people is he traveling with?"

"Two. Selina Klein and John B. Smith."

I laugh out loud. John B. Smith is one of the pseudonyms agreed in the Religious Freedom treaty with the States to allow a citizen of Norope to travel to North America without their real name entered in the flight manifest, should it be deemed necessary in the protection of their right to religious freedom. Travis must have made a deal with Collindale to get him out of the country without his husband finding out.

"Is there any debt recorded against Travis Gabor?"

"None."

So that "master" mentioned in the fake conversation was a just a sexual thing. I recall the way Stefan grabbed his husband in the restaurant, the desperation in Travis's eyes.

"When does their flight leave?"

"In two hours."

So Travis is still in the country. I see no reason to report his absence; he's been ruled out of the investigation already. There's no debt to any corporation filed against him, so this is a purely civil matter that's outside of my remit. By the time his husband's car arrives to pick him up, he'll be on a plane to America and then God knows where. "Good luck, Travis," I say, and leave his room as I found it.

21

A COUPLE OF hours later the report is filed and I'm back for a grilling in the virtual meeting room with the lawyers and reps.

"So it was suicide all along," says the representative for Europe.

"Yes, ma'am," I say.

"I'm not satisfied," she says. "You mentioned this woman, Arlington, in your final report. What was she doing in that room?"

After what Delaney told me, I was reluctant to include her, but I needed to present an undoctored version of the spy-cam footage. Now, seeing the look on the American lawyer's face, I regret the decision. "As I said, I think she . . ." I pause. "I'm not sure how, but I believe she knew that Alejandro had taken his own life and went there to do something, but was interrupted by Theo Buckingham."

"How did she know that he had hanged himself?"

"Does it matter?" says the American rep, this time alone,

as Collindale is now somewhere over the Atlantic. "We all saw the film. We read the pathologist's report and the forensics. He hanged himself and the case is over."

"That woman did something," the European persists, this time staring at the lawyer representing the Circle who has resorted to simply staring at the table to avoid all eye contact. "She clearly went over to—"

"As SDCI Moreno speculated, probably DNA theft, and that's hardly anything that can be prosecuted now." The American smiles at me as the Circle's lawyer remains deafeningly silent. "You did excellent work."

"Don't talk like this is all over," the woman from Norope speaks now. "I agree with my European colleague. The involvement of this woman who hacked the local node and—"

"I'd like to draw your attention to clause one forty-three, subsection B on page fifty-seven of the contract," he says, still smiling. "It states, very clearly, that the remit of the investigation is to identify the cause of death of Alejandro Casales, and should it prove to be murder, the identification and capture of the party or parties responsible. That has been successfully actioned. Theo Buckingham mutilated a dead body and subsequently committed suicide. Case closed. Would you like to discuss a new contract to deal with any further investigation into events tangential to these deaths?"

Both the European and Noropean representatives shake their heads, exchanging a look somewhere between frustration and defeat.

"Excellent. Well, I think that's everything, then." The American stands and extends a hand to Milsom. "May I commend you on your department's speed and efficiency. You said Moreno was one of the best and I would like it to be on record that I wholeheartedly agree."

"Thank you," Milsom says. She's scowling far less than when I last saw her.

"Thank *you*," says the Circle's lawyer, but she says it to me. I stare at her hand for a second and then lurch forward to shake it. "You're welcome to come to the memorial service for Alejandro Casales. Ms. Klein assured me that the other members of the Circle would be very happy to have you attend, and I could organize the visa very swiftly in these circumstances."

The American gov-corp lawyer glares at her and Milsom sees it too. "I'm afraid SDCI Moreno's skills are in great demand."

"Oh. Well, consider the offer still on the table if you can make it," says the Circle's lawyer, and heads for the door.

"There is just one more detail I'd like to draw everyone's attention to," says the American representative, having regained his composure, before the Circle lawyer can leave. "With regard to the final clause of the contract, which outlines press coverage, we have decided that it would be detrimental to the interests of the Circle to have suicide reported in relation to the death of Alejandro Casales. Therefore, the narrative agreed to with the Circle's representative—who, as you will note, has final sign-off on the press release regarding these unfortunate events—is that Theodore Buckingham committed the murder and subsequently committed suicide. I'm sure you'll agree that it's very close to the truth, and out of respect of the religious needs of the Circle, we feel it's the best way to go."

The narrative? The fucking *narrative*? I want to shout but everyone in the room is nodding in agreement.

"The Ministry of Justice will issue the agreed statement," Milsom says. "If you don't mind, we'll make the announcement to the press once the official release has been signed off by all parties and after the staff at the Moor Hotel have been fully briefed. I'll make sure our best press-liaison officer works with them."

No one objects. Milsom comes and stands next to me as the lawyers and representatives file out, the Noropean saying nothing about my work, as it's only what was expected of me anyway, and the European too angry with the American to make any positive comments. When the last one leaves Milsom shuts the door and turns to me.

"Well, case closed."

"Is it?"

She looks up at the ceiling. "Carlos—"

"Something else is going on here. They were right to pick that hole in my report. How did Arlington know Casales had just killed himself? It would only make sense if he were chipped but he wasn't, and that's just . . . It's just untidy. And there's the fact he committed suicide in the first place. Why? Why do that? What really happened in London to make Alejandro hang himself?"

"Carlos—"

"And did you see the way the American was just shutting it down from the moment the Q and A started? I bet he knows who Arlington is and doesn't want anyone to—"

"Moreno!" Milsom shouts, and I jump and stand straight and clasp my hands behind my back, mouth shut. "You need to walk away from this now. The case is closed. Why he committed suicide is irrelevant now." She must see how much that sticks in my craw, because she comes over and rests a hand on my shoulder. "You have to figure out a way to live without knowing why he did it, just like everyone else who knew him will. Your professional involvement is over."

I sag. Then I remember the invitation. "I wouldn't normally ask, boss, but I would like to take up the offer from the Circle's lawyer to attend the funeral." She pulls her hand away from my shoulder. "Would you give me permission to attend? Please?"

She looks at me for a long moment as she thinks it over.

"I'd like to see my father again," I add. "I didn't have the chance to make amends with Alejandro but I still have the chance with my father, if you'd just let me go and—"

"No. Permission denied."

My mouth drops open. "But—"

"Casales wasn't immediate family. Besides, there's no guarantee you'd get permission for that either. It's not in the interests of the MoJ to allow you to make a trip to the Circle."

"Please," I say one last time, trampling my pride under my own heels. "I've never asked for anything for myself. Not once in almost twenty years. Please let me see him."

"I said no, Moreno, and I don't want to hear another word about it. Ms. Patel has offered you a night at the hotel for free as a gesture of goodwill toward the MoJ. You're to return to London first thing tomorrow and report immediately to your case officer at MoJ HQ for a full debriefing and psychiatric assessment." She looks at me like I'm a car engine that's been making a strange noise. "You clearly need recalibration."

I open my eyes and look up at the inside of the bed's canopy. For the first time since the day I left the Circle, I want to go back there. I left thinking there had to be something better than being stuck in the middle of nowhere with a father who didn't want me, living a life so simple it made me want to burn everything down out of sheer boredom. I needed more than they could give me, and at the age of sixteen, the logical place to look for it was Out There, past the boundary. My sixteen-year-old self wouldn't understand that what I really needed could never be found anywhere but inside me. I'm still not even sure I believe that now. Sounds like the sort of bullshit my psych supervisor would say.

I want to see my father and talk to him as an adult, instead of the angry, fucked-up teenager I was back then. I'm still angry—if it weren't for him and Alejandro, I wouldn't be the property of the Ministry of Justice—but I feel like I need to try to get past that now. My life is what it is, and if my father dies before I can reconcile this rage into something . . . easier, I'll never heal. I tut and tuck my hands under my head, trying to relax. Reconciling my rage? That's definitely the kind of bullshit my psych supervisor would come up with.

Yet the pull back to the Circle remains. I want to say good-bye to Alejandro. Properly. As myself and not as someone investigating his death. And, if I am truthful with myself, I want to see if there is anything there to explain the suicide, no matter how unlikely that is. I think about what that fuck from the US gov-corp said about the narrative and wonder whether Selina will be told the truth. Probably not. And what use would it serve, anyway? He's dead. Theo wanted everyone to think it was murder. Perhaps, in the most shit way possible, everyone is going to make that last desire of his true.

Now Alejandro has left them all behind. I don't believe he's gone on to some other place, be it heaven or not, but the people at the Circle have been abandoned. Perhaps it will be easier for them to think he was taken from them, rather than his choice to leave them. Would I have found it easier if my mother had been slaughtered by a madman instead of choosing to get on Atlas and leaving me behind?

Yeah. Maybe I would.

No. I won't think about that. I'm not the man the press want me to be. I am not the victim here.

A notification pops up from Tia, informing me that there have been more than a million mentions of Alejandro Casales in the public news feeds and social streams in the last minute. A link invites me to explore but I dismiss the notification. So the press release has gone out. I just hope it will take the vultures a few hours to descend upon the hotel. No doubt they'll be whipping themselves up into a fervor about the timing of it all, so close to the capsule being opened. The conspiracy theorists are probably having a field day.

I consider going down to the bar. But with the embargo lifted, the current guests are just as likely to harass me for the gory details as any hacks would be. I'll spend the night up here, maybe order a couple more meals and desserts just to get the most out of this, and go back to London after a king's breakfast.

Sometimes I have as much as a week between cases. With less than a day between this one and the one before, I reckon Milsom won't begrudge me at least a day or two of downtime. Even the MoJ recognize the need to let their workhorses rest in the pasture once in a while. Otherwise we burn out, and that wouldn't be the most efficient use of an asset as expensive as me. With more than thirty years left on my contract, my debt must still be in the hundreds of thousands. Certainly at the inflated prices and levels of interest those bastard hothousers arranged. No. Don't think about it. As Dee always said, getting angry does nothing except waste *our* energy. It doesn't punish the ones who exploited us. The ones who did that to us are still exploiting homeless kids now and still making huge profits from shaping them into assets to order. My anger isn't going to do a fucking thing for any of them.

I roll onto my side, planning to get up and go for a walk before the press hounds start barking at the door. I feel the plastic box beneath my hip and remember the gingerbread.

"Lights, twenty percent," I say, realizing the room has slipped into the same dark as my mood. I sit up, pull the lid off the box and breathe in the scent of fresh ginger.

There's a note resting on top of the biscuits with a "C" written on it. I unfold it to find neat handwriting that slants to the right, as if the letters are leaning into a headwind and trying to reach the end of the line.

A story for you, it says at the top, and I wonder if she mixed up my box with the one intended for her niece. Does her name begin with a "C" too? I pluck out one of the biscuits and read on while I eat it.

> *Once upon a time there was a priest of a secret religion. He lived in a world where everyone had magic gems stitched into their heads that let them speak to each other and sometimes lots of people all at once. The priest didn't have one of the magic gems stitched into his head though, because he thought that talking to everyone else meant that you never listened to yourself anymore. He was so good at speaking without a magic gem, he persuaded others to have their gems taken out and to follow him wherever he went.*

I stop chewing as the sense that this is actually a story for me sends a cold, creeping shiver down my back.

> *With so many people following this priest, he became rich and powerful, and other kings and queens watched him very carefully. Then one day, the priest died very suddenly in a foreign kingdom, and the people there had to make sure they knew what had happened to him before he could be laid to rest. A medicine woman was brought in to read his body's final days, and she found that the*

priest had secretly sewn in a magic gem. Even though the gem itself was missing, she could see the stitching and the hole where it had been, even after someone else had tried to cover the hole and stitches with a spell. She was so shocked, she told the noble lady who owned the land about it right away.

"Linda, you are one sharp cookie," I mutter. The case was still open when she brought the gingerbread to me. She wrote this to convey meaning through metaphor, avoiding critical keywords so that my APA wouldn't detect any relationship between the content and the case.

Before the medicine woman had even finished preparing the priest for burial, powerful knights came and took the priest away and made the medicine woman promise to keep silent about the magic gem. Being a good and loyal citizen of the kingdom, she swore an oath and waved them good-bye from her door. She never told another soul about the secret gem sewn into the priest's head, and lived a long and happy life, riding her old horse and baking cakes for handsome young men who visited from the capital of the kingdom. The end.

I smile before the implications sink in. So Delaney wasn't lying and Alejandro did get himself chipped in London after all. If Linda was standing here right now, I'd kiss her. Instead, I finish the biscuit, put the letter back inside the box and snap the lid on tight.

After double-checking that the case status really is closed and that any keywords relating to Alejandro are no longer being automatically recorded and placed in the case file, I stand up and start to pace. Delaney said the server at the place where Alejandro got illegally chipped was destroyed in the fire—probably set by Arlington—and that Alejandro's data was lost with it. I didn't believe that at the time and I certainly don't believe that now.

"Tia, apparently there was a fire at a warehouse in Wandsworth last Sunday. Can you find anything on that?"

"There are several hundred mentions that fit your parameters in news feeds and one related case file currently open for an arson investigation."

"Can I access that file?"

"State your justification."

I scratch the stubble on my chin. "Possible connection to secondary criminal activity. Casual inquiry."

Tia provides a link to the file and I grin. No one is protecting this arson case—presumably to make it look as normal as possible. At my pay grade, and thanks to the bits and pieces murder inquiries always churn up, I have more freedom to poke about in other cases than many officers do. Listing it as a casual inquiry will enable me to look without copying any of the data to my personal MoJ files. If I want to do that, I'll have to involve Milsom and I don't want her to know about this. The moment she suspects I'm following up on anything to do with Alejandro, she'll roast my balls.

I stop pacing and focus on the contents of the file. Three people died in the fire, thanks to the external doors being locked before the fire was set. The fact that it hasn't been opened up to the murder team stinks, but with so many cases on at any one time, the odds are that no one will actually notice unless they are specifically looking. The arson specialist notes that the fire was started at about eight a.m., which is unusual—most arsonists like the cover of darkness—and even though it was a gloomy winter morning, there was still far more risk of being seen than most serial arsonists would like. The report states that no suspects were detected on any of the local public cams on the streets around the warehouse, but when I dig deeper I can't find any evidence of the footage being pulled together for review. It takes me only ten minutes to isolate a picture of a petite individual wearing a dark hat and black clothes approaching one of the windows of the warehouse, holding something that looks like a bottle with a rag stuffed into it. I would bet a month's allocation that it was Arlington.

I look up the details on the arson officer who wrote the report and find that he's been reassigned to another department and had his pay grade raised. There hasn't been any activity on the arson file since he submitted the report on initial findings. It's been left to languish until a standard data cleanup archives it under "dormant" and it's forgotten. Nicely done, dodgy high-up MoJ person, I think. It's the best way to hide data these days: right in the open.

Even though the local node in the building was destroyed, along with the server that probably supported Alejandro's illegal chip, I don't believe the data has been lost. Alejandro must have continued to use his chip when he returned to the hotel; it would explain the behavior that Klein described and would account for his last words as an instruction to his Artificial Personal Assistant to send that letter, whatever it was. If his cloud storage had been housed on the warehouse server alone (which is pretty bloody unlikely anyway) Alejandro wouldn't have been able to continue to use the chip without knowing something was wrong.

Crim-orgs that sell illegal chipping services are outside of my direct experience, but there's a wealth of information stored in the MoJ archives. And while my search will be registered along with the thousands of other searches made by MoJ staff and AIs every hour, I'm prepared to argue the toss if it comes up. I'm officially between cases, and in the past I've dug about the archives, looking up whatever has taken my fancy or plugging gaps left by hot-housing and my unconventional adolescence. This isn't unusual behavior for me, so it won't be flagged up.

Delaney clearly hasn't been doing hir homework—or didn't want to let on how much ze knew—but it rapidly becomes clear that a full illegal edentity provided by these services includes the provision of the full data backup, public in-box and basic digital rights that any legitimate chip provides by law. They have to; anything else and that kind of bizarre online activity would be picked up almost instantly by the MoJ bots that look for this kind of thing. So Alejandro's data is still out there somewhere. All I need to do to find it is isolate the false edentity.

The crim-orgs make use of the fact that even though the vast majority of people are chipped at age sixteen, sometimes things go wrong and people need a new chip, and in rare instances a new edentity. Whether they are victims of cybercrime, have been placed in a witness-protection program or have just paid a ton of money to wipe their online slate clean, there are ways to set up new edentities without any previous data being moved over.

"Tia, is the location of the origin server filed with the creation of new edentities?"

"No."

I look up, my eyes drifting toward the ceiling rose and then swiftly darting away. "How many new edentities were activated during the time period between Wednesday ten a.m. and Saturday morning ten a.m. last week?"

"Approximately three-point-two million."

"What the fuck? Oh, I mean registered to . . ." I pause. Where would his fake edentity be registered? Norope? London?

Somewhere completely different? With no way to know, that angle won't work either.

"No, I got it. Tia, identify all of the local nodes connected to the Internet within a kilometer radius of the Wandsworth warehouse fire that sent data last week on Saturday between nine a.m. and ten p.m."

"Eleven local nodes detected."

"Eliminate the public street nodes."

"Five remaining."

"Okay, out of those five, did any of them stop sending data after nine a.m. on the Sunday morning and remain silent since then?"

"Yes. One local node within the radius specified meets your parameters."

I get that thrill, right in my chest, when I know I'm onto something. "I want access to the data sent by that specific node to the Internet between noon on Tuesday and midnight last Saturday. Justification: possible connection to secondary criminal activity. Casual inquiry."

There's a pause, long enough for me to worry that someone at the MoJ is onto me; then Tia gives me a link and I realize the delay was simply finding data from that source that would have been sent to disparate locations in the cloud and pulling it into one virtual location for review. The data is always there. It's just a matter of knowing where to look.

I select the link. There's so much data it's overwhelming, represented as a list of files and numbers with time stamps that seems to go on forever. Time to start eliminating.

"Tia, move any data uploaded by edentities that have time stamps on the Tuesday into a separate temp folder called 'Staff.'" Alejandro was still in Devon, unchipped, so anything uploaded then would have been by the people who worked at the warehouse and who may have been connected to the crim-org.

About eighty percent of the data is moved out of the list. Good. Now I just need to narrow it down to a manageable number of edentities that could plausibly be Alejandro's. I think back to what Selina told me about his trip. She said he went up to London on Wednesday afternoon. Even if he went straight to the crim-org, it's unlikely he would have been chipped and online much before five p.m. that evening. I take a breath to start using that as a new parameter, but, of course, the crim who set up the identity could have done that anytime and simply transferred it to Alejandro once his chip was functional.

Shit.

A different approach is required. Maybe the sort of data uploaded within this twenty percent can lead me to his space on the cloud.

"Tia, isolate any data uploaded by edentities that came online from noon on Wednesday onward, and filter for pornographic-content tags. Remove any with those tags." I doubt very much that Alejandro got himself chipped to jerk himself off.

Another five percent gets eliminated. There's still far too much to go through myself.

Envía la carta.

Of course. I've lived in England too long.

"Tia, list the edentities that either read Internet content in Spanish or that uploaded text in Spanish."

The list shrinks before my eyes to three edentities. One leaps out at me. "El Don de la Mancha," with a string of numbers in faded text beneath it to distinguish it from all the other thousands of that name.

"Tia, I want to see the data stored in the cloud by that edentity," I say, selecting it with a point of my index finger.

"There is no data stored in the cloud by that edentity."

"What?"

"There is no—"

"But how did you know the content was Spanish if it's not there anymore?"

"I deduced the content was Spanish from the use of queries relating to creation of punctuation required to create Spanish questions with a v-keyboard, answered by the local node's automated help function, not from the content itself."

The thrill in my chest fizzles out. Sometimes Tia is too good.

"I take it the content was really, properly deleted?"

"Yes. I am unable to retrieve any backups mirrored to any other locations in the cloud. If a backup exists, the data relating to the transfer of the data has been deleted."

"But, theoretically, it could still be out there?"

"Yes. Theoretically."

There has to be another copy somewhere. He was still using it just before he died. "Right. I want you to search the Moor Hotel local node for any data uploaded to the cloud by that edentity."

I chew my lip. This is getting very close to the stuff I'm supposed to put behind me.

"No data uploaded by that edentity."

"Fuck!"

Arlington. She must have scrubbed all traces of his activity. Then it comes to me: what she did when her back was to the camera, after Theo had done his work with the ax and left the Diamond Suite. She wasn't stealing DNA. She was removing his chip. The Yanks knew he was chipped all along; of course they removed it and tried to hide any traces. The "spell" in Linda's story was probably just a dab of glue and makeup. Linda was too efficient, discovering traces of the changes to the brain caused by the recent addition of a chip before they could recover the body. They—either the Americans or the

MoJ pressured by the Americans—silenced her with a simple order, most probably had her remove the mention of it from her final report, and thought it was over. After all, no one would ever suspect him to be chipped in the first place. It would have been successfully covered up if Linda were only an average pathologist. I'd send her a note if it wouldn't raise suspicion. Maybe I will in a few days, when I'm on my next case and Milsom isn't twitchy anymore.

I start on a second biscuit. I need to rest but that's not a possibility. I need to think about what I'm going to say to my case officer to make sure there isn't any serious intervention. I need to put this behind me, like Milsom said.

There's no chance of that. I'm not some fucking walking AI that can switch this shit off just because it inconveniences the MoJ. I have to know why Alejandro got himself chipped after building an entire cult on the basis that it's the worst thing people can ever do to themselves. I need to know what he wrote in that last letter. Theo must have destroyed the paper suicide note he stole from the desk before he got to the cottage—or Arlington took it after making sure Theo died—but the electronic version has to be out there somewhere.

The frustration of leaving this unsolved makes me want to tear the chip out of my own brain. The fucking MoJ have me made into someone who pursues an investigation thoroughly, doggedly, someone who has instincts beyond anything an AI can give them. But they only want that when it suits them. Bastards!

No. I have to rein in this anger. Do the best I can under their radar before recalibration. JeeMuh, just the thought of the machine makes sweat prickle beneath my collar, so I force it away. I focus on the next step instead.

My only hope is to track down an illegal copy made of the data without Alejandro's or Arlington's knowledge. There's a chance she was siphoning off the data after she torched the original server, so he could keep using the chip seamlessly, but I don't rate my chances at being to find a trail from her. If the case was still open I could start working with the hacking specialist who analyzed the hotel's local node, but that's not going to happen.

I think back to the archive content on illegal-chipping outfits. One of the many dangers of going to them instead of an approved gov-corp operation is that the crim-org will steal your data. Surely they knew who he was—even if he lied to them about his identity when he bought the service. Surely they would want to steal his data.

I go back to the original data that Tia gathered for me that was routed through the torched local node in the window when Alejandro was there. The edentities of the crims that died in the fire are there, and using them I may be able to find people connected to them who are still alive, one of whom may well have access to any data copied from Alejandro's cloud space.

It's a long shot, I know it is, but if there's anything I've learned in the years in this job, it's that whatever you need is in the data. You just have to know which paths through it to follow and how to eliminate the extraneous without losing patterns.

It occurs to me that this is the same crim-org that Delaney has been investigating and ze would probably do despicable things to gain the same data-access privileges as me. With hir knowledge and my data access, we could probably make a very good team on this and narrow in on some decent leads much faster. But even if ze wasn't a scum-of-the-earth journo, I couldn't get in touch with hir about this anyway. Too risky.

I get Tia to order another meal to my room in an hour and a half, knowing that I could easily get lost in the task and forget. I drink a glass of water for the same reason and lie on the bed.

There's always a moment when I feel overwhelmed at the start of any data-tunneling process. There's too much to see any kind of pattern but I know it's in there. I take a deep breath and hold my palm level with my chest, pushing downward. I will work this out. I've never met a puzzle I cannot solve. This is no different.

An hour in, I have three names connected to those who died and they are solid leads. I pick one to drill down into and then the data disappears.

"Level-two data privileges revoked," Tia says.

I break into a sweat. Milsom has discovered what I'm doing. I hold my breath, waiting for her call, but it doesn't come.

"Did Milsom do that?"

Tia doesn't reply.

"Tia?"

"Please wait."

I sit up and wipe the sweat from my top lip. This is going to be a black mark if I don't think of something quick.

"All MoJ privileges revoked."

"What the fuck?"

"Access to MoJ personal case space revoked."

"Tia, what the fuck is going on?"

I go to stab at the icon that's usually in the bottom right-hand corner of my vision, but before I can select it, it disappears.

22

"TIA?" I HOLD my breath, as if waiting for someone I fear dead to call from the next room. "Tia?"

I squeeze my eyes shut and knuckle them, feeling the dark corners of the room pressing in. "Lights one hundred percent," I say, and then realize Tia isn't there to make it happen. Did I lock the door? With paranoia blooming in my gut, I swipe the key fob off the chest of drawers and lock it, imagining Arlington on her way to kill me, having somehow shut down my chip. A brief tap on the standard lamp switches it on fully and the added brightness makes me feel slightly better.

It can't be Milsom doing this; she would leave Tia active so she could send a message to bollock me. Was Tia being hacked and shut itself down as a fail-safe?

"Please stand by," Tia says, and I yelp and then laugh with relief.

"Did someone try to hack you?"

"Please stand by."

A new icon appears in the top right of my vision. A solid-gold letter "G" in a blocky three-dimensional logo slowly spins clockwise. I try to swipe it away but it remains. A spoken "delete" command is just as ineffectual. None of my other icons have reappeared.

"Incoming call from Stefan Gabor."

"Reject it and tell me what the ever-living fuck is going on."

"You do not have call-rejection privileges," Tia says, and there's the little beep that signals voice connection.

"Good evening, Mr. Moreno."

I stay silent, too many thoughts and fears rushing through my head for me to be able to reply in any way that won't bring Milsom's wrath down on my arse.

"I take it you've noticed the icon?"

My guts clench so sharply it's painful.

"I bought your contract from the Ministry of Justice."

"But it was a nontransferable con—"

"The word 'nontransferable' doesn't apply to 'billionaire twats' like me. Surely you know that. Prepare yourself for immersion. I prefer to see someone's face when I break their life into little pieces."

The call ends and it feels like I'm going to vomit up my intestines.

"Immersion in thirty seconds," Tia says.

"What? I don't want to immerse—"

"Please sit or recline in a comfortable space and confirm that you are not operating machinery."

"I'm not sitting! I don't want to immerse!"

A countdown appears in the left-hand corner of my vision in red numerals. "25, 24, 23—"

"This immersion is compulsory. Please comply with safety protocols."

Is that even legal? "Fuck this shit! Tia, get me Milsom. I need to speak to her!" Maybe if I don't comply, the immersion won't be able to happen.

"Failure to comply with safety protocols will put you at risk of injury. Any injuries sustained that subsequently interfere with the completion of your duties to the Gabor corporation will result in extension of your indentured status."

"16, 15—"

"Tia," I say, my voice hoarse with panic as I sit down on the bed. "Get me Milsom; tag it urgent."

"You are not permitted to contact former Ministry of Justice colleagues unless given explicit permission by Stefan Gabor."

"Then call the fucking police!"

"No crime is in progress. Please confirm you are not driving a vehicle."

I can't stop shaking. I can feel my pulse in my neck, compressing my throat with each beat. A notification flashes up with "No vehicle detected" and Tia starts warning me of the potential of heart attacks, depression, PTSD. And then the hotel room disappears.

I'M sitting in a chair covered in white leather, the real stuff, with a high back and generous arms. The room is huge, with a gleaming white marble floor and a central fireplace as big as my entire bathroom at home. There are flames, though they are a cold blue and look holographic. There's an L-shaped sofa that must be bigger than the car in which I was driven to Devon, a rug on the floor that looks like a polar bear skin with a sickeningly realistic head still attached.

The rest of the furniture is made of crystal, cut with facets at the edges to catch the sunlight pouring through the window. There isn't a speck of dust, as expected for a virtual space, and no attempt whatsoever to make this place feel welcoming.

On the wall opposite me there's a portrait of Stefan Gabor that's at least three meters high, either created in his younger days or by a digital artist who was prepared to sacrifice realism for the sake of client satisfaction. It's the kind of portrait that has eyes that seem to stare at you from the canvas. The painted Gabor is wearing a white suit and silky white cravat, like some sort of smug modern God very pleased with himself for being so goddamn rich.

To my left there is a window instead of a wall, overlooking a city with a skyline I don't immediately recognize. It could be an imaginary one, for all I know. The sky is blue with cotton-wool clouds scudding across it as if it's blowing a gale out there.

There is total silence; no fake crackle from the pseudo fire and no sound of the wind programmed to penetrate the triple glazing. All the while as I take in the room, that fucking golden "G" spins, forcing me to consciously try to ignore it. I close my eyes and it's still there, spinning in my private darkness.

Unable to bear it, I twist to peer around the high back of the chair and see a painting of Travis, this one two meters tall—of course—wearing a white suit in a different cut. The artist didn't have to fake his beauty. It almost looks like something from an advert. He is too handsome to seem real.

"It doesn't do him justice," Stefan Gabor says, and I start so violently the chair scrapes against the floor with a squeak. I turn back toward the fire to see him standing next to it, looking just as he did in the hotel restaurant, only disgustingly satisfied with himself. "I sacked the artist who made that. He's designing condom packaging now. I like the picture well enough, but I asked for something special." He fixes his eyes on me, made small by the flabby expanse of his jowls. "He'll never create portraits again. I made sure of that."

"You're trying to intimidate me," I say, dredging up some sort of sludgy courage from the place deep inside me that I haven't needed for a long time. "Surely you have better things to do with your time."

He smiles and opens his arms with an expansive gesture. "So, there is the real Carlos Moreno! I was wondering whether there was anything more to you than class envy and deductive reasoning. I knew there must be. Not many survive what you did and make your pay grade, even if you only get to pay off your debt with it."

I keep my mouth shut, remembering the way he treated Travis in the restaurant. This is one sadistic bastard and I don't want to give him anything he can use against me.

"That will change now," he continues. "The MoJ contract was incredibly generous. I see no reason why my property needs to have an allowance."

He's talking about my allowance like it's a salary, or something granted to me by my owner as a kindness, not part of the debt I'm paying off with servitude. Then the rest of his words sink in. Oh God, now he holds my contract. He owns me, and for the first time since the hot-housers caught me, I feel genuine terror.

My adrenaline levels, already high, spike and the old training kicks in. I push all the panic aside, fixating on the facts before me. "If I don't have an allowance anymore, I take it the length of the contract has been shortened accordingly," I say.

"No." He smiles. "Ten years were added by the MoJ just before I bought it, as punishment for your transgressions."

I stand, clenching my fists. "What transgressions?"

"Failure to report the disappearance of my husband. Failure to notify me in a timely fashion that he'd left the hotel."

"Bullshit! That was a civil matter outside of my remit. There's no fucking way that—"

He holds up a hand. "You forget who you're speaking to. Do you want me to remind you of your status here?" When I stay silent, with great difficulty, that smug smile returns. "Better. If you raise your voice in my presence again you will be punished. I can be very creative." I rage at him within the confines of my skull but my mouth stays shut. "Yes, the commissioner herself added those years and gave me her personal apologies for your conduct. I think she was relieved to have you taken off her hands." He points at the chair. "Sit down, Moreno. If I wanted you to stand I would have told you."

I sit and watch him stride over to the window, looking out at the shorter skyscrapers and parks below like a king surveying his domain.

"You have a private apartment with a generous space allocation. This isn't a permissible arrangement under your new contract. I have many properties in my portfolio and accommodation will be assigned to you, something more suited to your circumstances. This will be arranged while you're traveling. I understand you don't have any personal effects of note, which is just as well, as your accommodation will be smaller than what you've grown accustomed to."

"Traveling?" I ask the question to stop myself imagining the box he'll put me in, along with thousands of other poor bastards without any real choice about where they live.

"I'll get to that shortly. I think it's necessary for you to understand your change in circumstances first."

This is really about him getting to gloat. I assume he's seen my previous comments about him that I asked Milsom to bury for me. He wants to revel in the power he has over me and then this will be done. I just have to stay quiet and not give him the slightest chance to dig his claws in any deeper.

"You will be given new clothes. You will represent me when you fulfill your duties in public and online, and I will not have you dressed like a bloody plod who thinks any old suit is smart."

Something shifts and I look down at my clothes. My suit has been replaced by one I'd never be able to afford, one with narrow-cut legs and a high, uncomfortable collar. The tie has a thick, fashionable knot that feels like it's trying to choke me. I feel like a fraud in it and I realize he's taken just a sliver more from me. The MoJ let me choose the clothes they were obligated to provide for me from a wide selection. Even though I never wanted to incur more debt to extend that range, I never realized how much the decision about what to wear meant to my sense of self until it was gone.

Only now do I appreciate the leniency of the contract with the MoJ. I was able to apply for extensions to my debt and that's gone now, by the sound of it. Even though I hated having to ask permission to be trapped in my contract for longer—as if it were some sort of privilege to have to apply for the money to make my life bearable and then pay for it with my own freedom—at least I could. It was shit having to weigh up the need to eat with the prospect of dying indentured, but it feels like it was something precious, now lost.

"When you travel you will only have an allowance for food if you're staying somewhere without access to a printer," Gabor continues. "When you're not traveling, you will be able to use the printer in your new accommodation."

He turns and looks at me when he says that, as if waiting for the dismay to leak out onto my face. Gabor knows how important I feel it is to eat well and he wants me to know that he has taken that from me. Even though I can feel a new despair pooling within my stomach, I keep my features blank, like Dee taught me to, practiced under the gaze of my psych supervisor to avoid the machine. I may not be in the MoJ anymore but I'm not going to forget what I learned there or in hot-housing. When he doesn't get what he hoped for, he turns back to look out of the window.

"Your APA has been updated in line with the change in ownership, so you'll learn many of the everyday details as you go. If you do as I wish, to the best of your ability, without hesitation, then I will not punish you. If you carry out your duties in an exemplary fashion I may reward you. If you disobey me . . ." He pauses to look at me again, a predatory smile spreading across his face. "You don't want to disobey me. And you should know that if I discover that you have deliberately acted against my interests, I will have you serve out the rest of your contract in a brothel specializing in satisfying the most sordid tastes. I understand you have some limited experience in that area already."

I want to slam his head into the glass, grab his hair as he reels from the blow and throw him to the floor and remind him, as I smash his face into a pulp, that the use of indentured persons in brothels or any other aspects of the sex industry is illegal. But he already knows this and I know better than to express my opinion. He bought a nontransferable contract, for fuck's sake, one that was supposed to protect me from bastards like him, to protect me from ever having to do anything like what I had to when I was desperate. One I had to work hard to merit—the irony of which didn't escape me at the time. I worked so damn hard to be owned by the right kind of corporate entity and he has rendered that worthless without even trying. He could throw me in a brothel, maim or disfigure me or even kill me. The paltry number of fundamental human rights I struggled to keep are now gone.

I think of Alejandro swinging from that cord and I am filled with a visceral flash of rage. How could he have squandered all the privileges he had? What could possibly have been so bad that he couldn't face finding a way through? He had power, wealth and respect and he just chucked it all away, when I have nothing. Because of him. I don't even have the choice to take my own life. Even with the MoJ, if I did anything to deliberately endanger my life Tia would have shut me down. I'm certain Gabor won't have changed those settings.

"I am right about your experience, aren't I?" he says, and I struggle to bring myself back to his misery fest. "There wasn't a great deal of detail about that part of your life just after the Circle. Your psych supervisor thought you might be a repressed homosexual—understandable considering all the cock you sucked to buy passage across the Atlantic, and the string of girlfriends you failed to keep all those years since."

I'm on my feet before I realize it, about to leap at his throat before the old training kicks in at the last moment.

"He also talked about the constant battle to keep your anger under control. So much of it. Are you feeling angry with me now, Moreno?"

I straighten my back, clasp my hands behind it. "No. Sir."

"I should think not. I'm not the mother who abandoned you. I'm not the father who couldn't provide for you because he was too fucking weak to cope with life. I'm not the cult leader who sucked him in and took everything he owned and wouldn't give you a red cent when you asserted your right to leave. I'm not the pimp who said he would help you when you were lost in America, unchipped, starving, penniless, and then sold you to the man who wanted a rent boy all to himself while he sailed across the Atlantic. I'm not the traffickers who masqueraded as a charity and sold you to the hot-housers. Why would you be angry at me?"

He knows everything. Not even Milsom knew how I got

out of the States. I feel naked in front of this monstrous man. The anger dissolves in liquid shame and I look at the floor so he doesn't see it in my eyes. I sit down before he tells me to.

"I, on the other hand," he continues, walking toward me, "have every fucking right in the world to be angry. You knew my husband was in a car on the way to Heathrow and you did nothing. You knew he had been stalking that cult leader and you said nothing. You had no intention of interviewing my husband and yet you didn't tell me. If you had bothered to tell *him*, you could have stopped him making a terrible mistake. If I didn't need you to fix this, I'd take great pleasure in expressing my anger." His hand comes out of nowhere, grasping my tie and hauling me to my feet. "I hope you appreciate just how lucky you are that you are worth more to me intact and functioning."

"I do, sir."

He drops me back into the chair. I tug my tie and jacket back into place.

"You are also lucky because I know exactly where he is going and you are the one person in the world who can—and will—bring him back to me. As far as the Circle and the rest of the world who might take an interest in you are concerned, you are still working for the Ministry of Justice, and the commissioner agreed that it was best to keep your public status as before, just until interest in this case blows over. You are going to accept the Circle's invitation to attend that idiot's funeral and you are going to bring my husband back to me. From the moment you land on American soil you will have forty-eight hours to deliver my husband into my care. For every hour past that deadline I will add a year to your contract. If you fail, I'll get my money's worth out of you via whatever unsavory means I decide."

The fear of failure churns with the bittersweet satisfaction of getting my wish to return to the Circle after all.

"Any questions?"

"What if he doesn't want to come back to you?"

"That's irrelevant. What he thinks he wants is very different to what is best for him. If he refuses, bring him back anyway. All you need to do is get him to a rendezvous at the edge of the Circle's land, and my people will be waiting for you. If you need to knock him out and carry him over your shoulder, so be it."

"What if he isn't there? Just because he was stalking Alejandro, it doesn't mean he cares about the cult. A religious-protection visa was the best way to get away from . . . Norope."

"He's going to the Circle." Gabor speaks with total certainty. "Anything else?"

"When I bring him back," I say, not wanting to appear anything less than confident, "what will my duties be?"

Gabor's hateful smile returns. "Whatever the fuck I want them to be. Now go and bring my husband back, or I'll make your trip across the Atlantic in the bottom of a pervert's boat seem like a fucking holiday." His smile becomes wicked. "No pun intended."

23

MY FEET ARE on the floor, my knees are bent and the rest of my body is lying on the bed where it fell. I have the most horrendous headache. MyPhys reports that it's due to muscular tension in my shoulders and neck. No shit.

I sit up, pulled between two extremes. I could fly into a rampage, smashing everything in this room and ideally hurting myself in the process before Tia would shut me down. Just as easily, the last dregs of any fight left in me could leach out of the soles of my feet, into the carpet, staining it as brown as the mark in the Diamond Suite that death left behind.

I've been fighting since I was sixteen, in one way or another, struggling to just make it to somewhere safe. Whether it was stealing food, hitching rides or having to trust someone I knew would betray me at some point, I was always moving forward at least. I could always imagine a way out. Even in the bottom of that fucking boat, trying not to vomit as that disgusting man did what he liked with my body, I knew it couldn't last forever. Eventually we would reach the port and I would get away from him. Even when he chained my leg to the galley table when we reached Falmouth and said he'd changed his mind and wanted to keep me after all, I still got away. When the hot-housers made it clear that if I didn't attain a certain standard the best they'd be able to find me was a contract with a forced labor gang, I still fought my way out.

Now? Now I feel like my own skull is my prison and Tia my jailer. Even if I find Travis and somehow manage to get him to his husband's mooks, I doubt my new owner will have any interest in keeping me in good health. Anyone else, and I would have some hope that my experience in the MoJ and the highly specialized skills I honed there would be of enough value to ensure my survival. But Gabor? He already has an army of lawyers who know the law and the workings of the MoJ as well as—if not better than—I do. He must have investigators on his staff already, dotted all over the world, no doubt. As soon as I bring Travis out of the Circle, I'll be nothing more than another mouth to feed.

This is what it is to be meat, then. That's what they called low-value assets in hot-housing and the word terrified me. And now that's what I am to Gabor. There isn't a single aspect of myself or my skill set that will be of any value to him once Travis is back. I wouldn't put it past that fuck to have me shot and dumped somewhere, if it works out cheaper to kill me than keep me fed. No, he'd sell me on to someone else—he is a businessman after all.

There's no chance my bringing Travis back will earn forgiveness either. Gabor is clearly a man who enjoys power over others, especially those who have pissed him off. He'll get his husband back, then make me suffer, and he'll relish every moment of it.

I have to find a way out of this. I draw in a deep breath, feeling myself rally. That fight isn't gone yet.

"Tia, call Dee for me."

"You do not have permission to contact Dee Whittaker."

"Who do I have permission to contact?"

"Stefan Gabor's Artificial Personal Assistant."

"That's it?"

"Yes."

JeeMuh. Feeling nauseous, I go into the bathroom to wash my face. As I dry myself off a message arrives from Gabor's APA. The message is a travel itinerary and details of the hotel I'll be staying at in the States while I wait for the Circle to come out and pick me up. Probably where the US gov-corp will keep an eye on me too. Tia has accepted the invitation to the funeral on my behalf without my even knowing, which chills me to my core.

I've been on a plane only once in my life, from London to Oslo. I have a brief fantasy of approaching one of the Met officers who'll be stationed at Heathrow, begging them for help. Or, even better, telling them I'm a terrorist so they shut down my chip. Then in the interview I could—

No. Gabor will know and he'll send people to take care of it. If I'd been bought by that fucker with the boat again, I'd be free of him in seconds, but not Gabor.

I scan the itinerary and see that I'm not even going to Heathrow anyway; I'm being flown over by one of Gabor's private jets. Of course I am. Gabor wouldn't want me to have even the slimmest chance to try to break away from him. I have ten minutes before the driver who came to pick up Travis will drive me to an airfield less than an hour away. I'm fucked.

There's nothing to do except pack and lament the fact that I don't get the night in this hotel to myself. I never had a chance to try the soufflé. I cancel the meal order, not wanting that delicious food to go to waste. My thoughts run on to the flight and the worry there won't be any real food on board, and then I'm hunched over the toilet, trying not to heave my guts up at the thought of having to eat printed food again. I'm panicking and then I'm not, echoes of the machine still working its magic on me. I stand and nod to myself. Hold it together. Don't throw up. What kind of dumb-ass would want to lose the last good meal that way, for fuck's sake?

I still have seven minutes to go when all of my things are packed in my tiny case. I stand at the window and look out at the skeletal trees picked out by floodlights at their bases. The sky is pitch-black and it's not even six in the evening. In the distance I can see headlights from a car and wonder if it's a guest on their way to the hotel, or some journo, perhaps, sent by some boss to get the story straight from the source. Only then do I remember that I left that beef in the microwave at my flat and all those vegetables half-chopped for the casserole. That man's kindness at the market, left to rot on my countertop.

A knock at my door makes me jump. The bastard is early. I take my time to unlock it, only to find Naal Delaney standing there. I blink at hir, thrown by the surprise of hir not being the driver, and then check that my status is set to the highest level of privacy. My public profile still lists me as an SDCI, as Gabor said it would. He evidently has no fucks to give about the crime of impersonating a police officer.

"It's bedlam down there," ze says. "Every journo south of bloody Watford is here in person or in virtu. Can I come in?" When I pause, ze adds, "It's okay. The MoJ won't have any idea I'm here. I'm using my privacy tech."

I beckon hir inside and use the time ze takes to come in to check if Tia is still connected to the cloud. I'm cut off and unable to record, just like before. I actually have a chance to really talk!

"Where did you get that tech?" I'm desperate enough to ask without thinking.

Delaney laughs. "I'm not going to tell you that. Even though you're between cases, I'm sure you would still leap at the chance to prosecute some illegal tech on the side."

I watch Delaney nod with approval as ze takes in the room, while I try to decide whether to confide the disastrous turn of events. Back at the café in town, ze said that if I didn't report the attempted bribery, I'd be owed a favor. I just need to work out what to ask for.

"Thanks for holding up your side of the deal," Delaney says, sitting on the bed and bouncing up and down a couple of times. "I got here nice and early, first journalist on the scene after the embargo was lifted, and I've just had a very interesting chat with a cleaner." Ze stops and frowns at me. "Are you all right?"

I'm sweating. The driver is going to be here any minute and I still haven't decided how to call in the favor. Ideally I want that privacy tech, but there's no way Delaney will pass on hir supplier as long as ze thinks I'm still with the MoJ. If I reveal I've been bought by Gabor it would be just as unlikely; Delaney made hir low opinion of Gabor clear the last time we spoke. My worth as a contact would be massively devalued too.

"I always get the shakes after a case," I say. "Like a delayed stress reaction. It'll pass."

"So one of the Circle did it," ze says. "I popped up to see if you'd consider giving me a statement. It's not my usual bag but seeing as I'm here anyway . . ."

"Sorry, no. Everything I could possibly say about the case is covered by the MoJ press release."

Delaney shrugs. "I thought as much. I figure the murderer was in the pay of the US gov-corp. I don't suppose you dug down on his connection to the US gov-corp, in light of our conversation?"

"The Yanks blocked it before I could get anything conclusive," I say, concentrating hard on hir face to stop my eyes from being drawn away by that fucking Gabor logo. "And the MoJ have closed the case. I caught the bad guy; everyone gets to go home. The ones who benefit the most remain nameless and free. You know how it is."

"But you're not satisfied." Delaney smiles. "I can see it. You're still hungry."

I neither agree with nor deny hir appraisal. That training will be with me forever. "Look, I've only got a couple of minutes. I've managed to get the MoJ to let me go to Alejandro's funeral at the Circle. The driver will be here any minute."

Delaney stands, rubbing hir hands together. "Now we're talking. I wish I could come with you. I don't suppose we could come to some sort of arrangement? I'm very interested in them."

Surely Tia is spying on me now? I need to be careful not to mention anything that could trigger an alert to Gabor. I need to avoid names and just hope that Gabor isn't watching every single thing I do. It's worth the risk and yet I still hesitate. Can I trust this person? Like every other time I've taken the first step on the path to betrayal, I probably can't. There's no other choice. "Actually, I have something in mind. With the case officially closed, I can't look into everything I want to, and, besides, once I'm at the Circle I'll be offline. Would you follow up on a lead I got tracking down the data stored by that illegal chip?"

Delaney's eyes, already large and dramatic, widen until I can see all white around the irises. "Are you shitting me?"

"No, straight up. On one condition: you keep anything you

find confidential until I've seen it. I'm sure I don't have to explain why."

"Because both of our necks would be on the line; you working with a journo and me following MoJ leads would look bad for both of us." Delaney smiles with a theatrical flutter of eyelashes. "You can depend on my discretion."

I go to the desk and pull out the pen and hotel notepaper within. A flash of Alejandro penning his suicide note fills me as I unscrew the cap. "This is where I'll be staying. Don't assume it's secure. Don't send me anything unless it's encrypted to fuck."

"My dear man, there isn't an encryption algorithm that could keep out the US and Noropean gov-corps if they really wanted to read our shit. But I have other means, should it be necessary. I do research dangerous and powerful people for a living, you know."

I write three names below the hotel details, with their edentities alongside them. "These people are connected to the crimorg that chipped the victim and they aren't on any watch lists. I had to dig pretty fucking deep into private data to get to them. If you tracked them down and—"

Delaney holds up a hand. "This isn't my first rodeo. This is very helpful, thank you. And in return, you'll tell me what it's like inside the Circle now?"

I nod. I have no idea how I will get that information to hir, but I'll worry about that later. "Is there a place I can get a message to you? I'm always on the move and I don't want anything from you landing in my public in-box."

Ze gives me a physical drop-box address in London. "There's nothing online that connects it to me," ze says. "Don't ask. How long will you be in the States?"

"All being well, I should be back in Norope in three or four days. Depends on how hospitable the Circle decides to be," I add hastily. I hand over the piece of paper. For the first time in years, I have a flashback to when I handed over the temporary visa—one I'd waited months to secure after leaving the Circle—to the pimp who'd been grooming me. He promised he'd find someone looking for hired help on one of the millionaire's yachts that still crossed the Atlantic for fun, giving me a way to pay for my own travel back to Europe. Back then I was naive and desperate. I don't have that excuse now. "I'm taking a really fucking big risk giving this to you," I say. "If you screw me over . . ."

"You'll fuck me over twice as hard. I get it." Delaney reads the note and then tucks it into hir jacket pocket. "For what it's worth, it's in my interest to cultivate a mutually beneficial working relationship with you. And I don't want you to bring the MoJ down on my head either."

"I'd love to chat but my driver is going to be here any second and I don't want to have to explain you being in my room to my boss."

"Take care at the Circle," Delaney says, heading for the door.

"They're harmless," I say.

"They were twenty-odd years ago," ze says, pausing with a hand over the door handle. "But one of their own just killed their leader. Something immensely fucked-up must be going on there for that to happen."

I say nothing and Delaney leaves. Theo may not really have been the murderer, but his response to the suicide was certainly . . . unusual. He was brought up in a highly restrictive religious sect, by all accounts, so he probably had more things repressed than most people could even name. One extreme grief reaction doesn't mean the entire cult is dangerous.

Thinking back, the most dangerous thing I encountered

there was boredom. I was always busy—Alejandro made sure that all of us were working on something all the time—but it was all physical work. Tending the fields with old-fashioned tools, driving horses with plows, repairing buildings, making clothes . . . The business of keeping everyone fed and housed and clothed without buying anything from the outside was hellishly time-consuming and did nothing to keep my thoughts from turning in on themselves. I needed to be fed, and in the absence of intellectual satisfaction my mind was like an echo chamber for the anger and frustration. Why were so many clever people wasting their lives with their hands in mud when there were machines to do that for us? Why couldn't we enjoy all the entertainment the world had to give us? Why was it more important to listen to Alejandro or some other boring old bastard talking about the dangers of being chipped than having a laugh or learning about the world? I hated them all by the time I escaped.

Escape? Yes, that's how I saw it then. Would I have made the same decision now, having seen the real world? Would I see it as a sanctuary if I knew then what I do now? Could it be a place of sanctuary to me now?

No. Alejandro made it painfully clear that if I left, I would never be accepted there again. My father stood next to him as he said it. Neither of them asked me to stay. Neither of them suggested I sample the world outside first with the option to come back if I needed to. If anything, they seemed glad to see me go.

I don't want to see my father again.

There's a knock at the door and it opens before I have a chance to speak. A bald man dressed in an expensive black suit with a cap tucked under his arm fills the doorway. "Time to go, Moreno."

———

THERE'S a glass screen between the driver and me so there's nothing to do but settle into the cocooned luxury of the limousine interior and regret not being able to say a proper goodbye to Nadia. She'll think I'm rude. Strangely, I find myself caring about that.

None of my usual icons have returned and Tia won't respond to any requests to restore them. I ask for music; it tells me that it's not permitted. I ask for my mail, a summary of news headlines, a dip in the social stream. All are denied. There's nothing but the black outside the windows or behind my eyelids and that fucking logo. Even that isn't enough to keep me awake now that the adrenaline is leaving my body.

I'm woken by the car pulling to a stop and am instantly alert. We're at the airfield, the limo brought within meters of the private jet, engines already fired and waiting for me to board. I'm ushered up the steps by the driver, who carries my bag for me out of what I presume is habit. He makes it look like a handbag, he's so big.

The flight attendant is a tall blond man with an unfeasibly white smile that dazzles me as I step into the craft.

"Welcome aboard, Mr. Moreno. If you'd like to follow me."

I'm shown to one of the six seats inside the main body of the craft. I feel like I'm in some sort of shallow mersive made for people who like to spend their evenings living as though they are billionaires to help themselves forget they're living in a gov-corp-approved box and will never achieve anything more meaningful in life than clawing their way to a higher pay grade than their neighbors. If a prostitute appears from behind the curtain at the far end, offering to give me a blow job, I'll know that none of this is real. A second flight attendant, a black woman with legs that go on forever and another dazzling smile, chooses that moment to sweep aside the curtain and clip it back. She walks past me after welcoming me on board and all too realistically ignoring my trousers. It's just as well. I hate those kinds of mersives.

My case is stowed somewhere farther down the plane; no overhead bins are in this section. I'm told to fasten my belt. The chair feels more like one that should be beside a huge fireplace in the Moor Hotel than any seat I'd expect to find in a plane.

Outside the window I see the lights of the tiny terminal building, so small it looks more like a private house. The driver is walking back to the limousine and will probably be driving back to London to ferry that toad around. I have an acute sense of living Travis's former life, being taken from one place to another—probably with just as much say in the matter—in extreme luxury and quiet misery. Did he fall for Gabor when he was young and desperate, willing to overlook the age gap and paunch in return for a life of champagne and silk? Or was he simply picked out and made an offer he couldn't refuse even if he wanted to? Either way, it's clear that at some point Travis realized that the lifestyle wasn't compensation enough. How long will it be before he realizes the same at the Circle?

Within minutes the plane starts to taxi to the airstrip and the flight attendants go to belt themselves in somewhere at the back. Tia starts talking me through the safety briefing, using augmented reality to highlight exits and how the individual life pods will work in the event of ditching in the sea. The pods are stored within the seats and will automatically activate should a crash be imminent. As far as I can tell, it will inflate a structure around me and my chair, protecting me from impact and fire, before I'm ejected out of the plane, to be found by rescue services. It seems ridiculous, but apparently it's one of the wonderful inventions "gifted to the world" by the Gabor R&D branch and has a "one hundred percent success rate in crash simulations." With air travel being so safe—no loss of life in the past ten years or so—I wonder if this was a pet project initiated by Gabor himself. It seems absurdly overengineered, like something more suited to protecting scientific equipment sent down to the surface of Mars than passengers in private jets that never crash.

The flight time is just over nine hours, Tia informs me, and then ignores another request for access to any distractions. Then the acceleration of the craft pressing me into my seat and the sensations caused by the lift into the air are enough to keep me occupied for a while.

The male attendant reappears once we level out. I accept the offer of a drink, choosing a large whisky before being told that no alcohol has been authorized for the flight. Sparkling apple and pomegranate juice is suggested and I acquiesce, some pitiful part of me hoping that the in-flight food will be good. After another abortive attempt to contact Dee, Tia offers me approved in-flight reading that's just arrived from Gabor's APA. Peevishly, I ignore the link, trying to find something interesting to look at other than the flight attendants. I last about ten minutes before caving, appalled at my inability to cope without music or something to research. I've become what Alejandro deplored so vocally: a person incapable of sitting within his own skin.

To my surprise, the material sent by the toad's APA is actually of great interest. It's evident that Gabor has had others look into the Circle, though how they managed to dig up so much in a matter of hours puzzles me, until I suspect Stefan has been interested in the Circle for some time. Perhaps he was already aware of Travis's fascination with Alejandro and just didn't believe his husband would actually have the guts to break away.

If that was the case, surely the alarm bells would have rung when Travis had to have his chip removed? Perhaps that's why Stefan is so furious, because he knows he should have seen it coming.

The file contains detailed information about ten members of the Circle, none of whom I recognize from my time there. They have several things in common: all joined in the past ten years, all were greatly respected in their individual fields—all in the sciences, interestingly enough—and every single one has something to hide. Several have criminal activity that has hitherto avoided prosecution, a couple made poor choices in their youth involving porn, and one falsified data to support a scientific paper early in his career and then covered it up. Several of the names are familiar, thanks to my brief research into the patents held by the Circle, reminding me of the money that it brings into the States every year. Two things rapidly become apparent as I dig down in the data Gabor sent: a significant proportion of this data was obtained illegally and the Circle isn't just a religious cult anymore.

24

AS HOTELS GO, the one I've been deposited at by a dull US Gabor corp liaison isn't too bad. As with all things American, it's on a bigger scale than anything in Norope and has an affiliation to a particular church stated proudly on a stone plaque next to the entrance. When Tia handles the handshake with the hotel node and the check-in, it informs me that my behavior at the hotel mustn't contravene any of the guidelines provided (via a link I don't select) for the comfort and religious freedom of all guests. What it neglects to mention is that they mean the particular brand of religious freedom that they approve of.

I checked in eight hours, forty-seven minutes and twenty seconds ago, according to the stopwatch counter that appeared without my permission on the left-hand side of my vision as soon as I stepped onto US soil. Below that counter is a second one informing me of how many hours, minutes and seconds remain before the toad's forty-eight-hour deadline expires and each additional hour will mean a year added to my contract.

Collindale sent a message mere moments after I checked in, saying he'll escort me to the Circle but not detailing exactly when. Even though I know I can't expect to be taken there much before the funeral, the wait and uncertainty are agonizing. I've memorized the pictures and bios of those Circle members as best I can, and now I'm too tired to work yet too restless to relax. It's two o'clock local time, but my body thinks I should be going to bed. My stomach rumbles, but I can't bring myself to eat anything produced by the printer in my room.

Gabor obviously thinks I'll be able to use the information on those people as leverage, should it be necessary to find an ally at the Circle to get Travis out. Even though I don't have much faith Gabor will keep me alive once his husband is delivered back to him, I still can't take the risk of ignoring his order. At some point after the funeral the Circle will boot me back out again, and if I don't have Travis with me, Gabor could have me killed then and there if he wishes. I don't want to be a kidnapper, but if a choice has to be made, I doubt I will put Travis's marital happiness above my own life. He made his choice years ago. I've never had the pleasure of knowing what that's like.

I'm pacing again, even though my legs are aching and my head feels stuffed with cotton wool. I think about the bios Gabor sent me, the patents, the way Collindale and the US gov-corp got so twitchy about anyone knowing about the suicide. What Alejandro founded as an oasis of simple godliness in the Texas wilderness has mutated into some sort of elite research facility raking in a huge amount of money from the products of its scientific endeavors. I try to fit that idea of it into my memories of the aging hippies with tanned beer guts and sagging breasts, either sitting around praying and talking about how God worked through Alejandro to save them from the evils of the modern world or working the fields to grow real food for everyone there. I don't remember anyone other than my dad having a background in science, and he couldn't even wash and dress himself without being reminded to, let alone carry out research. I try to persuade Tia to do a search on his name and any of the Circle's patents, but it won't comply. I can't decide if Gabor has restricted my access out of spite or fear that I'll get a message for help out there somehow. Probably both.

I try to imagine what it will be like to see my father again. Will he be pleased to see me? We parted on such bad terms. Has that festered inside him as it has in me, mutating into an emotional cancer that fucked up his life as much as mine? Or will he throw his arms wide and behave like nothing happened? I don't know which of those possibilities I dread the most.

Eventually I can't pace anymore and flop onto the bed, thinking I'll just rest my eyes for a few minutes. I wake some hours later. The light from the window is the dull bronze of a Texas sunset and does nothing to help my disorientation. Tia informs me that no contact has been made from the Circle or US gov-corp. I've been in the States for more than twelve hours now and have nothing to show for it except jet lag and a headache the size of the Atlantic. MyPhys recommends I drink water and eat.

The water is easy enough. The chemical aftertaste is unpleasant but better than being ill. Evidently the hotel's water supply is pumped in from one of the older reclamation plants. I try not to think about it too much.

The food issue is harder. I sit on the edge of the bed, my stomach long past the stage of rumbling, staring at the printer fitted into the wall. It's a typical generic model and only a couple of years old by the look of it. "Any cuisine, anytime!" boasts the tagline beneath the company logo. I think of the meat and vegetables rotting in my apartment, the look on Gabor's face

when he made it clear I'd never eat real food again, the consequences of not using the printer. If I don't eat and fall ill or cease
to function properly as a result, MyPhys will no doubt escalate
this. For those in better circumstances than I, it would simply
be a notification sent to a health-care provider. In the MoJ, I
would have been sent to my psych supervisor and no doubt given
a recalibration session. But now? Now I wouldn't be surprised
if MyPhys reporting into Gabor's APA would result in some of
his goons coming in here and force-feeding me. He must have
people nearby, waiting for me to emerge with Travis.

I instruct Tia to open the menu for me. As expected, there
are thousands of meals available. All are described in ludi-
crously poetic language and a picture of the dish presented
restaurant style, with equally fake steam and the kind of metal
cutlery you never get printed with one of these hotel models.

It doesn't fool me. I know that those dishes are all just different combinations of protein, oil and powdered chemicals
injected in the appropriate ratios and then built layer by layer
into the correct shape and texture by the nozzles. Behind that
shiny black plasglass are the same sorts of tubes that would
have been in that machine in my childhood home, packaged
so that you never see how horribly artificial and inedible the
contents really look.

Surely it's different now. More advanced than back then.
No. The formula may be more advanced, the chemicals better
at fooling the palate and the manufacturers making more
sophisticated combinations, but it's still not real food.

I need to eat though. I select a lasagna and pace the room
as it prints behind the opaque plasglass screen. A soft musical
tone tells me it's ready and the screen slides open as I approach.
I pull out the tray, nothing more than shiny cardboard, and
peer at the newly printed "lasagna" resting on a plastic plate

with a horribly kitschy flower pattern running round the edge and a logo for the affiliated church. I pull a plastic fork from the slot at the side of the printer and push the "food" around with it, unable to bring myself to put any of it in my mouth. It smells good. It's hot. It looks like a fake lasagna; not nearly as good as the picture but better than I expected. I carve off a corner and hold it on the fork, my traitorous stomach rumbling loudly. Finally, I close my eyes and shove it in my mouth.

Each forkful brings a memory of the house in Spain. Crying in front of the printer when it wouldn't make chorizo anymore, the timid tapping on my father's bedroom door that evolved into banging thumps when the printer just fired out spurts of lumpy goop into the tray.

Bear hearing me crying and trying to solve the problem, and waiting for the social team to come and take me away as the sound of police sirens and the smell of smoke filled the house. The riots stopped three streets away, I learned many years later, and Bear's report to the social team was lost in the tumultuous collapse of democratic government.

I don't notice the tears on my cheeks until the plastic plate is empty. Beneath the "sauce" smears a new logo has been revealed, one for the printer company, with a cartoon animal holding a sign saying "God loves you!" next to it.

I dump the tray in the recycling bin and then fall into another restless sleep. Several times I wake from dreams of boats and chains, filled with the sense I'm going to die that grows, unchallenged, in the darkness.

I wake before dawn with no sense of the actual time nor what my body thinks it should be. The counter is approaching twenty-four hours and still no contact from the US gov-corp.

Collindale said he would collect me when it was time to go, and that would be determined by the funeral arrangements at the Circle. I guess they don't want me hanging around for hours, being curious and poking my investigator's nose where they don't want it. I'd be the same.

A shower helps, even though it's not the lengthy indulgence that it was at the Moor Hotel. By the time I'm dressed and caffeinated there's a faint pink glow brushing the bottom of the clouds on the horizon. The headache has eased but the hunger is building again. I just need to wait a little longer; then I can eat something real at the wake. Fuck, am I really looking forward to a wake now? I need to get out of this hotel room and feel the wind on my face.

There are apples for sale in the lobby café for twenty dollars each, grown at a local orchard, if the sales display is to be believed. I walk past them, the question of whether to incur more debt to buy one having been made irrelevant by my new contract, and head toward a courtyard-garden sign posted from all the elevators on the ground floor. Tinny Muzak plays as I walk, trying to shrug off the sense of shaky disembodiment caused by the jet lag and hunger, and I notice a woman watching me as I go past. My first thought is that she's from the US gov-corp, assigned to make sure I don't leave the hotel without an escort. My second is that she's actually a Gabor employee with the same brief. My third is that I'm evidently paranoid. JeeMuh, what I wouldn't do to have that Moor Hotel breakfast again. Was that only yesterday? Or the day before? I'd even welcome small talk with Alex the SOCO. Hell, even a grilling from Milsom would be good right now, if it meant I was back in the MoJ for real.

The courtyard garden is the most inappropriately named outdoor space I've even been in. There are a few planters with brittle-looking cacti and some artificial ferns that have seen better days. At least there is a crisp chill in the air to refresh me. It will have to do.

I sit there, thoughts of Dee and Mars floating through my mind like the clouds passing over my head, until I start to feel too cold. I shuffle back into the hotel, hands in my pockets, hating this limbo. I stop next to the lobby café, staring at the apples, until a ping comes from Collindale telling me that he'll be at the hotel in five minutes and I need to be ready to leave.

The adrenaline kicks back in as I walk briskly to the elevator and then down the seemingly endless corridor to my room. Without knowing how long it will take to find Travis, it's useless trying to plan my approach. There are fewer than twenty-four hours left and about four of those will be eaten up by travel into the heart of the Circle and back out again—assuming I can get a car to bring him back out to the rendezvous. It's going to be tight.

I don't notice the package on my bed until I've shut the door behind me and gotten halfway to the en-suite. I stop and stare at it, half expecting it to blow up. It's only three centimeters or so thick, about thirty centimeters by twenty, wrapped in thick brown paper covered with a protective bio-film wrapper. I pick it up, turn it over to see that there's nothing written on the outside anywhere, and then get a ping from Collindale telling me he's in a car outside.

Hoping it's from Delaney, I stuff it into my case underneath everything else and suppress the worry that they will search my bag again. I hurry down to the lobby as Tia checks me out of the hotel. Collindale is parked to the left of the main entrance and is leaning against a predictably large car. I return his wave.

Collindale looks exactly as he did in Devon and gives me

the same smile and sense of being short as he shakes my hand. "Good flight over?"

"Not bad. I could do without the jet lag though."

"You wait till you fly back," he says, opening the boot.

I put my case in and watch as he waves a customs wand over it, checking for any electronics. I hold my breath, fearful that the package actually contains an old tablet, but he seems satisfied and switches the wand off after waving it over my body. "I know you're not dumb enough to try to sneak some personal tech into the Circle," he says. "Just gotta make sure I can tell my boss I followed procedure. You know how it is."

"Yup," I say as casually as I can, wishing that Milsom were still my boss.

He opens the passenger's door for me and I climb in and buckle up as he walks round to the driver's side. Being on the other side of the car adds to the background noise of disorientation.

"So, I guess they must have told you that the Circle has strict guidelines about who can go into their"—he struggles to find the least loaded word—"territory."

I nod. "The last time I was there I wasn't chipped. I understand there's some sort of thing I have to wear?"

He reaches into the backseat and retrieves a very small plastic case. Inside is a plain solid-metal bracelet. "This," he says, pulling it out and chucking the empty box back onto the backseat. "It locks on and you won't be able to take it off until you leave the territory. I have the key, but any US gov-corp employee of my pay grade and above can unlock it for you. No one at the Circle can, I should add. Obviously."

"Does it cut off my connection to the cloud?"

"No, it shuts your APA down altogether and stops you from

reactivating it. I know it seems kinda full-on, but the Circle insists on it. They said you'd understand."

"It's fine," I say.

"Ankle or wrist?"

I shudder and remind myself there is no boat, no chain, no leering pervert here. "Wrist is fine."

"It emits an alarm of one hundred and twenty decibels if you or anyone else there tries to deactivate it or tries to physically cut it off you. It's made of a high-tensile alloy that can't be cut with conventional tools." He makes a small gesture, as if selecting something from his own APA's menu, and it clicks open. "You sure you wanna go to this funeral?"

"Yes," I say, after making a note of the time and the amount I have left until the deadline, and he puts it on my wrist. The spinning Gabor logo disappears and I breathe a sigh of relief.

"Were you expecting it to hurt?" he asks.

I shake my head, reveling in a visual field free of the marking of slavery. "I thought it would be more uncomfortable."

"It's about an hour to the border. I can play some music, seeing as your APA is down," he offers, and I beam at him.

"That would be great," I say, hoping that a plan involving this bracelet and my permanent freedom will form soon. Gabor has no way to track me now and Tia can't police me either. I have to make the most of it.

25

BY THE TIME we reach the border of the Circle's land I've re-appraised my opinion of Collindale. Without the pressure of the case hanging over us and tainting our interactions he turns out to be quite good company. He doesn't talk too much, which always helps, and doesn't make small talk about the capsule, which helps even more. He has an infectious enthusiasm for an obscure form of jazz that came from the part of New York he grew up in. After listening to it for an hour, I'm coming round to it too.

"I'll send you some links, once you're back online," he says, and I smile and thank him as if nothing is wrong, as if he's going to unlock the bracelet in a few hours and wave me off from the airport. For the briefest moment I'm tempted to tell him what's happened and beg him for help, but either pride or fear or the sheer ridiculous need to see the Circle again and work out what the fuck is going on there stops me.

The final road ends at a gate, there for symbolism more than anything else. There's no fence on either side of it, just posts at regular intervals that would jam a car engine and make a chip go haywire in someone's head while notifying the Circle of trespass. They put it up the year I left, replacing the old, rusting barbed wire that had a habit of trapping tumbleweeds and made the place feel like a gulag for anyone who liked going for long walks.

I ready myself for some surge in emotion, some horrible memory or at least a stirring of something long buried. There's nothing. I feel numb. Distanced. My pysch supervisor would probably bleat on about repression and how harmful it is. At least I won't see that sanctimonious bastard ever again.

The land here is flat and dominated by agriculture. For the past hour I haven't seen another soul. The only movement has been a few birds wheeling in the sky and a few farming drones spraying something onto fields lying fallow over the winter. The last time I was here, I was walking down this road in the opposite direction, leaving the Circle behind me with nothing more than the clothes on my back, a few days' worth of food that I'd stolen from the kitchen and a rage that kept me walking long after many would have turned back.

I had slept rough for two weeks before finding civilization and was immediately picked up by local law enforcement, who were ultimately sympathetic but unable to help me. Cult escapees aren't that common, but one of the officers had clearly had some relevant experience, because she stopped the other one from taking me back, pointing out that at my age I had the right to choose. They took me to a local church and some nice people there put me up in a simple room at the back of the church hall in return for light labor as I waited for my temporary visa to come through. When the daughter of the pastor came to my room in the middle of the night and made it clear there would be other responsibilities, I ran away.

Maybe if I'd stuck it out there, I wouldn't be in the mess I'm in now. But, then again, maybe I'd have just ended up in another one.

"There she is," Collindale says, snapping me out of the bitter memory. He points to a car on the other side of the gate, a modest, old-fashioned car powered by solar panels attached to its roof by fraying rope. Selina Klein is leaning against it, wearing a long black dress and coat. Collindale flashes the lights and she heads over to the gate, unlocking it by the time our car pulls up. I push down the disappointment—and the relief—that it's not my father who has come out to meet me.

"Good morning, ma'am," Collindale says, and she smiles at his quaint manners.

"Hello, Mark." She turns to me as Collindale gets my bag. "Hi."

"Hi," I say back, seeing the sadness in her eyes. "I seem to be making a habit of seeing you under terrible circumstances."

She smiles weakly and I wish I hadn't said it. Collindale sets my bag down next to me and shakes my hand. "I did all the checks and the bracelet is active," he tells her. To me he says, "I'll see you later."

"I'll make sure he gets here in one piece," Selina replies, and she heads to the old car.

I give Collindale a last wave, feeling the metal bracelet slapping my wrist as I do so, and then put my case in the car.

"It's old but reliable," Selina says when I get inside. "It'll take us another hour to get to—" She stops, shaking her head at herself. "You know that already. Your dad said sorry for not picking you up, but he couldn't get away."

"I suppose there's a lot to do."

"Yes."

"So, now you know I used to be in the Circle."

She nods. "I mentioned your name and your dad told me. He's so proud you made—"

"I'm sorry I didn't tell you before," I cut in, unable to stomach even a secondhand report of my father's pride. "I couldn't risk altering your opinion of me during the investigation."

"I understand," she says. "I hope you don't mind, but there won't be time for you to see your room before the funeral."

"That's fine."

"I'll take you there after the wake. If there's anything you need, just let me know."

"Thanks."

"It must be a relief. Closing the case, I mean."

I look at her but her eyes are fixed on the road ahead. "Of a sort." I look out over fields I once dug in, lying fallow. "I thought I'd be walking. There weren't any cars the last time I was here."

"We choose to live without personal tech," she says. "We're not the Amish." After a pause, she adds, "The car is a tool, not a distraction."

There's an edge to her voice. Perhaps she thought I was judging them, comparing them to the Circle I left and finding them wanting.

The rest of the journey is in silence. It's far from comfortable and companionable. I've seen her at her most vulnerable and I think that makes her feel awkward around me, like she wants to put on a show of being fine when she clearly isn't and knows that I'll see through it. Her makeup and styled hair make her look glamorous compared to when I last saw her, but she's still far from her best.

There's nothing to be said anyway. I barely know her. I want to know if Travis is going to be at the funeral. I don't ask, lest I make it obvious that I'm here for him as well as Alejandro. I want to ask her about my father but no clear question crystallizes. So I sit there, looking out at the gray sky, wondering what the fuck I am going to say to people about the case and my part in it. Am I even still bound by that insane contract? I can't imagine something as legally trivial as a change in ownership would make any difference to those lawyers.

The farther we go, the more dread and nervous anticipation fill the car, shared by both of us but for very different reasons. I find myself looking out for the silhouette of the huge house and converted barn that I spent eight years of my life hating, as if seeing it at a distance will somehow help prepare me and stop it from catching me emotionally unready.

Eventually I pick out blocky shapes on the horizon. But there are six instead of two.

"It's changed quite a bit," I comment as they grow larger with our approach.

"There are almost four hundred of us now."

"JeeMuh! There were barely a hundred when I arrived and not many more when I left."

"That was more than twenty years ago, Mr. Moreno. And . . . and could I ask you not to use that word? I don't have a problem with it, but I think there are several here who wouldn't like Christ and Muhammad's names taken in vain."

"Right. Sorry." I try to remember whether she said it herself, back in England, but without Tia to remind me, I give up. America is not the place to police hypocrisy.

The four newer buildings are far from what I'd expect the Circle to build. For one thing, they're all different from one another and the original two buildings, so different they could almost have been plucked out of different cities from around the world and just dropped here. The old farmhouse where I slept when we first arrived looks neglected, and the old barn, containing the dining hall and dormitories Dad and I moved into, doesn't look that much better. I remember sanding those sills and repainting the window frames every two years. Did Alejandro just lose interest in them?

The new buildings have something of the experimental about them. Now that we're getting closer I can see how each one seems to have incorporated basic elements—little more than a block with a high-pitch roof on it and then a steel structure weaving in and out of it to form what I assume is a fire escape—and added something new each time. They are a world away from the traditional wooden structures that stand near them.

"Are the new ones accommodation blocks, then?"

"The one on the right is a meeting hall as well as some rooms."

"Will I be sleeping in my old dorm?"

"Oh, we don't have dormitories now. Everyone has their own room in the new buildings. We don't use the old ones anymore. They're not energy efficient."

"But Alejandro loved the old farmhouse."

After a long pause, she says, "He loved the new buildings more."

The new roofs look like they're made of solar-sensitive material and one of the buildings looks like it's completely covered in the stuff. I've never seen it shaped that way before. I think back to the list of patents, how several were classed under energy storage. Maybe this is where ideas are tested. Then it strikes me that this place looks more like a scientific research facility than anything homey. These buildings would look more at home on university campuses.

We're less than a mile away now and I realize the fields around us have crops. It's hard to tell which are maize and which are corn. In November? "Milder winters here too now," I say, jerking a thumb toward one.

"Oh, those are some ultrahardy varieties we're testing out. They're doing better than we thought they would."

I see a movement in the corn and wait for a child to come running out. But when we pass I catch a glimpse of a wheeled drone doing something with the soil. "You have farming drones here?"

"A few. I suppose you had to do everything by hand when you were here."

"Well, yeah. I was told it was kind of the point."

"Alejandro said he used to be pretty hard-core. This must be a bit of a shock for you."

I remember him teaching me how to plant. I must have been nine and still intimidated by that huge sky and the silence at night. Bear was gone, I couldn't connect with the man who was supposed to be my father and Alejandro was trying his best to draw me out of myself. He'd decided to take me out into the fields with a watering can, a couple of tools and a bag of seeds. When we reached the edge of a plowed field he laid his hand on the small of my back and propelled me between the freshly plowed furrows I'd thought were out-of-bounds.

"Do you know what this is?" He held out a seed on his palm.

"It's one of the bits you have to spit out." I hated them. I hated the food that needed to be chewed more thoroughly, that had alien textures and uneven coloration and bits that couldn't be eaten. Some of the teenagers had laughed at me when I'd tried to eat an orange without peeling it and put all sorts of fruit in front of me, telling me I could eat every part. After I took two bites out of a lemon, peel and all, my father had come across us and yelled at the teens until their parents had come and taken them away. I didn't stay for the offered lesson, unable to spend more than a minute in his presence without wanting to burn everything to the ground.

"It's a seed," Alejandro said. "And sometimes we do spit them out. Do you know what they are for?" At my sullen shrug he smiled and reached for my hand to drop it onto my palm. "You plant them in the soil and they grow into a whole new plant."

I stared at the seed, trying to work out if he was trying to catch me out. "Why?"

"Because God made them that way." He smiled at my unimpressed scowl. "And because the genes inside them are programmed to do that. When they are in the right kind of soil that has the right kind of nutrients, all they need is water and sunlight to start growing."

"I don't believe you."

"Where do you think all the food comes from?"

"Real food comes from the printer. Your wrong food comes from the kitchen."

He looked so sad then, just for a moment, before he smiled and crouched down. "I shall prove it to you. We will plant these seeds together. Then you'll see them grow, and at the end of the summer you'll eat the corn."

I wrinkled my nose at the soil. "After it's been in the dirt?"

"Everything we eat comes from the dirt. Even a lot of the things they put in those printers. It all comes from somewhere, chico. This way," he said, and pressed the seed into the little hole he'd made while talking, "we feel a connection to what we eat."

"But there are drones that do this," I said, having seen them in a cartoon.

"If we use machines to plant and tend and harvest, we cut ourselves off from the source of life. We need to touch the soil, smell the rain, feel an ache in our back at the end of the day. It keeps us connected and grateful."

I think back to that man so in love with creation, willing to spend hours trying to find something worth saving in a screwed-up child, and am filled with a sudden and terrible sense of loss. I simply can't reconcile that memory with what I see now. Seeing the drone wheel out of the field feels like an erasure, an underlining of his death that marks not just the absence of him but the end of men like him. Nothing of him has endured.

Perhaps I'm sinking into a nostalgic grief. Did he simply think that was all bullshit back then and just got over himself? How did he get from a man who liked the drafts in the old farmhouse to one who preferred those ultramodern structures? Energy efficient? He didn't give a fuck about that sort of thing—in fact, he probably would have felt cut off from the land and weather in one of those fake cocoons. Did science simply overtake the spiritual at some point?

"The funeral will be starting in about ten minutes," Selina says, when we're still half a mile away. "It's in the new hall. I feel you should know that not everyone is very . . . comfortable with you being here."

"Let me guess: my dad is one of them."

"Oh no, he's been one of the most enthusiastic. He's been so excited the last couple of days."

I try to imagine him excited. It's like trying to visualize a green sky with purple polka dots: possible but far from a realistic mental image.

"I'll stay close and make sure no one gives you a hard time," she says when I don't reply. "I've told everyone how kind you were to me and how sensitively you managed the case. It's just that . . . Well, we're not used to strangers here."

"I should know quite a lot of people," I say.

"Not as many as you might think," she replies, and parks the car. "It was a long time ago, Mr. Moreno."

But I'm the only one who left. At least, that's what Gabor said, and he'd obviously had people look into the Circle. Then the most awful thought occurs to me. Perhaps I'm the only person who left alive.

BEHIND the buildings there's a large carport with space for about ten cars, but only two others are there, both old and one of them battered as if it's been through a crash and not been fully repaired. Selina asks if it's all right for me to leave my bag in the car until after the funeral and I agree. I need privacy to open that package, anyway. I feel happier with my case locked away in a car rather than in a room anyone could go and poke about in. Then she simply tucks the keys into the pocket in the driver's side door and leaves it unlocked. I guess they don't worry about thieves out here.

While I'm worried about my case, at least one problem has been solved: how to get out to the rendezvous. All I need to do is either persuade Travis to go home or, more likely, hit him over the head and bundle him into the car boot in the small hours. Either way, I see a way out now.

There is an alternative, one that is feeling better every moment. I could just steal the car and make a run for it. I'd never be able to take the bracelet off—and as a result I'd never be able to use my chip again—but it would be worth it to get away from Gabor. What I would do after getting out of the States—and how I'd do that—remains unanswered. Everything may have changed here in the Circle, but in this country, the treatment of nonperson-status men with my heritage is still just as bad as it ever was.

Now isn't the time to consider this, anyway. I have to face my father. And my grief.

"It's quite safe in there—don't worry," Selina says, thinking I'm still concerned about my bag.

"I've lived in London too long," I say, and I fall into step alongside her as she heads for the right building.

Now that I'm up close, I see the buildings are made from some unrecognizable material rather than stone, as they looked from a distance. The pieces are uniform in size and shape and it seems like the building construction has been subdivided into modular sections that can be fitted together easily. I've seen similar ideas in printed buildings in London, built quickly to replace homes destroyed in riots years before; temporary solutions that poverty made permanent. These are far more impressive and more solid, but the principle seems the same.

Surely Alejandro would have preferred timber to be shipped in and to get everyone to build them together. Some sort of cheesy teamwork lesson or bollocks like that. Perhaps printed modules are cheaper. But it isn't like the Circle is short of money, and the printed pieces would still have to be transported there. I can't imagine Alejandro allowing a printer on-site. Then I remember the farm drone. Perhaps a large-scale industrial printer would be seen as a tool too. It still doesn't feel right though.

I can hear the low murmur of gathered people before Selina opens the doors into the hall, and I steel myself to see my father. There are at least a couple hundred people sitting in rows of interlocking seats arranged in church-like pews. At the far end of the room there is a huge cross made of oak mounted on the wall. It's a plain, functional room with large windows that look over the fields and doesn't feel particularly chapel-like.

The murmur dies away as everyone turns to stare at me. I scan the faces, struggling to recognize anyone other than those whose bios I read on the way over, only to discover my father isn't among them.

"This is Gabriel's son," Selina says. "Carlos."

No one says anything. Neither do I. I'm struck by how young so many of them are, most in their twenties, some in their thirties and only a handful over forty. They all look so . . . healthy. All are slim and look incredibly fit, and it feels like I've walked into a personal-trainer convention. Very few of them are wearing black; most are wearing a kind of dark blue coverall that looks more like a uniform than anything else. I've heard of cults where everyone wears the same thing but I would imagine robes or something looser and more comfortable, not this. Not even when I was a kid did Alejandro insist everyone wear the same clothes. I feel like I've been brought back to the wrong place.

A man in his late forties stands up. "Welcome back to the Circle, Carlos. You might not remember me. I'm Ethan. I was older than you by a few years when you were here as a child. I look a bit different now."

I struggle to place him and wish I had Tia to help. He might have been one of the teenagers who laughed at me for eating fruit wrong. It doesn't matter. I force a smile, appreciative of the fact he's trying to break the tension and make it clear to me that at least one person is happy with my being here.

"Welcome, Carlos," says a woman in her twenties, brown skinned and smiling, and then others join in, some more convincing than others.

"Thanks," I say, feeling eight again, an outsider disbelieving the smiles.

Many of the people waiting have reddened eyes; some are openly weeping. The attention shifts away from me as they gradually turn back to face the front of the hall, waiting for the ceremony to start.

Selina sets off down the aisle, but I slip into the back row, needing to feel a wall behind me instead of eyes. When she realizes I haven't followed her, she turns back and comes to sit next to me.

"You can sit at the front if you like," I whisper. She shakes her head. "I'll be fine."

"No, it's okay," she replies.

More people start filing in. Some are in more traditional funeral clothing but the majority are wearing the coveralls. I look for familiar faces, even hoping to see some of the people I used to actively dislike—just to feel like I'm really in the same place I was before—but there's only a handful of older people who I barely recall. I was too busy staring at my own miserable navel to have formed any proper relationships here, and even though twenty years or so have gone by, it's still disconcerting that I can't remember their names.

Then Travis walks in. He's wearing a black suit without the ostentatious styling I saw before and his hair has been cut too. He doesn't notice me as he heads down the aisle to sit next to the young woman who greeted me earlier. He seems relaxed and much more comfortable here than I am.

"Your father is one of the pallbearers," Selina whispers to me as I continually tense up every time someone comes into the room. "I doubt he'll have a chance to say hello before the start."

That eases some of the tension. I study the faces of another group walking in and one of them, a woman in her late thirties, is someone I recognize instantly. Not because I've met her before; I've seen her photo in the MoJ archive. Her name is Aliette Sorel, a brilliant physicist who went missing about five years ago. Her face stood out from the missing-persons file because of the scar running from her left earlobe to her chin, something she refused to have removed with cosmetic surgery.

She won a Nobel Prize for physics at the age of twenty and was seen as a wunderkind in her field, so her disappearance made headlines all over Europe and Norope too. She was last sighted in London, hence the MoJ entry. Did she defect from her high-profile position in Europe because she'd had enough of the modern obsession with connectivity, drawn here by Alejandro? Or was there the opportunity to conduct research here that she didn't have elsewhere?

Moments after she sits down a man enters with a friend, whom I also recognize from an MoJ file; he was one of several scientists who supposedly died in a terrorist attack at an artificial-intelligence conference in Los Angeles almost ten years ago. I remember him only because his daughter was under investigation in relation to the attack and the case spilled over into Norope as members of the terrorist cell were tracked down. She was cleared but committed suicide soon afterward. Does he even know about that?

Those two, plus the scientists Gabor sent the file on, plus the drones in the fields and the experimental architecture, all contribute to the feeling of this being a research facility now rather than the cult I left. It's a clever way to avoid industrial espionage: remove the chips, lock down the perimeter and use the US gov-corp's hard-core religious protection rules to keep prying eyes out. But what could possibly draw so many to this place? Money? Dedication? A particular project?

My thoughts turn to Selina. I had the impression that Alejandro tempted her here with charm and a way to put her failed marriage behind her. The baggage she had regarding personal chips could be left at the gates; no one at the Circle would ever be able to fall in love with anything unreal, so she could be safe to form close relationships again without the risk of being hurt like that twice. But is that the whole story? She was a UX designer and information architect before she left New York—valuable skills in the coordination of multiple scientific projects and the pooling of knowledge gained from them. And Travis too; I assumed he was here to escape his husband—and understandably so—but he also has a tech background and he may have kept his hand in more than I thought. My father, a former scientist put back together again by Alejandro. The patents in engineering and energy storage—it's all pointing to the Circle being so much more than the outside world believes.

The doors to the hall shut and then someone at the front stands and everyone else follows suit. In moments the doors open again and four men and two women enter with the coffin on their shoulders. The man at the front left is my father. He's almost bald, his thick black hair lost in the years since I last saw him, and that which remains is a pale gray. He looks like an old man now, shaking the very core of me, as if some childish part of me thought he would be young for the whole of my life.

But he looks like he's in better shape than I ever saw him in. He walks with ease, no more hampered by the weight of the coffin than the younger man behind him. His eyes, wet with tears, are fixed on the cross ahead of him and then he's walked past me.

They set the coffin down reverentially on a couple of trestles at the front and everyone except my father goes and sits down, along with everyone else. I realize he's one of the oldest people in the room.

He turns and stands at the front to address us all, scanning the rows of seats as everyone settles back into place. His eyes finally meet mine and they brighten as a broad smile lifts his brow and ten years off his face.

"My friends," he says. "Forgive me, but I've just seen my son for the first time in twenty-three years and I need to embrace him."

He walks up the aisle and Selina makes room for me to go to the end of the row. There are tears on his cheeks by the time he reaches me and throws his arms about me. I return the bear hug, feeling tears prick my own eyes, a thousand things on my lips and none of them worth saying. Something that has always hurt, all these years, feels soothed, and for the first time I appreciate how heavily I've carried our separation.

He pulls away enough to cup my face in his hands and kiss me on the forehead. "I'll speak to you soon, hijo," he whispers, and then lets me go.

I return to my seat with a lump in my throat and shaking knees as he returns to the front. Travis is twisted round in his seat, staring at me with blushing cheeks, until I look directly at him and he faces front again.

"My friends, you know I'm not a man who speaks well, so I hope you will forgive me if I struggle. I never thought I would see this day. I never thought I'd have to face what's ahead of us without Alejandro. Every single one of us was drawn here by him. We were inspired by his vision, guided by his gentle wisdom and given strength when we needed it most. God worked wonders through him. I would not be standing here today were it not for this man we loved so deeply, and I know there are several of you who can say the same. I . . ." He pauses as his voice breaks, looking up at the high ceiling to compose himself. "I cannot pretend to understand what happened and, I'm ashamed to say, I haven't found it in myself to forgive. I will try, but not yet. Alejandro was taken from us too soon. There is so much left to do and we all need to lean on each other as we come to terms with the fact that we will go on without him.

When we despair, we have to remember that we will see things for him, discover for him, learn for him, just as much as we learned from him. His vision will live on through us." After another long pause, he clears his throat. "Alejandro told me once, years ago, when Breanna died, that he too wanted to be buried rather than cremated. He said he liked the idea of his body nourishing the Earth as the Earth once nourished him. Perhaps that can offer some small comfort now. If you feel you want to, take a moment to come up to the front and touch the coffin, say good-bye in your own way. Then we'll take him outside and say good-bye to him one last time."

I stay seated and watch as dozens of people shuffle forward from their seats to weep over the coffin, my father gently moving them aside one by one to allow the next to have their moment. I can tell Selina wants to go up there but she keeps hesitating.

"Go up," I whisper to her. "You'll only regret it if you don't."

"I keep imagining him inside the coffin," she says, tears breaking free. "Like he was in that room."

I reach across and take her hand. "He isn't like that now. They'll have cleaned him up and . . . He'll be intact. The pathologist and the undertakers would have made sure of that, okay?"

She nods and squeezes my hand. When the mourners thin out she goes up there too and breaks down as she touches the plain, unvarnished wood. My father lets her have a minute or two and gently pulls her away. She sobs on his shoulder for a few seconds and then pulls herself together enough to walk back to her seat. She blows her nose and covers her face with her hands, and I realize that if I'm going to go say good-bye, the time is now.

I stay seated. I think I'll go up, say good-bye, but the

moment passes and I am still seated, watching the last people get up and weep over that box. Like Selina, I too think of him inside, of the stitches holding the pieces of his body together that Theo split apart with his devotion and grief. All I can do is fight the urge to go and shout at that damn box. *Why?* I want to scream through the wood. Why did you kill yourself? How can a man who gathered up the lost from all over the world and brought them together and gave them peace be so unable to do that for himself?

He gathered me up, but he didn't give me peace.

I stay in my seat, fearing I'll do more than ask that question. I fear I'll curse him, spit this hatred and hurt at him that still burns beneath the memories of love. Of course my father did what he did the day I left. I expected—and still expect—nothing less than parental incompetence from him. I expected more from Alejandro though. When I looked into his eyes that last time, silently begging him for help, for some kindness to help me find a way back into the world he stole us from, he simply looked back as if I were nothing. He had failed to make me love him more than anything else in the world and he preferred to see that failure leave than help him find another path safely.

And then I am in that field again, a child again, watching him twist off the cob of corn and press it into my hands. "Here. You grew this. This is only here because of you. You gave it time and water and kept the pests and weeds at bay, and now it gives this to you. Now I'll show you how to cook it and we'll eat it with fresh butter."

"Just us?"

"Just us."

I cover my face with a hand, twisting away from the aisle as people pass me, pressed into the seat by the storm front of bitter, loving grief. I feel a hand on my shoulder and I ignore it, wanting nothing of these people, wanting to stay in my private space, where I can wrestle with this alone. The hand slips away after a few moments and in the instant of relief I realize it was always thus. I was always turned inward when the people here tried to reach out. Perhaps Alejandro knew there was no way to help me and thought it was better to let me go and damn myself than waste any more time on me.

I watch them carry the box out, suppressing the brief regret that I didn't have my moment with him. Selina is waiting at the end of the aisle and I stand to give her the signal that I'm leaving, in the hope she'll follow the coffin out and get on with her grief.

They bury him on the other side of the farmhouse in the center of a lawn that wasn't there the last time I was here. It used to be a vegetable patch, but in the intervening years the space was made into a more traditional garden. At my frown, Selina mentions how Alejandro used to sit on the porch and look out over it in the evenings, and I feel like she's talking about someone else. But Alejandro got older, changed, much more than I have. Maybe he wanted a space that was just beautiful and nothing more.

I stand back as prayers are said and people throw in their own handfuls of earth. My father invites me to do the same, eliciting some frowns from a few of the mourners. I almost refuse but a combination of social pressure and the fear that I'll regret it if I don't moves me forward. I try to think of something nice about him when I stand over the hole with my fistful of dirt, but nothing comes to me except the image of him standing on that chair, putting his head in the noose. I throw the soil in and it clatters on the lid of the coffin. My father seems satisfied and I go back to my place, aware of Travis watching me carefully.

Several people grab shovels once the personal good-byes are finished and begin to fill in the grave. Some are almost screaming with grief, making me step even farther back. I have an acute awareness of not being one of them and I'm possessed by the desire to go and steal that car right now. Selina is comforting one of the mourners while weeping herself and no one's eyes are on me. I take a few more steps back and then turn to head to the carport, desperate to remove myself from this wrong place, these wrong people, this wrong time.

"Carlos!" she calls, and I stop. "The wake is back in the hall we were just in."

I turn and nod. "My mistake," I say, and head toward it.

"I'll see you there, son," my father says, and I nod and wave an acknowledgment as I walk, hoping he doesn't see the disappointment in my eyes.

26

THERE ARE PEOPLE stacking chairs in the hall, transforming the space from one in which people sit and stare at the front to one in which they stand and stare at the floor. A few are already doing that, shivering and holding cups of something steaming, tears still running down their faces.

I haven't been to many funerals and all of the ones I've attended were as part of my job. As in all of those, I find myself standing at the edge of the room, watching the faces of the mourners, working out their relationships with the deceased and those left behind, only this time it's as much to stop thinking about my own relationship with him. I can spot the women who were Alejandro's lovers and the men who wanted to be, the ones he saved and the ones who are panicking at the thought of life without him.

Selina soon arrives and guides her friend over to another who's serving the warm drinks to distract him out of his distress. She comes straight over and the feeling of being actively minded grows. A few people start to approach me, only to have her practically intercept and deflect them. Has someone told her to make sure I don't speak to anyone properly? Or has she just decided to take it upon herself to keep me on the outside?

In some ways it's a relief. Small talk is hard enough, but at a wake it's even worse. I'm given a coffee and a tiny sandwich made with real bread and thick-cut, fresh ham. It's gone in two bites. Wordlessly, Selina beckons the person with the tray back, and without shame I take four more and shove another in my mouth as she watches. Then Travis Gabor walks in.

He heads straight for me as soon as Selina is taken up with steering someone else away.

"I didn't expect to see you here," he says, white teeth gleaming against his tan.

Behind him, Selina turns and I see a flash of worry in her eyes as she realizes someone got past her.

I muster a smile after I swallow the last of the second sandwich. "I can't say the same."

He winces theatrically, like a busted teenager who's been hiding a pile of empty condom packets under his mattress and is actually pleased I've discovered what a stud he is. "I want to apologize."

"Is everything okay here?" Selina asks, her voice a little too high.

"Oh, it's perfect," Travis says, crisping his accent up a notch for the American ear to enjoy. "Could you give us a few minutes? I have something I need to talk to the nice policeman about."

Selina hesitates, caught between wanting to deny him and not being able to think of a good-enough reason. I start on the third sandwich, wanting to eat them before I talk with Travis. "I'll just be over there," she says to me, as if I'm a new intern at a scary office.

I eat the fourth too fast and suppress a belch. "The 'nice policeman' is listening."

"I'm sorry I messed you about. Really. You must think I'm such a . . . a . . ."

"Desperate man?" It's a risk, making him think about why he left, but if I want to keep my options open, I need him to trust me.

The performance smile falters and a glimpse of the real Travis can be seen at last. "It wasn't a happy marriage. I suppose you guessed that. Being a detective and all."

"That's why you had the chip removed," I say. "You knew that if you left him with that still in your skull, he'd track you down."

He looks down at his shoes and nods. His head snaps back up. "But that's not the only reason. I did it so I could come here."

I fold my arms and raise an eyebrow, a silent invitation to try to convince me.

"Seriously!"

"You don't strike me as a god-fearing man, Mr. Gabor."

"Don't call me that. And why do you say that? You don't know anything about what I believe." He searches my eyes for some sort of response but I don't give anything away. "I'm where I'm supposed to be now. And he can't do a bloody thing about it." The grin that spreads across his face is devilish. "And I bet he is going absolutely insane about it."

I remain silent.

"So, when did you realize I was gone?"

"While you were being driven to Heathrow. I went to your room and found the tablet you programmed. Cute."

"Did you tell him?"

"I didn't tell anyone. It was none of my business. I'd eliminated you from the investigation by then. I was only going to interview you so he'd stop giving my boss an earful about keeping you at the hotel."

He looks genuinely touched. "Thanks. That was what I was most afraid of: you finding out before I was on the plane and telling him. He would have been able to ground it if he'd known I was on it."

"I know. Truth be told, I wanted you to get away from him."

He blinks and leans closer. There's something so desperate about him, so vulnerable. The first hint I may be on his side and he's hungry for more. "Why?"

"I saw the way he treated you in the restaurant."

He smiles, this time with a hint of the flirtatious. "You wanted to rescue me?"

"I didn't want to get in the way of you rescuing yourself."

The smile fades and he just stares at me, uncertain how to play this. I wonder who the real Travis is. It's not the coquette and it's not the primping dandy that his husband shaped him into. Neither role has fully fallen away yet. I suppose he doesn't know who to be yet either.

"Did you bribe a doctor to give you the reason to have the chip removed?"

"I don't want to get anyone into trouble."

"I'm just curious. Sorry. It's my training. I hate loose ends."

After a pause, he nods. "I couldn't tell Stefan I needed it removed to come here. I couldn't tell him I was planning to leave him either. It took months to arrange. And it all worked perfectly, apart from . . . well. I hoped to fly back here with Alejandro. I wanted to have a real conversation with him, without worrying about Stefan." He looks down, frowning. "So awful. That Theo just seemed a bit of a man-child, not a lunatic."

There's the real Travis. I suspect he's more of an introvert than perhaps even he appreciates. "Can I ask you a question? It's personal and not part of any case. Just for my satisfaction."

He looks back up at me. "All right. Go on, then."

"How did you end up with Stefan? I . . . I just don't see it."

"The age gap, you mean?"

"The humanity gap."

The intensity of his gaze borders on the erotic. I find myself wondering if he's going to kiss me as he searches for something in my eyes, and with a detached curiosity I find myself hoping he will, just to see what it feels like.

He leans back and breaks eye contact to take in the room, as if he'd forgotten about it. "Let's go outside."

Travis leads me through a side door as mourners are still coming in through the main entrance. The carport is in sight and that desire to run returns, but where would I go? How could I survive? I've clawed my way out of being a nonperson before and I don't know if I have it in me to do that again. If I take Travis back to his husband, I could get a message to Delaney, forge a relationship with hir that could lead to real freedom. But can I bring myself to do that to this man, someone who has escaped himself?

Travis rests a hand on the small of my back and guides me round the corner to a bench with a view of the crops swaying in the breeze.

"It's very peaceful here, isn't it?" he says as we sit on the bench.

"If you like that sort of thing."

"Is it true that you used to be here when you were a child?" After I nod, he asks, "Why did you leave?"

I frown. "I'd rather talk about you."

He laughs. "You don't have the monopoly on curiosity. You tell me why you left and I'll tell you how I got involved with Satan on Earth."

I shift, unable to find a comfortable position. I don't know how to frame this conversation. It has the fumbling awkwardness of a first date, not the tail end of an investigation or the preamble to a kidnapping. "My dad brought me here with him when I was eight. He . . . he hadn't been well for a long time. He'd had a nervous breakdown and stuff wasn't great, and, anyway, long story short, Alejandro found him and brought him to be in the Circle and I had to come too."

"What about your mum?"

"She wasn't around."

"Is she dead?"

I snap my head to look at him. "I'm not a fucking NPC in a mersive."

His mouth opens and his eyes widen as the blush returns. "I'm so sorry. That was . . . I'm sorry."

"She left on Atlas. With that Pathfinder woman. She left us behind."

"That *was* you!" He must have seen the documentary. His hand rests on my arm and I stare at it, paralyzed in the place between wanting comfort and hating his pity. "That must have been hard."

I shrug, as if that dumb movement can brush it all off. "I was a baby. I never knew her. Dad was the one it was hard for. He applied to go too, got through to the last round and didn't make the final cut. They had a policy of no preferential treatment for married couples, which is fucking cold, when you think about it, but I guess the mission was more important than feelings, so that's the way it was."

It's the most I've ever spoken about it and it leaves me breathless and wanting to kill alien robots or something equally violent and free from consequences.

"She must have been . . ."

"Selfish." I don't wait to state a judgment I've already made.

"Driven," he says. "It could have been worse if she'd stayed. She might have resented you and your dad." He waits for me to respond but I'm keeping my mouth shut, appalled by how much I've said already. "So, you came here when you were eight. Why did you leave?"

"Why are you so interested?"

Now he shrugs. "I find you hard to fathom. You don't give much away. I suppose they train you well in the MoJ."

I almost tell him I learned it before I even got there, but what is this? Some fucking interview? I stare back out at the crops. "I wasn't happy here," I finally say.

"But you didn't want to stay and find out if—" He stops himself. "Hang on. When did you leave?"

"When I was sixteen."

"Oh. Right." He nods to himself, as if I'd answered another question as well as the one I'd heard. He bites his lip, weighing something up. "And then you joined the Ministry of Justice in Norope?" His tone has changed to breezy curiosity again. I've missed something here.

"I didn't want to stay and find out what?"

His smile is fake. "Whether it would get better. I suppose teens don't think that way though, right? Shame really."

He's not going to give me more. Something changed here after I left, that much is already obvious. Something about that change is what he thinks I should have stayed for, had I known about it. I file that away to dig at later.

"So, the Ministry of Justice," he says again. "How on Earth did you end up there?"

"It's a long and not-very-interesting story. Your turn."

"Well, that's fair," he says, leaning back to cross his arms. "I've been married to Stefan since I was twenty-two. He was forty-three." The perfect curve of his upper lip distorts as he thinks back with obvious disgust. "I've always hated him. It wasn't ever a love match."

"Money, then?"

"God, no. You think I'd marry that slug for bloody money?"

"Lots of people would. Money and power. Never having to be afraid."

"That only works if you're not afraid of your spouse. Look, I suppose I'm going to tell you the whole sordid affair, but please don't take any of this back to the MoJ."

"I won't. Civil matter, remember? Out of my jurisdiction."

"I studied at Cambridge. While I was there I met some people . . . through my don. They liked me, I liked them and, well, one thing led to another and I got myself a real education at the real university. The one that's been there for hundreds of years."

"You've lost me."

He smiles. "You know that the gov-corps and subsidiaries dictate what's on university syllabi, don't you?"

"I can't say I've ever given it much thought."

"Well, they do. Paris has the only university in Europe that sets its own curriculum. Oxford held out for a while, but when things got really bad during the riots, they caved. Cambridge lost independence fifty years earlier. The tabs always were a cowardly lot. At least, that's what they wanted everyone to think. But there's a network there, like a university within a university, where they actually teach real stuff. Not just the gov-corp-approved bullshit. That's where I learned how to think properly."

I twist round to watch him as he speaks. What I thought was the real Travis was only empathy. This is a different man altogether. Someone fiercely intelligent who's been hiding it for years.

"It's where I learned how to hack. And I'm not talking about that bollocks you see in the mersives, with some nerd—or some really sexy girl with a pixie haircut and attitude—frantically typing away on a v-keyboard. I mean the real thing. A hacker looks like an orchestra conductor when he's working. It can be a beautiful thing to watch."

"Yeah, all that crime can be so elegant." I make no effort to hide my sarcasm. "There's no victims, right, when it's—"

"Look, if you're going to be a twat about this, I'll shut up now."

"Sorry. I just don't think it's romantic to hack. As you said, it's not like the mersives."

"And it's not just like the propaganda you read in your Ministry files either. Oh, there are wankers in the hacking world—of course there are. But that wasn't the sort of stuff we were into."

"And what was that, exactly?"

"Exposing corporate injustice."

I try not to laugh. "The what, now?"

"It isn't funny."

I hold up my hands. "No, you're right. It's not funny. But corporate injustice is just . . . it's the way things are now. Who are you going to expose it to? There are no people who aren't already in it. And those who say they're independent just don't know who owns them."

"Wow. Were you this jaded before you joined, or did the MoJ do it to you?"

"What has all of this got to do with Gabor?"

"I hacked him. I followed some threads back to him when I was at uni, so when I left I got a job at one of his many, many companies so it would be easier to get deeper inside. It just didn't work out the way I wanted it to."

"So you weren't as good as you thought you were and got caught?"

He smirks. "No, I was too good. The hack was easy. It was

what to do with the knowledge afterward that was the problem. That's where I fucked up. And to cut a very long story short, as you're fond of doing, Gabor outplayed me and gave me a choice."

I scratch the back of my neck, not seeing how he could get from hacking to unhappy marriage. "Hang on. He gave you a choice to marry him or—what?—ruin him. This isn't making any sense."

"The choice was to be owned or to be killed, Mr. Moreno. Perhaps if I were a more courageous man I would have chosen the latter, but it wasn't just my life in the balance. He said he would kill my family too. He's done much worse. So I said I would be bought off. Bought, I should say. And, lucky me, being a handsome man that he took a fancy to meant that it wasn't just a standard corporate-indenture arrangement that he could have forced through the courts. He made me his husband and kept me close. At all times. I hacked for him then. For years. Screwing over competitors left, right and center and making my jailer even more rich and even more powerful. He put a new chip in me, one he thought would stop me being able to screw him over too. But he underestimated me." He gazes out at the horizon, a subtle smile flickering in and out of existence. "He got complacent. I made him think I fell in love with him. It wasn't hard; he's such a fucking narcissist it fit with his worldview. I found a weakness in the security on my chip, got in touch with some old uni friends and planned my escape and here I am. Free at last."

"But what about your family? Aren't you worried about what he'll do to them?"

"Oh, they're all dead now. Dad was old when I was born, so he went first. Mum drank herself to death, and my sister was killed in the nuclear accident out in Shanghai last year. So there was only me left to fight for. He didn't let me get close to anyone else, after all. You could argue I brought it all on myself, and I'd agree. But I wasn't a gold digger and I wasn't some weak man marrying for comfort and security. I made a mistake when I was young and didn't know how the world worked and I have paid for it. Many, many times over."

I let the silence sit between us. He is one of the few people I know who would understand the mess I'm in now. I could tell him, perhaps, ask for his help to escape too. But somehow the words don't make it out of my mouth.

"Wait. If you're so good at hacking and all that, why didn't you take more care with your search history? It took the MoJ AI milliseconds to pull your searches on Alejandro."

He laughs. "Oh, that was there because I wanted the Ministry to think I was stalking him once Gabor flagged up my disappearance. If I didn't get away before he noticed, I hoped an investigator would take pity on me and let me run off with my religious savior. And it was evidence in support of my religious application to the States immigration department."

"So, if it wasn't an obsession with Alejandro that brought you here, what was it?"

He looks at me then, a distance in his eyes, as if he is looking at me on the other side of a bridge he won't let me cross. "You're so easy to talk to. I shouldn't have said all I have. All I will say is that the reason I'm here is bigger than Alejandro, bigger than any one man ever could be. But you don't need to worry about that. You'll finish up here and go home in time to watch the capsule being opened and soon forget about me."

He stands, deciding the conversation is over, no sign of that desperate need to connect ever having happened.

"Won't you want to know what's inside it?" I ask, standing too. "You'll miss it all, being here."

He turns to face me, eyes sparkling. "Oh, I already know

what's inside it. And if I hadn't been such a cock in my early twenties, I wouldn't have lived through hell and the world would already know too. What was it Cillian Mackenzie said when they announced that Atlas was planning to follow those coordinates the Pathfinder knew? Oh yes: 'Don't believe anything on the news feeds. It's all just a circus for the masses.' The capsule is just part of that circus, Mr. Moreno. And even though Alejandro is gone now, the show must go on."

27

"THERE YOU ARE!"

My father has rounded the corner without me noticing, Selina behind him, with the skin between her brows pinched deep. She sees my face, the confusion and slow dawning of suspicion upon it, and then fires a fierce glare at Travis.

"I've been looking everywhere for you," my father continues, oblivious, as Travis gives Selina an innocent smile.

"Me too. I was just about to take you back to the border," Selina says.

My father rounds on her. "Don't be ridiculous—he's only just arrived. I think he should stay the night."

"But the funeral is over and that's what he came for and—"

"What kind of a welcome is this?" My father comes and wraps an arm around me. "This is my son. I haven't even had a chance to have a conversation with him. He'll stay for the wake and he'll stay for the night and that's the end of it." When Selina draws a breath to argue, he carries on over her. "He knew Alejandro. We can't just pack him off, and anyway, you're in no state to drive, Selina. None of us are."

"I'm not sure that Carl wants to stay," she says, looking at me in the hope I'll take the cue and ask to leave. I don't know whether it's because I was on edge when we arrived and she thinks I'll leap at the chance to go, or whether she's so desperate to get rid of me she isn't thinking straight. Either way, I'm not ready to leave yet.

"I'd really appreciate being able to stay. Thanks, Dad," I say, feeling his hand tighten and crush me into his side.

Travis slinks off round the corner as Selina sighs, seeing that she's not going to win. I don't know if it's because he's one of the oldest or if it's been agreed upon, but it seems my father is de facto leader here now and she's not going to challenge him. At least not today.

"We'll be back in the hall soon," Dad says to her. "I just want five minutes with my son."

He holds me at arm's length as Selina rushes off, calling Travis's name, no doubt about to quiz him on what we discussed. Her concern goes beyond any kind of basic social decision to keep me on the outside. Maybe Collindale briefed her to keep me at arm's length from the rest of the Circle, worried that I would tell them what really happened. That doesn't sit right with me though. It would make more sense if she was someone the US gov-corp had here on the inside. If she's one of them, more than being one of the Circle, does that mean they told her what happened to Alejandro?

"You look well," my father says, and I realize I haven't really been looking at him. "Tired, but healthy."

So many times I've fantasized about laying into him. Sometimes it's punching him, but more often it's telling him exactly what I went through because of him. But now I am here, in front of him, it feels like a barrier is between us, one of my making. He looks so happy, and while that enrages a part of me, it also makes me reluctant to shatter something so fragile. So I say nothing, knowing he will speak soon enough.

"I was so afraid I wouldn't get the chance to see you again," he says, letting go and steering me out toward the fields. "But God led you back."

"It wasn't God," I can't stop myself from saying.

"Still not a believer, then?" He glances at me and I see genuine worry in his eyes. "Do you still shout at people when they talk about their faith?"

I shake my head. "I grew out of that. Now I mostly let them damn themselves with their own ignorance."

He winces. "Well, I suppose that's better than nothing." He leads us between two rows of maize, brushing the stalks with his fingertips. "There's so much I've wanted to say to you, and now that I have the chance, I can't think of any of it."

"Yeah." I give him that much.

"I was so worried about you. But look at you. You landed on your feet. Made a career for yourself. The Noropean Ministry of Justice! That's fantastic, son, absolutely fantastic!"

The anger builds. I'm waiting for an apology I fear will never come and all the while, behind the tidal surge of shit, that highly trained part of my brain is working on what Travis said. If he hacked Gabor and found out whatever is in the capsule—I knew it wasn't possible to keep its contents secret all this time—then my owner has known what the contents were for even longer.

"You were a late bloomer, that's all." My dad's chatter cuts through the processing. "I was so afraid that attitude of yours would be the undoing of you, but—"

"Just stop there," I say, unable to listen to this shit any

longer. "That attitude of mine? Haven't you thought about why I was the way I was?"

"Oh, teenagers just—"

"No. Just . . . no. You stayed in bed for—what?—two years. You stopped caring for me when I was six, Dad. And I know you had a breakdown and it wasn't a deliberate thing, but, fuck. You don't get to stand here now and say *I* had some fucking attitude problem."

"But, son—"

"You switched off and then some guy turns up, speaks with you for—what?—an hour. Then you sell everything and move us to another country to live with fucking morons who think that living in a commune in the middle of nowhere is the best way to cope with the world. And not only that. What's the first thing you do when we arrive? You take away the one thing that kept me going when you checked out."

"Are you still upset about the damn bear, Carlos?"

"It's not the bear. It's not the chip that was inside it; it's not the fact you took away the best start for me in the real world. It's not that. It's . . . it's . . . ."

"Because it sounds like you're still angry about that. I told you at the time, those things aren't good for you. Listening in on you while you grow up, feeding all those gov-corp lies to you—"

"That data would have gone into my adult chip, Dad. I would have had a head start. My APA would have known what I was good at before I even did!"

"It's not natural. I can't believe you're still bearing a grudge about this."

"Fuck!" I yell at the sky, stepping away from him. "It's not the fucking bear, Dad. It's the fact you think it was me that had a problem here. I was a child you just uprooted and dumped in this backward cult and every goddamn time I tried to talk to you about stuff, you just spouted shit about God or just told me to go away because you were with Alejandro. You didn't give a shit about me. No wonder I was angry! No wonder I had an attitude!"

His mouth has fallen open and he's staring at me like I'm an alien.

"And then when I can finally leave you're just like, 'Well, see ya, son. Good luck!' and you didn't even give me a single fucking dollar. I had to steal the food I took with me. And you stood there with that righteous fuck and just waved me off?"

"I couldn't stop you from leaving."

"You could have made sure I was okay! You could have given me enough cash to last long enough to get a visa! I was a nonperson, Dad. Do you know what it's like out there when you're not lily-white and don't officially exist?"

"I hoped that you'd come back." His voice is barely a croak. "I thought you'd walk it off for a couple of days and then when you got hungry you'd be back."

"What, like some dog? Some fucking dog without a mind of its own?"

"No, like a boy who didn't know what he wanted."

"But you didn't come after me, did you?" His stupid, staring eyes infuriate me. "Did you? Not one letter, not one fucking phone call. I could have been dead, for all you knew!"

He shakes his head. "No, Carlos, I always asked Alejandro to check up on you when he traveled. When he told me you were recruited by the Noropean Ministry of Justice I knew you'd be okay."

"Recruited?" The last sticks of the dam inside me break. "They bought me from corporate-sanctioned slavers. The last real choice I had was when I walked out of this place. Then it was one exploitative fuck after the next and now . . ."

I rein myself in, stopping myself in time. I'm shaking like I'm on far too many stims and I have to keep swallowing down a lump in my throat that feels like an orange is stuck there.

"Oh, God, I didn't know," he whispers. "Alejandro said there are charities, that one of them probably—"

"No. There wasn't any fairy-tale rescue. I've spent twenty-three years being fucked over by one person or another, and when I think about it, Dad, when I look back and think about how I got to the place I am now, I see you at the root of it. You and that man in the ground over there."

"I'm sorry," he whispers, new tears falling down his cheeks now. Are they for me or for himself?

I wait for some moment of glorious release, for those two small words to make me feel whole again. But nothing happens. "Is that it?"

"Lo siento, hijo," he says again, reaching toward me. "I had no idea. No idea at all. I'm so sorry."

He touches my shoulder and I swipe his hand away. But he reaches for me again, weeping and sniveling, and I ball my fist but his arms draw me into an embrace and then the fight goes out of me and I sob, really sob, for the first time in years.

When I come back to myself I feel quieter inside. And so tired. I pull away from him and just sit down in the dust, exhausted. He sits beside me and blows his nose loudly.

"I'm a terrible father. I knew I was, but not how much. Now I do. You're right. I switched off and then I ruined your life. I wish I could say I thought I was doing the best thing for both of us, but really I was thinking about myself and just . . . telling myself it was good for you too." He sniffs loudly. "I nearly fell apart when Carmen went off on Atlas and they left us behind. But I hung on and hung on and tried to get by. And then those journalists, they wouldn't leave me alone and . . . Well, I don't have any excuse. I should have asked for help. I should have been there for you. Your mother wasn't. I had to be and I wasn't, and I'll never forgive myself for that." He blows his nose again and shifts on his backside so he's facing me. "You're healthy, aren't you, Carlos? No illnesses?"

"Is this supposed to make you feel better?"

"Answer the question."

"I'm fine. I'm healthy and I'm fit too. It's one of the terms of the contract. I have to keep myself fit and well otherwise . . . otherwise it's not good."

His mouth narrows to a thin, down-curved line. "This contract. You don't have to worry about that anymore."

"Dad, it's not that simple. I can't just not go back. There would be trouble."

"Fuck the Ministry of Noropean Justice. Fuck this contract of theirs. You're staying here."

I pull my hand down my face, the fatigue making it such an effort. "I don't belong here. Christ, after all I've been through to get away from this place, you think I want to just stay and—"

"You're staying here, Carlos, until I sort some things out. I wasn't there for you before. I am now. I've already put some things into motion, now I know I'm doing the right thing. But I can't say anything until tomorrow morning, no matter how much I want to. I just can't. Okay? But trust me. I won't let you down now."

"I'll think about it." I don't have the heart to tell him that all his paternal will and bluster can't fight my real owner. Nor can I tell him I'll wait until the morning, not when I might decide to take Travis in the night, or just make a run for it by myself. "Look, this jet lag is kicking my ass. I just want to have a rest, maybe come back to the wake later. Is that okay?"

He nods, stands and helps pull me to my feet. "I'll show you where your room is."

"I need my bag," I say as we start back, thinking about the package inside it.

"Anything you need, son," my father says, his arm back around my shoulders. "It's all going to be fine now."

I don't have the heart to tell him I think he's a fool. The world just doesn't work the way he thinks it does.

I follow him back past the buildings to the carport, drawing into myself. I feel like I'm in some bizarre fugue state, the winter sunshine at odds with the sense I should be fast asleep in my bed on the other side of the world, my surroundings shifting into nothing but a poorly rendered background in a shitty mersive I don't want to be in.

It doesn't stop me churning through the evidence, even though there's no case here. I'm a product of my training and right now the constant analysis is a comfort. It's the only thing I can be sure of about myself: what I can do, rather than the nebulous, dissatisfying and frankly narcissistic bullshit of feeling uncertain about who I am.

My father's behavior is new grist for this inner mill as he chatters on the way to the car. He is nothing like the man who lurked at the back of my memory all these years. There's an energy to him I associate with Alejandro, and, more than that, he seems to be filled with . . . What is it? A hopefulness for the future? Is that because I'm now fitting into the role of the prodigal son? I'm here and able to give him the chance to make good. No, it's more than that.

He's at least three stone lighter. He moves like a man in his prime, with purpose and vigor. He's filling the air between us with the most inane crap and it makes me wonder what he really wants to say and can't. What has transformed him so? This is more than a man healed; this is one with renewed purpose. Travis said he was here for a reason bigger than any one man. Is that reason the same thing that has rejuvenated my father?

And then there is that moment every investigator craves, that perfect clarity that comes when the discomfort of ill-fitting pieces suddenly reposition themselves into the cohesive shape of a previously hidden truth. Like I've been scraping away in the dirt, revealing jagged edges, not knowing if they all belong to the same thing, and then all of a sudden the soil has fallen away and the object has been pulled free. Those edges are no longer isolated oddities. The whole piece is visible.

Travis said he already knew what is in the capsule . . .

If the capsule isn't, in fact, just the cruelest joke being played against humanity, it can contain only one or all of three things: religious messages from the Pathfinder, details of the tech advances they made in the building of Atlas, and the famously secret coordinates of the place they thought they would find God. If Travis knows those contents already, others could too. Someone like Alejandro, who has been traveling the world, finding the best disillusioned scientists and plucking them from their miserable lives to plant them here instead.

And of course Gabor knew the capsule contents all this time too. The life pod built into my seat on the airplane slots into place. It was insanely overengineered because that wasn't what it was designed for. Gabor had the capsule contents for at least ten years, probably even more. A huge number of his companies were involved in the Mars mission, one that has famously made a loss. A man like that doesn't go into ventures for love. He was testing the technology left behind by the insane genius that was the Pathfinder.

Travis bought his way here—the Circle wouldn't let in an outsider that close to someone as powerful as Gabor with rival interests without a big sweetener. Perhaps Travis brought details he learned from Gabor's operation that the Circle didn't get hold of. Perhaps Travis has simply told the Americans how far Gabor's project is coming along.

Like a crude paper plane drifting into the same airspace as two supersonic passenger airliners racing each other, I stumbled into rival projects racing to follow the Pathfinder. My owner isn't a love-struck obsessive with strange ideas about what marriage is; he's a man terrified that his pet hacker, his renegade slave, is going to scupper his plans.

No wonder this place feels so different. It's evolved from the gentle sanctuary for those unable to cope with modern life that Alejandro founded into a research facility pursuing a goal of marrying their religious faith with their skills. These people, many who were at the top of their scientific field, are in the peak health and fitness required of those about to undergo something physically demanding. The patents, the crop experimentation, the farming drones—it's all obvious now. They're preparing to leave Earth and follow Atlas.

The bang of the car door being slammed shut makes me jump. My father has my bag and smiles at me as I blink at him. He hasn't mentioned any of this. Is he planning to leave me behind, like my mother? My jaw clenches so hard my teeth ache. He said he'd put things into motion—did he mean I didn't need to worry about the MoJ contract because he plans to take me with them? Do I even want to go?

I follow him into one of the new buildings, wrestling these fucking useless emotions back into place, and with them the speculation about his plans. Regardless of whatever hopes he may have, it's clear Selina wants to get me out of here. I need to be careful. I am not in a safe place.

The corridors are narrow, the interior more like a warren than the inside of a building this size. Of course; they're preparing for life on board a ship where space will be at a premium, and probably testing print and build techniques for when they reach their destination. The room my father leads me to reminds me of a cabin I had in a game set on an old twentieth-century submarine. There's not even a window.

"It's small but comfortable," he says, putting my bag on the bed. "There's a bathroom through that door. Is there anything else you need?"

I shake my head.

"Well, rest up and come back to the wake when you're ready. I'd love to introduce you to some people here." He turns for the door and then pauses. "It's not like when you were here before, son. These people are quite brilliant and not just hiding from the world. Don't write them off."

"When did it change?"

"We got our act together a couple of years after you left." His eyes are shadowed by a deep frown. "It was so hard, not being able to share it with you. I think you would have been much happier here. Alejandro, he . . . Some things became clear to him and he . . . he led the changes here. I wish I'd handled things differently with you. But I am going to put it right now, son. You don't need to be afraid anymore."

"You could have sent a letter."

"By the time Alejandro found you again you were in the Ministry of Justice. It wasn't possible."

I frown at him. Not possible? Then I realize Alejandro would have been afraid I'd tell my superiors, ones belonging to a different gov-corp. I probably would have back then. I would have done anything to kill his dreams and he knew it. Then I remember the American lawyers and Collindale's pressure during the investigation. Of course the Circle isn't acting alone—how could it be? The US gov-corp is backing this project and protecting its secrets. The last thing they would have permitted is contact with a young man recently acquired by a rival gov-corp law-enforcement agency.

"I understand," I say.

He leaves the room and bids me good-bye from the corridor and I close the door on the sound of his receding footsteps. I sit on the bed, trying not to think of this room as a prison cell. I last a minute before opening the door. As if my own father would lock me in. I look both ways down the corridor, satisfied that I'm alone here, and close it again. This time I lock it from the inside and feel better for it.

There's only one facet of this object I still can't see clearly: why Alejandro killed himself. I'm torn between needing to remove the last bit of dirt and see the whole goddamn thing before me for what it is, and, just as much, running away from it all. I notice a tiny digital readout set into the wall near the pillow displaying the time and date. There are six and a half hours left before my forty-eight are up. I have to make a decision. Do I trust my father—the man who has never once in my entire life come through for me—to come up with some sort of solution as promised (do I even want what I think he's planning?), or do I kidnap another slave and take him back to his tormentor in the hope I'll be tormented less? Or do I just cut loose and go on the run, back to being a nonperson again, unprotected by any laws, devoid of any rights?

There's another choice. If I'm right and there are two rival space programs created using knowledge that was supposed to be gifted to the entirety of humanity, surely there's a moral obligation to tell the world? There are scientists here who could have been working on something for the benefit of everyone. There are resources being pumped into this instead of combating so many ills in the world. Is it right for an elite few to just fuck off and leave everyone behind again? Some pundits claim that Atlas set back global health and scientific development by more than fifty years, simply by stealing the best and brightest and a hell of a lot of natural resources too. Should I just let that happen again?

I lean back until my head rests against the wall. Run away or kidnap a fellow slave; stay quiet or blow the lid off a potential global conspiracy . . . Are these the first genuine choices I've had in so many years? It feels so much harder than I ever fantasized it would. Some small, fearful nugget inside me craves Milsom standing over me, in person or virtually, telling me what to do. Is that because I'm weak or because it's been trained into me so deeply I don't know how to live as a truly free individual anymore? Does anyone?

"Come on, Carl!" I say out loud to myself. No amount of longing or worrying or philosophizing is going to do a fucking thing for me. I break it down into several smaller choices and consider the first: whether to open the package or not.

The thought of not knowing what's inside soon overrides any concern about being upset by its contents. Whether that's my natural curiosity or the years of MoJ conditioning to never be able to leave a case incomplete, I don't know and I don't have any fucks left to give about it. I unzip my case and take out the package.

It's plain on the outside—no name nor any hotel details, presumably hand delivered by someone capable of breaking into a hotel room. Having done that myself many times, I know how easy that is.

I tear it open at one end, tip the box inside onto the bed and open that. I expected it all to be paper inside but, in fact, there are only a few sheets, folded in half. The rest of the package is made up of small packets wrapped in plastic with a strange bobbled texture. They're numbered, each numeral handwritten with a thick black pen. An envelope rests on top of the packets and the sheets of paper. "Read this first" is written on the front. I untuck the flap at the back and pull out a couple of sheets of letter paper.

These packets contain a satellite phone that can be used without a chip, which has been disassembled and wrapped in a special plastic to make it invisible to scanners. Enclosed is a list of instructions to put it back together again. On the other sheets of paper are what I pulled from the cloud space belonging to a certain individual whom I thought was murdered. It makes interesting reading. When you get to the end, call me on the number below. ND.

The number is based in England, a long string of digits. I've never made a phone call with a handset before, but I've seen numbers like this being dialed in old films and period-setting mersives. I lay the letter and instructions to one side and pick up the sheaf of papers.

Two of them are just lists of names. Collindale's leaps out, as do a few very high-profile US gov-corp CEOs and other higher-ups. The third sheet is a list of mining companies and mining sites all over the world, along with details about how each of them is owned clandestinely by the US gov-corp. The fourth is a list of accidents and "natural disasters" that have taken place in Russia, Saudi Arabia, China, Korea, various locations across the African continent and even Australia. The last page is text and my eye skips to the end to see "Alejandro." It's a printout of the digital version of his suicide note.

I look away, letting the flicker of dread calm. I want to know so badly and yet I'm afraid of what it was that pushed him to that point of no return. If I know the same as he did, will I be destroyed too?

I need to know.

To the leaders of the world's nations and governing corporations,

Everything you have been told about the security of the capsule left behind by the Pathfinder is a lie.

The contents of the capsule have been known by the US gov-corp for the past forty years. They stole it from Cillian Mackenzie's computer before the capsule was sealed and buried. They just took some time to work out what to do with it.

During that time, ignorant of plans being made, I was trying to put my life back together after failing to make the final cut and leave on Atlas. I pulled through. I helped a couple of other rejects and I realized I actually had a gift Cillian Mackenzie overlooked: I knew how to help people that others had discarded. I founded the Circle, and I went and found all of the other people he and the Pathfinder threw away. I gave them somewhere safe to heal. I gave them a place to reevaluate their lives and reconnect with God. We were happy.

Then the US gov-corp approached me and said that they wanted to build a second Atlas and follow the first. We talked. They knew I had the skills to lead the project and a lot of the people already at the Circle would be ideal to carry on the work they'd started. We were secure—no security risks from chips and no way for outsiders to come spy. I made a deal with them. I'd form the project team and keep it all secret and they would bankroll it and give us the raw materials and resources we needed.

Nine days from now the capsule will be opened and you will be led to believe that this is the first time the knowledge within will be available to benefit the whole world. Sixteen days from now, project Rapture will reach its fruition. The Circle, and almost ten thousand people selected by the US gov-corp, will leave Earth in one hundred pods. They will connect in orbit to form Atlas 2 and go to follow the path forged by Lee Suh-Mi forty years ago.

I was supposed to leave with them but last week I discovered a secret US gov-corp memo detailing how I will be left behind. They don't want to me be on Atlas 2. They believe my power and influence with the core of Rapture, made up of members of what the world thinks is still the religious cult called the Circle, could be a destabilizing influence on the ship and ultimately on the final colony. They plan to tell me that they want me to stay behind and put together a team for a second Rapture.

I looked into this. There is no second Rapture planned. The US gov-corp has systematically stripped certain global resources to near-total depletion. They have falsified records to hide the resources they've been buying, and in many cases stealing, from other gov-corps and minor governments. Contained is a list of mining projects that, if any of you investigate thoroughly, will prove my point. The US gov-corp has also taken care to remove any other threats to this project in countries deemed unsavory. I enclose a list of so-called accidents and fake natural disasters that have been carried out to either kill key foreign scientists or deprive those entities of resources to enable them to build their own rival programs. All of this took place without the knowledge of me or my fellows at the Circle. I suspect that Europe has their own program, as they have approached me but haven't provided details, as I refused to deal with them. I will not give my expertise to a gov-corp that treated so many I care about so poorly when democracy failed in my country of birth.

And so I am forced to face the prospect of being left behind a second time and I cannot go through that again. I cannot. I will not. To the Circle, I say this: I am sorry. I cannot go with you and I cannot, in all good conscience, hide what I have learned in recent days about our sponsors. To the US gov-corp, I say this: how can you choose ten thousand people and leave billions behind to war and struggle? To the remaining world leaders to whom this letter will be sent on completion, I say this: pursuing Atlas to find God is something all of us should have the right to do. The Circle can help the world, not just an immoral elite. Save them and you will save yourselves.

I thought I was a godly man but I have been a servant of Satan, and now I go to hell in the hope my death and this letter will save the rest of you from being consigned to the same fate on Earth. God save your souls. Madre de Dios, forgive me.

Alejandro Casales

Beneath the printout of Alejandro's suicide letter is another handwritten note from Delaney.

Tell the Circle that if they give me a space on Atlas 2, I won't give this to the press and stop Rapture from happening. I'll give you until 24 hours before Rapture, and then I'm blowing it all open. The way I see it, Moreno, is that Alejandro and Theo are dead. They all thought Alejandro was going with them, so there must be two spaces on that ship. They should be ours. Naal.

I set the paper down next to the little packages and rest my head in my hands. There was a lot of unresolved shit between Alejandro and me but I'm not so cold that I feel no sympathy for him. I know what it feels like to be left behind.

In all of the documentaries, all of the articles, all of the ridiculously inappropriate "think pieces" about who Atlas left behind, there were two characters they built up for their puerile narratives. I was one, the tragic abandoned child with the appalling mother willing to put herself before her own baby, the victim of the ultimate maternal crime in the eyes of a misogynistic media. The other was Alejandro. A brilliant man tipped to be Suh's second in some of the articles written before Atlas left. Written before it was apparent just how well Cillian Mackenzie positioned himself in the project and how powerful his influence was. Alejandro and he were too similar, too good at manipulating people for there to be room for both of them. Alejandro had the religious faith but it seemed that wasn't necessarily a desirable trait to have in Mackenzie's fabled personality tests. When Alejandro was excluded from the final pick, he was cast as the lesser man, the one outplayed by Mackenzie and left behind to nurse the proof of his inadequacy.

Of course, when Alejandro turned it all around and founded a cult he wasn't the loser anymore. The Americans applauded his strength and faith as a visionary when he left Europe to settle his chosen few—and his rapidly increasing wealth—in the US. The Europeans called him a fraud and the Noropeans laughed at him, thinking he was nothing more than a narcissist gathering sheep to adore him and assuage those insecurities caused by being left behind.

But he was none of those things. He genuinely wanted to heal others that Atlas left behind, and in doing so, heal himself. Of course he said yes when the Americans gave him the chance to follow the Pathfinder. He loved her. He thought she was God's finger, pointing the way to him. He was being given the chance to follow God's plan without Mackenzie getting in his way.

All that, only to discover that he was being left behind a second time. No wonder he broke. It was his life. He put everything into following that woman, twice, only to have someone else deny him what he felt was his destiny.

My abandonment is nothing in comparison. I just existed. He devoted himself, worked so hard, only to have it all destroyed again.

And finally I understand. The anger evaporates. All of that petty bitterness about the way he was living, about the luxury he was squandering, and he was carrying this the whole time. It was nothing to do with the love of those he'd saved not being enough. How could he live while ten thousand people raced to God off the back of his efforts? How could he ever look up at the sky without being crushed with bitterness? What would he have left to live for when the Rapture left him behind?

Now that brilliant man is gone and those who drove him to suicide are sitting smug and happy, thinking that his desperate attempt to take them down with him has failed.

Rapture. The name says it all. Tired of waiting for God to do it, the Americans have decided to manufacture their own ascent into the heavens as the chosen few. If they plan to take ten thousand, as Alejandro said, they're not planning to come back. The first Atlas was a one-way trip, but it took only a thousand people, and they were from all over the world. If the US sends up their top ten thousand—as judged by gov-corp standards and religious bullshit—the ones left behind will be thrown into chaos. There's no way the US could have made a plan for those people without blowing their cover. They are just fucking off and damning the ones left behind.

And what of Gabor's project? He's managed to keep it under wraps thus far, but now that Travis is here, the US knows. How long will it be before some "natural disasters" befall key locations and people in Europe?

Delaney has to release the information. The rest of the world needs to know. Gabor will be taken down and I'll go back to the MoJ having busted the biggest global criminal conspiracy of this generation. My forced debt to them will have been paid off and I will be free. Really, truly free to live where I want, to grow my own food and—JeeMuh—to find someone to love.

Alejandro's death won't have been for nothing.

I put the phone together and switch it on. It works, to my relief, so I dial the number. It rings three times before being picked up.

There's silence for a moment. "Hello?" I say.

A pause. "Who's speaking, please?"

It's a woman's voice. My hackles go up. "I want to speak to Naal Delaney."

"That isn't possible, sir. Naal Delaney was found dead this morning. This is the investigating officer and your voice will be run through—"

I end the call. Poor fucker. In less than a minute the Noropean MoJ will know I phoned a recently murdered journalist with a piece of archaic technology from the other side of the world. I wonder what Milsom will make of that.

If either the US gov-corp or Gabor found out enough to want hir dead, they'll clean up the data trail leading to the contents of this package. I grow cold at the thought of being the only person in the world who has the chance to blow it all open. I have a phone but no numbers to call. I have all this knowledge but no means to disseminate it. I have to leave.

I pack it all back into my case and unlock the door, but just as I'm about to open it there's a knock.

"It's Selina. We need to talk, Mr. Moreno."

28

I OPEN THE door and Selina stands there, all tight smile and tension. "Hi," she says. I don't believe the cheeriness.

"Ms. Klein."

"Look, this is kinda awkward, but I really do think you need to go. I know your dad wants you to stay, but we need to be the realistic ones here. The MoJ and the US gov-corp agreed that you could be here for the funeral as long as you leave the same day. I promised Collindale I'd get you back to the border, and if I don't, I'll be in trouble with him and you'll be in trouble with your boss. So . . ."

"You're absolutely right," I say, grabbing my case. "Let's go."

She beams with relief. "I'm so glad you understand. I feel so bad about this."

We set off for the car and as I follow her through the warren, I turn my mind to my next steps. I slow down as I realize my options are as narrow as this corridor. If she drives me to the border, Collindale will remove the bracelet and that fucking golden G will be back and I'll get grief from Gabor about where his husband is. And with his APA controlling my access to the Internet, I can't release the data to all the global news agencies I need to at once.

If I refuse to have the bracelet taken off, Collindale will get suspicious, so that's not an option. If I dump Selina and steal the car, I'll be a nonperson trying to find a way to get this information out into the world without any Internet access, in the country most motivated to keep it covered up. And if whoever killed Delaney tracked that far, there's every chance they'll be looking for me too. Hell, if it was the US who killed hir, Collindale could be waiting to kill me too.

Fuck!

There's no way to get this out in the open in time. It was just a little heroic fantasy, just as ready to crumble in the face of reality as any other fairy tale. The expansive hope that filled me but minutes before has been popped like a balloon. I've never wanted my freedom so keenly, so *painfully*, as I do in this moment. I want to see Gabor taken down but that's not going to happen, and that bitter kernel that's taken root inside me feels comforted by that thought. I know the way the world works and there's no justice that can touch a creature like him. As perversely satisfying as it is to be proven right, there's no solace in having one's utter powerlessness confirmed.

There will be resource wars again, once the conspiracy comes to light, but there's nothing I can do about that. It wasn't my doing and I cannot undo it either. Like every other person struggling through life, in the end it comes down to protecting myself and the ones I love. I cannot save the world.

By the time I've figured this out, we're outside, walking past the hall. I can see she's watching me carefully, no doubt worried I'll insist on saying good-bye to my father and causing a confrontation between them.

My choices are shrinking, along with my ability to think calmly. I can't leave with her. I won't kidnap Travis. I couldn't live with myself for one thing, and for another I don't think Gabor will treat me any better. There's the outside chance the US will kill him, but this close to Rapture, they may just decide to leave him be. Going on the run as a nonperson would mean I'd still be stuck in the US when Rapture happens, and this is the last place on Earth I'd want to be then.

I either blow it all open to the people in that hall and let them force the US to stop it, or I try to get on that ship and leave this shitty planet behind.

I stop. My heart booms in my ears and my breath chokes in my tight throat, constricted by this simple and horribly complex choice. I raise my palm until it's level with my chest and push it downward, desperately clinging to the old technique in the hope of salvaging a rational thought from this bubbling mass of panic. I breathe in deeply. Now able to examine the base assumptions beneath this choice once more, it becomes painfully apparent to me that a room full of angry scientists are as capable of stopping the US gov-corp's plans as a cluster of gnats are capable of stopping a hurricane.

"Selina," I say, and she stops. "I can't go with you."

The blood rush of making the decision threatens this brittle calm. I don't want to leave Earth, but not as much as I don't want to be left behind again. And in that moment I share that pure fear across the divide of death. I understand now, in a way I simply couldn't before, why Alejandro felt it was better to die than be abandoned a second time.

Selina is staring at me, weighing the risks of escalation.

"I can't leave the Circle now." I keep my voice soft. "I know about Rapture."

Her eyes widen and then she nods slowly. "Shit," she says with a half smile. "We were worried you'd figure it out."

For a moment I'm scared she's just going to kill me, but there's nothing in her body language to suggest it. "You're with the US gov-corp, aren't you? They briefed you to keep me from finding anything out here, right?"

She nods again. "Look, if you know, it changes everything. I need to—"

"I want to take Theo's place on Atlas Two."

Selina half laughs and looks away. "It's not a cruise liner, Mr. Moreno. Everyone is handpicked. Did your dad tell you about Rapture? Did he say he'd get you a place?"

"No. I found out through my investigation. But I think my dad would want me to go with you all."

She folds her arms. "He's put in an application, but it'll be turned down. He doesn't know that yet. He doesn't understand how complex it all is. So I'm sorry, but you just . . . You have to just accept you can't come with us."

A ferocious surge of primal self-protection floods my body with more adrenaline. I'm not going to let yet another person steal my future away from me again. "Did they tell you what really happened in England? To Alejandro?"

Her face creases with the echoes of grief. "Yes. I know he killed himself. Collindale debriefed me on the plane coming back. What's that got to do with—"

"Did Collindale tell you *why* he killed himself?"

Her arms shift position, moving to hold herself tight. "He said it was the pressure. He couldn't face the thought of leading us up in space."

"You didn't believe that, did you? I can see you don't."

She looks down at the dust between us. "Something changed. I don't know what. Maybe he just snapped."

"You're not stupid." I put down my case and close the distance between us. "He killed himself because he found out the US gov-corp was going to force him to stay behind. He couldn't handle it."

"But that doesn't make any sense!"

"They didn't want someone with all that power and influence over the most important people in Rapture to continue to have that power and influence off-world. The US gov-corp has a hierarchy they fully intend to maintain long after Earth is left behind."

She covers her mouth and I see the horror in her eyes as she finally understands the truth. Tears well and I take another step closer, dropping my voice.

"This is the way it's going to play out: you're going to back my father's application for my place on board, and for one other person from Norope. And don't tell me the MoJ contract is going to be a problem, because it fucking won't be—trust me on that. If you don't get me those two places on board, I'll go into that room and tell everyone there what your wonderful gov-corp did to the man they loved, and we'll see how long this project holds together. Your brief is to make sure I don't fuck up Rapture, right? This is the way to make that happen. Do we have a deal?"

29

I NEVER WOULD have thought that being hot-housed would turn out to be an advantage. When it became apparent that between us, Dee and I could rapidly acquire the skills and knowledge that Theo would have brought to the team, people stopped shouting and started planning. We had ten days to prepare for launch, and without our experience of drug-assisted assimilation of vast amounts of knowledge, it wouldn't have been viable.

It wasn't just factual knowledge we needed to acquire, but also muscle memory. Learning how to move in zero g, albeit only temporarily, was part of the training, along with memorizing the layout of the pod in which we'd leave Earth to dock with Atlas 2, already in orbit.

When she arrived, Dee asked me who'd been bumped out of the program to make room for the two of us, but there was no way to find out and neither of us really wanted to. There wasn't time to think about the wider implications. Just like when we first met, getting through the intense training program meant our survival, and we spent our energy on that alone. Cocooned in the underground facility built beneath the old farmhouse, for us the outside world ceased to exist days before we left the planet. Gabor, the capsule, the Noropean MoJ and the questions that were no doubt being asked about my phone call to Naal Delaney—all were deliciously irrelevant. Training, sleeping, eating were all that mattered.

Dee is grinning at me. She hasn't stopped since we climbed into the pod in Texas and strapped in next to each other. "It's like being in a mersive," she whispered to me once we'd broken Earth's gravitational pull. "Only so much scarier!"

As the start of new lives go, this one could have been better. My ribs ache from the vomiting caused by going from too much g to no g and then readjusting to being back in almost one g again. The pod that I had traveled in with Dee, my dad, Travis and a few others from the Circle docked with the main hub. Apparently we're a lot less likely to die now. I remain unconvinced.

Dee's sitting on my bed in a cabin, which is exactly the same as the room at the Circle where I read Alejandro's suicide note. Her cabin is next door but she hasn't been in it yet, having offered to stay with me until I feel better. Travis's is on the other side and my dad's cabin is opposite. The last time I lived in such close proximity to people was during hot-housing. At least the rooms are nicer here and we're free to leave them whenever we want.

That's what I keep trying to tell myself but I can't shake the feeling I've taken a step backward. I'm free of Gabor and of any sort of contract—and the relief made me weep—but now I'm trapped in a glorified tin can with thousands of people. One that I can't leave for twenty years.

"You're not going to throw up again, are you?" Dee asks. "'Cos I reckon there isn't anything left inside you."

I shake my head.

"Want to try eating something?"

The only food is printed. That's all I'll eat now. Forever.

I'm retching into the toilet bowl again. Dee comes in and rubs my back. "JeeMuh, Carl. Maybe we should call for a doctor."

"It'll pass," I say, trying to convince myself as much as her. "Just . . . just talk to me about something that isn't food."

"I wanted to ask you something, actually."

"Okay," I say, leaning against the sink to look in the mirror. I look like I'm going to die.

"Why me?"

"Oh, that's easy." I smile. "I needed a gaming buddy." I don't tell her that it was because she's my only friend. I don't mention the fact that she got me through one of the hardest times in my life; she knows that already. "Don't look at me like that. It wasn't a marriage proposal or anything. It's just, you know, interstellar travel. Adventure. Freedom."

She smirks. "Seriously though, Carl. Thanks. I don't know how you swung it, but I'm glad you did."

She's standing in the doorway, twisting the security bangle that's exactly the same as the one I still wear from my visit to the Circle. The bathroom is too small for the two of us to stand in when I'm not hunched over the toilet. The light from the cabin's screen on the wall behind her filters through her hair, giving her a golden halo. I want to confide my fears to her. I want to ask her if she is just as terrified as I am and if she wonders whether she made the right decision as much as I do.

Instead I reach for the toothbrush and paste that were already in the bathroom, wrapped in bioplastic, and start brushing my teeth. She watches for a moment then goes back to sitting on the bed.

"We need to be careful here," she says when I'm done, still looking at the bangle. "There's a network on the ship—your dad told me that practically the sum of human knowledge is being taken with us—but we're cut off from it. I'm not convinced they're going to take these off us. New game. New rules." She looks at me. "I've still got your back."

I sit next to her. "And I've got yours. Travis is okay, I think. He's not what he pretends to be. You should give him a chance."

"He's not one of us though. You're the only one I trust."

I almost tell her he gave me the money to pay off her contract, making it easier for the US gov-corp to bring her over straightaway, but I don't want her to feel beholden to him. Persuading the Americans to bring her over was easy when they saw her skill set. I, on the other hand, am seen as an unknown quantity. I know they'll need my skills soon enough. There are more than 10,400 people on this ship. Someone is bound to lose it and kill someone at some point.

Dee smiles, as if worried she's been too serious. "If they ever do take these damn things off us, we'll go back to Mars and see how sexy those scientists can be."

I take her hand. "You don't owe me anything, okay? You don't have to be here for me because I got you the place. No debts here. It's a fresh start for both of us."

She nods, the grin gone. She knows exactly what I mean. "No debts."

There's a knock on the door and we let go of each other's hands. "Come in," I call, and Travis enters.

"Want to see something beautiful? Oh, hi, Dee."

"I'll go."

"No, stay," I say, making room for Travis on the bed. There isn't anything else to sit on. I pat the space between Dee and me and he sits down.

"I hacked into a satellite array in Earth's orbit," he says. "I thought you might like a last glimpse of the mother planet before we go out of range."

He taps a space in the air in front of him, presumably an icon in his vision alone, and the far wall of the cabin shifts from a view of the sea that Dee chose earlier to several live-cam feeds looking down on Europe, Russia and the Americas.

"It looks like a mersive cut scene," I say, and he agrees. He smells freshly showered.

"Can anyone else see this?" Dee asks.

"Theoretically, but no one else is watching as far as I can tell."

"I'll be right back," Dee says, and goes into the bathroom. The door locks with a satisfying clunk.

"I like Dee," he says. "She's fun."

"Thanks for lending me that money."

"I didn't lend it. I gifted it. And besides, it wasn't mine. It was that fuck's money that I tucked away for when I needed it."

He looks at the bathroom door and I find myself worrying he's got the wrong idea. "Dee's not my girlfriend."

"I know. I asked her. She said you went through some tough stuff together way back."

"Hot-housing. She got me through it. Travis, I wasn't working for the MoJ when I met you at the hotel. I was owned by them."

He twists round, shocked. "I had no idea."

I shrug. "Assets aren't permitted to discuss their status with real people. Look, there's something I didn't tell you when I came back to the Circle for the funeral." I pause. Why do I want to tell him this? Is it part of cleaning the slate, ready for the next phase of my life? Or is it because I'm starting to appreciate that I care about how he sees me? I don't want him to find out some other way. "Your husband bought my contract illegally. He sent me to the Circle to bring you back to him. Whether you liked it or not."

Travis pales, even now; not even on the same planet as that man, he looks frightened. "But you didn't."

"No."

He leans over and kisses my cheek. "Thank you."

My face flushes with heat. I need to check the environmental controls. It's obviously too warm in here. "What did you give the Yanks to get into the Circle?"

"A full update on where Stefan's project was. He was at least a year behind—it was harder to keep it quiet without the US religious-protection laws to keep things hidden without questions, so his operation moved slower. And I told them where it was based. They wanted to know everything. I was all too happy to oblige."

We sit in companionable silence, watching the last live images of Earth. The toilet flushes and Dee joins us again. It's less than two hours since we left orbit but it feels like we left days ago. I feel light-headed, hollow in my stomach and my chest aches, but sitting here, Travis on one side, Dee on the other, I find I'm able to start thinking about being here without wanting to throw up. It's not just a tin can. There's meters and meters of shielding between us and space—there has to be; otherwise the radiation will kill us before we reach our destination. That, or we'll be destroyed by grains of dust at the speed we'll reach. As for the food . . . my stomach lurches again and I swallow rapidly. I'll just have to cope.

"Somewhere down there," Travis says, pointing to the cam over Europe, "my ex-husband is losing his shit on an epic scale. Fuck, that is just the best thought."

"They'll have opened that capsule by now," Dee says. "Shit, now I'll never know what was in it."

A tiny smirk tugs at the corner of Travis's mouth but he doesn't say anything.

"Weird to think I've been scheduling coverage of that for months and now I'm in the middle of the only news item that might crowd it out."

I look at the clouds over the Atlantic, the jagged edges of the European coast, the odd little speck of the British Isles. I wonder what Milsom is doing and if she ever tried to find me after I was bought by Gabor. Probably not. The MoJ will carry on as if I were never there. She'll get someone in to replace me and the business of death will go on. I think of Linda and her sparkling red boots. I liked her. I wonder what she made of Rapture.

I try to imagine all those lives and find it just as difficult as imagining the ship I'm traveling in right now. Every truth I try to grasp has an immediate counter, keeping me off balance. We're spinning around a central hub but it doesn't feel like it. I'm free yet more confined than I've been for years. I'm finally following my mother to her destination, with no idea if she even made it there. Did she feel as frightened? Or did her religious conviction insulate her against such fears?

I'm watching the planet I've lived on all my life on a screen as I travel away from it, never to return. I stare at it, trying to hold that thought in my mind, but it's too big, too fundamental, too frightening. I want to go to Mars and shoot fake aliens inside robots. It feels like the only sane thing to do right now.

"What's that?" Travis says, pointing at a flash of bright

light over Spain. The clouds around it race away in a perfect circle as a new one grows.

"Can you zoom?" Dee asks.

Europe fills the screen and the top of a mushroom cloud over a small town in southern Andalusia blooms into its terrifying fullness as a second bright flash bursts into being near Madrid.

"Oh Jesus! Oh fuck!" Travis yells, leaping to his feet. "Those are his factories and the silos where he has the— Oh God, no!"

He stabs at invisible icons in the air before him. Another cam feed fills the screen, showing North America with a time stamp of seconds before, zoomed in to show the missiles leaving for Europe.

I watch it in total silence as Travis wails at the images, dropping the tablet and sinking to his knees. Dee's hand wraps around mine and we squeeze so tight it hurts.

"Is this real?" she asks, but I can't reply. "Of course it is," she says, moments later. "They didn't want anyone to follow us. They didn't want anyone to beat us to the Pathfinder." She crawls over to sit behind me, wrapping her arms around my shoulders, pressing her cheek against my ear. She's shivering and then I realize I am too.

More pinpricks of light pepper the screen, one in England, two in France, more in Russia, then America, as the retaliation begins. We watch the deaths of millions in seconds, divorced from the carnage by distance and the screen. At first, shock and the old training keep me from falling apart as some ridiculous part of my brain thinks it must be a cut scene.

Then I remember the gingerbread biscuits in that tub and the story Linda wrote for me. The way she slurped her tea and grinned at the copper who'd brought it to her. I think of my ex looking up at a mushroom cloud on the horizon and feeling the blast of the shock wave. Then image upon image of trees being flattened, of Alejandro's farmhouse being scattered to the wind, of the grave where Bear is buried being scoured by the raging destruction, and I'm crying, my whole body shaking with each sob as Dee's arms tighten around me. I hold on to her, as if she can keep some part of me anchored, as I imagine the man with the grandson who gave me the vegetables being burned alive, his kindness obliterated.

And yet I cannot tear my eyes from the screen. The destruction of all we left behind surely cannot look so beautiful, cannot look so serene, as that perfect green and blue orb is decorated with hundreds of its own tiny stars before the cams cut out.

My mind tumbles back to that hallway at the Circle, at the moment I decided it was better to leave than be left behind, only now understanding how monumental that was for us. As Travis weeps on his knees I clutch Dee, needing her more than I ever have before. I know she feels the same, as she crushes me to her just as tightly. It's us and them. It's us, trapped inside this ship with them, with those capable of such an unimaginably cruel act. How can we be safe with people so ready to kill those who are not like them?

Are we the only ones who know about this other than those who gave the order?

"We can't tell anyone," I say, my voice hoarse, alien. "And we have to make sure the ones at the top don't know we've seen this."

Travis nods eventually, as does Dee. We are left staring at the black screen as if staring into our own deaths, flying away from murder on a mass corporate scale toward a future created for and owned by this elite, godly few. No one will follow us now, with their rival claims and alien religions and cultural dissonance.

There is nothing to come from Earth after Atlas.

Emma Newman is the author of *Planetfall* and a professional audiobook narrator who reads short stories and novels in all genres. She also cowrites and hosts the Hugo-nominated podcast "Tea and Jeopardy." Emma is a keen role-player, gamer and designer-dressmaker. Visit her online at enewman.co.uk.